For Aspen, Hudson and Landon

This book is a work of fiction. Names, characters, businesses, organizations, places, events and incidents are either the product of the author's imagination or, in the case of historical events or persons, used fictitiously. Any resemblance to actual events or persons, living or dead, is likewise intended fictitiously.

For further information, contact:

Tumblehome, Inc.

201 Newbury St, Suite 201

Boston, MA 02116

http://tumblehomebooks.org/

Library of Congress Control Number 2020930149

ISBN-13 978-1-943431-56-4

ISBN-10 943431-56-6

Pell, Eva J.

ResQ Takes On The Takhi / Eva J. Pell - 1st ed

Illustrated by Alexa Lindauer

Printed in Taiwan

10 9 8 7 6 5 4 3 2 1

ResQ Takes On The Takhi

SAVING ONE ANIMAL AT A TIME

Eva J. Pell

Illustrated by

Alexa Lindauer

TUMBLEHOME, Inc.

CONTENTS

Hövsgöl Nuur
Lake Baykal
RUSSIA
Uvs Nuur
Höh Nuur
CHINA
Mongolia
ALTAY
Hustai Nuruu National Park
ULAANBAATAR
CHINA
GOBI DESERT
0 100 200 km
0 100 200 mi

1. *Dynochute* Express

It's a long way from here in Hoboken, New Jersey, to my cousin Stowe's house in Vermont. We only get to see each other once in a while when our parents have time to drive us. But those days are over—thanks to the Dynochute.

After texting Stowe to let her know I'm sending my latest invention to bring her down for a visit, I head up to the rooftop of 12 River Road. It's kind of windy up here, but with my feet firmly planted on the tar-papered surface I hit the STRETCH button on the computer screen and watch my beautiful transporter tube extend from its home in the dilapidated old chimney. Small thrusters guide the Dynochute in an arc above the treetops. In two minutes and thirteen seconds it arrives at its destination—Stowe's front porch in Vermont. I send a text. "DYNOCHUTE HAS LANDED. PREPARE 4 DEPARTURE."

A camera is mounted on the Dynochute opening. I hear a

door slam, and seconds later my cousin appears on screen. Must be warm in the house. All she has on are leggings, a t-shirt and her pink fluffy slippers.

Then I send another text message. "HERE COMES TRANSIT SUIT. CALL 4 FURTHER INSTRUCTIONS."

A large container lands with a thud on Stowe's wooden porch.

Stowe, with her phone now perched under her chin, inspects the brown transit suit and bright red helmet I've sent to protect her. "Quite the color combination. I'm going to look like an apple tree."

"But you love trees. Anyway, put it on so I can get you down here. A guy from Mongolia left a phone message at ResQ headquarters and said he's calling back soon. Ariella's out and you're better at talking to people than me." Plus, twelve-year-old girls sound a lot more grown up than eleven-year-old boys.

"Okay. Timing's perfect," she says. "I'm so ready to escape from the mountain of schoolwork Mom's piled on me. Give me a sec. I need to go back to the house and grab some stuff I want to bring along."

Stowe returns lugging an over-stuffed backpack. She kicks off her slippers and pulls on the suit.

"Put your pack in the compression-proof box the transit suit came in," I tell her.

"Check. I'm ready, but are you positive the Dynochute is strong enough to hold me?"

"No worries," I assure Stowe. "It's shape-memory polymer. Gets stronger as it stretches."

"No worries for *you,* Wheaton Ivan Guinto, mighty inventor. You're standing on the roof waiting for me. I still remember that chocolate bar you sent through the Dynochute. It arrived here as a pile of chocolate chips."

"That was before I perfected the slow-down for landing. And the crazy way you ski is way more dangerous than a little ride in the Dynochute."

"Yeah, but on skis, I'm in control."

"Stowe, trust me, you'll be fine. Remember to seal the compression suit and lock your visor in place on the helmet. I'll be watching through the camera mounted by your right ear. Are you ready?"

"Ready as I'll ever be." She marches to the opening and in preparation for the trip sets the compression box on the ledge of the Dynochute, with her legs straddling the sides.

There is no prep time. As soon as I push the TRANSIT button, the box catapults forward and she's sucked in feet first, zipping through the tunnel. The howling wind coming out of the Dynochute sounds like a souped-up vacuum cleaner.

In 75.2 seconds, Stowe decelerates, landing inside the chimney as she crashes into the container that preceded her.

Stowe shoves the box out of her way as she crawls out the exit door. "Phew, it stinks like something died in there," she says, flipping up her helmet. "How old is this stack?"

"Old. But who cares about a little smell. How'd you like the Dynochute? Pretty cool, huh?"

"Well, it beats the long bus ride."

I can't believe that's all she can say. 260 miles divided by 75.2 seconds is 3.46 miles per second.

"You were flying at 12,456 miles per hour. That's a speed that would make Superman jealous."

"Sorry Wig, I don't want to hurt your feelings." Stowe rubs her hand through my mop of hair and gives me a grin. "But hurling through the Dynochute—*in the dark*—it's a little hard to know where you're going to end up, or in what condition."

"Well, now you know." Of the two of us I'm not usually the one who's doing the reassuring.

"Next time, how about a pillow for the landing," Stowe says, rubbing her bottom.

Stowe flips off her helmet. Her scrambled-egg hair is standing straight up. She yanks her legs out of the transit suit and we both look down at her glittery toenails.

"I assume you have shoes in your backpack?" Not waiting for an answer, I hoist it out of the transit box and hand it to her. "What's in this? It weighs a ton."

"You did say something about a call from Mongolia. I figured I better be ready. Now let's get to the phone before that guy calls back."

2. Welcome To ResQ Headquarters

"Let's go down the outside stairs," I say, leading the way.

Stowe's bare feet slam the spiral steps, skipping every other metal rung. I take a little longer, hitting each step. Don't want to twist my ankle.

We reach the street and I tell Stowe to close her eyes. "I've got a surprise for you. Hold on to me and I'll make sure you don't step in any dog souvenirs." I guide Stowe to the storefront at the entrance of the old building Ariella, our grandmother, inherited from her father. "Okay, you can open them now."

"OMG," she cries. "It's one of GG Gordino's old pizza shops!" And then Stowe zeroes in on the hand-carved wooden sign mounted above the door.

Below is a collage of pictures—animals from all over the world.

"*Yes!!* Ariella's done it. Like she promised her father she would." But then Stowe's happy face turns sad. "I miss GG so much. Remember all the times he took us to the National Zoo."

"Yeah and his l-o-n-g stories about animals going extinct around the world." We both laugh, remembering how it sometimes took GG a while to get to his point.

"Do you think he wanted to start ResQ himself?" Stowe asks.

"Nah. He loved the pizza business. But that was his thing. He'd be fine with his daughter selling the stores—"

"To save animals," Stowe finishes the sentence.

"He'd be happy knowing that with the money Ariella got from selling Gordino's Pizza, she'll be able to fund ResQ for decades. And who knows, maybe I'll get royalties from my inventions to help keep us going too."

I push open the front door and wave to the guys who work in the pizza shop. "This is my cousin Stowe. We're heading upstairs." They nod and glance down at her bare feet. There is a sign in the window that says NO SHOES NO SERVICE. Wonder what they'd think if they knew she's just come out of the chimney!

We exit through the back of the store and run up the stone steps. By now Stowe's feet have to be beyond cold.

The building's got four floors. On the second landing I unlock the door and stretch out my arm. "Welcome to ResQ headquarters."

Stowe looks around and takes a deep breath. "That must be extra garlic on the pizza. Smells awesome." Good old Stowe, always focused on food.

"Yeah, maybe the smell is creeping upstairs, but here we're in Command Central." Our grandmother has knocked out interior walls so what used to be an apartment is now a big open space. We're just getting started, so all we have are a few desks and a worktable.

Stowe lays her phone face down. As she walks away I hear a text vibration, which she ignores. Looks like the ringer's been turned off.

Stowe goes over to photographs our grandmother hung on the wall from our first rescue. "Wonder how the little orangutans are doing these days?"

She starts to say something else, but we're interrupted by the ringing of the ResQ phone.

3. Needed In Mongolia

As the ringing continues, I look at Stowe and point to the phone.

"Okay, I'll answer," she says, picking up the receiver. "Hello! *Emergency Service for the Rescue of Endangered Species,* Stowe LeBlond, naturalist, speaking." She switches the phone to speaker.

"Hello. My name is Batar Munkherdene, calling from Mongolia to speak with Ariella Gordon, wildlife photographer. Do I have right number?" The man speaks slowly, but we have to listen hard to understand him.

"Yes, you do," Stowe says in her most mature voice. "She isn't here at the moment but I can speak for ResQ. Wheaton Guinto, our engineer, is with me on speaker phone."

"Hi Mr. Munkherdene," I say, trying to make my voice sound deep.

By now he may have figured out we're kids, and could be wondering why the two of us aren't in school. If he needs to know, we'll explain that I'm in grad school and Stowe's home-schooled.

"I would prefer to speak with Ms. Gordon, but I will describe problem to you." The caller does sound a little unsure of us.

"What kind of rescue do you need Mr. Munk...her ... deneee?" Stowe asks.

"You can call me Munuu. I am director of a project for Preservation and Protection of Takhi."

"Takhi?" I mouth to Stowe.

Stowe does what looks like a little galloping motion, but then holds up her hand, signaling she'll explain later.

Munuu continues. "I work with team of people from around world who are involved in breeding these beautiful horses. We are in process of reintroducing this endangered species back into the wild."

I get it now, and give Stowe a nod.

"The horses live in what are called harems—one stallion, group of mares and some foals. We conduct annual census of all reintroduced horses to see how many we have and how they are doing in natural habitat," Munuu tells us. "For few years, two American scientists who work for a wildlife organization have been coming to Hustai Nuruu National Park to conduct surveys. This year they let me know that one harem is missing."

"What do you think happened? Did they all die?" Stowe butts in.

"It seems unlikely. Last time they were counted, harem had ten members. If they died we would have found remains. We guess they left park. There is a lot of uninhabited territory around park. Based on when they were last seen, we guess they are somewhere east of park and west of Khentii mountains."

"ResQ's pretty good at finding missing animals," I say.

"Yes, I read about you and your advanced search tools on internet," Munuu says. "Part of what we need is to locate harem to see how many horses are still alive. But if you find takhi, we would also like you to figure out how to drive group back into park. Long-term, an isolated harem will not survive."

Hmm. I think the problem just got a whole lot more interesting.

"How much time do you think this will take?" Stowe asks a good question. We've both got school. This sounds like a big project.

Munuu's speech starts to speed up. "It is end of October, so we only have little time before winter comes and we have to stop. Temperatures here get very cold, too dangerous to search. Hail and snow can become problem. If we do not find horses soon, it will be too late to go into field. Takhi maybe roam even farther away from rest of horses.

"Can ResQ help us find these horses and figure out way to bring them back to park?"

Stowe and I look at each other and stick our thumbs up at the same time.

"You betcha, Munuu," Stowe blurts out. "Give us 'til tomorrow to get organized, and we'll be there. Wheaton's developed something called the Finder —a bionic dog on a drone."

"It'll be useful in locating the lost horses," I add. "We'll think about how to move them. I have a few ideas."

"This is outstanding news." Munuu seems to hesitate a moment and then asks, "Can you tell me, what are your fees?"

"Oh, don't worry about that. Ariella, um, Ms. Gordon, requests that our clients make a donation to support the next rescue," Stowe tells him.

No time to worry about fees now. We need to seal the deal.

"Munuu, we'll be flying in on a super-speed private aircraft."

Stowe gives me a nod. She knows I'm referring to the ECAPS, our mini space shuttle.

"You want to fly into Chinggis Khaan Airport in Ulaanbaatar, Mongolia's capital," Munuu says. "It is about 60 miles from Hustai Nuruu National Park. I will let the authorities know you are coming.

"When you get here I will fill you in on details about park, and provide special maps and anything else you might need. Please text me when you know your arrival time. I look forward to meeting you."

"Same here. See you soon," I say.

As I hang up we see our grandmother Ariella, in her usual black jeans and black shirt, leaning against the wall on the other side of the room. Her long white braid is swung over her shoulder, and her arms are folded across her chest. Wonder how long she's been standing there?

"Well, hello, Stowe. How did *you* get here? And who are you two seeing soon?"

4. Ariella Enters The Picture

"Hiya," Stowe says, giving her a big hug. "Wheaton brought me down here in the Dynochute. Now we can hang out together all the time."

"Is that so." Ariella's steel blue eyes lock into mine, at least until I decide the floor is more interesting. "Wheaton, I thought we agreed that the first time Stowe was transported in the Dynochute, we'd work it together in case something went wrong?"

"I guess... But you weren't here, and I wanted her to see all the cool stuff going on. Nothing bad happened. And while you were out, we got a rescue job. In Mongolia."

Ariella points to the chairs, and we sit.

"Mongolia? Doing what?" she asks.

Stowe jumps in. "This guy, Munuu, heads up an organization to save the takhi."

"Batar Munkherdene? I met him years ago, before you two were born. I was in Mongolia working on an article about the takhi. It was early days in the reintroduction effort, and Munuu took me out on horseback to see what was going on. Emptiest place I ever went to. I remember him as a very serious man."

Our grandmother is a famous wildlife photographer who's traveled the world writing stories for different magazines.

Stowe describes the problem in Mongolia, and how we agreed that ResQ would help locate the missing takhi and try to drive them back to the park. I hope Ariella thinks Stowe should come with us.

"If this search needs to happen right away, I don't see any way we can get organized fast enough," Ariella says to me.

"The equipment is totally ready to go." I hope I sound convincing.

"Tomorrow in Mongolia is awfully soon. You do realize they're 13 time zones ahead of us?"

"That makes it easier," Stowe says. "We can have pizza for lunch and then spend the afternoon packing up whatever we'll need. If we leave around 6:00 PM we can be there before 9:00 AM tomorrow morning, right in time to get started."

"And if Munuu was helpful to you, shouldn't you try to help him out now?" This seems like a good argument to me.

Ariella shakes her head again, but this time she's laughing. "You two always remind me so much of GG. Wheaton, not only do you have his flying-saucer brown eyes and jet-black hair, but you always have a rational argument to bring to the debate. And Stowe, you're impatient like he was. Seeing you charge ahead would have made him very happy."

Okay. Ariella seems like she's going to agree to the rescue. I have to keep pushing. "So, Stowe can come with us, right? If we find the horses, herding them back into the park is going to take a few people."

Instead of answering my question, Ariella turns to Stowe. "What did you tell your mother before you *flew* down here?"

As if it heard us, Stowe's cell phone vibrates. She flips it over and there's a text from her mom saying 'FOUND YOUR SLIPPERS. WHERE ARE YOU?' followed by a bunch more repeating 'WHERE ARE YOU?' The texts look steamed and worried – a bad combination.

"Mom was busy doing yoga when I left, and she doesn't like to be disturbed. I did leave her a note. Maybe she didn't see it." Now it's Stowe's turn to check out the cracks in the floor.

"You better call her right now to explain how you got here. We can discuss the possibility of your coming with us to Mongolia, but your mother may have other plans for you. And put the phone on speaker, so I can hear what she's saying."

Stowe's cheeks have turned bright red. She doesn't like getting in trouble, especially with our grandmother. She hits speed dial and her mom answers before the first ring is over.

"Hi, Mom. Don't be angry, I can explain."

"I'm listening," a voice says on the other end of the phone.

Stowe tells her about the trip in the Dynochute, and ResQ's next mission to Mongolia.

"Auntie, please let Stowe come. We can't do this without her," I blurt out.

I need Stowe to come. Growing up on the side of a mountain, she knows way more than me about the natural world. Besides, I love Ariella, but this adventure won't be the same if it's only me and her.

"Hello to you too, Wheaton. Mother, are you there? If so, please take the phone off speaker so we can talk."

Ariella and Stowe's mom talk for a while and then we hear my aunt's voice again.

"All right, Stowe. Ski training doesn't start until November, so you can go to Mongolia."

Stowe rolls her eyes when her mother mentions skiing. That's odd. She lives for that sport.

My aunt isn't quite finished. "You've left a lot of unfinished schoolwork here, so be prepared to work very hard when you get home. And I expect you to keep daily logs like you did when you went to Borneo."

"Thanks, Mom." Stowe's face gets a little long realizing there's no escaping her mother's assignments. She's a really smart girl, but she isn't happy learning at a table. Get Stowe outdoors, and she can solve any problem. I guess you could say we're opposites.

"Kids, remember to listen to your grandmother," my aunt tells to us.

And then in the softest, calmest voice I've ever heard coming out of a mom she says, "*Namaste.*"

"*Namaste,*" Stowe says back, and they hang up.

"What's *Namaste*?" I ask, totally confused by that quiet ending to the conversation.

"Oh it's a yoga saying, something about gratitude. But who cares! We're going to Mongolia!"

"Not so fast." My grandmother turns to me. "Young man, you still need to make sure *your* parents are all right with this trip."

Oh boy, my mom is not the quiet, *Namaste* type.

"I know. Let me run home, pack my gear, and check with them."

"Wheaton, can you get me one of the minicomputer headsets before you go," Stowe requests, "in case I want to get started on my logs. I love that invention. My mom was so impressed with how good my spelling and grammar were from the logs on the Borneo trip."

"It's over here in the storage cabinet." I get a chair and climb up to reach the shelf where I put it after our last trip. "Here you go. And don't forget you can do Google searches for extra information." Stowe is dyslexic, so having this helper that corrects her English saves her time and frustration.

But now I have to go home and face *my* mother. This could be harder than the whole trip to Mongolia.

STOWE LEBLOND'S LOG

Hoboken, New Jersey

October 25

1:00 PM

Wheaton brought me from Vermont to Hoboken in his Dynochute. *I zipped south like I was on the longest, fastest slide ever. Unreal. No more 5-hour car trips to get here!*

Wheaton told me all about his Dynochute invention. It's this tube—looks a little like a covered slinky, made of something called shape-memory polymer. As it extends, crystals form and link to each other, making it way stronger than when it's parked in the chimney. Guess that's how it supported me in my journey.

The coolest part is getting the Dynochute *back into the stack. You hit a button on a remote, sending a blast of hot air through the* Dynochute. *When it's heated up, the whole thing pulls back to its original shape inside the stack. Guess that's why it's called "shape-memory" polymer. Who could imagine that there are materials capable of doing stuff like that? People like Wheaton who are studying to become doctors of Material Science and Engineering!*

I didn't tell Wheaton how awesome his invention is. No point in him getting a swelled head. He already knows he's the smartest kid anywhere.

5. Preparing For Departure

It took a while, but I was able to convince my mother to let me go to Mongolia. Well, I didn't convince her, Ariella did. Sometimes I feel like my grandmother's this big old tree anchored in the ground, and my mother's some sort of wild wind blowing through the branches. If I hold on and wait, things usually calm down without me falling out.

Anyway, I'm back at headquarters, with a long list of stuff to watch out for in Mongolia and instructions on eating three meals a day.

Ariella tells us to make sure we pack everything we're going to need. "The landscape is rugged, with broad plains and uninhabited mountains. I've never been there at this time of the year, but the brutal cold on the Mongolian steppes is well known, and there will be very few people in the area."

"But you have seen the takhi, right?" Stowe asks.

"Oh yes. I was in Mongolia in the spring and summer to

photograph the first takhi being released into the wild."

"What do they look like? Are they beautiful?"

"They are spectacular—shorter than domestic horses, often with a few light stripes on their legs. They have short, spiky manes, and their tails are very long."

"Sounds like those Przew something or other horses at the National Zoo," I blurt out.

"One and the same. In the West we call them P-r-z-e-w-a-l-s-k-i horses." Ariella goes over and writes it out on the whiteboard. "You pronounce it shu-VAL-skee, but many people just call it the P-horse."

Ariella gives us more background on the horses. "The P-horse, the zebra and the domesticated horse we know, are all related—similar but with definite differences. The P-horse and the zebra are wild and have never been tamed."

"Reminds me of you." I give Stowe a little shove.

"The P-horses almost went extinct," Ariella tells us.

"Like millions of years ago?"

"No Wheaton, in the late 1960s. Scientists are breeding them and reintroducing them into parks where they used to live. The problem is, once the P-horses are freed, they need to fend for themselves, and face whatever nature dishes out."

"I get it," Stowe says. "The surveys are done to figure out how the P-horses are doing on their own."

Ariella nods. "Now, since Wheaton promised Munuu that ResQ will be there tomorrow, we better move it along.

"Stowe, you study our route to Mongolia, and the two of you gather up everything we're going to need."

While Stowe pulls things together, I run over to my school, the Stevens Institute, for some electronic gear. It sounds like it's going to be tricky to steer the horses in the right direction, but I can think of a few ways to do it. Rummaging around in my professor's lab, I find a bunch of stuff that could be useful—random items like wires and batteries, nothing expensive. Besides, I'll return everything.

When I get back to ResQ headquarters, Stowe has packed up the rest of the supplies we should need, including a stack of chocolate bars for emergencies.

I lay down my cardboard box. "You forgot the Finder." I walk over to one of our storage closets and pull out a silver-colored metal suitcase containing our bionic dog. "We're going to need it to track the horses."

"Looks like you've got everything assembled, kids," Ariella says. "Let me grab my cameras and I'll meet you on the roof."

As Ariella leaves I start to slip something into the storage closet.

"Hey, what's that?" Stowe never misses a thing.

I open my palm and show Stowe a little porcelain horse with its leg broken. "When I went home I accidentally stepped on it. I think it's one of those collectibles Ariella used to bring to our moms whenever she went on trips. My brother must have been playing with it and left it on the floor. When we get back, I'll try and repair it."

"Hope your mom doesn't notice it's missing."

"Whatever," I say, shoving the miniature into the closet. "Let's get going."

We're headed to a military base in Lakehurst, New Jersey, 70 miles away, where the special vehicles I've invented are stored. It's a private spot so we don't attract the attention of neighbors.

Balancing our gear, we make our way back to the roof. Stowe's changed into blue fleece pants and a sweatshirt, not to mention shoes and socks. Ariella joins us and adds her cameras to the pile. We pack everything into the carriers for transport. I've thrown in a pillow to improve the landing experience.

I open my computer and send the Dynochute to Hangar # 36 at the base. "Now hop into your transport suits, and let's go."

STOWE LEBLOND'S LOG

Hoboken, New Jersey

October 25

4:30 PM

ResQ is going to search for a rogue harem of Przewalski horses.

It is pronounced shu-VAL-skee, which makes no sense. Grandma said the word is Polish, named for an explorer, Colonel Nikolai Przewalski, who kind of discovered the horse in 1881. Mongolians knew about the horses all along and called them takhi, which means spirit. I like that name a lot better than Przewalski.

Most wild horses aren't wild—just domestic horses that escape and become feral. There is some debate, but the takhi seem to be the real thing.

Here's why they went extinct in the wild. When Przewalski first "discovered" them, people hunted the takhi down and put a lot of them in zoos. Some were shot for food by soldiers during big world wars. Eating horses of any type... that's disgusting! Other takhi died from starvation because they had to compete with sheep and cattle that grazed on their food. And there were several EXTREMELY cold winters! One winter the temperature reached -40°, leaving the takhi with very little to eat.

In most countries temperature is measured in Celsius (C), not Fahrenheit (F) the way we do in the USA. If you want to convert C to F you multiply the C by 9/5 and add

+32. Here's how the equation looks for -40°C:

(-40°C x 9/5) + 32 = ?

-360/5 +32 = ?

-72 + 32 = - 40°F

As it turns out -40 is the only temperature where C and F are the same. Either way that is cold, even in Vermont. (Mom, see: keeping up with my math.)

By the late 1950s the takhi were almost extinct except for 30 animals, and they were in zoos!

There's this big international program to breed the horses and return them to the wild. When we get to Mongolia we're going to meet the people involved in this work, and I'll have more to report.

6. Loaded Up And Ready To Go

I send the transport box into the Dynochute and follow right behind. Now I see why Stowe complained about the hard landing.

After throwing the pillow down at the Dynochute exit, I talk to Stowe through the remote headset in her helmet. "Everything is ready for you two. Come through now."

In a matter of minutes the three of us and our gear are all on the ground—everything intact. Stowe turns around and looks skyward. "Weird. It's such a clear, sunny day. Why can't I see the Dynochute?"

"Guess you didn't notice. It's invisible when airborne. I wrapped it in a metamaterial that bends light so you can't see it."

"It reminds me of the skin you have for the HeliBoaJee, except you can't see through this one," Stowe says.

"You got it." I pull out my laptop and send the signal to retract the Dynochute back to Hoboken.

"Ariella, Stowe and I can take care of loading up the ECAPS."

After a nod from our grandmother, we walk over to the hangar. I punch in the code, and the large overhead door slides up with a metallic groan. We head over to the ECAPS, our space ship/transporter, and open the storage compartment. Working together, we get all our supplies secured.

"Wheaton, can I drive the HeliBoaJee into the ECAPS? I drive Dad's pickup truck on our property all the time."

"All right, but you better be careful. It's one of a kind." I pull out the ramp Stowe will need to drive the HeliBoaJee up into our aircraft. Even though it's in jeep mode, the HeliBoaJee's got odd angles, like the pointy speedboat front. And it's a little higher than an ordinary jeep, since the rotor blades for the helicopter form are stored on top.

"Wheaton, couldn't the ECAPS door be a little bigger?" Stowe complains as she moves forward.

I stand next to the doorway and try to guide her. *"Go slow."* She's making me nervous with her rushing.

"Stop, you're going to hit the door frame," I yell. "Move a little to the left. Now straighten out and come forward."

Stowe locks the HeliBoaJee in place at the base of the ECAPS and I can breathe again.

Ariella rejoins us. "Maybe you should text Munuu to let him know our plans."

"Will do," I say, pulling out my phone.

"IT'S 6:30 PM. LEAVING SOON. SHOULD BE IN ULAANBAATAR 1 HOUR AFTER DEPARTURE. RESQ TEAM."

Munuu writes back immediately, "MEET YOU AT AIR-PORT. USE RUNWAY #3. FOR PRIVATE PLANES. LESS BUSY. YOU WILL GET HERE AFTER SUNRISE. CHECK TIME CHANGE. BRING WARM COATS. GETTING COLD OUT IN PARK."

"Sunrise! Ugh, we'll lose a night's sleep."

"Poor baby." Stowe pats my head.

I hate missing out on sleep. But no more time to think about short nights. I disconnect the ECAPS from the solar panel that's generated the hydrogen we'll need for take-off and confirm that the tanks with garbage-generated methane are secure to help us maneuver in space.

The three of us remove our jackets and pull on our space suits.

"Hit the program button on your sleeve once you're sealed up," I remind my traveling companions. "We need to stay pressurized." They know all this, but you can't be too careful when you leave the earth's surface.

Ariella and Stowe give me a thumbs up.

I move the ECAPS out to an open area we've designated for launch. The three of us climb aboard. I'm in the pilot seat, Ariella beside me, and Stowe behind us, all set to navigate. It's time to head into space.

7. Fast Trip To Mongolia

I check in with the control tower. We're clear for liftoff.

"Are we ready?" I ask.

"Yes, Captain," Stowe belts out.

"Yes," Ariella says after checking all the gauges in front of her.

The ignition sequence starts. I fire up the solar-generated hydrogen and count down. "Ten, nine, eight, seven, six, five, four, three, two, one."

There's a rumble, and our craft leaves the earth. "We have liftoff."

As we travel east, it gets dark right away. The city lights below become fainter as we soar in the direction of the stars. I turn the ECAPS so it can follow the shape of the earth.

"Remember, we're pretty much weightless now, so stay

belted in. We've got an hour, so if you want to, take off your helmets. Secure them so they don't float away."

I'm not a fan of this sensation of free falling. Glad I resisted having pizza back at headquarters.

Ariella hooks her helmet to the arm of the seat and pulls her braid into place. She laughs as it floats away from her, brushing Stowe's nose.

As she reaches back to reclaim her tail, I decide to ask a question I'm guessing won't be popular. "I know we're on our way to carry out this mission, but what's the big deal about this one harem? Can't they make it on their own? And what if they don't?"

"If your family got separated from everyone, it wouldn't matter if you all died?" Stowe blurts out.

"That's a little dramatic," I tell my cousin.

Ariella turns to us. "The two of you are touching on important points. Stowe is right that each family has value. The things that make a harem unique are found in the genes of the individuals. If a harem is separated from the larger population, the genes of this group will be lost."

"Yeah Wheaton, look at all your brainy genes. Who'd want to lose those."

Our grandmother shakes her head at us and continues. "Reintroduction is not easy. With the harsh weather, a certain number of animals will die each year. And there are diseases and predators to contend with. Conservation biologists say that you need at least 100 takhi to have a population that will last. The lost harem will not survive long on its own."

Stowe adds, "And if it was so much work and money to raise the horses, why wouldn't you do whatever you could to keep them alive?"

Having gotten the last word, she starts whispering into her headset.

"Have you been watching to make sure we're still on track?" I ask.

"Of course I have," Stowe says, turning her head to look straight at the screen.

Lucky for her, we haven't gone in the wrong direction.

Now, staring at the GPS, she tells us, "We've just passed Ukraine. The sun is rising over that mountain range down there."

Stowe pauses as we look at the changing landscape below us. "That should be the Altai Mountains that sit at the western end of Mongolia near Russia and China."

A few minutes later our navigator has more to say, "Look down, guys. That's got to be the Gobi Desert. It's huge!"

We all peer below at this massive texture of browns. There are swirls of lighter brown that might be a dust storm, and grooves where bare rock is exposed. And already in October there are pockets of white where snow has dotted the landscape.

"The desert is located in southern Mongolia and northwestern China, so we're close to Ulaanbaatar now," Stowe reports. "Wheaton, prepare for landing."

I turn the ECAPS north, remind my passengers to get their helmets back on, and begin to slow the vehicle down.

As we descend, the capital lies ahead of us, with the airport at the western edge of the city. The sun is shining above. Good thing we have GPS, because below all I can see is a blanket of black smog.

"It's landing time," I tell my passengers.

The runway sits in the middle of a long, flat valley. My heart races as we descend through the haze into the Chinggis Khaan Airport. Even though I've done this before, my leg is shaking like crazy.

I cut the engine while parachute one opens. With the ECAPS tilted and the landing gear engaged, we come down the runway like the big space shuttles. Everything is under control and the landing is smooth.

"Phew, we made it." Why is Stowe surprised?

"How long did the trip take?" she asks.

"Sixty-one minutes, exactly as Wheaton projected," Ariella says. "Good job."

As I sit there, still gripping the landing shifter, Stowe shouts, "Come on, hotshot, let's get going. That must be Munuu waiting for us on the tarmac."

We climb down the ladder and pull off our space suits. It's cold out here. Wish I'd unpacked my heavy coat.

A short man in a parka waves us over. "*Sain uu/Hello*. Welcome to Ulaanbaatar.

Ariella, it is wonderful to see you again." Munuu shakes our grandmother's hand. Then he turns to us.

"So you are Wheaton Guinto and Stowe LeBlond." It's obvious he's just realized we're kids.

"You got here very fast." Munuu says. He walks around the ECAPS looking at it from every side. "This is what you referred to as your private aircraft? And you built it for rescue business? Hmm."

"The ECAPS is a good little vehicle," I say, trying to sound cool, and not as young as I look (or am). "I do work for another organization back in the States, and something like it was originally built for them. Would you like to peek inside?"

"Yes. Thank you. " Munuu climbs in to have a closer look. "How do you power this thing?"

I give him the short version of how our technology works.

"For departure," I tell him, "we'll need a clean source of water to generate the return fuel." I explain about my aluminum-laser system that will split the water to create the needed hydrogen.

"Don't worry. You will have adequate water supply." Munuu assures me.

Now it's my turn to ask a question. "Is this smog going to clear? We have a portable solar fuel cell system to generate methane for our land-based vehicle. But we'll need some sun."

Munuu shakes his head. "This air pollution is terrible. Many people who live in this city burn low-grade coal, and they send it straight out of their chimneys. At this time of year they only do this at night, so in few hours, when it warms up, air will clear. And out in park there is no smog, so if that is where you plan to use it, you will be fine."

Munuu glances at his watch. Must be interested in moving us along.

"Go store your space ship in there"—he points to a hangar—"in case the weather turns. Then rejoin me at passport control."

While the others follow our host, I jump back on board and motor our aircraft inside. There's a long line when I meet up with the group, but Munuu waves us off to a side door where we're cleared right through.

Now it's off to Munuu's office. I look back, glad the ECAPS is safe from people snooping around, and relieved that everything has gone okay.

At least so far.

STOWE LEBLOND'S LOG

Traveling to Ulaanbaatar, Mongolia

(arriving) October 26

9:00 AM

Another fast trip in the ECAPS, *and now we're in Mongolia. The country's around 604,000 square miles, one-fifth the size of the USA (minus Hawaii and Alaska).*

Mongolia's landlocked with Russia to the north. China makes an arc around the rest of the country. It has several mountain ranges including the Altai Mountains in the west and the Khentii Mountains, in the central region, that come down from Russia toward Ulaanbaatar, the capital.

Ariella told us some archeologists think skiing started in Mongolia's Altai Mountains, maybe 5,000-10,000 years ago. Skis were just curved planks. Good enough to hunt in the winter, I guess, but not designed for racing.

Even though the country is pretty big, the population is small—around three million. (We have more than 100 times as many in the U.S.) Almost half the people live in the capital.

There's a big air pollution problem in Ulaanbaatar. They burn coal for heat and electricity. A lot of particulates, sulfur dioxide, and nitrogen dioxide are released into the atmosphere. To make matters worse, the capital sits in a valley between mountains. In the winter, warm air at the surface of the earth is trapped under a blanket of colder air. Scientists call this a thermal inversion. Since the air doesn't mix normally, the pollutants get concentrated, which is very unhealthy. The U.S. has problems like this too, but they used to be worse. Today we have laws that set standards for how much air pollution is allowed. We don't have that many coal-fired power plants anymore, but where they exist, scrubbers are placed in smoke stacks to remove most of these pollutants. Of course, when you burn coal you also emit carbon dioxide, which causes global warming, and no one has solved that problem yet.

The majority of the people who don't live in the capital are semi-nomadic, following their herds from one grazing place to another. It doesn't rain much, so Mongolians eat dairy and meat, not many vegetables. I'll survive as long as we aren't here too long.

Horses are important in Mongolian life. The country has more horses than people. But the horses people own are different from the wild takhi. I need to find out how you tell them apart. I hope we meet the scientists who are conducting a survey out in the park. They can give me some of this information.

I can't wait to get started on the rescue and see these takhi up close. Just not tooo close.

Mongolian Words I am learning. Before I list my new words I have to tell you that the spellings are phonetic. The Mongolian language is written in a different alphabet called Cyrillic. For fun I'm going to try and copy the letters for Cyrillic too.

Hello – Sain uu – Сайн уу

Gold – Alt – алт *(Like the Altai mountains)*

8. Munuu Preps Resq

Munuu drives through the crowded streets of Ulaanbaatar, trading horn honking with the other crazy drivers. I guess you have to be an aggressive driver to get anywhere in this city. It's kind of a relief when we arrive at the Mongolian Wildlife Service Headquarters.

We head into Munuu's office cluttered with piles of notebooks, laminated pages with pictures of plants and animals, carry-cases full of equipment, and maps and charts lining the walls.

"I realize it is your dinner time, but here in Mongolia, it's time for late breakfast." Munuu points to the food on a side table and makes space for us to sit. "Eat, please."

"I can't believe we're stopping for a meal when there's so much to do," I whisper to Stowe.

"Shush. Munuu put this out for us."

Stowe zeroes in on something grainy. "Mmmm, this food is great. I love this roasted millet. Tastes nutty."

Nutty like you. There's nothing at the breakfast table I've ever seen. But I better eat something or I'll hear about it later.

"Some *sarlagiin tos* for your bun?" Munuu offers. "Yak butter. Comes from high up in mountains."

O-k-a-y—yak butter, this should be interesting. I put a little on my bun and take a bite. The salty taste makes my tongue shrivel up, but the bun's not bad. "What's that?" I whisper to Stowe, pointing at the white stuff.

Munuu hears me. "*Tarag,*" he starts to say.

Before he can translate, Stowe kicks me under the table. "Haven't you ever seen yogurt before?"

I swirl my spoon around and take a bite. The yogurt's thick and tart, but I can't find any fruit at the bottom. Oh well...

Eating reminds me of my mom. "This might be a good time to text our parents."

We both send short informative messages.

While we're all chowing down, Munuu starts to get into what we need to know about this rescue.

"As I told you on phone, we are trying to locate takhi family we lost track of since last season. We think they went east in direction of Khentii mountain range."

"Why would the takhi leave the park?" Stowe asks.

"Not sure. Range is close to park border, and southern

slopes of mountains are covered in grass. There are a few rivers out there." Munuu shows us the area on a map. "Water and food could be attractive to takhi. If they strayed into that area, they could get cut off from park during period of flooding, maybe in spring. Or, maybe they ran off if something scared them. These animals are easily . . . I think you use word spooked."

Ariella makes eye contact with Munuu and then follows up. "You don't think the horses might have gone up into the mountains?"

"No," he shakes his head. "They like open plains. But I am worried that they could have strayed north along western edge of the Khan Khentii range. There is big mining area up there, and many railroad lines. All could present danger for takhi family group."

"You've got a lot of things named Khan here. Any relation to that warrior Genghis Khan?"

"Really, Wig," Stowe mutters. "Munuu's in the middle of telling us something important."

"Yes, Wheaton," Munuu says. "Chinggis Khaan, or Genghis Khan, as you call him, came from that region, and it is said he was buried high up in mountains. But no one has ever found burial site."

"Munuu, you were telling us where you thought the harem might have gone." Stowe gives me another look for getting us off topic.

"All guesses. Might be best if you start by looking for American colleagues, Dr. Abdoulaye Babacar, wildlife ecologist, and veterinarian Dr. Mai Chen, who have been out in field doing surveys of all harem in park. They can tell you more about this family group and where they might have gone." Munuu brings up pictures of Dr. Babacar and Dr. Chen on his cell phone.

Abdoulaye Babacar sounds like an African name. He's tall with long hair in dreadlocks pulled into a ponytail. Mai Chen is way shorter, but she has a ponytail too. They seem old, around my parents' age.

"How big is the park? Any idea where we should start? Do the scientists have a satellite phone?" Stowe's in her question-firing mode.

"Yes they do, but they have not called in for a while. This is phone frequency number they are using." Munuu thrusts a slip of paper at us with the number on it. "I hope their phone is working.

"Hustai Nuruu is quite large—52,000 hectares." Munuu points to the location, in the middle of the park, where the scientists were the last time they called in.

"If I remember right it's about 100 kilometers from here to the park." Ariella says.

"Yes," Munuu replies. "And there is only one road to get there. 'Doulaye and Mai will be off-road doing their surveys."

"We'll fly there. It'll be faster, and easier to scan the park from the air."

"Fly?" Munuu asks.

I did mention our land-based vehicle, but no reason he would think it can fly. I give Munuu a description of the HeliBoaJee, which seems to satisfy him.

"Not to change the subject," Stowe says, as she changes the subject. "Are the P-horses, I mean takhi, fitted with tracking collars before they're released?"

"Yes, they are," Munuu tells us. "Each horse collar has its own signal with VHF beacon that can be located using radio telemetry."

"Very High Frequency, in case you were wondering."

No kidding. Stowe can be quite a showoff.

"There are some things to be aware of," Munuu continues. "You can only pick up VHF signal if you are within few miles of horses. Will be difficult to do from air. And batteries in collars don't last for that long, maybe one, two years. We do not want horses to wear collars forever, so they are designed to fall off when batteries die."

"Do the takhi in the rogue harem still have collars on them?" Stowe's asking the right question.

"I cannot answer this question, but 'Doulaye and Mai may be able to tell you."

Munuu turns to me. "Now it is my turn to asks some questions."

9. Gear Readied For Rescue

"When we spoke on phone you mentioned special technology that might help locate harem," Munuu reminds us. "What do you have?"

He sounds a little skeptical, so here goes.

"It's called the Finder, a kind of bionic dog—"

"Mounted on a drone," Stowe interjects.

"Yes, that's what you said." Munuu's not a guy for small talk.

I go over to one of our packs and pull out our wonder pup.

"This is it," I say, holding it for Munuu to see.

Stowe cannot contain her enthusiasm. "We used this in Borneo to search for a poached baby orangutan and a lost person."

As the words escape Stowe's mouth, she remembers we didn't share everything that happened in Borneo—in particular, losing a member of our team. I glance over at Ariella, whose eyebrows have arched. I need to jump in here.

"I'll tell you how the Finder works. It recognizes the scent of missing people or animals like a real dog, but it's made of a collection of billions of carbon nanotubes standing side by side. You can't see the nanotubes, since each one is about 50,000 times smaller than the diameter of a human hair. We need something that will give us the scent of one or more of the takhi from the harem. We'll use a vacuum to pull air over the object. The molecules that create the signature smell of the missing takhi will stick to the inside of the tubes in the Finder."

Stowe is getting impatient and decides to complete my detailed explanation. "Then when we get to the park we'll release our bionic dog. It'll fly right above the ground so the air passes through it. If the harem was there, chemicals in the air will match what's in the Finder and it will stop in its tracks. Depending on where we are, we'll also get a signal."

Munuu stares at the Finder. "This is quite interesting. I hope 'Doulaye and Mai have something you can use for tracking."

"Speaking of the scientists," I say, "do you have any items of theirs? It would great to get their scents plugged into the Finder. Might help speed up locating them."

Munuu yells down the hall. "Can someone hurry up and get me 'Doulaye and Mai's luggage?"

One of the staff hands Munuu two duffel bags.

He plops them on the table with a thud. "Can you get what you need from these? Scientists left some of their clothes behind when they went out to park."

"But that's their private stuff," Stowe blurts out.

"We're doing this to locate them. And besides, no one's interested in their stinky laundry." Sometimes Stowe can be so dramatic.

I pull a pump out of my pack and suck air from the duffels through the Finder.

"This gives us a start," I say, sliding the cover back over my invention.

We begin to pack up, but Munuu isn't quite finished. "What are your plans for herding the takhi back to the park if you do locate them?"

All eyes are on me now. "How do they respond to sound?"

"Horses have excellent hearing," Munuu tells us. "They can hear sound 4 kilometers away. And they have wide range, much wider than humans. Because takhi live in wild, they are very sensitive to noise, very easily frightened."

"That's helpful. I'm still designing a device in my head. It will include sounds to encourage the horses to move."

Munuu lifts his eyebrows and mouth in a shape that says *we'll see*. "It is possible that you will locate harem but not be able to get them back to park. If you find them, please conduct brief survey first, so at least we will know their health."

Munuu hands us a list with the things he wants us to observe:

Number of horses – stallions/mares

Number of foal

Estimated size of each horse

Appearance – color of coat, mane etc.

Impression of health/vigor

"Should we pay attention to what they're eating?" Stowe asks, as she glances over the list.

"Yes. Do you know plant species?"

"I do." Stowe says. "We live on the side of a mountain, and my mother taught me how to identify everything that grows around our house."

Munuu goes to a shelf and retrieves a book for Stowe. "Since there is vegetation you may never have seen before, here is field guide of Mongolian plants. And if you cannot identify one, take picture, and we can figure out what it is later."

Munuu isn't so sure about Stowe's plant smarts. He'll be surprised when he finds out how much she knows.

"And speaking of what goes into the takhi, do you collect poop samples on the other end?" Stowe asks.

Collect poop! What is Stowe thinking?

"Yes, we do collect stool. It helps identify which animals are which, and if horses are healthy. Will you get these samples for us?" Munuu asks.

"Of course we will, won't we Wig?" Stowe flashes me a cheesy smile.

"Sounds like your sort of thing." I stare hard at Stowe. "Nothing you like better than giving kisses to your slimy salamanders and pet frogs."

Ariella shakes her head at us before turning to Munuu. "Do you have pictures of the takhi groups from earlier surveys? Maybe members of the rogue harem?"

"We do. Of course, they do not compare with ones you have taken in past." You can tell Munuu admires Ariella.

Our grandmother waves her hand at Munuu. "You are very kind."

"Here they are." Munuu brings up a series of pictures of a stallion, six mares, and three foals. "'Doulaye took these photos last year when he and Mai were here doing annual survey, and group was still in park."

Stowe's surprisingly quiet while she stares at the pictures. I'm never certain what her next question will be, but when she launches in, I understand her change of mood.

"Munuu, besides the horses, I am sure there are other park mammals. Are any of them predators of the takhi?"

"Yes, the Mongolian wolf, we call it *chono*. These wolves can be problem, especially for reintroduced takhi. But we don't see them often," he tells her.

Stowe says nothing for a very long minute. She sucks in a whole lot of air, but I don't hear much coming out. My guess is she's remembering when an 80-pound coyote stared in the window at her house. And the next morning

Fiddlehead, Stowe's favorite chicken, was gone. Ever since then, the idea of coyotes and wolves has terrified her.

Stowe remains quiet for a few more seconds, takes one more deep breath, grabs another bun and stands up.

"I think we have our orders."

10. Off To Hustai Nuruu National Park

Munuu hands us detailed maps. "Keep them with you. Remember there is no cell service in most of park, and depending on weather, GPS and satellite transmission can be problem. We don't want to lose you too. Now let us head back to airport. I reserved vehicle for you but sounds like you have your own."

"Yes, it's still in the ECAPS. Wait till you see it!" Stowe is in orbit again.

Munuu drives us back to the airport and parks his car. He walks back to the hangar with Ariella and me. Stowe's gone ahead of us, talking into her headset.

As we approach the landing strip, Stowe comes zooming out of the ECAPS in the HeliBoaJee, skidding to a stop inches in front of us.

I hope she didn't nick the door on the way out.

"These are our wheels," I tell Munuu, "the HeliBoaJee—part Helicopter, part Boat, part Jeep. Push a button and we can be in the air, on the road or in the water."

We've been with Munuu for a while, but all of a sudden he stares down at me like he's seeing me for the first time. "Wheaton, do you mind me asking; how old *are* you?"

"Eleven," I say, feeling my back straighten.

"He's a brainiac," Stowe tells Munuu. "He's a college graduate and enrolled in a Ph.D. program. One day he's going to be Dr. Wheaton Guinto."

Come on, Stowe. You know I can't stand being the center of attention.

Now Munuu's face has a giant question mark all over it. I feel like I have to explain myself. Urghh.

"It's a long, boring story. I had a kind of blood disease when I was 2, and I was stuck at home for a couple years. My parents claim I found designs from their engineering firm and started building them with my Legos. When my parents took me back to preschool, they kicked me out. Something about me being too advanced. Same thing kept happening until at nine I was in college. Anyway, that's my story," I say, looking down at my shoes.

Ariella's been standing next to me the whole time. She puts her arm around me for a second and gives me a hug. She knows how much I hate talking about this stuff.

Time to shine a light on my cousin. "Stowe's training to be a ski champ, may even go to the Olympics someday. And she's only twelve." Stowe is much taller than me, but I don't want Munuu to think she's a lot older.

Stowe gives me a funny look when I mention the skiing. Wonder what's going on. I guess she'll tell me later.

"Well, you two have surprised me. When we spoke on the phone I did not realize you were kids."

At least he didn't say just kids.

Munuu helps us load the supplies onto the HeliBoaJee. He hands each of us his satellite phone frequency. "Please update me daily and call if you run into any problems."

I climb into the pilot's seat and hit the CONVERSION button. The rotor blade pops up, landing skids slide out, and wheels retract. The tail rotor pushes into place, and the HeliBoaJee is ready to go.

We promise Munuu to keep in touch, and with that we head west to the Hustai Nuruu National Park air space.

STOWE LEBLOND'S LOG

Ulaanbaatar, Mongolia

October 26

11:00 AM

Our first day in Mongolia started with breakfast at Munuu's office. I'm guessing there'll be lots of meat to dodge later but I'm happy to say all we saw this AM were grains and dairy products. You should see how fast Wheaton finished eating. He said it was so we could get going. I'm guessing the food wasn't his favorite.

Our search is starting in Hustai Nuruu National Park. It's 52,000 hectares, which isn't even midsize for the U.S National Parks, but plenty big when you are looking for two people and ten horses.

TIME FOR A MATH PROBLEM:

1 hectare = 0.00386 square miles or 2.47 acres

52,000 hectares X 0.00386 = 201 square miles

For comparison purposes The Great Sand Dunes National Park in Colorado, where we went camping that one time, is 167 square miles, and Zion National Park in Utah is 230 square miles.

While I'm at it, 1 kilometer = 0.62 miles so if the park is 100 kilometers away that's

100 X 0.62 = 62 miles.

From what we're learning, it's pretty amazing that the

takhi are around at all. The last takhi anyone reported seeing in the wild before now was between 1966 and 1969. That's when scientists from countries including the United States, Netherlands, Czechoslovakia, and England started breeding them in captivity. Slowly the numbers started to grow. As of 2018 there are 2,000 takhi in the whole world, with 350-400 living in the wild, most of them in Hustai Nuruu National Park.

There's an organization called the International Union for Conservation of Nature (IUCN). It has 1,300 members from around the world, and they are dedicated to species survival and other related stuff. They grade animal populations from being in the worst shape to the best:

Extinct
Extinct in the wild
Critically Endangered
ENDANGERED
Vulnerable
Near Threatened
Least concern

For an individual takhi to be counted as a member of a surviving species, it has to be born in the wild, live at least five years, and produce an offspring that survives and reproduces in the wild. In 2008 takhi moved from being extinct in the wild to being critically endangered, and after 2011 there were enough takhi that passed the wild test to make it to the endangered list. Who thought being endangered would sound good! Of course a hard winter, disease or predators, and the species could be knocked down on the list again.

Every animal counts!

Mongolian Words I am learning.

yak butter – *sarlagiin tos* – сарлагийн тос

yogurt – *tarag* – тараг

wolf – *chono* – чоно

11. Some Dead Clues And A Collar

We get out of the crazy Ulaanbaatar air space and can relax a little.

"Munuu seemed almost cross with us," I say to Ariella. "He did ask us to come."

"From what I recall, Munuu has had a very hard life. He came from a poor family of goat herders and has been taking care of himself since he went to high school. He has rough edges, but I never met anyone in all my travels who cared more about preserving this country and all its resources."

"Okay. I understand." Now to the matter at hand. "Stowe, why don't you try and reach the scientists by satellite phone."

She dials and shakes her head. "No answer. Remember, Munuu was worried that their phone might not be working."

"We ought to try and find them," I suggest. "They know more about the harem than anyone. Munuu said the last time he heard from them, they were somewhere in the middle of the park."

"What if they're not sitting waiting for us?" Stowe asks. "We've got their scent programmed into the Finder. Let's launch it as soon as we get to the park boundary."

"It's a big place, Miss Impatience. If you were going to send out a search and rescue dog, you wouldn't drop it down in any old spot. We've got to find some clues first."

Stowe lets out a big sigh as she peers down below. "I guess... I've just never seen a place that looks so empty."

"Yes," Ariella says, "exactly like I remembered...."

The three of us stare ahead as we pass across the park perimeter. We see wide river valleys, and foothills of the bigger Khentii mountains. The broad, grassy areas are pretty brown at this time of year. There are pockets of snow, an indicator of how cold it is even though it's only October.

"There's no sign of life down there," I say.

Stowe laughs. "Don't tell that to the plants."

Before I can come back with a smart response, my cousin's body language changes. She leans forward peering through her binoculars. "Take a look. Are those takhi?"

Ariella grabs another pair of binocs and focuses on Stowe's sighting. "Yes, looks like them. Wheaton, can you circle the area so we can take a closer look?"

I fly in a wide arc so we don't scare the horses.

It looks like a diorama—nine tan-colored horses, almost

camouflaged against the remnants of last summer's pasture. The spiky dark brown manes crowning their heads bring these wild horses into three-dimensional relief. All alone down there, they look so peaceful grazing together. Hard to imagine that they can be wild or aggressive.

"There's no VHF signal," I say. "Must be an older group where the collars have fallen off, or we're not close enough. Either way, those takhi are inside the park so not the ones we're looking for. Let's head to the middle of the park. Maybe we'll see the scientists...."

Ariella nods and I turn the copter west.

On the first pass over the area we don't hear or see anything. I suggest we fly over in a zig-zag pattern. "Maybe by coming at a different angle, we'll pick up something."

The "middle" is pretty expansive when you're out here. Back and forth we go. Nothing. "I'm going to try something different," I say, as I begin flying in a spiral pattern.

We're about to give up when I hear what might be a signal. "Guys, is that a beep? It's really low." Everyone leans in. With the chopping sounds of the Heli-blades, none of us is sure. But maybe.

We continue flying in tighter and tighter circles. Straining to hear, we look at one another and nod. A pinging is coming from the VHF system, but it's so faint we're lucky we caught it.

"Wonder what's down there? Maybe takhi the scientists were studying? I wish we could see something." I look at Stowe. "This might be a good place to release the Finder. Let's land."

I touch down a little fast. All right, too fast. We bump pretty hard. “Sorry guys, I forgot how hard the ground gets when it freezes.”

“Let’s go find some takhi,” Stowe yells. “And, fingers crossed, ’Doulaye and Mai too. Grab the Finder, Wheaton.” She pulls on her down jacket as she darts off the HeliBoaJee.

“Why don’t you make a little more noise so the takhi know we’re coming,” I hiss.

“Wheaton’s right. We need to make our way as quietly as possible. We wouldn’t want to scare the horses,” Ariella whispers. “Let’s take our gear with us. We don’t know what we’ll find.”

What does that mean? I can imagine lots of bad things, but I’m not going to say them out loud.

We take our packs and start to fan out from the HeliBoaJee. I stop to zip up my jacket and yank on my hood. It feels like January in Hoboken out here.

Stowe wastes no time and charges over a field of rocks. There’s no trail. I hang onto Ariella. Wouldn’t want her to fall.

Despite being very careful, I trip.

“Ughh, what’s that?” I gasp, jumping back. “Looks like the skeleton of the family dog or something.”

Ariella crouches down. “No, I don’t think that’s a dog. The legs are short, the body’s chunky, and see how small the head is? Most likely it’s the remains of a tarbagan marmot.”

Stowe races back to join us. “Do you think a wolf got it?”

“Hard to know, but see how the skull is bashed in. Wolves don’t do that. More likely human hunters did in this little fella, quite a while ago.”

Ariella snaps a few photos of the skeleton and we continue on.

Stowe, who always seems to be few steps ahead of us, stops and turns around. “Munuu did say the scientists were somewhere in the middle of the park. Is there any reason you can’t get the Finder going now?”

“You’re right. I’m on it.” With the lid open, I program the remote to move the Finder back and forth across the valley floor. “Let’s go, puppy. Go find ‘Doulaye and Mai.”

Sitting on a rock, I follow the Finder's movement through my binoculars. For a while it zooms around with nothing to say for itself. But then it sits down on the ground and starts flashing positive signals. "Hey guys, the Finder says the scientists might be over there." I point in the direction of my brilliant device.

As we stare ahead, we notice a large dark bird circling overhead.

Ariella peers through her binoculars. "That's a cinereous vulture. Look at that wing-span. Must be 10 feet across."

We take turns looking at the bird while Ariella pulls out her camera, extending her telephoto to the max.

"I know it's exciting for you and Stowe to see new birds, but should we be worried about why a vulture is circling? I hope it doesn't think there's a good meal down here."

"It's a vulture. It eats dead stuff." Stowe gives me a shove.

"No kidding. Not us I was thinking about."

"We better see what the Finder has located," Ariella says.

Stowe takes off. She races about 100 yards (oops, around 100 meters here in Mongolia) ahead and shrieks.

"What's wrong?" Ariella and I run through the grass toward my cousin. She's standing like a statue, pointing at something large lying on the ground.

"Is it a horse?" From the distance all I can see is something big and brown, and what looks like blood on the grass.

"No, I don't think so, but a lot of it is missing." Stowe yells back in a high-pitched voice.

Ariella and I arrive at the site of a half-chewed-up carcass of something. It only has three legs.

"What is it?" I hold my nose. The stench reminds me of the way the garbage smelled that week the trash collectors went on strike.

Stowe's voice quivers. "It looks a little like a deer."

"No, it's a Mongolian gazelle, a type of antelope," Ariella tells us. "I'm pretty sure this animal *was* taken down by a wolf. See the teeth marks near its throat."

I wish I didn't have to look.

"Why did the Finder stop here? Wheaton, you said it would pick up the scientists' scents. Were they attacked by the wolf too?"

My leg shaking is not the response we need, but I have no answers for Stowe's questions.

"And we still can't explain the VHF signal Wheaton picked up from the air." Stowe turns away from the gazelle. "Why don't you get that Finder moving. Maybe there are more clues out here."

"No problem." Any excuse to leave this crime scene.

As we move away from the gazelle, we look back long enough to see the vulture land. We must have interrupted its meal.

Meanwhile the Finder begins to circle an area not too far from us.

"It's spinning again." Stowe looks ahead with her binoculars. "No sign of anything dead or alive," she reports, before moving toward our bionic dog, now settled down next to a small shrub.

"Look at this," she says, bending down to pick up what looks like a horse collar. "I don't get it. Didn't Munuu say they only fall off when the batteries die? But you got a VHF signal. This must be what it was coming from, don't you think?"

Ariella takes a look at the collar. "There's a number on it. #959. I bet Dr. Chen and Dr. Babacar will be able to tell us who this belongs to."

"Are those knife marks on the collar? The Finder says the scientists were here. Why would they cut it off?" Two dead animals and knife marks on a collar. I don't like this at all.

STOWE LEBLOND'S LOG

Hustai Nuruu National Park, Mongolia

October 26

3:30 PM

There are supposed to be many different animals in Hustai Nuruu National Park. But in October I guess a lot of them are already hibernating or lying low for the winter. We did see two dead animals. First, we found the skeleton of a tarbagan marmot that looked like it had its head bashed in. Ariella thinks that the marmot may have been killed by a human hunter who wanted its fur for making hats and coats. It's illegal but that doesn't stop everyone. Vultures probably made a meal of the carcass, leaving the skeleton for us to find.

Then we found a dead Mongolian gazelle. There are thousands of them, and they migrate in big herds in search of grazing pastures. The Mongolian gazelle is at risk for several reasons. Like with the marmots, humans hunt them. Another problem relates to mining, which is big business in Mongolia. The roads and railways used by the mining companies interrupt the gazelle's migration patterns and their search for food. The Trans-Mongolian railway connects Russia and China. It runs right through the Mongolian gazelle's migration path used every winter by thousands of animals looking for water and food. The barbed wire fences around the train lines prevent normal migration, and in 2016, 5,300 Mongolian gazelles died. I hope the missing takhi harem didn't get into that kind of trouble.

People aren't the only enemies of the gazelle. Based on the teeth marks on its neck, odds are the one we found was attacked by a wolf. It must have been a pretty fresh kill, because a lot of the carcass was still there. (So disgusting...)

Of course, one person's gross-out is another animal's feast. Ariella pointed out a cinereous vulture that was waiting for us to leave so it could dive into the gazelle. These vultures are not found in the Americas, just Europe and Asia. They are big vultures, as much as 30 pounds, mostly black with a white head. They have their own problems and are endangered in Europe, partly because their habitats are being destroyed. Lots of people means trees are cut down and no place for nests. And in places where rodents and wild dogs are poisoned on purpose, the vultures that feed on the carcasses are poisoned as well.

It's creepy to see these vultures circling overhead, but they are part of the cycle of life. I still hope we don't find any more dead animals or worse on this trip.

Mongolian Words I am learning

marmot – *tarvaga* – тарвага

Mongolian gazelle – *Mongol zeer* – монгол зээр

cinereous vulture – *torgon shuvuu* – Торгон шувуу

12. Stopping At A *Ger* Hotel

We look in every direction. No sign of another person anywhere. The sun is getting low on the horizon, but the sky is still so huge it feels like it could swallow us up.

"What do we do now? The scientists were here, otherwise the Finder would never have sniffed out this collar," I say.

"Or the dead gazelle," Stowe adds.

"When we go home I need to figure out how to have the Finder identify the timing of an encounter. But for now we need to decide where to go next."

"Let's start by going back to the HeliBoaJee, so we can analyze this collar a little further," Ariella suggests.

As soon as we get back, Stowe passes the broken collar by the VHF system, which starts to ping. "The batteries are still alive. What does that mean?"

"I don't know," I say. "This must be the signal we picked up from the air. And we know that the scientists handled the collar, since the Finder sniffed it out. I bet our pup will lead us to 'Doulaye and Mai."

Stowe and I are ready to continue the search, but Ariella steps in.

"Time to take a break. It's late in the afternoon, and soon it will be dark. We've lost a night's sleep. There's no telling what will happen tomorrow. When I was here before, there was a small tourist camp, kind of a hotel, near the south-central border of the park. It's late in the season, but I think they used to be open year-round. Let's see if we can find them."

"The scientists may be nearby. The sooner we find them, the quicker we'll know where the harem might have gone." Stowe's always in a rush, but this time I agree with her. And the thought of sleeping in a camp doesn't sound too comfortable.

"Finding the scientists is a priority, I agree, but as soon as the sun sets it will get very cold out here. And if we get too tired, we could end up in trouble of our own." Ariella cuts the air with her hand in a motion that's code for *end of discussion.*

Stowe and I learned a long time ago that debating, or as our grandmother would say, nagging, won't change her mind. With that, we pack up the Finder and the rest of our gear and get back in the HeliBoaJee.

Ariella directs me to the section of the park perimeter where she believes we will locate our lodging solution.

Stowe points. “Look.”

Below, a bunch of circular huts look like they're wrapped in puffy white sheets. They have some sort of pipe extending out of the roofs, and the doors are brightly colored. Off to the side are a few outbuildings painted turquoise.

Our grandmother smiles. “That's what I was hoping we'd find.”

As I land the HeliBoaJee, a few people come running out from one of the huts.

Ariella steps down and waves at the man coming toward us. “Chuluun, is that you? I am Ariella Gordon. *Sain uu*. I stayed with you about ten years ago,” she says.

The man is kind of stocky, but maybe he looks that way because he's wearing this long blue wool overcoat that gets wide below his knees. His black eyes are smiling as he greets her. “Yes, I remember. Photographer?” he says in a loud raspy voice. He motions with his hands, mimicking snapping a picture. He turns and says something to the two women behind him.

The older woman comes forward. She's wearing a beautiful red coat with a black velvet sash tied around her waist. “Hello, welcome,” she says to us. “My name Tuya.” She gestures to come inside.

We walk toward the door of the hut when the younger woman, more a girl of about seventeen, waves to us.

"Sarnai? You're all grown up," Ariella says. "How are the other children?" she asks Chuluun.

"Everyone good—getting big," he raises his hand high above his head. "Two young ones now at boarding school. They come home Friday. Oldest daughter is married. Lives in Ulaanbaatar. Elder son studies at university in China. He will be engineer."

Then Chuluun turns to Sarnai, who's around Stowe's height. He tugs on one of her braids sticking out of a gold-embroidered black cap that matches the sash on her turquoise coat. "She just finished school and helps with business."

"You American?" Sarnai asks. We nod and she claps her hands. "Good, I practice my English with you."

Chuluun holds the door open for us. Ariella explains that their home and the "rooms" they have for tourists are called *gers* in Mongolian.

"These look like the yurts we saw on vacation in Maine," I say to Ariella.

"It's the same idea. Yurt is the Russian word for these structures." Then she whispers etiquette instructions in our ears before we go inside.

Stowe enters first and walks clockwise, careful to avoid the center poles. Without turning her back on the altar with the statue of Buddha, she goes over and runs her hand over one of the orange and blue woven blankets decorating the walls. "These are so beautiful."

Beds for the family line the walls. The center of the room must be the kitchen. There's a stove and small table piled with clean pots and dishes. The family has another brief discussion. Sarnai speaks the most English, so she turns to us. "Please join us for dinner and then we go to *ger* you can stay in tonight."

"That sounds very good. *Bayarlalaa,*" Ariella says.

Tuya invites us to sit down on stools around a small table while she serves the evening meal. This is going to be interesting. Mongolia is not supposed to be a very vegetarian-friendly country. I glance sideways at Stowe, who's trying to size up what's in the different pots on the stove.

We each get a plate and bowl. Tuya puts out a spread of noodle soup, mutton stew, and dumplings filled with meat called *buuz*. Stowe is looking down at her lap, and it's not because she dropped food there.

"Phew, you're saved," I whisper to her, as Tuya comes out with a large plate of *byaslag*—cheese. Ariella did say it's rude not to try everything, but it's all right to sample something and leave the rest. Stowe takes so little of the meat it's hard to see under the cheese on her plate. Tuya pours each of us a glass of *süü* (that's milk). I'm not asking from what animal.

During dinner Ariella explains why we're here. When she mentions the scientists, Chuluun looks up.

"Two American scientists had reservation to stay here few days ago. Never came." He shrugs.

Ariella raises her eyebrows and looks at the two of us.

It's the second clue of the day, but the puzzle doesn't look any closer to being figured out.

We hear a sizzling sound from the stove. Tuya brings a jar of raspberry jam and what look like deep fried cookies to the table. "*Boortsog*," she says. "Dip in jam."

"These are amazing," Stowe says as we pop one after the other of these warm, sweet cookies into our mouths.

When we finish, we thank Tuya.

Sarnai turns to us. "Come. I show you *ger* where you sleep." She beckons, and we follow her out the door.

There are about fifteen guest quarters. She takes us to one with three beds. There's a gas stove in the middle, "to stay warm," she tells us.

That explains those pipes sticking out of each *ger*.

She pauses as she gets ready to leave. "You ride horses?"

"Do I ever!" Stowe says. "I help take care of horses at the stable of a friend back home, I don't have my own horse, but I ride whenever I can."

"And you?" Sarnai looks at me.

"I ride when I visit Stowe, but I'm not very good at it." That's an understatement. I'm getting nervous about where this discussion is heading.

She turns to Ariella. "Wheaton and Stowe come with me to see our horses. Okay?"

"All right. But only for a little while. And kids, get some warm clothing on. It's dark now and it will be cold outside."

"Wait here, I will be back soon," Sarnai says as she exits the *ger*. After a little while she returns, carrying two fur coats and hats. "Put these on. Better than your coats."

"What kind of fur is this? Stowe asks Sarnai. She glances over at me, her teeth clenched.

"Fox," Sarnai tells us. "Very warm."

Stowe's body gets a little straighter but she knows better than to comment. Glad these coats didn't turn out to be marmot. Not sure we need to be so warmly dressed, to walk over and *see* the horses. Why do I get the feeling we are going to do more than just look at them?

STOWE LEBLOND'S LOG

Hustai Nuruu National Park, Mongolia

October 26

7:00 PM

We are spending the night at a local "hotel,"—a cluster of yurts, or gers as they are called here. Ger means house or home, and Mongolian people have lived in them for thousands of years. The design is very useful for nomads, people who travel from place to place following their grazing animals. These houses are collapsible. They are circular with a lattice of wooden poles that expand to create a frame. With a round design there is no wasted space. You always say that corners are where dust goes to die ☺. The inside of the ger is insulated with felt, which is unwoven wool pressed into a fabric. An outside wrapping made of something waterproof, like animal skins, provides the cover. The dome-shaped roof has a hole in the middle for the pipe/chimney from the stove. The whole structure can be put up in an hour. Pretty good for something so complex. Some people can't get a simple tent up in that time.

We were surprised at the beautiful decorations in our host's ger. The door, facing south away from the worst of the winds, is wooden and painted orange with intricate blue designs. Inside all the furniture is painted orange.

There are still a lot of Mongolians who live a nomadic existence. Many of those people only live in their gers for part of the year. They move to permanent shelters for the winter. If you're driving around out here and see someone taking down a ger, you're supposed to stop and help. Idea is, you never know when you might need help—sounds like what you always tell me—"pay it forward."

Our hosts keep their hotel of gers open year-round. It feels pretty warm inside, but glad we won't be here in January. I almost forgot to mention that there are no bathrooms in the gers. They have separate bathrooms—outhouses really. Hope we don't have to "go" at night ☺.

Living so far from towns does limit what people eat. It's not like you can drive 20 minutes to your local supermarket. You know how we have five food groups? Well here they have a few grains and veggies but there are only two types of food that count—red and white. Red refers to meat, mostly boiled mutton. Needless to say I'm passing on that. White are all the milk products, including cheeses and yogurt. Milk comes from lots of animals, not just cows. We're talking horses, camels, sheep, goats and reindeer. Horse milk is supposed to be the most nutritious. I'm trying to be adventurous, but maybe I'll stick to good old cow's milk if I can get away with it.

Mongolian Words

Thank you – Bayarlalaa – баярлалаа

Milk – Süü – сүү

Horse – Mori – морь

Cheese – Byaslag – бяслаг

Home – Ger – гэр

13. Night Ride

We follow Sarnai out into the cold night air, nice and toasty in our fur coats.

"Your name is beautiful," Stowe says to our host.

Sarnai's cheeks turn a little redder, if that's possible. "Thanks, it means rose in English. I have met other Americans, but your names are quite different."

"They're kind of geographic," Stowe explains with a giggle. "I was named for a famous ski town in the state of Vermont where my dad was born. My family lives there now, so everyone remembers my name."

"And my parents named me for a river in the Yukon in Canada. They met there on a canoe trip during college," I tell Sarnai. "Everyone thinks our names are funny since our mothers' family comes from Italy, and Stowe's Dad is French Canadian and mine's Fiipino."

"So interesting," Sarnai says. "In America people come from so many places. In Mongolia all our families have lived here forever."

Our discussion of names and origins comes to a halt as we arrive at something that looks like an open corral. A few horses are tied to a simple fence post. The rest of the herd seems to be wandering off in the distance. Not clear what's going on. There aren't many horses around for us to "see."

Before I have time to wonder what Sarnai really has in mind she asks, "Would you like to go for little ride?"

I'm uncomfortable with the grin on her face, but of course Stowe doesn't leave much time to consider an answer.

"Are you kidding? Of course we want to ride."

I give my cousin an intense look. "I don't think Ariella will think this is such a good idea."

"Only short ride," Sarnai promises.

"If we have to do this, I'm going back to get my backpack, in case there's gear we need out there," I say, glaring at Stowe.

Ariella, Chuluun and Tuya are standing near the family *ger* with their backs to me. Unnoticed, I creep into our "hotel room" and grab my pack. I see one of Ariella's cameras and take that too. Never know when it might come in handy.

In no time I'm back with the horsewomen. Sarnai's produced a few saddles. She hoists one to Stowe, and then passes another to me. She points to the tethered horses. Swinging her arm in the air like she's lassoing, she explains that she has brought two in for us to ride. The third, already saddled up, is obviously hers.

Sarnai walks over to a jet-black horse, takes the saddle from me, and gets it positioned. "This is *Khar*. He is old. You ride him."

I pull myself up onto *Khar's* back. He stands stock-still. That's a relief. The saddle is comfy. It has a back support and a high front. This might not be so bad.

Looks like Stowe's getting a brown horse. "This is *Khüren*. He is for you," Sarnai says.

Then she walks over to the milk-white horse. "This my horse, *Tsagaan*."

Once the three of us are mounted, Sarnai trots off and we follow.

Khar strolls along at a nice slow pace. The horse is short, so I don't feel like the ground's that far away, and he's solid like a rock. I should be able to stay right-side up. The sky is clear, and with the full moon we don't need headlamps to see where we're going. Wherever that is.

Stowe has slowed down and is now riding beside me. "Want to be sure you're okay. These horses are a dream to ride, aren't they?"

"It's not bad. Almost relaxing." My answer surprises me. "You ride like you were born on a horse. How much time did you spend at that barn last summer?"

"I was there every day, even weekends. Mostly I cleaned the stalls, groomed the horses, and kept the hay bins full," Stowe tells me. "But when someone wasn't taking a horse for a lesson that day, I got to give it some exercise. When the stable owner had extra time we'd go trail riding together. It was the best summer ever."

"Sounds like you like horseback riding almost as much as skiing." I say to Stowe.

She gets that weird look on her face again, but before she can respond we notice that Sarnai has turned around and is riding back to join us, her fingers to her lips. "Look. Takhi," she whispers, as she points not more than a hundred meters in front of us.

"Nine of them. I wonder if 'Doulaye and Mai have surveyed them?" Stowe says.

I hand her Ariella's camera. "Why don't you try to take their pictures."

Stowe's eyebrows rise. "Did you ask before you took this?"

"No. I figured it would be all right. Besides, then I would have had to tell them about the plans for our little riding adventure."

Stowe takes the camera and dismounts. "It's pretty dark even with the amazing moonlight. I don't want to use a flash and spook the horses. Get off your horse and come over here," she orders me. "Stand still so you can be my tripod."

While Stowe's snapping pictures of the family of mares and the stallion, Sarnai has ridden off a distance from us.

"Psst," we hear. "You guys," she calls. "Come here."

14. What's Wrong With That Mare?

Stowe finishes taking her last picture. The two of us mount up and make our way to the sound of Sarnai's call.

"Look," she's pointing at another takhi and a foal.

"Why are they off by themselves?" Stowe asks.

Sarnai shakes her head. "Mare is acting strange, and foal does not look so good either."

We watch the adult lie down. "Looks tired and sick. So thin. Maybe family is deserting them," our guide suggests.

"We ought to let Munuu know there's a sick takhi out here," Stowe says to me.

"Agree. Let's go back before Ariella wonders where we are." I'm thinking a predator could be out here licking its chops.

"Did you bring a plastic bag?" Stowe asks. "We should collect stool samples before we leave."

"Lucky for you, the sampling kits are in my pack." I yank out a few of the bags Munuu gave us for this purpose, and hand them to Stowe. "Don't get too close to the horses. Remember they're not going to be friendly like *Khüren*."

"I won't." Stowe jumps off her horse and makes a wide circle around the sad-looking takhi and her foal. The mare follows with her eyes.

Stowe bends down to scoop up some poop when the horse rises from the ground.

"Don't make any fast moves," I warn from my perch on *Khar*.

Stowe doesn't utter a word as she stands up. She pauses and snaps a few photos of the pair. That was *not* necessary right now.

The mare flinches at the click of the camera and lets out a snort. She takes a step in Stowe's direction. I stop breathing as my cousin walks backwards, never taking her gaze off the takhi. The horse doesn't advance any further but follows the retreating human with her eyes. Sarnai is waiting with *Khüren's* reins outstretched.

Stowe gets up on her stallion as fast as her legs allow. "That was a little scary. Let's get out of here."

Sarnai waves her arm for us to depart.

I hope that means heading to her parents' place.

As we retreat, the mare lies back down. The three of us ride side by side, looking back from time to time to be sure the takhi haven't decided to follow.

We don't talk for a while, and then out of the silence we hear an awful piercing noise. Not once, but at regular intervals. And in between there's this scary ghost-like whirring.

I look in Stowe's direction. "What is that? Where's it coming from?"

I don't like this situation at all. And to make matters worse, large clouds have covered the moon and it's dark out here.

We pull out our headlamps and an extra one for Sarnai. When we're all illuminated, we notice our guide is smirking. I don't see how this could be anything to smile about.

Sarnai beckons for us to follow her to a nearby tree. She points into the canopy. "Look up there."

At first I see nothing, but then the clouds recede and the moonlight reveals a tiny owl with bright yellow eyes. That piercing sound is coming from a bird not more than nine inches tall.

"Sorry I panicked. It sounded like something in trouble." I feel kind of dumb. I should've been able to tell an owl cry from a person. "I thought owls say hoo-hoo."

"That's fine," Stowe says, as she squints to get a glimpse at the bird. "It's a *Little Owl*—a new bird to add to my list."

The silence out here is broken again—by a long, deep howl. This time it's Stowe who turns chalk white.

"That's a wolf's cry, isn't it?" she asks Sarnai.

"Yes. Still far away, but it will find takhi if mare doesn't get up soon. Maybe we hurry back to your *Emee*."

We mount our steeds and ride back, a lot faster than we left.

15. Explaining Ourselves

Arriving back at the horse pen we see Ariella, Tuya and Chuluun talking with two other people. "Prepare for an interrogation," I whisper to my companions.

"Where have you been?" Ariella calls, before we even dismount. The lines on her face are so tight they could slice her skin. "You said you were going to *check out* the horses, not go off riding in the night."

We try to explain what happened on our ride, but our grandmother doesn't seem interested.

While we're getting chewed out for the escapade, I notice Chuluun has taken Sarnai off to the side. His loud voice sounds like a bark now, and not a friendly one. But unlike us, Sarnai seems able to input some information on what happened out there. After more arm waving between father and daughter, he turns to Ariella.

"Please go have tea. Children will give us whole story."

Inside we shed our skins. That's when we take a closer look at the tall guy with the crazy dreadlocks, and the short lean woman squinting out of her glasses.

"You're Dr. Babacar and Dr. Chen," Stowe says, sticking out her hand for a shake. "I'm Stowe LeBlond. This is Wheaton Guinto."

Ariella interrupts. Not a good sign. "They were finishing up their surveys at the eastern end of the park. They always planned to stay here but were delayed a few days. They can tell you more later, but for now I still want an explanation..."

Stowe describes how we found the family of takhi, and the lone mare and her foal that seemed sick. She holds up the poop samples we've collected.

Dr. Babacar's looking at us with his head cocked. "Guys, you didn't try to ride those wild horses did you? You know they could make you sick."

"Really. How?" I ask.

"They could give you bronco-itis."

Dr. Chen shakes her head. I have a feeling she's heard that joke before.

Stowe ignores the joke and continues. "On our way back we heard a wolf howl. Dr. Chen, you don't think it would attack a sick animal, do you?"

"Please call me Mai." The vet's eyes and nose wrinkle, the way they do when you're worried. "A wolf would happily prey on a weakened animal. And foals are always an easy mark. 'Doulaye, I think we should head out and see what's going on."

"Agree. But you know how easy it is to get lost out there, especially at night." He doesn't seem to be kidding any more as he turns to Sarnai. "Can you help us find these animals?"

"No problem," she replies.

Stowe goes for her coat. "We need to come too."

"I don't think so. You kids have had enough adventure for one night. We'll see everyone again in the morning." Ariella isn't inviting any more discussion, but Stowe seems to miss that point.

"Are you sure?"

"Quite." Then our grandmother turns to the others. "I hope things go smoothly. We look forward to catching up tomorrow."

The three of them depart, and while we finish drinking our tea, Tuya starts clearing the dishes.

"In morning you come for breakfast to *ger* restaurant. Sign on outside so you know which one."

Tuya's given us a cue that it's time to leave. She's pretty quiet compared to her husband and daughter, but she seems to be the one who keeps everything organized around here.

"Good night and thank you, *bayarlalaa,*" Ariella says to our host.

The night air has gotten colder. Glad it's only a few steps to our *ger*.

Ariella lights the stove to warm things up. Stowe goes for the camera and decides to show our grandmother the photographs she's taken of the takhi. Not the best time for that....

Ariella looks closely at the pictures Stowe has taken.

"You did a very good job. It's not easy photographing in the dark. But next time ask before you help yourself to my cameras."

"Sorry," we say at the same time. I can't let Stowe take all the blame for this one.

"Did you ask 'Doulaye and Mai if they know where the rogue harem might be?" Seems like a good time to change subjects.

"Yes. They have some ideas, but we'll pick this conversation up in the morning. For now, you get ready for bed. Send your parents texts to let them know you're fine." Our grandmother leans over and gives us both a kiss on our heads and walks toward her bed.

Stowe blabs into her headset for a while. Log time I guess. I'm ready to go to sleep. Last thing I remember is Ariella whispering, "Lights out."

STOWE LEBLOND'S LOG

Hustai Nuruu National Park, Mongolia

October 26

10:00 PM

Tonight we got to ride Mongolian horses. Not the takhi, of course, but domesticated ones. Mongolia is all about horses. They have about 3 million people in the whole country and at least as many horses. The history and culture of this country were built around these animals. It's only because of the horse that Mongolians could live a nomadic lifestyle. It also gave them an edge as warriors. Some people think that the Great Wall of China was built to keep out the horses.

The Mongolian horses are squatter than ours, not so different from the takhi, but much better behaved. The mares are kept mostly to produce milk. The stallions are the ones that people ride. When the horses aren't being ridden or milked, they roam freely, grazing on whatever they can find. In the winter they dig beneath the snow to find food and eat the snow for water.

Mongolians love horse racing. It's a national sport. Their races can be 15-30 kilometers long. That's 9 - 18 miles! Much longer than the Kentucky Derby track, which is only 1 1/4 miles.

Wheaton did well. The horse he rode is called Khar because it's black. The Mongolians don't name their horses—just call them by their color. They probably have too many to come up with names for all of them. Khar was on the older side. That may have made him easier to ride.

Mongolian Words

black – Khar – хар

brown – Khüren – хүрэн

white – Tsagaan – цагаан

grandmother – Emee – эмээ

16. Sick Foal Headed To Ulaanbaatar

The sun hasn't risen yet but I can see Ariella standing by the door of the *ger* whispering to someone.

"What's happening?" I call out.

Stowe rolls over and opens her eyes. "Who's out there? Is it morning already?"

Ariella shuts the door and turns on one of the lamps. She comes over and sits on the side of Stowe's bed.

"That was Mai. Seems they found your takhi mare and foal. They did get there before any wolves located the pair." She pauses for a second and takes a breath. "Unfortunately, the mare was very ill and Mai had to put her down. It sounds like the foal is quite sick too."

"Oh, no. Where is the foal now? What's Mai going to do to it?" Stowe bolts up, wide awake now.

Ariella strokes my cousin's cheek. "The foal is here. Get

yourselves dressed and we'll learn more from the scientists over breakfast."

No time to brush hair or do anything else. We pull on our clothes and hurry over to the restaurant *ger*. Tuya is already there, fixing food for the guests.

"Where are they?" Stowe looks all around. "And Sarnai?"

"They will be here very soon," Ariella says. They've been up all night, taking turns with the foal."

"While waiting for rest, would you like *Suutei tsai*? Green tea with milk." Tuya's face has a still patience that reminds me of the way Stowe's mother looks sometimes.

"Sounds wonderful," Ariella says. "And if you have *tarag* and biscuits we 'll be very happy. *Bayarlala*."

Sarnai arrives and comes to sit with us.

She starts to relay what happened last night. "We got back to spot where we saw takhi mare. It was on ground hardly moving. Mai is very brave..."

"No, she's not." The vet walks in, her backpack still slung over her shoulder.

Mai puts her gear off to the side and joins us. "What Sarnai is saying is that I was able to approach the mare from behind and examine her. I could see she was in no condition to get on her feet. Believe me, I would never risk approaching a takhi if it were standing. Before I started working with 'Doulaye, I worked for a zoo that studied takhi. A keeper thought he could go into a pen with one of them for a second to pick up something he'd dropped. I won't go into the details, but he was out of work for six months after that encounter."

"Ariella said you put the mare down?" Stowe's blue eyes are wide and wet.

"Yes, I'm pretty sure she had *piroplasmosis*. It's a tick-borne disease that is very hard on takhi. I've taken samples and will confirm when we're back in Ulaanbaatar. Even if I could have treated her, the chances of recovery were slim, and with the wolves out here, she'd be killed before the antibiotics ever had a chance to work."

"That's so sad. I guess you're used to animals dying," Stowe says to the vet.

"You never get used to losing one," Mai tells my cousin, "but you do learn to accept it."

"And what about her foal?" Stowe asks.

"She's really sick too," the vet says. "Seems like the same disease. We have two choices. We can put her down as well, or take her back to Ulaanbaatar where I can treat the foal properly in an infirmary and she can be observed."

"She's going to survive, right?" Stowe's face is wrinkled up, and her voice is soft.

"It's a long shot, the foal's very sick. And to be honest, after reintroduction, we often let nature takes its course. I'm only intervening because I think we can gain important information that will help us understand and manage this disease."

While Mai's been talking, 'Doulaye joins us. "The foal took a bottle of horse milk and she's sleeping now. We need to decide what to do."

"I've talked with Chuluun," Mai tells her colleague. "He has a trailer we can borrow and hook up to the jeep. We need three people to transport this foal safely. One to drive, and two to sit with the foal—give her a bottle and watch her legs if she starts to kick."

"Can I go?" Stowe asks before Mai even finishes her sentence.

"This mission needs three adults." She sees Stowe's hurt look. "No offense. I know you're very capable, but not for this task. I need Ariella to drive the jeep while I monitor the foal. She's very young, maybe only three months old, but she still has enough strength that I need 'Doulaye to help keep her from hurting herself."

"Okay, I get it." Stowe's head droops a little.

"You still want us to look for the rogue harem, right?" I ask.

"Not until we're back, Wheaton." Ariella focuses an intense stare in my direction.

"Can you guys give us an idea of where you think the group might be?" I ask. "So we can start thinking about how this rescue might work."

"We didn't see any sign of them this year, and we've covered every square foot of Hustai Nuruu," 'Doulaye tells us. "Some tourists claim they saw a takhi harem not far from a mining town northeast of the park perimeter."

Stowe looks at me. "Sounds like a job for the Finder."

"Which is—?" Mai sounds skeptical, and she doesn't even know what it is. She's talking to us like we're a random eleven and twelve-year-old trailing along with their grandmother. What else is new?

"It's a bionic dog mounted on a drone," Stowe volunteers.

I give a quick explanation of how our device works. "If we could get some sort of scent from this takhi harem, and pass it through the Finder, it could help sniff them out."

"We got your smells from luggage you left with Munuu," Stowe blurts out, "and it helped us find the collar for takhi #959."

"But you didn't find us." Mai doesn't seem all that impressed.

"We sort of did." Stowe plows on, explaining how we found the dead marmot, gazelle, and the collar. "You did handle them, didn't you?"

"You got me there." Mai holds up her hands. "I remember that gazelle. We interrupted the wolf's meal. And I haven't thought of that collar for quite a while. I cut it off a takhi mare a little more than a year ago, when we were here for our last survey. We were observing a harem and one of the takhi, #959 could have been the number, had a welt on her neck. I darted her with a tranquilizer gun and cut off her collar. I'm surprised the batteries still work. They've got to be at least two years old."

"Must be the cold weather out here," 'Doulaye says. It's good for battery life. If we stayed out there for two years we'd be preserved too, but without a signal."

Mai gives 'Doulaye a look. She's all business. "The weather is exactly why I forgot about the collar. As you will learn if you spend much time out here, storms come in pretty fast and they can be wicked. That afternoon the weather got wild and we had to pack up in a hurry. In our rush, I dropped the collar, but we were back in Ulaanbaatar before I noticed it was missing. It wasn't realistic to go back to retrieve it."

I assume the story's done, when Mai puts her finger in the air and points it in my direction.

"I hadn't stopped to think about this until now. I'm almost positive that "welty" takhi is a member of the missing harem. Wonder if her wound healed..."

"Hope so. And if she survived, the collar might provide you the scent you need," 'Doulaye suggests.

"There was a little hair stuck to it," I say, "so maybe even though #959's been separated from the collar for a year, there could be enough scent to help the Finder."

"And what about poop?—oops, stool samples from the harem?" Stowe asks. "Are there any back in Ulaanbaatar that would be a match? That would give us a good scent too. The scent will be disgusting, but it'll give us something to work with. You know what I mean."

Mai grins at Stowe. "We did collect the samples you're asking about. It's been quite a while, but I'll check with Munuu to see if, after they were analyzed, he kept what was left in the freezer."

"Will the scents survive freezing?" Stowe asks me.

"Good question. Maybe. But the samples won't do us any good in Ulaanbaatar." Am I the only one worried about getting this mission completed before it gets too cold out here?

"You know how to pull scents off samples," I say to Ariella. "Since you're going with the foal, could you take the Finder, and vacuum the air space off any "appropriate" harem poop before coming back. And please see if you can get a scent off the collar too."

"I can do that. And *once I'm back,*" our grandmother says with more emphasis than necessary, "we can use the Finder to continue the search. Now, come back to our *ger* and help me gather up all the gear I need."

She turns to Mai and 'Doulaye. "I'll meet you down at the pen shortly."

Stowe doesn't come with us but follows Mai out the door. I wonder what they're discussing....

I help Ariella pack what she'll need and we make our way back to the others.

'Doulaye coaxes the foal up into the carrier. Looks like they're ready to leave, but Mai stops in her tracks.

"Darn, I left my field pack at breakfast." She pauses for a second. "Look, I've got my personal stuff on me, and there's nothing in it I'll need in Ulaanbaatar. Please put it out of the way until we get back."

Ariella gives both of us a kiss and focuses her eyes right into ours. "While I'm gone, you two *work on a plan* to locate the takhi and herd them back to the park. See you soon."

We join Sarnai and her parents as we watch the scientists and Ariella drive down the road with their sick little foal.

"Do you think she'll make it?" Stowe asks.

STOWE LEBLOND'S LOG

Hustai Nuruu National Park, Mongolia

October 27

9:00 AM

Last night we found a sick mare and her foal. Mai had to put the mare down but maybe the foal can be saved. She thinks the foal has piroplasmosis. That's a disease caused by a single-cell organism that attacks the blood. It's transmitted by ticks, sort of like Lyme disease, but way worse. For some reason, even though this disease is found in domesticated horses and takhi, it only seems to kill the takhi.

Mai and 'Doulaye described a few of the differences between domesticated horses (the ones we ride at home) and takhi. They are related, evolving around 500,000 years ago from a common ancestor. The science of genetics helps figure that out. One way to tell the animals apart is the number of chromosomes each has. Chromosomes are found in every cell of our body, and they contain the codes—genes—that make each species unique. Humans have 23 pairs of chromosomes or 46 in each cell. Domesticated horses have a total of 64 chromosomes per cell, and the takhi have 66. If a domesticated horse and a Takhi mate, the offspring will have 65 chromosomes and look like a takhi.

Remember I told you about the breeding program to save these wild horses from extinction? Well, all the takhi alive today come from 14 individuals. One of the challenges is to make sure that the genes keep getting mixed by mating different animals together. It's worked so far, but that's the reason we need to get that harem back into the park—so the foals find other takhi to mate with when they grow up.

Of course, that's not always easy. Takhi live for about 36 years in small family groups with one stallion. When the males grow up, they get kicked out and have to form their own group. Sometimes the young stallion chases a weaker stallion away from its family and takes its place. (And I think competing with other girls is hard!)

'Doulaye and Mai are awesome. 'Doulaye comes from Senegal. He moved to the United States when he was a student, and now he works in Virginia at the Smithsonian Conservation Biology Institute. That's where he learned everything there is to know about the takhi.

Mai's a veterinarian at the same organization with 'Doulaye. She told me that very few vets work on wildlife. But when she was in school she did an internship at the National Zoo and decided wildlife needs her more than the family dog or cat does.

Someday maybe I could do one of their jobs.

17. Designing A Herding Device

"Brrr, it's cold out here," I say, in case someone missed the obvious. "Let's go back to our *ger* so I can do some research and see how this rescue might work."

"Want to come, Sarnai?" Stowe asks. "Wheaton could use our help."

"It's true," I tell her. "Plus, I'm going to need access to your Wi-Fi. Can you get me the code?"

"I will join you for a while. The code is in our Cyrillic alphabet. I think I know how to type it on your laptop so I can enter for you."

This *ger* hotel is in the middle of no place, but they've got a satellite dish. It's powered by solar panels. These people are called nomads, but they have Wi-Fi, TV and lots of modern stuff.

The three of us plop down in a cozy corner of the *ger*, and Sarnai gets me set up online.

Before I can start to design a herding system, I need to understand these animals a little better.

"Are the takhi as jumpy and aggressive as Mai said? Your horses are so nice." Sometimes people exaggerate. Worth a reality check.

"Oh yes," our friend tells us. "We only got close to takhi last night because she was sick. Otherwise she would most likely run away. Or maybe charge us."

"So if we wanted to herd them in one direction, it would be hard? What kinds of things scare them the most?" I ask.

"Wolves," Sarnai says without hesitation.

Stowe shudders, her shoulders lifting to her earlobes.

"That gives me an idea," I say.

"No, Wig, we are not dressing up in wolf costumes." I guess Stowe's not that freaked out.

"Ha, ha. I was thinking that maybe I could create a speaker system that would have a wolf call. We could ride behind the takhi and scare them into moving away from us toward the park."

"Could be a problem," Sarnai points out. "You need to know something about wolf calls. One wolf calling could mean looking for mate."

"Great, so we make matters worse by pulling wolves in." Stowe gives me a look.

"But," Sarnai continues, "several wolves howling, could mean it is their territory and others should stay away. And a wolf growl means do not come any closer."

"What other noises do you think would scare the takhi into running?"

"I don't know about takhi," Stowe interjects, "but the horses I took care of last summer were terrified during the fireworks at Fourth of July. We ended up putting stoppers in their ears to muffle the noise."

"I heard 'Doulaye say that in another park, a group of takhi ran away because they were scared by explosions at nearby mine," Sarnai tells us.

This conversation has given me some ideas. "Here's what I'm thinking. I need to record sounds that might get the horses to run. Then I need to figure out how to amplify the sound and control its direction. I see the problem with the wolf calls, but I wonder how far the horses will run in response to a fake explosion, and if they'll get used to it after a while."

"Maybe we need a few options," Stowe suggests.

"Great minds think alike."

"If you let off a scary noise, takhi may scatter. How will you control where they run?" Sarnai raises a good point.

"Maybe if we have three systems—"

"But we only have one HeliBoaJee." Stowe points out.

"I was thinking we'd do this on horseback. We'd stay far enough back not to freak out the takhi, but be positioned so we could steer them toward the park."

Stowe points at Sarnai, herself and me. "One, two, three. One night of riding and you're ready to take this on. Pretty soon you'll be a regular cowboy."

She's right. I'm not what you'd call a seasoned equestrian. But we've got to get the job done.

"Okay, oh brilliant one. What's your plan?" Stowe asks.

"First step, we'll need devices to record the sounds."

I peer into the box I've brought and pull out a couple of old smart phones. I don't throw electronics away. You never know when something will come in handy.

"I have one too." Sarnai hands me her device. The three of us watch a bunch of YouTube videos and select a few dramatic explosions and a series of wolf howls that Sarnai says fit the "stay away" message.

Our new friend lets out a big yawn. "I've been up most of night. Do you mind if I go take nap?"

"No problem. It's going to take me a while to put these devices together. By the time you're rested, maybe I'll have something we can test out."

Sarnai waves and walks out the door.

"Wheaton, if you don't need me, I'm going down to where the horses are, to see if anyone needs help."

"Go ahead. But before you leave—I was wondering—what were you talking about with Mai while I was getting the Finder?"

I feel a little silly asking Stowe, but at school and even at home, I always seem so different, people tend to leave me out of stuff.

"Oh, I was asking her questions about the horses. The type of stuff my mom wants to see in my log. No secrets, I promise." She gives me a hug that says she understands me better than anyone. Then she runs out the door.

"Have fun," I call after her. "Come back when you get cold."

18. Takhi-Herding-Sound System Ready To Go

With the girls gone for a while, I focus on putting together the devices. I've got the sound source from our recordings, and a bunch of amplifiers we'll need. There won't be any Wi-Fi or cell service where we're going, so I make sure each system is connected with a USB cable.

I'm missing something to direct the sound. Lucky for me Chuluun lets me borrow megaphones he has for their horse racing and eagle hunting competitions.

It's well into the afternoon when Stowe and Sarnai reappear. I show them my latest invention—the **T**akhi-**H**erding-**S**ound **S**ystem.

"What is **THiSS**?" Stowe is so clever.

"It's pretty simple." I hand them each one of the smart phones. "If you go to the Notes App you'll see buttons to select the sound and the decibels—"

"That's a measure of loudness," Stowe tells Sarnai.

"Oh, *changa duu chime,*" she nods.

"The sound will come out through the megaphones your dad let me borrow. By rotating them, we can target its direction," I explain.

"We'll each strap a THSS to our waist. Energy generators I put together, made of piezoceramics, will sit on our saddles to keep the equipment charged."

Stowe leans over to take a closer look. "We'll need those. It might take a few days, to herd these horses back to the park."

"Exactly," I say. "When we find the rogue harem, we'll need to experiment with how to herd the takhi in the right direction—which sounds will work best, and at what volume."

"We better take ear protection for our horses, or they get scared too," Sarnai suggests.

"Do you have foam rubber, maybe from packing material?" Stowe asks Sarnai.

"I think so. Let me go look."

"And please bring back some old tights or thin socks too if you have them," my cousin requests.

Sarnai produces the necessary items and Stowe stuffs the toes of the tights with foam rubber about the size of a golf ball. She ties knots at the end of the ball and cuts the tights back to around the knee area. "Ta-daa—here you have three sets of ear plugs for our trusty steeds. You're not the only creative one." Stowe flashes me a smile.

"We'll need to test them out before we start the herding," I tell Stowe. "Make sure you have extra foam rubber if they're too small for any of our horses."

Tuya peeks into the *ger,* and we notice it's dark outside. I guess we've lost track of time. "There you are. Come to dinner. You must be hungry."

We wash up and head back to the restaurant for an evening meal.

"Let's call Ariella to find out how the foal's doing," Stowe says to me.

She takes advantage of the strong Wi-Fi signal in the restaurant and reaches our grandmother.

"Hi, Ariella. How was the trip to Ulaanbaatar? How's the foal? Are you coming back tonight?"

Stowe stops her cascade of questions and puts the phone on speaker so we can all hear what's happening.

"Hi, kids. It was a rough ride back to the city. 'Doulaye had his work cut out for him. The foal was very agitated—had trouble drinking from the bottle and kicked like crazy. Munuu met us and we took the foal to a quarantine area where she will be tested and cared for."

"Is she going to be all right?"

"I'll be honest with you. It doesn't look good. The young horse is very weak. And she has no mother. Not a good combination. But it will take at least another day to complete the diagnosis, and for Mai to put her on a treatment plan, if she makes it."

"So you're not coming back tonight?"

"Afraid not, Wheaton. The three of us drove here together, and I need to wait until Mai and 'Doulaye are ready. I hope we can return by tomorrow evening. What have you kids been up to?"

Stowe proceeds to describe how we developed the THSS and the horse earplugs, and how we're going to be able to drive the harem back into the park. After we find them, of course.

"Impressive," Ariella says. "Let's hope we can be back as planned and get on with our mission. Have a good night."

"Night. Love you," Stowe and I respond.

After we hang up Stowe glances off to the side where there are a pile of games and activities for kids.

"Wheaton, check it out. They have Jenga."

Sarnai looks over. "Oh, those were some blocks a tourist left for us."

"Actually, that's a really fun game. Do we have time for a few rounds?" Stowe asks.

"We do," Sarnai says. "How do you play?"

"It's easy. At least the idea is," Stowe tells her. "We stack up the blocks, three on a level, any way we want. Then we take turns pulling out one block at a time from a lower level and putting it on top. First one to cause the tower to crash loses." It's kind of an upside-down game.

The three of us sit down on the floor. I'm an engineer so I have the game figured out pretty well. Sarnai's new to it, so she brings down quite a few towers.

Stowe's played a lot but her impatience gets the best of

her. Because she's so competitive, all this losing is starting to bug her.

"Since this is a game of losers instead of winners," she sticks her tongue out at me, "let's add another twist. Wheaton, you have the advantage because you're an engineer. How about whoever loses gets to ask you a question? Unless you lose, of course. Then you can ask one of us something."

"Fine with me," I say.

We start taking turns removing blocks. The girls must have been watching my strategy because when my turn comes around I can see they've got me. I pull out a block and everything topples.

"Yahoo," Stowe hollers. "What's your question, dude?"

"Sarnai, how much longer before the weather turns scary cold?"

She checks the weather app on her cell phone. "Looks like couple of good days left. Then temperatures go to zero and maybe snow."

Stowe's eyebrows raise. "Okay, one more round. Let's try and beat Wheaton again."

I change my game plan, and when it's Stowe's turn she pulls out a block and the game is over.

"Achh," she grumbles. But then she turns serious. "Maybe that block is the rogue harem for the takhi population. We have to get them back with the others to keep their tower standing."

"That's not a question is it?" I ask.

"I know," she responds, giving me a penetrating look. "Do we really have to wait to start looking for the harem?"

19. No More Time To Wait

It's after 7:00 AM and the sun is inching up over the horizon. I peer outside and check the weather.

"Stowe, get up. I've been thinking about your question last night. It's -8°C (20°F) but it's going to feel pretty toasty later on. Might get to 10°C (50°F). Maybe we should take the HeliBoaJee for a ride, to see if we can spot the rogue harem."

My cousin bolts up in bed. "What harm can it do?"

"And we'd only be doing surveillance," I add, for further justification.

"Could we invite Sarnai to come with us? She knows the area."

"Good idea. Let's get breakfast and ask her."

We clean up and make our way to the restaurant.

"Morning," Stowe calls out as we enter.

Sarnai is already there to greet us.

"Where's your mom?" Stowe inquires.

"Oh, my parents went to visit my sister who lives in Ulaanbaatar," she tells us. "They sleep there. Good time to get away since so few guests. Tomorrow they stop to pick up my brother and sister from boarding school. Kids come home for weekend."

"Sarnai, we're thinking of taking the HeliBoaJee for a short ride east of the park—to see if we can locate the missing takhi harem. Would you like to come?" I ask.

Before she can answer, Stowe pipes in. "It would be a big help. You know the area, and we don't."

Can't tell what Sarnai's thinking, but from the way she smiles and lifts her eyebrows at us, I'm guessing she knows this may not be something the adults know about.

"Is it safe?"

"Totally. We've used it in a tropical rain forest, which is much trickier than the open spaces out here." I hope I sound confident. "The mountains are 60 miles, I mean 100 kilometers from here. It'll only be for a few hours."

"Okay, I will go with you."

"Yay. When do you finish up?" Stowe asks Sarnai.

"You are the only guests." Sarnai gives us a wink. "When you finish breakfast I will wash up and be ready to go."

With that Stowe and I chow down, grab our gear and head over to the HeliBoaJee. We're busy getting set up when Sarnai arrives.

"Before we take off, is there a place to get some water? I need to hook up our portable solar regeneration tree," I explain. "We have plenty of fuel for today, but we'll need more before returning to Ulaanbaatar."

"We get our water from a stream nearby. You come with me."

"How far do we have to go?" I'm thinking this is going to take a while and we really need to get going.

"Not far. We will take motorcycle."

I look at Stowe hoping she'll offer to go, but she already has her headset on. Guess she wants to write another log before we head out.

Sarnai grabs a couple of jugs and ties them to the motorcycle. She gives me a helmet hanging off the handlebars, and the two of us hop on.

This is something my mother will not want to hear about.

It's a bumpy ride, and a little fast for me, but as promised, a short distance away. As we fill our containers my hands and feet get wet. Better take extra socks and gloves wherever we go.

Sarnai delivers me and the water back to the village to set things up for fuel generation. I expand the solar tree like a giant umbrella and she helps me pour the water into the stalk—a big fat tank.

"Today's a great day to do this, since it'll be sunny all day," I explain, while attaching the generator to the methane storage tanks we'll need later. "The energy from the sun will run a small pump that will bubble air through the water.

That captures the carbon dioxide (CO_2). At the same time the solar cells are splitting water (H_2O) into hydrogen (H_2) and oxygen (O). When the H_2 and CO_2 react they produce methane, which will be pumped into our fuel tanks."

"Wow," Sarnai says.

"Oh, yeah," Stowe's rejoined us just in time to provided unneeded commentary. "That's our inventor boy..."

"Don't start," I warn her. "Let's get going." I lead the way to the HeliBoaJee. The others follow, and we all climb aboard.

"Here's the GPS system." I point at the screen in front of Sarnai. "It should work, but it'll help if you describe where we are—"

"And make suggestions on where to find the harem," Stowe adds.

"All set?" I ask my passengers. "Buckle up. We're out of here."

The rotor blades begin to whirl and we lift off, heading east in the direction of the Khentii mountains.

STOWE LEBLOND'S LOG

Hustai Nuruu National Park, Mongolia

October 28

8:00 AM

ResQ's mission is to find this rogue harem of takhi I told you about before, and chase them back into Hustai Nuruu Park. Assuming we can find them, getting wild horses where you want them to go could be a problem. But as always, Wheaton's come up with a plan. We're going to create sounds that will scare the horses into running, and with three of us on horseback, we'll be able to direct them where they need to go. He calls his invention the Takhi-Herding-Sound System. I nicknamed it THSS.

To put the device together you need to understand something about sound. It travels in waves. The tighter the waves, the higher the pitch. The longer the waves, the deeper the sound. The noise level depends on how tall the waves are. Sound is measured by something called a "hertz." One hertz is equal to one complete sound wave per second. Humans can hear in a range from 20 hertz to 20 kilohertz (kilo means a thousand times).

Horses have a bigger range from 14 hertz to 25 kilohertz, which means they can hear higher and lower pitch sounds than we can. They also have really good hearing—they can hear noise from 2.5 miles away. You know how people hold their hands around their ears to hear better? (Ariella does that sometimes.) Well, horses' ears are already shaped like cones, so they start out more tuned in. And then horses have 10 muscles connected to each ear. They can move their ears separately to focus on sounds. Most humans can't do that. We only have 3 muscles controlling movement of each ear, so maybe that's why some people don't listen so well ☺.

As with all of Wheaton's inventions, the THSS needs power to operate. We don't know how long we'll be in the field, and we'll be traveling by horseback. Carrying lots of batteries would add extra weight, and it's not like there will be power stations for recharging along the way. So Wheaton has designed this unit that's made of a piezoelectric material to create the needed energy. He told me that piezoelectric materials are types of crystals. Quartz is an example. If you put a thin layer of this material between two metal plates and squoosh it (Wheaton says apply mechanical pressure), negative charge goes to one plate and positive to the other. This creates a current that can now be sent to where it will be useful. Wheaton has designed our recharger by making small generators from a ceramic piezoelectric material in a metal plate sandwich. It sits on the front of our saddles, wired to the THSS. As we go up and down, the motion creates the current we need to drive our sound machines. Another invention that doesn't waste energy!!

Mongolian words I'm learning

Loudness – Changa duu chime – чанга дуу чимээ

20. Scoping Out The Terrain

For a while we follow the Tuul River on the southern edge of the park.

"Getting close to Ulaanbaatar," Sarnai tell us. "Start going north."

We fly over the only road that goes east-west.

"Down there is Trans-Mongolia train," Sarnai points. "Goes from China, north through Mongolia, into Russia. Tracks are surrounded by barbed wire in lot of places—"

"Why is that necessary?" Stowe blurts out in her indignant voice.

"To prevent livestock accidents. But can be big problem for wildlife."

Our guide tells us to head north as far as the Boroo Mine, around 100 kilometers (62 miles) from Ulaanbaatar.

For a while we fly east of the tracks. Below is what looks like a cloud of leaping brown dancers, only with four legs. Sarnai tells us these are Mongolian gazelles in search of a place to spend the winter. "They like to go to southern province, *Ömnögovi,* but they run into problems with mines there too."

"They look a lot nicer alive." Stowe tells Sarnai about the dismembered animal we found a few days ago.

"Let's go back over to the western side of the train track," I propose, "and hope it's a barrier the takhi haven't crossed. I don't want to run out of fuel. Let's make the mine the northern edge of our search and from there go back toward the park."

Stowe scans below, binoculars pressed to her face. "I don't see any horses, but looks like another train track going southwest."

Then she gasps. "That's the mine down there. It's hideous."

Talk about understatement. Below us are a series of huge pits. Each has terraces—more like giant scars, carved out of the land, littered with piles of smashed rocks and debris. If we squint, we can see what looks like a lake way at the bottom.

"Boroo is gold mine," Sarnai says. "It is used up. That water is full of bad chemicals. There is another mine, Gatsuurt, nearby, but no activity now. Worth a lot of money but bad for environment."

We fly around looking outside the fenced-in perimeter and see rows of holes dotting the adjacent landscape.

"What are those?" I ask. "Look like giant gopher or marmot holes."

"No, not caused by animals," Sarnai says. "People come from all over and dig, hoping to find gold. When they are done they leave without filling in holes or putting up fences. Dangerous for humans and animals."

We continue our flyover with no sign of the takhi. But to the west of the mines we see more outcroppings of trees and small rocky ridges. Great hiding places.

Back and forth I rotate our craft. We focus for a while on a small section between the railroad tracks, the mine and the road.

"Hold on. There's something down there. Can you hover for a bit?" Stowe points to a small clearing and hands the binocs to Sarnai.

"Look like takhi," our guide says. "Maybe seven or eight. I am not sure. Can you get any closer?"

I bank the HeliBoaJee for a clearer view.

"Good news." Stowe yells over the sound of the rotors. "Looks like we've got them in our sight."

Bad news is, horses have no trouble hearing the chopper sounds overhead. They stop for a moment and then, as if the harem were one animal, they pivot and take off down a passageway gouged out between the rocky ridges.

"Let's land and see if there is any way we can chase them in jeep mode."

Stowe gives me a look. "This sounds like more than just "finding" them, don't you think?"

"Yeah. But we know where they are. What if we could get this whole thing solved today?"

Stowe shrugs. Sarnai doesn't say anything. Guess she's curious to see how this vehicle conversion works.

Landing is easy compared to the challenges we faced in the tropical rainforest. Here there's lots of hard ground with tufts of last summers' grass and rocks scattered in no obvious pattern. When the girls step out, I get the wheels extended, landing gear up, rotor retracted, and the HeliBoaJee body squooshed together in jeep mode.

"Wow," Sarnai says, clapping her hands. "I wondered how you did that."

"Pile back in. Let's find some takhi," I yell.

Sarnai sits behind us. She points in the direction the horses went, and we're off.

There are no roads out here, but our guide suggests routes that the horses may have taken. We tool around for a while, but we've definitely lost the harem.

"Oh well, it was worth a try. At least we have a general idea where the horses are," I tell my companions. "Fuel's getting low, so let's fly back and plan our next move."

Back in heli mode, we return to home base well before being missed.

With the vehicle parked, the three of us head for the restaurant.

"We gave other staff day off," Sarnai tells us. "Come to kitchen and we can make ourselves lunch."

I check the weather again. "The five-day forecast for Ulaanbaatar says nice today and pretty good for the next 36 hours. Then it looks like a snowstorm's coming."

"It's still October. Snow so early?" Stowe asks Sarnai.

"Yes. It is October in Mongolia."

"We know the takhi are about 100 kilometers from here. Any idea how far they can travel in a day?" I ask.

"If they are strong," Sarnai says, "maybe 50 kilometers."

"That's a lot," Stowe comments. "I bet that's only when they're 'motivated'."

"THSS," we say in unison.

"Let's call Ariella and see when they'll be back. She needs to know about the weather forecast. We've got to get the harem drive started." I look at Stowe.

"I'll call," she says, picking up her cell phone. Service is pretty bad but she gets through.

"Hi. How's the foal?...Oh..." Stowe stops talking and her eyebrows crunch together. Then she puts the phone on speaker. "Could you repeat that for Wheaton and Sarnai."

"Hi kids. As I told Stowe, the little foal didn't make it. She did have piroplasmosis and the disease had gone too far before Mai could treat her."

Two dead takhi. Makes our getting the harem back into the park even more important.

"When are you coming back?" I ask.

Before Ariella can answer Stowe barrels ahead. "We found the rogue harem in the foothills of the Khentii mountains, like 'Doulaye mentioned. We need to get going on horseback to start herding them to the park."

Might have been smarter to ease into this.

"Excuse me? What part of *stay put* did the two of you not understand?" Ariella's voice is a little louder than necessary. The connection's not that bad.

"It's the weather," I say. "There are only a few good days left, so we figured we should try and locate the takhi. We were only in the HeliBoaJee for a few hours and we found them—"

"Well, we won't be back today," Ariella says. "Mai needs to perform an autopsy on the foal, and 'Doulaye went to get their jeep looked at. It was making some awful sounds on our way back to Ulaanbaatar. You'll have to wait to start the rescue for at least another day or two."

"We can't wait," Stowe blurts out.

I gesture, pulling my hand across my mouth, for Stowe to be quiet.

"What Stowe means is a snowstorm's coming in three or four days. If my invention works, we can drive the harem back into the park in about 48 hours. If we don't start right away, this rescue might not happen until next spring."

"And how will you get to the takhi if we aren't there to transport the horses?" Ariella has a good point.

That's when Sarnai weighs in. "My boyfriend lives nearby. His family has horse trailer. He can take us and horses to starting point tomorrow morning."

"And you are going to spend the night outside? Did you

hear what 'Doulaye said about the danger of being out in the cold over here?" Ariella never leaves anything to chance.

"I do. And remember, we brought a tent and my geothermal heater."

"I haven't forgotten. But I don't see you going out alone without an adult."

"I am adult." Sarnai says a little too fast, her mouth getting tight.

"I know you are." Ariella always finds a way to be understanding and kind. To a point. "But Stowe and Wheaton are not."

Stowe walks over to the corner where Mai left her backpack. A satellite phone is sticking out of one of the pockets. She waves to get my attention, as she points to it and then comes back to the phone.

"Ariella, how about if Sarnai's boyfriend gives us and our horses a ride to the area where the harem is? We'll bring along Mai's satellite phone so we can call and give you updates to tell you where we are. As soon as the jeep's repaired, the three of you can meet us. What do you think?"

There's some conversation in the background. "I don't love the idea, but okay.... Mai said to remind you that their sat phone needs to be charged, and let me know what you're doing in the morning."

"May I borrow one of your cameras?" Stowe asks. She's not making that mistake again.

"Yes. Take the one with the telephoto lens and a tripod," Ariella tells her.

With that we say goodbye. Sarnai calls Oktai, her boyfriend.

She talks to him for a few minutes. Of course, they're speaking Mongolian, so we have to wait for a translation. "He is busy tomorrow—"

Before Sarnai can finish what she has to say Stowe interrupts. "Could Oktai help us this afternoon? We can camp for the night and then we'd be ready to start first thing in the morning."

Sarnai talks to her boyfriend for a few more minutes, and then turns to us. "He says he can come in one hour."

"Sounds like a plan," I tell her.

She confirms and hangs up.

Stowe's been on the floor looking through Mai's pack.

"Hey, nosy girl. That's not yours."

"I know. But this is her field gear. When we went through her personal things back in Munuu's office, you didn't have a problem with that. I'm looking to see if there are any things beside the sat phone that we should take with us."

She starts pulling out all kinds of random items, a notebook, a first aid kit, tissues, chewing gum, flares, and a stack of laminated pages with pictures of Mongolian plants and animals.

"Check this out, *Medicinal Plants of Mongolia*. I'm going to ask Mai if I can take these home for my mom. You know how she's into herbal medicine."

Stowe reaches into the pack one more time and pulls out what looks like a rifle. "What's this?"

"Whoa, Stowe, put that back, we don't touch guns."

"Really? Thanks for telling me. This is a dart gun, doofus. Remember Mai said she tranquilized the horse to get the collar off."

"Guns are scary, I don't care what they're used for. Put it away."

"Whatever." Stowe shrugs but picks up the whole pack. "There's a lot of useful stuff in here and it's not too heavy. Let's take it with us."

STOWE LEBLOND'S LOG

Hustai Nuruu National Park, Mongolia

October 28

1:30 PM

The rogue takhi harem may have gone to an area near a gold mine. Mongolia has a lot of minerals—like gold, copper and tin. It's tricky. People all over the world need these minerals for lots of stuff, and it's a way to make money. Mongolia was a very poor country, and mining is making a difference. Unfortunately, when you bulldoze the land to find the ore, it leaves behind an environmental mess. Remember when we lived out West, we saw some huge strip mines? They scar the land and pollute the water and soil. Big companies from all over the world come here to take advantage of the minerals. Local farmers, who struggle when the winters are too cold, are getting into the game too. Sarnai told us that small groups of people dig what are called artisanal mines—basically holes in the ground from which they crush the soil and sift for gold or other valuable minerals. These people are called ninja miners! I don't get the name, except that ninja is a Japanese word that means sneaky or stealthy. I guess if they aren't following the rules that name might work. The sad thing is these minerals will only be around for a while, maybe 100 years, and then they'll be gone. I hope there will still be people raising goats and protecting the environment for their great-grandchildren.

Speaking of the natural environment, there is a real herbal medicine culture in Mongolia. (Mom—you would love it.) People here have been using plants for medicine since before Genghis Khan was the ruler, and they still do. There are plants used for fevers, for all kinds of sicknesses, even some for tonsillitis. That would be good for Wheaton. He gets it all the time. Don't worry, I won't be treating him. Herbal medicine is tricky, I remember. Too little won't help, and too much could be bad. Mai has a whole list of those plants. I'll bring them home for us to look at. Maybe we have some of them in Vermont.

21. Horses En Route To Find Horses

Around 2:30 PM we see Oktai approaching with a horse trailer pulled by a pickup that reminds me of the beat-up old Ford, Stowe's dad uses for hauling firewood.

"*Sain uu,*" Sarnai's friend says as he hops out of the cab.

He's a solid guy, around five feet four inches. His boots are caked with mud and his rust-colored sheepskin jacket is trimmed with a pattern we've seen on wall hangings in the *gers*.

Sarnai introduces us, and after a quick handshake, she takes charge. "Get your stuff and meet us back here ready to go."

With no room for more conversation, Stowe and I haul our things to the waiting vehicle. Oktai has already loaded up the horses. Sarnai's brought the fur coats and hats we wore last time we went riding. "You'll need these."

Then she pats her backpack. "Food for next few days."

With everything set, Stowe and I slide onto the bench behind the driver. It's warm inside and we shed some clothing. Sarnai pops in next to Oktai and we're off.

Oktai has long black hair, transparent blue eyes, and a big smile we can see when he glances back at us in the rear-view mirror.

The ride on the best and only road is pretty bouncy. As we approach the capital we see the smog again, but as soon as we turn north the air clears. I'm looking out at the terrain to the west. It looks like Hustai Nuruu.

Stowe is peering out of her window. "Is that the Khentii range?" She points to tall mountains off to the east.

"Yes," Oktai says.

"That's where Ghengis Khan is buried," I whisper to Stowe.

She shakes her head and gives me a shove.

A little later we pass a set of train tracks going northeast. I think we're close to our destination.

"What does that sign say?" I ask Sarnai.

"We are entering the *Selenge aimag,*" She tells us. "*Aimag* is what I think you call state or province. It's the one where the Boroo mine is located. The takhi were east of here somewhere, when we saw them yesterday from your HeliBoaBoa."

Stowe giggles.

I've been following along on GPS. "This might be a good place to start."

Oktai pulls the truck off to the side. The ground is pretty much frozen so he won't have any trouble getting back on the road afterwards.

We put all our layers back on and fasten our fur hats under our chins. Oktai and Sarnai bring out the horses and get them saddled up. They distribute the gear evenly in our saddle bags so no animal is overburdened.

"I think you have everything," our driver says. "Good luck."

He shakes hands with Stowe and me, and then turns and gives Sarnai a kiss. *"Ayuulgüi baigaarai."*

"Bidniig avch irsend bayarlalaa. Sarnai smiles and blushes, so that her whole face is the color of her cheeks.

Oktai hops back into the pickup, gives us a wave, and drives back south.

"He's so cute," Stowe says to Sarnai. "Is he a serious boyfriend?"

She nods and turns one shade redder.

Not to change the subject, but I'm changing the subject. "Sarnai, any ideas where we should start? Maybe we could spot the takhi before it gets dark, and then start the drive in the morning."

She gets up on her horse and beckons us to follow. Glad these horses are on the shorter side. Getting up and down isn't so bad.

Sarnai points to a nearby hillside. "If we are up little higher, maybe we will see something."

As we reach the crest in the hill, I see an odd structure—a

bunch of rocks in a heap with a branch sticking up in the middle. "What is that?"

"That," Sarnai tells us, "is called *ovoo*. They are shrines found in high places everywhere. You must walk around it three times, like clock, and place rock on pile."

"And if not?" Stowe asks.

"Bad luck."

"Can't afford that," my cousin announces, as she dismounts, circles the *ovoo*, and sets a small rock in place.

Sarnai follows. I feel stupid, but I do it too. Don't want to jinx anything.

We look out to the north and east. The mine site is in the distance, but no takhi. There are lots of little hills jutting out—great places for the horses to hide.

"Let's ride east for a while and stop to look and listen every few minutes," Stowe suggests.

Sarnai leads and I bring up the rear. *Khar* hasn't gotten any faster, which is fine with me. When we take breaks it's so still I can hear my heart beating. I don't think it is ever quiet like this in Hoboken.

As we turn south, Stowe points off in the distance. "Those are the train tracks we passed coming up here. Let's hope the takhi haven't gone that way."

We pause to get our bearings. I open the GPS on my cell

phone. The weather is mostly clear, and with this big sky, reception isn't a problem. I start to comment on our coordinates when Stowe puts her fingers to her lips.

"Hear that?"

We strain to hear neighing.

Stowe pulls out her binocs and scans the horizon in all directions. "There they are," she whispers, and passes the field glasses to our guide.

"Yes," Sarnai says. "One stallion, maybe eight mares and two foals."

The sun is setting, and the temperature is dropping fast.

"Let's set up camp," I suggest. "The horses don't look like they're going anywhere."

Sarnai has brought along a stake, which she pounds into the ground. It will serve as a hitching post for our horses.

The three of us get the tent pitched and bring our gear inside. I take out a geothermal heater I've designed for missions to cold places.

"It's another Wheaton-invention," Stowe tells Sarnai. "I haven't seen it in action."

"Come here. We'll get it going." I push a button and a long tube drills into the soil. "The tube is extending underground until it reaches soil that is warm, at least compared to the air. Then an exhaust fan is going to kick in to suck warmth into our tent."

"That explains why this tent has an opening in the middle of the floor. How long is this going to take?" Stowe asks, holding her hands over the outlet of the heater.

"A little patience, please. Maybe 15 minutes. And it's not going to feel like an electric heater. It'll get the temperature up to about 50°F."

"10°C," Stowe tells Sarnai.

"You have so much cool stuff." Sarnai rubs the top of my hat and laughs. She does enjoy that joke.

Even though it's not yet warm enough to take off our hats and coats, we do shove our gloves in our pockets so we can eat something. Sarnai's brought along dried meat—I guess the Mongolian version of beef jerky. Tastes good to me but Stowe is not happy. Luckily Sarnai has noticed my cousin's aversion to meat and also has rice to share. Then our guide passes out cups and pours tea from the thermos. We begin to feel a little warmer.

But that pleasant after-dinner feeling doesn't last long.

In the distance we hear a low whistling noise. With every passing second it gets louder.

"What 's going on?" Stowe goes to the tent flap and sticks her head out for an instant. She yanks it back inside, her hat glistening with moisture.

"That's one wicked storm," she reports, as if it weren't already obvious.

Sarnai gets up. "I go check on our horses. Be right back. You stay inside."

Our guide isn't gone long. "All fine with horses. They are used to being out in storms. I tied reins to stake a little tighter."

Huddling together close to the geothermal heater, we hear the wind howling and the shearing sound of the snow against the sides of our tent. I hope it doesn't turn our shelter into Swiss cheese.

There isn't much time to worry about the integrity of the tent. The wind blows like crazy and then starts swirling from the opposite direction. The front flap flies open and before we know what's happening, a gust blows in and starts to pull the tent out of the ground. We try to hold it down by standing on the flooring, but the force is too great and it's pulled away from us. We stand there with nothing but the heater in the ground, as the tent goes airborne.

22. Seeking Shelter

The tent flies off like a parachute in reverse and Stowe screams. “I thought you said the weather was going to be good for the next 36 hours.”

“It was,” I yell back. “Not like I can control some random cloud. And who staked down the tent, Missy?” This isn’t all my fault.

Stowe glares at me, pulls up her hood, yanks on her gloves, and without saying another word, races off chasing the tent.

I pause for a second, and then take off in pursuit.

The snow and wind are blinding, and I’ve already lost sight of her.

“Where are you?” I holler, calling Stowe’s name over and over again.

The storm is vicious. I can’t see a foot in front of me. I

forget how uneven the ground is, and stumble. "Oww," I scream as I feel my feet slip into a hole.

My hands scrape the ground as I grasp a tuft of grass to break the fall—my legs dangling in the unknown. Must be the coat, but I seem to be wedged in place. I can't pull myself out, but at least I'm not falling any farther.

"Help," I scream. "Stowe, where are you?"

The wind drives snow up against my neck. Wish I could protect my face, but if I lift my hands I might slip into whatever lies below. "Help! help!" I continue to shout.

And then I hear a familiar voice. "Wheaton, I hear you. Where are you? I'm coming!"

I don't see her approaching, but I keep shouting.

"Hold on," Stowe yells, appearing in front of me.

"I'm stuck," I cry. "Get me out of here."

She kneels down on the ground, weaves her arms under my armpits and tries to free me. "You're wedged in pretty tight."

"Don't let go," I beg. "My feet aren't touching the ground."

"This must be one of the ninja mine holes we saw from the air," she mutters. "Put your arms around my neck and hold tight," Stowe orders. When I start to pull, you wriggle if you can and *don't* let go."

The first few tries I seem totally stuck. I'm starting to panic . "If you can't get me out of here, I'm going to turn into a human popsicle." I'm remembering 'Doulaye's warning.

"That's not an option," Stowe barks at me. "Let's try again."

This time she squeezes me so hard that I break free of the hole. For a moment it feels like I'm going to slip, but with Stowe holding tight I slither out onto the frozen ground.

We sit there stunned. "You okay?" she asks.

I'm silent for a moment. I don't want to talk about how my heart is still pounding, so I change the subject. "Did you catch the tent?"

Stowe shakes her head. "I lost sight of it as soon as it flew off."

"What do we do now?" The storm hasn't let up. The driving snow feels like someone's speed skating across my face.

"The wind is going in that direction," Stowe points to our left.

I'm so turned around I don't know if that is east, west, north or south.

"The tent must have flown with the wind," Stowe says. "Let's follow. But hold my hand, so we don't get separated, or fall in any more holes!"

Having the wind behind us is good for our faces, but it's hard to put on the brakes. We don't see any more mine holes—a relief since we're being propelled, practically flying forward. And then we encounter another *ovoo*. Holding each other's hands tight, we come to a halt right before we plow into it. For some reason, we let go of each other and go around it in different directions—which means one of us went counterclockwise. Hope that won't bring bad luck.

Either way, we each deposit a rock to the pile before moving on.

It feels like we've been roaming out here a long time when the wind finally settles down and the precipitation stops. Now it's just wicked cold, and we're standing in an inch of snow.

There's no sign of the tent.

"Let's go back to camp," Stowe suggests. "Which way?"

"Good question." I pull out my phone. There is no cell service, which means no GPS.

"It must have gone down during the storm," I tell Stowe.

"What do we do now, Dr. Techno-Wizard?"

"Hey, I'm not the one who took off without thinking." No way she's pinning this on me. "At least I didn't let you go off and get lost by yourself."

"You're right, sorry." Stowe's face is red from the cold, but her eyes are squinting, a sign she's worried.

"What about Sarnai and our horses? What are they going to do?"

"I don't know," I say. "At least the horses were tied down. Hope they stayed that way. Maybe they can give Sarnai some warmth. How far do you think we've traveled? You think if we call out she might hear us?"

Stowe shrugs. "No clue, but we should try."

"Sarnai, Sarnai, Sarnai!" we holler, as we rotate our bodies, shouting in every direction.

It's so still now you'd think our voices would carry a long distance. But we get no response. We try a couple more rounds of shouting but the results are the same.

The clouds have disappeared, and whatever "warmth" was in the air is being sucked away at a rapid rate.

"We've got to find shelter," Stowe says. "It's dangerous to be out here in this cold."

We look around. I've never been in any place so empty. No houses, no people. Nothing.

"Are your hands cold?" I don't want to sound like a wuss, but my hands are aching.

"Yeah. Brush the snow off your gloves and pull your fingers into your palms," Stowe suggests. "And let's walk fast to keep our feet warm. But remember to watch where you step."

"What exactly are we looking for?"

"I'm not sure, but we don't want to fall asleep out here in this cold. I keep hoping if we explore these little hills, we'll find a protected area." Stowe doesn't sound like her usual confident self, and it's making me more nervous, if that's possible. Maybe going out here alone wasn't so smart after all.

We wander around for another hour or so. The moon is high in the sky, and the reflection off the snow provides an amazing amount of light. We pass areas with a few shrubs and a tree or two, but nothing you'd call a thicket that could provide any serious shelter. We haven't talked much for a while. I'm guessing Stowe's as scared as I am. What are we going to do if we don't find someplace to shelter for the night?

We trudge over another hill and are coming down the other side when Stowe stops in her tracks. "Wheaton, see that outcropping?" Her chin points about 300 yards ahead of us. "Let's make our way over there. If we huddle against the side, maybe it'll reduce our exposure."

This doesn't sound like a perfect solution, but it's the best—no, the only—option we seem to have. So, hand in hand, we hustle our way over to the rocky spot.

As we get closer Stowe notices something. "Is that a space between the rocks?"

She drops my hand, races over, and crouches down. "Wheaton, I think this might be some sort of cave. Let's see if we can get in."

"Is that such a good idea? Our headlamps are back at camp. Could we fall down into a hole? And maybe there's water at the bottom." We're both shivering like crazy. I want to believe Stowe's found someplace for us to escape this awful cold, but I'm worried we could get into more trouble.

"I'll use the flashlight on my cell phone to take a peek." Before I can stop her, Stowe slides into the opening and disappears.

She's gone longer than I like. I crouch down and yell in, "Are you okay?"

Stowe pokes her head out of the opening. "Sorry. I'm fine. This place is kind of cool." She giggles. "Probably not the best word to choose. It's actually not as cold in here." She sticks out her hand for me to join her.

I creep in and hug the wall. It's still cold, but not freezing like outside. Without the wind, we should be able to survive. But that doesn't make me comfortable. "Are you positive there's no hole to fall into?"

Stowe flashes her phone's light across an area maybe 30 feet by 30 feet. "We're fine. This is more like a rock shelter."

She reaches over and starts brushing the snow off my coat. "One thing about this fur, it keeps you dry. I guess otherwise animals would be soaked to the skin half the time."

Then she points to the side farthest away from where we're standing. "Take a look over there."

Small brown blobs dot the cave wall.

"Come closer. They're awesome." Stowe shines her light and I walk across to where she's standing.

"Bats? Aren't they sometimes rabid?"

"Yeah, they can be. But these are hibernating. Best way to avoid the cold," Stowe reassures me.

I get close enough to see what they look like. Their bodies, covered in smoky-brown fur, are hanging upside down. Underneath, they're more yellowish-brown. Their wings are tucked in and seem to be a darker color. I can't see their faces, which is fine with me.

I look around our new home away from home and notice some hard round balls on the ground. "What do you think that is?"

"Fossilized poop," Stowe says. "Your favorite."

"Hope it's not from a wolf." I can tease as well as my cousin.

She shrugs. "Whatever. If they weren't here during the storm, not likely they'll show up tonight. Anyway, this is as good as it's going to get."

Not sure good would be the word I'd choose, but this will make it possible to survive until morning.

"Let's go over to the far wall, away from the opening," Stowe suggests. "It'll be a little warmer there. But before we settle down for the night, let's exercise to get our blood flowing."

My cousin starts running in place, doing jumping jacks and a bunch of crazy maneuvers, first with her arms and then her legs. "Get moving, buddy. These ski drills will warm you right up."

With blood flowing through our veins again we sit down, sliding our fur coats under our bottoms.

Stowe lets out a yawn and plops her head on my shoulder. Thinking about the events of the last few hours, I'm not quite ready to close my eyes. But then tiredness overtakes my fear, and I too drift off to sleep.

23. Reunited

Sleeping wasn't easy, but we managed to catch a few zzz's. One thing about a cave, it stays pretty dark. The rising sun sends a few rays of light in through the entrance of our limestone shelter, signaling that we can resume our search for Sarnai.

I nudge Stowe, who's still nodding off. "Sun's up. Let's go outside and check our GPS again."

We stand up and I'm surprised how stiff we are, and cold. Guess we don't down-regulate our body temperatures like those hibernating bats. After running a few laps inside the rock shelter, we scooch out of our nighttime hideout. Hit by the frigid morning air, we jump up and down and do some air kickboxing to get our bodies ready for what lies ahead. Whatever that will be.

Good news. The GPS is working again, and in the daylight we're able to orient ourselves. "The Boroo mine is south of us and to the east. I think if we walk due south, we'll be heading the right way."

The ground is pretty slippery from last night's storm, so we have to watch our step. At least I do. We haven't gone too far when we hear three explosions, each louder than the one before.

"THSS!" we say in unison. We can tell where the sound is coming from.

"Sarnai! Sarnai!" we call out.

No answer. We must still be out of earshot.

Moving south, we scream her name every few seconds. The air is still so cold that it stings to breathe, and we need to take a quick break. We're about ready to start up again when a voice calls out.

"Stowe, Wheaton, is that you?"

"Sarnai, we're coming!" we yell, as we fly, slipping and sliding, in her direction.

"There she is." Stowe points. We see Sarnai sitting on *Tsagaan,* waving her arm as she rides towards us. She's got *Khar* and *Khüren* in tow.

Jumping off her horse, Sarnai runs over and throws her arms around us. "I am so glad you are okay."

"You're happy to see *us*? We were so worried about *you,*" Stowe says. "How did you get through the night without a tent?"

"I had a tent."

"You did? You found the one that blew away?" I don't know how this could be possible.

"No. But you left your backpacks. I hope you don't mind, I looked inside and found sleeping bags. I used my saddle as little bed, and with sleeping bag I made tent over your heating thing. Not a lot of room, but I was fine. Except I was so scared about what happened to you two."

We tell Sarnai all about the cave we found.

"Oh good. There are many caves all over Mongolia." She takes a deep breath. "I am responsible for you guys. Maybe we keep this adventure between us."

Stowe and I agree.

Sarnai tells us she left most of our gear at the camp, so we mount the horses and follow her lead back toward home base.

We've been traveling for a short while when Stowe veers off track, headed for a small cluster of bushes. She hops off *Khüren* and grabs at something. "Look what I found," she hollers back to us.

Sarnai races over to where Stowe is busy disentangling our tent.

"It's in pretty good shape, considering the trip it's taken," Stowe reports, rolling the tent up tight. "We should be able to use it tonight."

We make our way back to the campsite where we down some breakfast. The tea Sarnai's brought along in one of the thermoses is still pretty warm. I hope we don't face a night this cold again anytime soon.

"Good thinking to use the THSS system. Hearing the explosion sounds made it a lot easier to find you," I tell Sarnai. "And you figured out how to set it up."

Stowe's been busy getting things repacked so we can take off in search of the harem. "Do you think the takhi are still around? Or did the storm scare them away?"

"When I got up this morning I saw harem same place it was yesterday," Sarnai tells us. "I put megaphone for THSS facing in opposite direction from takhi so I would not scare them. Come. We go see if they are still over there."

We walk up a small hill near our campsite and Sarnai looks through her binoculars. She points to the harem. They are grazing as if nothing big happened last night.

The three of us walk back to our horses. "Time to start the drive," I say.

24. Herding Horses Begins

"You already have your THSS connected," I say to Sarnai. "But you want to fix one of these electric generators to the pommel of your saddle." Sarnai gives me a quizzical look.

"Sorry, your English is so good—but that's a goofy word. Pommel is the English word for that front upward curving part of the saddle."

Sarnai nods and attaches the generator.

Stowe and I do the same, and then secure our belts with the amplifiers and sound sources attached. We plug the megaphones into the amplifiers and strap them to our shoulders with an additional harness.

"When we get back on the horses remember to plug your generator into the amplifier," I tell my companions.

"What sound are we starting with?" Stowe asks.

"Let's use the explosion noise," I suggest, "but we'll start at a low sound level and see if the horses respond."

"Remember, don't get too close to takhi," Sarnai warns.

"How about we do this? I'm going to be in the middle. Stowe, you be to my left, and Sarnai to my right," I say to the girls. "We need to spread out so that we form an arc as we approach the horses. The two of you should ride a bit in front of me. We're going to have to be separated because when the takhi start to run they need to stay ahead of us. We don't want them to scatter."

"What level do we start at?" Stowe asks.

"We'll have to experiment. I think you two should broadcast a louder noise than me so we direct the harem to run forward, but together. I'll start with level #1 and you both with #2. If that doesn't move them, we'll ramp it up one notch at a time. Sound like a plan?"

Stowe reminds us to put the ear protectors on our horses so they don't get scared.

"Do we know they'll work?" I ask her. "You were going to test them before we went out into the field—"

Sarnai interrupts. "I tested them before using THSS to help find you. I had to get bigger piece of foam rubber to sit tight in *Tsagaan's* ears. The plugs fit fine for the other two horses. And when I made explosion sound, I used highest level, since I wanted you to hear it wherever you were. Horses didn't move. It worked!"

"Sounds like we're ready to give THSS a try."

Stowe gives me a thumbs up.

I hand the girls both headlamps and put on a double headlamp, one bulb mounted above each of my ears.

"Move out until you are barely in eyeshot of the harem," I tell them. "When you're in position flash a light at me. I'll come forward about half as far and beam back to you both simultaneously. That'll be the signal to send out the first sound blasts. I'll follow one second behind."

We teach Sarnai to bump fists, and the two of them ride off to establish position.

With the sun so bright, it's a little difficult to make out the headlamp flash, but I see a flicker at a 45-degree angle in each direction. I give *Khar* a nudge with my legs and we move forward. "We're in position," I whisper to my steed. Of course, with the ear plugs in he can't hear me. At least I hope he can't.

Here goes. I signal Stowe and Sarnai and hold my breath. I hear the *boom* coming from my left and right. I send my sound out immediately after.

The takhi look up in our direction and shift around. But they don't go anywhere. I send the headlamp signal again and we send out the sounds, one level louder. This time the horses take off. We follow, keeping our distance. They move a short way and then stop. I wave for Stowe and Sarnai to come back.

"The idea worked but the takhi didn't go too far. I've got a monitor on *Khar's* leg, and we've gone maybe half a mile."

"Less than a kilometer," Stowe tells Sarnai.

"At that rate we'll be here for a month."

"Should we switch to a wolf sound?" Stowe asks, her shoulders hunched in a way that says, please no.

"Nah. Let's leave that for last. The noise level we used so far hardly sounds like a scary explosion. Let's amp up the system. Dial to #4 and I'll go to #3. We can still increase the volume plenty. And if we do get the takhi going, you guys see if you can stay at their outer borders. *Khar's* not going to move fast, so I'll catch up."

With that we repeat the process. This time the sound is pretty impressive and the harem takes off for real. They run hard for about five minutes and then stop. Two of the mares and their foals have fallen behind and the harem waits for them to catch up. This turns out to be good for *Khar* and me.

We reconvene. "That worked pretty well. We covered more than 3 kilometers in five minutes. Let's give the horses some time to rest and then push them farther."

"Can I see GPS?" Sarnai requests. She looks at the map and turns to show us where we are. "We are approaching north-south road, and then another short train track. When we move takhi again, let's get them across road and head south so we avoid barbed wire fence."

I'm worried about crossing the road, but Sarnai assures me that it doesn't get a lot of traffic, and because the area is so open, the horses can be seen for miles ahead. Not like deer jumping out of the forest into traffic back home.

Another "explosion" and we drive the takhi across the road, veering south-west. After a few more starts and stops the harem seems to lose interest in our prodding sounds. We've covered about 25 percent of the total distance we need to travel, so it's a good time to take a break, feed our horses and ourselves.

"Do we need to turn it up a notch?" Stowe asks.

"I think so. And we may have to change the tune at some point." Stowe knows I'm suggesting going to the wolf growls.

"If we are going to use wolf noises, we should do it, in middle of day," Sarnai suggests. "Wolves hunt more at night so chances that real wolves come join us is lower now."

"All right. Let's give it a try," I say to the horsewomen.

They take their positions. We exchange signals with our headlamps and let out some howls. We don't need to get as loud with these sounds to get the takhi to respond. The stallion lets off a powerful neigh and charges ahead with the rest of the harem following as fast at their foals allow. It's hard to hear over the hoof beats of our horses, but we don't seem to be attracting any neighboring wolf calls. At least I hope not.

These THSS sounds are very effective in moving the takhi along. It only takes a few prods to get the harem to the halfway mark back to the park.

"It's almost 4:00 PM. Time to give everyone, including the takhi, a rest," I announce. "Looks like we've gone close to 40 kilometers (25 miles). If we stop here, do you think the takhi will run off?"

"I do not think so," Sarnai says. "Too tired and hungry."

She points to a nearby hillside. "They will be able to graze over there."

"I'll call Ariella and give her an update on today's progress," Stowe offers. She digs up the satellite phone and gets our grandmother right away.

Stowe relays how we herded the takhi and gives her the coordinates of our camp. She puts her hand over the receiver and whispers to us that the jeep repairs should be done first thing tomorrow, and they'll leave as soon as they pick it up.

"We'll call you again in the morning to figure out where to meet." Stowe says goodbye and turns to us.

"We have enough time before dark. Let's collect some survey data for Munuu and I'll take photos of the harem."

"While you do that, I will set up camp and stake our horses," Sarnai offers.

"You don't have to do that for us," Wheaton says. "Wait and we'll do our part."

"Don't worry, it is fine. I work faster alone," she says. "Besides, I don't want you to miss chance to collect some poop."

Stowe and I pull out the gear we need and walk over to a couple of rocks. We climb to a level spot where we can observe. We both get our binocs focused. There, not very far away, we have a perfect view of the last of the truly wild horses in the world.

25. Unwanted Guest

I take a deep breath. My nose hairs feel like they're turning into icicles. Good thing we have flip top mittens, so we can work our equipment without our hands freezing off. It's a little after 5:00 PM, and the sun is getting low on the horizon. Stowe grabs the camera and tripod. She sets up and snaps pictures as fast as she can.

I show her how to dial one channel on her headset to record data for Munuu to study later, and another channel for her log.

"The family group has eight mares, one stallion and two foals. The stallion's off to the side by himself." Stowe continues, "Stallion – shiny tan coat, maybe 18 hands long and 12 hands tall, tail around 9 hands long, mane beautiful dark-brown and thick, light stripes on the legs."

"What's that hand stuff all about?" I interrupt.

"Space Cadet, you don't know? Horses are measured in hands. One hand is 4 inches. You do the math."

The horse specialist goes on to call out what she sees for each of the animals as she clicks their pictures from every angle. "They're shorter than the domestic horses in America, aren't they? But they're so beautiful," Stowe says as much to herself as to me.

"Do any of them still have collars?" I ask.

"No. I guess either they've been out here for a while, or the younger members of the harem were born here and were never collared.

"Check out that mare over toward the left," Stowe says. She has a lump on her neck. Wonder if that could be 959?"

Her interest is diverted by one of the foals. "Look how cute he is. The setting sun looks like a spotlight shining on him."

Stowe focuses the camera. "Okay, little Sunshine, I'm taking your picture for Ariella. Maybe she'll include you in a story she writes someday."

I'm busy watching the rest of the harem. The takhi have big, sharp hooves, which they're using to dig for water now that the ground is frozen and last night's snow has blown away. In between, they're chowing down on a couple of shrubs over by a rocky outcropping, and some dead-looking weedy stuff. Summer's leftovers, I guess.

"Stowe, can you make out the plants the horses are eating?"

Stowe grabs a set of binoculars and says, both to me and into her headset, "One takhi is munching on some orchard grass, another's eating tufted vetch and what's left of the red clover. Not sure what the shrubs are."

"These takhi have quite the stomachs," I say to Stowe. "We couldn't keep all of that down. Look at all the poop out there, and one of the mares is adding to the collection now. Maybe you can go scoop up some of the plops and put them in Munuu's sample bags."

"Is that so? I thought maybe this time you could get your hands dirty."

Ughh, the thought of collecting poop is so gross. But I can't stand it when Stowe makes me feel like a wimp. "Okay, I'll do it," I say, pulling a stiff pair of leather gloves out of my pack. These will be perfect for the task.

"Oh, Wig, give me a break. Aren't those the ratty old things you wear to take the hooks out of fishes' mouths? You know you aren't going to pick the stuff up with your hands. We've got disposable scoopers for that.

"Give me the kits," Stowe says, her impatience showing. "I'll take care of the collection."

With that, she seems to forget where she is and starts to move from behind the tree right toward the group.

The horses seem to startle, but I don't think it's because of the poop collector's moves.

"Stowe, come back," I call in the loudest whisper imaginable.

"What now?" Stowe says.

"Get back here *now*." I'm not watching the group anymore or worrying about their poop.

"Wheaton, why is your leg shaking like that? What's wrong?"

"Grab your binoculars and take a look up on that hill to the east." It's hard to tell distances in this huge open space. "That's not a dog, is it?"

As Stowe peers into her binoculars, she starts moving closer to me. Before you know it, she's so close to me her binoculars are resting on my head. I can feel her wrists on my scalp, moving in harmony with my leg.

"I'm pretty sure that's a Mongolian wolf," she whispers. "It's bigger than a coyote."

With all the shaking I'm having a little trouble focusing my binocs. We've talked a lot about wolves being dangerous predators out here, but somehow it didn't seem real 'til now. I wish Ariella were here.

Stowe doesn't say a thing.

As we watch, everything changes.

The takhi stop grazing. The mares stick their heads straight up, and their ears flatten as they move close to their foals. The stallion starts to circle the harem.

The wolf creeps down the hill, its belly close to the grass.

"Do you see any more wolves or just one?" Stowe asks.

"Only one," I whisper. "Don't wolves usually hunt in packs?"

"Not always," Stowe says, her voice quivering.

As we size up the situation, Stowe's foal scampers away

from the group to sample some tufted vetch. The wolf's on the move too. We see it slinking toward the harem. Its eyes are focused on the foal.

No longer concerned about startling the takhi, I scream for Sarnai. Meanwhile, we start throwing rocks in the wolf's direction. Neither of us is an ace pitcher, and the rocks don't go nearly far enough to scare it.

All at once, the wolf tears toward the foal. It opens its mouth wide, and with a final leap it latches onto the young takhi's leg. The little horse lets out a high-pitched squeal.

"Oh, no, Sunshine!" Stowe cries.

I'm about to hurl another rock when Sarnai stops my arm. She points in the direction of a thunderous noise—the oncoming stallion galloping toward the wolf.

His nostrils flare. He's snorting. He rears up on his hind legs, threatening to land on the wolf. It backs up, and the stallion comes down on all fours, his head aimed right at the attacker. The wolf bares its big teeth as it snarls at the stallion. Steam's coming out of the stallion's nostrils. He kicks his heels so hard that dirt flies everywhere. And then, as quickly as it arrived, the wolf backs off and disappears behind the hill.

The foal whinnies like a crying baby. A mare, I'm guessing his mother, comes over and nuzzles her offspring. The rest of the group also approaches. They walk around the foal for a while. The stallion's ears lift and he snorts. Maybe he senses that the wolf hasn't gone far. He mills around the perimeter of the harem. Then the stallion gives off a neigh. The takhi lift their heads and begin to move in the direction

of the leader. Little Sunshine tries to get up, wobbles for a moment, and sinks back down to the ground. At the orders of the stallion, the group turns single file and heads west.

The mother lingers behind as her foal strains to move toward her. With the others leaving, she turns to follow, but then stops and returns one more time to try and coax the young horse. He tries so hard to stand, but it's impossible. Finally the mare backs away, takes one last look at her offspring, and trots off to join the rest of the harem as the group disappears over the horizon.

"Oh Wheaton, they're leaving Sunshine behind."

26. Taking Care Of Sunshine

Stowe turns away. I know she doesn't want me to see the tears rolling down her face. She sniffles, "I can't believe they left Sunshine all alone. We've got to do something."

Not waiting for further discussion, she grabs her stuff and starts to move toward the foal.

This time Sarnai stops her. "He is injured, but still wild. We all go together and take a closer look. But approach from behind."

Following our guide's instructions, the three of us make our way to the foal. He's lying on the ground kicking his three good legs like crazy. I wouldn't want to be on the receiving end of one of those powerful limbs.

We squat down behind the little guy. From close up the hooves look even more dangerous than from a distance.

"Poor Sunshine, I wish we could do something to help you," Stowe says, crouching as close to his injured leg as she dares.

It's dark now and we can't see where the wolf has gone. I wish we had a plan. "Wolves are nocturnal, aren't they? Will the wolf come back for the foal now that the stallion's gone?"

"I hope not. That wolf was mangy-looking. Maybe it was old and thrown out of the pack. I hope it's on *its* last legs." Stowe's sadness is converting into anger.

The foal continues to whimper. He sounds like a crying baby.

Stowe tilts her head as she looks at the young animal. "We need to treat Sunshine's wound. He's still bleeding and he's only going to get weaker."

"Should we be interfering with nature here? Aren't wolves endangered too?"

"Yeah, they are. But there are still so few takhi, if we have to choose between the horse and a meal for the wolf, I think we should save Sunshine."

I don't know if Stowe's right, but it's what she wants.

"We aren't going to be able to take a look at the foal's leg injury," Stowe says, "unless we quiet him down. I'm going to go get the dart gun."

"Are you nuts, you can't use that thing. You could miss and hit me!"

"Relax, Wheaton. Ever hear of the biathlon competition? You ski and target shoot. There's at least one good thing about all my training, I've had lots of target practice."

Stowe brings over Mai's backpack and unloads the supplies. "Wonder which dart to put in the gun? That foal is pretty small."

"Don't ask me." I hope she's thinking twice about this crazy idea.

"I'm a little scared to pick the wrong dose. Maybe we should start by trying an herbal medicine," Stowe suggests. "Remember that list in Mai's backpack? Let's see if there's anything that might help Sunshine."

Stowe pulls it out and shows it to Sarnai. "Do you know these plants?"

"Some of them. My grandmother taught me all about them when was little."

Stowe scans the information. "Says here that the rough chervil plant has roots that can be calming. The foal could use some of that. Any chance we'll find chervil around here?"

"Could be. I think it grows on rocky areas. Let me see what I can find," Sarnai says. With her headlamp showing the way, she runs up onto a rocky ledge around 50 yards away. Before I can stop her, Stowe follows.

How could they leave me alone with the foal? It's 6:00 PM and dark. Even with the full moon and my extra-strength dual headlamp on, it's creepy. To distract myself I collect nearby poop samples. That'll surprise Stowe. Then I go back to waiting.

Right around the time I start thinking it's too quiet, I hear a howl. In fact, sounds like more than one howl.

How far away are the wolves? I hope Sarnai's right that they aren't going to bother us.

"Guys, did you hear that?" I raise my voice. "Stowe? Sarnai? Where are you?"

For a few moments the howling stops. Then it starts again. "You two hurry up and get back here!" I yell. They don't answer. Distances out here are farther than they seem.

The howling stops again for another few minutes.

Maybe the wolves don't like the sound of my voice. Maybe I should sing an evil song. All I can think of is the Wizard of Oz, so here goes:

"*Ding Dong,* the witch is dead, the wicked witch, the wicked witch," I sing. I'm bellowing out the song at the top of my lungs when the girls get back carrying bunches of what I assume is rough chervil.

"That's quite a set of pipes you have, Wheaton." This time Stowe isn't picking on me. In the light of my headlamp, her face shines eggshell-white.

The howling starts again and we glance over to the next ridge. It's hard to count, but we see maybe six yellow eyes reflecting in the moonlight.

"A pack of wolves," we all say at the same time.

"Do we have to worry about our horses?" Stowe's asking a good question. "Sarnai, how do you keep wolves away from your livestock?"

"Our horses will be fine," she tell us. "Biggest problem is with young animals like foals and calves. We try to use dogs to scare them off. For us the wolf represents freedom so we only shoot it if we have to."

Stowe shrugs. "Well, we don't have any dogs or a shotgun. Back home when we want to scare off coyotes we build a fire with lots of smoke. Could we do that? Looks like there are some woody shrubs and dead leaves around."

This sounds like our only option. Stowe and Sarnai start to move.

"No way you two are going to collect that wood without me. Can't take a chance the wolf might attack you." Or me...

"Wolves almost never attack people. Someone has to stay with foal. If not, one of them may come down and finish off little one." Sarnai makes a sweeping gesture across her neck.

"I'll watch over Sunshine while you two collect the firewood as fast as you can." Stowe's taking charge.

I don't like this idea at all, but before I can argue with her, Stowe continues. "We'll all keep singing at the top of our lungs, and twirl around once in a while so our headlamps make it look like there are lots more of us.

"All right," I say to Sarnai. "Let's hurry."

We hurry off to a nearby outcropping where there's enough firewood and smoke-generating leaves to do the job. Sarnai and I break off shrub limbs and load up with anything on the ground that looks like it can burn. With our arms full, we race back down the slope, continuing our chorus as loudly as we can. I notice that the wolves are not as far away as a while ago.

"We don't have matches, Camping Princess. The wolves are closing in. I could short out a battery." No pretending now. I'm panicked.

"No need for that. There were flares in Mai's backpack." Stowe pulls one out, removes the cap and strikes it on a nearby rock. She's careful to hold it at the base as she touches the sizzling tip to the kindling.

We stand upwind from the smoke and fire, watching as those yellow eyes begin to recede. Once again the howling stops. Let's hope that means they're going to stay away.

"We've solved one problem," Stowe says. "Now we have to check on our patient."

With all the excitement, I haven't been paying too much attention to Sunshine. Looks like there's more blood than before. And the little guy's still whinnying and kicking. Wonder if it's because of the pain, or if the foal senses danger.

Stowe shows me the rough chervil they've picked. She rips off the roots and starts to stick out her hand to feed the foal.

I knock her hand aside. "You can't hand feed it. It'll bite you!"

"You're right." Stowe grabs a stick and pushes the roots close to the foal's mouth.

"Here you go, Sunshine. See if this helps."

"Come on, Sunshine, take a bite," I try urging the foal. "Stowe and Sarnai looked all over to find that for you."

After some more coaxing, he sticks out his tongue and takes a little of the roots. But like a sick kid, the foal loses interest and starts to whinny again.

"This Mongolian medicine isn't going to do the job if we can't get the foal to eat more of it. And if he keeps kicking like that, he's going to injure himself more," Stowe declares. "I'm going to have to tranquilize him."

I was afraid she'd say that. "Let's think this through before you take aim. Sunshine's a lot smaller than the adults. What's the difference in dosage of those darts?"

Stowe reads the labels. "Here's one that's half as much as the biggest. I'm going to use that."

"You're sure you know what you're doing? I don't want to be the one out cold."

"Relax, Wheaton. I'll get the foal in its rump. I'd like to tranquilize you, but I won't."

I swallow hard. Two ways this can go, very good or very bad. But I don't have a better option.

Stowe pulls out Mai's gun and loads the tranquilizer into the dart. She moves back a bit and lies down prone on the ground, as if she were in a biathlon competition, I guess. She takes aim at the foal's bottom and fires. Sunshine lets out a squeal I won't forget soon, but then he falls asleep almost instantly.

Stowe and Sarnai run right up to the foal. I stand back for a minute. Want to be certain he's not going to wake up.

My cousin crouches down close to the injured leg. "Look at that wound. You can see the teeth marks, and the leg is at a funny angle. Looks broken. Sunshine needs a vet. Wish Mai were here."

"Maybe this will help," Sarnai says, as she produces another plant root. "We call it *gishuugene*. It is for wound treatments."

Sarnai uses a rock to grind the root while Stowe pulls antiseptic cream from Mai's pack. "Maybe we can use both?"

Mixing things may not be a good idea, but the two medicine women get to work covering the ugly wound.

"Maybe we should bandage the leg, so the foal can't do any more damage to himself," Stowe suggests. "Wheaton, see what you can find in Mai's bag."

I follow orders and come up with a roll of gauze that Stowe winds around the foal's leg to stabilize it.

"This is no way near good enough, but at least it'll keep things from getting worse until we get Sunshine to a vet," Stowe says.

She rubs Sunshine's back. "The little guy smells like wet earth, even though the ground is pretty frozen."

"Maybe from what he was eating," Sarnai suggests.

"Wheaton, come here and feel his fur, it's so thick," Stowe says, stroking the long hair on the foal's back.

I guess it's okay to touch the foal while he's sleeping. My hands sink into what feels like two layers of soft, dense wool. "Guess he's prepared for this cold climate."

For a second Stowe buries her head in the foal's back. "Do you think we can save this little guy?"

27. Another Long Night

The temperature is dropping fast. Even with our fur coats on we're aware of the cold air colliding with our hot breath.

"Let's move the tent and our horses closer to the foal," Sarnai suggests.

While Sarnai repositions the hitching post and our trusty steeds, Stowe and I get the tent set up a few paces from Sunshine. With the geothermal heater in place, the three of us sit down for the first time in quite a while.

"We need to call Ariella and tell her what's going on," Stowe says. "And Sarnai, you might want to call your parents, too."

Stowe places a call to our grandmother and puts it on speaker so we all hear the conversation. "Hi. I know we weren't going to call 'til the morning, but something has happened. It's not us. We're all fine," she reassures Ariella before describing the wolf attack on Sunshine.

"We need Mai to take a look at the foal and see if he's going to make it. I couldn't bear it if we lost two foals on this trip. How early can you guys get here?"

Mai's been listening in on their side. "Our vehicle is ready, so we'll leave before sunrise. You're probably far from the road, so give us your coordinates and we'll find you. Be near your phone after 6:00 AM if we need to call. Keep the fire going all night, and the wolves won't come in. They aren't that interested in humans, so you should be fine."

"Is there anything else we can do for the foal?" Stowe asks.

"If the foal can't stand," Mai says, "you might want to cover it."

"There's one other thing you need to know." My turn to weigh in. "When the wolf attacked the foal, the rest of the harem ran off. They may not have gone far, but don't forget the Finder. It'll make locating them again a lot easier. They left plenty of fresh poop behind so we won't have any trouble getting a scent."

"No problem. It's already packed," Ariella assures me.

"Hi. Sarnai here. Could you call my parents and tell them what is happening?" She repeats her parent's cell phone number twice.

"Yes, of course," Ariella says.

I provide our location and we hang up.

The first thing Stowe does is get a sleeping bag and unzip it. She goes outside and covers the foal, who's no longer asleep. She pushes the chervil his way, and this time he takes a little more. Maybe that will help get him through the night.

It's been quite a while since we've eaten, and Sarnai takes out a bag of what look like white curds. "This is *aaruul*, made from milk, no meat," she tells us while looking at Stowe.

Following our grandmother's instructions about trying everything, we both take a bite. "Interesting," Stowe says.

That's one way to describe it. I don't want to be obnoxious, but there has to be something else we can eat. I dig into our bag and find some nuts and a bunch of chocolate bars. "We have food to share too," I offer.

Stowe flashes a big smile at me, and we all chow down.

We agree to take two-hour shifts watching over Sunshine and feeding the fire. I go first. The foal's pretty quiet, and with the fire producing warmth, I'm finally able to let my mind wander a little. For a while it's me and this vast empty country, until Stowe breaks the silence.

"How's it going?"

I startle out of my dream. "Wow, you scared me. I was far away, trying to imagine what it was like when Genghis Khan and his soldiers crossed these plains."

"I think you need some sleep." Stowe wraps her arm around me. "Go into the tent. I'll keep an eye on Sunshine and catch up with my logs."

STOWE LEBLOND'S LOG

Hustai Nuruu National Park, Mongolia

October 29

Midnight

We're spending the night out here on the Mongolian steppes. It is really cold. Good news: Wheaton invented a geothermal heater so it's not too bad. The heater takes advantage of the constant temperature of the earth below the frost line. It sucks the warmth up into our tent.

We're not in the tent all the time since we're taking turns watching over Sunshine, a foal that was attacked by a wolf. We watched the whole thing happen. I admit, I'm terrified of wolves. But at the same time, they're awesome. The Mongolian wolf is what they call a subspecies of the gray wolf, sometimes called the woolly wolf because of its thick undercoat. It's got amazing golden eyes, which pierce the darkness, almost like a laser pointer. Legs are supposedly shorter than the gray wolf, but I wasn't about to measure them. Some scientists think that the Mongolian wolf is the ancestor of the domestic dog. Sarnai told us that there's a legend that Genghis Khan and his family descended from the spirit of the wolf. Even though I hate the wolf that attacked Sunshine, I know that wolves are important animals with a part to play in keeping nature in balance.

Speaking of Genghis Khan, he's supposed to be buried somewhere up in the Khentii mountains east of where we are. Munuu said Chinggis (Genghis to us) Khan purposely had his family bury him in an unmarked grave so he couldn't be found, even after he was dead. Eight hundred years later, odds are that grave's pretty well overgrown.

Most people say he was a really bad dude, but the truth is Genghis Khan also did a lot of good. Guess it depends on which side you were on.

He invented a postal service, more like a pony express, to deliver mail throughout the empire. That was very cool back in the 1200s. No email or texting in those days.

Genghis Kahn gave rights to women in making important decisions ☺, spared people who were illiterate, and protected doctors and craftsman. I guess the problem came if people didn't let him have his way. And there were lots of those. His army of 129,000 men conquered 12 million square miles of territory and killed millions of people. That wasn't his good side.

Genghis Khan's picture is on Mongolian money. I guess people wouldn't have done that if they thought he was all bad.

Mongolian words I'm learning – Sarnai has a boyfriend and before he left they said some things to each other in Mongolian. I know I was being nosy, but I asked her what they said. Nothing romantic ☺.

> *Be safe – Ayuulgüi baigaarai* – Аюулгүй байгаарай
>
> *Thanks for taking us – Bidniig avch irsend bayarlalaa* – Биднийг авч ирсэнд баярлалаа
>
> *Milk curds – Aaruul* – Ааруул

STOWE LEBLOND'S NOTE TO HER PARENTS

Hustai Nuruu National Park, Mongolia

October 30

1:00 AM

Dear Mom and Dad,

I've got another hour to go in my shift watching Sunshine before Sarnai takes over. My log is done for tonight but there's something that's been on my mind and it's easier to share this way. I know you and Dad have supported my competitive skiing for years, and I know it was my idea to begin with. But this past summer I started thinking that I don't want to do it anymore. I don't like feeling that I'm only as good as my last race. I still love to ski, but I don't like the whole competition scene—the clothes or the pushy parents. Not you and Dad—you are great.

There's another, maybe better, reason. You know how I helped the Filmores out at their horse stable? Well, I loved everything about it. Not only trail riding with Mrs. Filmore, but grooming the horses, feeding them, even cleaning the stables. (I know that's surprising ☺). It's hard to describe, but when I arrived in the morning the horses seemed to know me. When I rubbed their coats they'd nuzzle me—I just love them.

Being out here, riding the Mongolian horses and watching these amazing wild horses, makes me more sure that I don't want to live for skiing anymore. Meeting Mai and

'Doulaye, and seeing how they are helping horses and other endangered species has got me thinking. Maybe I could do what they do.

I'm sitting here watching over this little foal and it seemed like a good time to put my thoughts together. I hope you and Dad won't be disappointed in me.

Love,

Stowe

28. Another Foal Headed To Ulaanbaatar

It's five AM and we're all up. The three of us and Sunshine. Well, the foal's awake, not "up." The threat of the wolves seems to have disappeared. Sarnai has gathered some more of the vetch and clover the takhi seemed to like, and she's busy pushing the food in the direction of our patient's mouth.

Stowe strokes the little horse's back while we wait for Ariella and the others to arrive.

As promised, an hour later we hear the sound of a vehicle and see two high beams coming our way. As they get closer the horse trailer comes into view. It's our guys.

Mai hops out first and heads right to Sunshine. Ariella and 'Doulaye follow.

Stowe wastes no time in letting the vet know how she and Sarnai treated our patient.

Mai crouches down behind the foal's head to take a look. "You kids did a terrific job dressing this wound, but I need to get him to Ulaanbaatar where I can do more for him."

"He's not going to die?" Stowe asks.

"There are no guarantees, but I think he'll make it. Lucky the wolf didn't go for his neck."

"Say thank you to stallion," Sarnai tells Mai.

Stowe stares down at the foal for a moment, but then continues with her questions. "When Sunshine's well again, will he go back to his family?"

Mai shakes her head. "That won't be possible. If we try to put him together with the other P-horses he'd fall behind. Another wolf would finish him off. We'll have to see if Munuu can find this P-horse a home."

"What happens now?" I ask.

"We quiet the foal down and get him loaded into the trailer," Mai says, as she turns and heads to the jeep. She brings back a sack of supplies. "Stowe, why don't you help me mix this tranquilizer with the food we brought for the foal."

My cousin follows instructions and then, with Mai's guidance, gives the sleep-inducing meal to Sunshine. "We didn't have any medicine, so I had to dart Sunshine with your gun before we could treat him. Hope that was okay?" Stowe asks.

"Yeah, turns out downhill-racer girl is also a biathlete," I inform everyone.

"You did what you had to do in an emergency," Mai says

to her pupil, "but darting can be dangerous for the animals. With oral sedatives we can control the dose better, and it enters the system more slowly. That tranquilizer will work well. He'll be asleep in around 45 minutes."

Next challenge—moving a 350-pound animal. He's about twice as old as the little foal that died. Even sleeping, moving him is going to be difficult.

'Doulaye takes charge. He brings over a big tarp. The six of us struggle, but we manage to work it under Sunshine. Then we drag him to the trailer.

'Doulaye opens the back and guides a beautiful sand-colored horse out to make room for our little foal.

"That is our *Eis*, I think," Sarnai says. "What is he doing here?"

"We stopped at the hotel first. Your parents suggested we take a horse for Ariella so she can be with you for the rest of the drive," 'Doulaye explains.

Our grandmother looks at us. "You didn't think I was going to miss out on all the adventure? But first, we need to figure out how to get Sunshine into that trailer."

This is going to be tricky.

"Could you pop the hubcaps off your tires?" I ask 'Doulaye. "If I lash two pairs of hubcaps together, I think we can create a channel for the rope and make a pulley to get Sunshine in there."

Mai and 'Doulaye give me a hand. With the pulley secured to the top of the truck, the six of us wrap the tarp around the foal like a sling and tie it to our hoisting apparatus. We connect the sling to the pulley, and all of us haul on the rope to lift the foal. At one point it's dangling in the air. While 'Doulaye, Mai and Ariella hang on to the pulley, the rest of us guide the foal to his bedroom, where we deposit Sunshine safely on the floor of the trailer.

That wasn't easy. We take a break to catch our breath.

"There's still a job to finish," I remind everyone.

"I hear you," 'Doulaye says, as he gets a saddle from the trailer and positions it on *Eis* for Ariella.

Then 'Doulaye points at me. "Be careful when you find that harem. You know what to do if one of those takhi charges?"

"Not really," I say.

"Take away its credit card."

"Here we go again," Mai says giving her colleague a little punch in the arm. "We better move along and get this foal back to Ulaanbaatar."

"Yup." 'Doulaye gives Mai a salute. "We're getting good at this."

The two scientists hop into their vehicle, give us a wave, and head down the road.

"Bye, Sunshine. We'll see you in a few days," Stowe calls after them.

Ariella's bundled up in a fur coat that she's managed to borrow. She pulls out some buns and a thermos of hot milk. We're so hungry we polish off every last drop.

With our bellies full, we pack up the tent and stomp out the fire. It's time to finish the job we came here to do.

29. Driving The Herd Home

Ariella gives me the Finder and tells me she managed to get some scent pulled out of the frozen stool samples. I take our pup down to the area where the takhi pooped before the wolf disturbed their activities and pull the air around the paddies into our bionic dog. "Sorry, buddy. I know it stinks." Wish I could hold my nose, but my hands are occupied.

After finishing my task I return to our camp and compare these fresh signals with the ones we know come from the harem the scientists studied a year ago. "Good news. The scent from the fresh stool matches those from before. So now we can be positive we've tracked down the right group."

"Phew. Would have been bad if there was more than one stray bunch. Are we ready to find the harem, Dr. Smellmeister?" Stowe says.

"Yes, we are." For the first time I'm feeling confident. "There hasn't been much wind overnight so the Finder should be able to pick up the horses' trail."

We mount up and I release our pup. Ariella rides next to me. The other two follow and Stowe explains to Sarnai how the Finder works.

It doesn't take long for our search engine to start spinning. No horses in sight.

"Oh well, Wheaton, Hansel and Gretel had bread crumbs, we have poop." Stowe points down to the takhi leavings on the ground.

I direct the Finder to move along.

Sarnai's been quiet for a while. "How will takhi react if Finder gets close to them?"

Good question. I hope we have an answer soon.

Over the next hour, we travel around ten miles, trailing the scent. We ride west between two different train tracks. No sign of any catastrophe along the barbed wire fence.

I've been watching the Finder through binoculars off and on, and it looks like it's stopped again. We trot toward our bionic dog.

"Yes! Another successful search!" I say. But before getting too excited, I observe one of the mares charging the Finder.

"Yikes." I holler. "She going to kill our pup." Time to call it home.

Using the remote, I signal the Finder to come back to

where we're standing. I make sure the attacker doesn't follow before jumping off my steed to scoop it up.

"It's been bumped around, but I think the guts should be okay." I hope.

The mare watches but doesn't come toward me. Meanwhile the rest of the harem has huddled together.

"I want to check on something. That angry mare's the one with the bump on its neck." I pull out my laptop to see what matches there are for the Finder signal.

"Do you have to do that now?" Stowe hisses at me. "We're in the middle of a rescue."

I ignore her impatience and zero in on an answer right away. "Guys, the mare that butted heads with the Finder is the owner of collar #959 , you know, the one we found a few days ago."

"That'll make Mai happy," Stowe says. "Wonder why the mare still has a welt two years after the collar fell off?"

"Could be scar tissue," Ariella suggests.

No more time for analysis. We need to drive these takhi back into the park.

I go to unpack the THSS apparatus. "After all these horses have been through, I feel bad about having to scare them into running again."

"Me too," Stowe says.

I show Ariella how the THSS works. "We only have three setups, and Sarnai and Stowe know how to operate them, so maybe ride along with me."

"That's fine. I'd like to take some action shots along the way." Ariella pats her saddlebag. She hasn't had too much time for photography on this mission.

We assume our positions and head out.

Once again the takhi respond to our prodding sounds. This time Ariella gallops on ahead, and with her reins in one hand and her camera in the other, she photographs this harem we've gotten to know so well.

Things seem to be going smoothly for a change, until we notice Sarnai pointing ahead and yelling. She's too far away and I can't hear what she's saying. One glance through the binoculars and the problem is obvious. The takhi are charging ahead in the direction of railroad tracks—bordered by one of those barbed wire fences.

There's no time to hatch a plan. Lucky for the takhi, and for us, Sarnai is an amazing horsewoman. Her position has been to the right of the harem and a bit behind them. We see her pull off her horse's ear protectors, yell something to him, and gallop forward. Next thing we know she's caught up to the takhi. Standing up in her saddle with one hand on the reins and the other waving at the harem, she slips between them and the treacherous barbed wire. The horses are running so hard and fast that the ground vibrates beneath their hooves.

The takhi better turn soon or Sarnai's going to be in trouble. And then, as if on cue, the horses change course, veering away from danger.

She rejoins us, her cheeks flushed, her hat blown back in the wind.

"Wow," Stowe says. "You are amazing. Where'd you learn to ride like that?

"Oh. When little I raced horses. I wanted to be real jockey but my father said I need to help with business. Oktai and I have plans. We'll see," Sarnai says.

Ariella rejoins us in time to hear the end of our conversation. "You are a remarkable rider. I took some photos of you in action. I'll select the best ones and email them to you. Maybe you can use them."

The wild ride avoiding the barbed wire has gotten the horses almost to the finish line. Over the next three hours we drive the horses well past the boundary deep into Hustai Nuruu National Park.

"You three did a great job. The harem will now have a chance to interact with other families. Our work is completed."

We high-five each other and Ariella too.

Then Ariella suggests that Sarnai lead us back to the *ger* hotel.

"It will take about hour to get home," our guide tells us. Then she looks at me and laughs. "Maybe hour and half."

It's about 3:00 PM when we arrive back where we started a few days ago. Chuluun and Tuya are there, and they help get the horses unpacked.

When we dismount I realize that I'm no horseman. I am so sore—my bum, my knees, my legs—I can hardly walk.

"You need a few more riding lessons," Stowe whispers in my ear.

"Maybe, but not right away, please."

The days seem to have gotten a lot shorter, even in this brief stay. But tonight no one needs an excuse to go to sleep early.

Tomorrow we go home.

30. Saying Good Bye

In the morning we have one last breakfast with our hosts. Before leaving, we hand out gifts for everyone—special t-shirts. Stowe came up with the idea. The front of the shirt has our logo—different animals connected in a circle, with the word RESQ printed on top.

The family models them for us, and we snap a few photos of everyone as a reminder of our visit.

Stowe grabs one more t-shirt and walks over to Sarnai. "This one's for Oktai. Tell him thanks from us. Hope your plans work out."

After hugs all around we climb into our vehicle and take off for Ulaanbaatar.

We've been in touch with Munuu, and he and Mai meet us at the airport. Munuu tells us, "Airport has series of quarantine pens for animals that are brought into country.

They happen to be empty, so I received permission for foal to rest here until we take him to his new home."

"Which will be where?" Stowe's eyes are begging for an answer she isn't going to get.

"Conservation scientist friends of mine have agreed to nurse foal back to health, and then take him to a wildlife sanctuary dedicated to endangered species. They will come for Sunshine tomorrow."

Stowe still looks sad. "What's the point to saving him so he can spend the rest of his life in captivity?"

Mai responds. "I understand how you feel. But remember, when Sunshine matures into a stallion, he will be able to breed, so we won't lose his genes for the future. And when people come to visit the sanctuary, Sunshine will help tell the story of this magnificent species."

Munuu steps up, and his face softens as he looks directly at Stowe. "Would you like to go and say goodbye to foal before you leave?"

"Oh yes, please."

Munuu drives us to the end of the runway where the quarantine pens are located. We walk into the enclosed area.

"He's standing." Stowe sounds happy for the first time. "Mai, what did you have to do?"

"I operated on his leg as soon as we got back. For now it's important that he's standing. In a few months he'll be able to walk and run, but not well enough to be set free and survive."

"Time to say goodbye." Ariella puts her arm around Stowe.

Mai turns to us. "'Doulaye had a meeting at the local University but said to be sure and tell you guys goodbye."

"Tell him bye from us too," Stowe says. "Maybe we'll visit you both in Washington D.C. someday."

Mai gives us all hugs and departs.

As we get ready to leave, Munuu pulls out gifts for all of us. Opening my present, I do a double take. We've gotten little porcelain takhi. Exactly like the one from my mother's collection.

"Thanks, this is perfect," I blurt out. Stowe looks at me and winks.

Then Munuu turns to Ariella and hands her an envelope. "I hope ResQ Foundation can use this donation to help in other rescues."

"This is wonderful. Thank you." Ariella slips the envelope into her pack.

"*Bayartai*/Goodbye." Munuu shakes hands with all of us.

"*Bayartai,*" we reply and wave as Munuu drives away.

Thanks to the ECAPS and Dynochute we're back at ResQ headquarters in a few hours.

"Wonder where we'll go next," Stowe says, yawning.

"There's a world of possibilities." Ariella takes a big stretch. "For now I think we all better go home and get some sleep."

Ariella gives us both big hugs and heads upstairs.

Stowe follows me to the roof for her trip back to Vermont.

"Here," I say, handing her a stack of printed pages. "I downloaded your logs and the note to your parents."

Stowe wrinkles her nose and gives me a hug. "I'll talk to you more about that later."

She jumps in the Dynochute and heads north.

I hop on my scooter and cruise home. It doesn't feel so cold after being in Mongolia.

It's 7:00 PM Wednesday night when I unlock the front door to the apartment. The 13-hour time change has moved us back a day on the trip home. Sounds like Mom's giving my brother a bath, and Dad's on a business call in the bedroom.

Everything in the living room is pretty much like I left it a few days ago. I slip the little porcelain horse onto my mother's shelf.

I wish it were that simple to fix the real world.

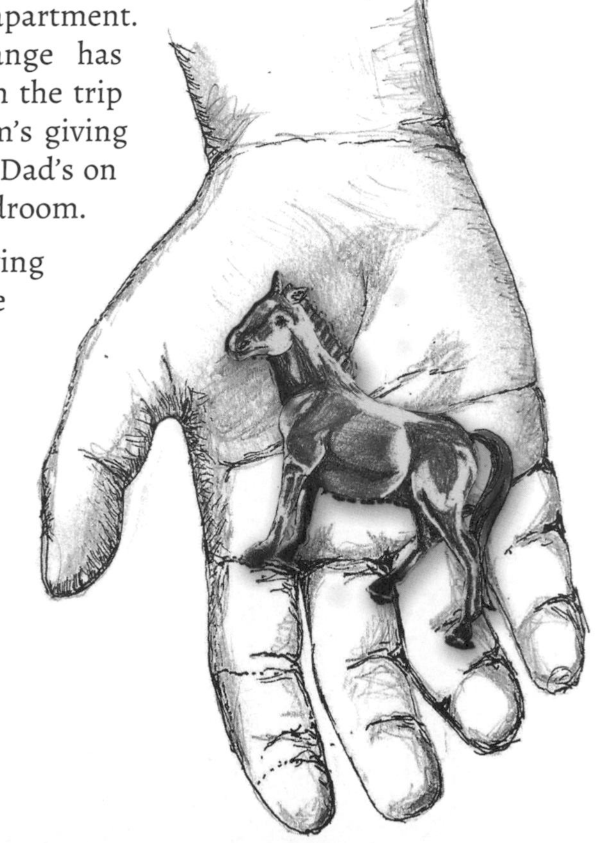

Acknowledgments

This story and the characters are fictitious. My inspiration comes from the wonderful scientists and keepers at the Smithsonian's National Zoo and Conservation Biology Institute. The natural history described in this book is based upon fact as determined through the literature, and first-hand accounting of people who know the Przewalski horse (Takhi) and the environment in Mongolia. Special thanks to Suzan Murray,Program Director, Smithsonian Wildlife Health Program, for her detailed reading of this manuscript, and to Melissa Songer, Conservation Biologist, Smithsonian Conservation Biology Institute, who read early versions and provided significant insight into the behavior or these remarkable creatures. Thanks to Michael E. VonFricken of the Department of Global and Community Health, George Mason University, Jeff Erickson, Penn State Law School, and Bayer Dashpurev, a Mongolian National studying Environmental Law at Penn State, for their personal insights regarding life in Mongolia. The Materials Research Institute at Penn State provided the inspiration for Wheaton's futuristic inventions. Thanks to Carlo Pantano and Edward Liszka for brainstorming with me and helping me understand the underlying principles of the materials used in the story. Thanks to all the readers of this manuscript from its inception—especially the Writers4Kids of State College, my exceptional editor/publisher, Pendred Noyce, my husband Ira for all his encouragement, and Hudson Jeremy Pell-Gibson, together with whom, the whole idea of ResQ started.

About The Author

Eva Pell is a PhD biologist, internationally known for her study of air pollution effects on plants. She was the Sr. Vice President for Research and Dean of the Graduate School at the Pennsylvania State University and was Under Secretary for Science at the Smithsonian Institution. She and her husband have three grandchildren, and reside in State College, Pennsylvania. This is her second book in the ResQ series.

Protean Literacy: Extending the Discourse on Empowerment

I happily dedicate this book to Maya, my little angel and to all children for their enduring hope and love which have been the inspiration for my work.

Protean Literacy: Extending the Discourse on Empowerment

Concha Delgado-Gaitan

Falmer Press
(A member of the Taylor & Francis Group)
London • Washington, D.C.

UK The Falmer Press, 4 John Street, London WC1N 2ET
USA The Falmer Press, Taylor & Francis Inc., 1900 Frost Road, Suite 101, Bristol, PA 19007

First published in 1996

A catalogue record for this book is available from the British Library

Library of Congress Cataloging-in-Publication Data are available on request

ISBN 0 7507 0469 1 cased
ISBN 0 7507 0470 5 paper

Jacket design by Caroline Archer

Typeset in 10/12 pt Garamond
Graphicraft Typesetters Ltd., Hong Kong.

Printed in Great Britain by Burgess Science Press, Basingstoke on paper which has a specified pH value on final paper manufacture of not less than 7.5 and is therefore 'acid free'.

Contents

Acknowledgments

During the ten years I spent conducting research in Carpinteria, I received funds from numerous sources to assist me in completing specific sections of this project, and to these organizations, I am deeply grateful. In chronological order they are: Academic Senate at the University of California, Santa Barbara (UCSB) (1986); Pearl Chase Foundation (1988); Linguistic Minority Research Project (1988); Johns Hopkins Center for Social Organization of Schools (1988–93); University of California President's Award for Research most leading to Improvement in Education (1990); Academic Senate at the University of California, Davis (UCD) (1990–3); Spencer Foundation (1991). This book represents a decade of data collection which was assisted at different periods by numerous graduate students at UCSB and UCD whom I wish to recognize: Martha Allexsaht-Snider, Francisca Gonzalez, Hector Mendez, David Sanchez, Alina Rodriguez and Frances Escobar.

Profoundest gratitude goes to my special friends and collaborators in Carpinteria: Cristina Aguilar and her family, Magdalena Alonzo and her family, Javier and Lupe Alvarez and their family, David and Maria Andrade and their family, Marta Meza and her family, and Teresa and Miguel Gutiérrez and their family.

Karen Stanley, an excellent teacher/researcher, deserves special mention for her time in data collection and analysis. I also extend my sincerest and warmest appreciation to Robert Keatinge, administrator and committed advocate of families and of the Latino community. I especially thank the Carpinteria School District administration for all of its cooperation during the years of my research in Carpinteria.

In addition to the devoted attention and support received from my collaborators in Carpinteria, I am compelled to recognize numerous friends and colleagues who have enhanced my thinking about my work. Daniel Rudman, playwright and friend deserves a big 'Thank you!' for sharing his precious time and insights on earlier versions of my manuscripts especially the sections of the children's stories. Lubna Chaudhry also deserves special acknowledgment for her total support of me and for her refreshing perspectives and conversations. And, to Bernice Zamora, poet, literary scholar and friend, I extend my genuine appreciation for her editorial assistance and her generous time in helping me prioritize my attention. I also thank my friend and mentor, Luis

DelAguila, whose sage teachings over a decade, have shown me how empowerment is a lifelong process.

And, of course, I wish to acknowledge my devoted family and friends at home and in many distant parts, who have supported me totally through the toughest crisis of this SLE illness which has transformed my life the past four years. Through their loving actions, they continuously express the heart of my work — our connection to one another.

Introduction

'Sembrando Semillas Juntos'

Había una vez un viejito que tenía una semilla y la sembró en la tierra y le tardó en crecer. Entonces un niño le echo agua y creció y creció y el viejito necesitaba ayuda. El niño le dijó que el le ayudaba a cortar el árbol que había crecido tan grande. Le dijó que lo cortaba con un cerrucho. Cuando terminaron de cuidar al árbol dió manzanas. Y después niños se juntaron para ayudarle al señor. Cuando ya todos los niños agarraron toda las manzanas, él le dió a cada quien un dolar. Después el viejito les dijó, 'Gracias' y todos los niños se hicieron amigos del viejito y el viejito fue a su casa contento.

'Planting Seeds Together'
(Story told by 7-year-old, Maria)
Once there was an old man who had one seed to plant it in the earth and it delayed in growing. Then a little boy watered it and it grew and grew and the old man needed help. The young boy told him that he would help him cut the tree that had grown so big. He told him to cut it with a saw. When they finished taking care of the tree, the tree produced apples. Then children gathered to help the man. When all the children collected all of the apples, he gave each one a dollar. Later the old man said, 'Thank you', and all of children became friends with the old man and the old man went home happy.

Convinced that stories about our lives provide a continuity for humankind to relate, I realize the compelling message which this Carpinteria story represents. By learning about each other's worlds we become more knowledgeable about the sociocultural, socioeconomic and sociopolitical nature of our discontinuities while simultaneously embracing our commonalities.

Without question the act of writing this book challenged many of my earlier understandings of culture, research and my presence as an ethnographer in the field. The importance of delivering this portrayal of a decade of study involving people's complex lives and their process of learning literacy prevailed.[1] An expressive logic at the center of their daily lives allowed me to confront the contradictions of conducting research in linguistically and ethnically diverse communities in the United States in this historical period. After concretized thinking, talking and reading with the people in Carpinteria, I become convinced that no single theory of culture suffices to understand the family values that influenced the cultural transformation and their relationship within their families, schools and the community. The people's cultural identity, language and common historical immigrant experience sustained their activism which simultaneously challenged and affirmed their beliefs and values as they placed children and literacy at center stage.

Issues which have long concerned me as standards for measuring literacy and family–school relationships remain bound by competitive, capitalistic principles of the educational system.[2] My research convinces me that many attempts to promote literacy and family–school relationships have limited effectiveness because they are driven by modernistic capitalist premises void of cultural affirmation and engagement of the local communities. The school system demands that parents advocate for their children in order to achieve academic success. A basic tenet holds that those with greater knowledge of how the system operates increase their access to educational resources.

Conducting research on literacy and family–school relationships in Latino communities has meant that I have had to wrestle with the dualities of modern and postmodern theories related to the educational arena because post-modern tenets reject modernistic scientific theories.[3] Although major academic trends locate themselves in either modernity or postmodernity discourses, concurrently, we need to remain open to alternative possibilities for people who choose to build communities founded on their particular cultural experience. I considered carefully the thinking of the people in Carpinteria in order to capture a more holistic understanding of the potential they envisioned for themselves in creating a dynamic community. These are people that even modernity forgot with respect to educational options. And where postmodern analyses also ignores their cultural history or possibilities for new social constellations. When there was an educational option, it was as an exit from racial, linguistic and economic oppressive conditions.

I assert that formulas based on positivistic assumptions in research limit our understanding about Latinos in the United States. Our real work begins in learning how Latinos perceive their cultural, historical, political and social experience which receives little attention in the sphere of social science, social policy and education. Our social mandate urges another consideration — to revisit and reconsider the outcome in the era that precedes the current postmodern period. Put differently, postmodern narrative discards past explanations of deficits but generates primarily critique and query with respect to marginalized communities. I believe that today's poor women, immigrants, people of color and other underrepresented cultural groups who have profited little from the prescriptive theories and projects of modernity deserve a place in the economic, social, political and educational arenas construed from their own perspective in order to claim their identity in this nation's history.[4] A truly democratic society must account for the complexity of all its groups. When the oppressive systems move beyond the denial of differences, equity and justice, peace may begin to evolve — inspired only by the inclusion of all our histories in this country. This means that the cohesion we all desire will surface only from our particular yet complex history inclusive of all peoples as participants in a truly democratic process. Critical theory and pedagogy have addressed participatory pedagogies but as yet, much of the critical pedagogy narrative fails to incorporate the day-to-day experience of people of color in a local setting where they have achieved great works of empowerment through collective political labor.[5a] Collective community efforts form a fundamental component of a democracy, and Carpinteria Latinos embrace the Comite de Padres Latinos (COPLA) as a crucial process of their empowerment.

Empowerment for Latinos in Carpinteria extends far beyond the simplistic impression of 'feeling good about themselves'. It has meant a cultural transformation. The trivialization of empowerment defined as merely any change, dismisses the perception of self that is influenced by sociocultural and sociopolitical conditions. Empowerment is not something that one does to another. No one can empower someone else. Power, the pivotal construct in empowerment is inherent in every person as an inner source of knowledge, strength and ability. The potential, to exercise power resides within everyone and is developed through one's life journey — dislodged everytime we deal with common issues. Critical reflection is the expression of people's cultural experience in a collective context. It characterizes the concept of empowerment which I believe describes the lives of the people I observed during the ten years of research in Carpinteria.

When people challenge their thinking about the obstacles that impede their participation in their communities and opportunities for growth, unpredictable possibilities occur. The following interaction took place during one of the first meetings held by Latino parents who later became COPLA. Present at the initial meeting were Maria Rosario, Rebeca Cortina, Manuel Peña, Rosa Martinez, Roberto Rodriguez, Antonia Juarez, and Juan Ramirez.

Rebeca: Ay muchos problemas que tenemos que confrentar entre nosotros. Es decir, no podemos alegarle mucho a las escuelas porque no tenemos medios ni conocimiento ni idioma con que hacerlo.

We have many problems to confront among ourselves. That is, we cannot argue with the schools because we have neither the means nor the language with which to do it.

Antonia: Yo digo que lo importante es el querer hacerlo y es por eso que entre todos unidos podemos aprender lo que tenemos que saber para ayudar a nuestros hijos.

I would say that the important thing is to want to do it and it is for that reason that collectively we can learn what we need to know to help our children.

Maria: Pues, ya sabemos como criar nuestros hijos. Nadie nos tiene que enseñar como amar a nuestros niños.

Well, we already know how to raise our children. Nobody needs to teach us how to love our children.

Roberto: A mi me parece que algunas familias Latinas aquí si tienen que aprender como cuidar a sus hijos porque yo veo algunos niños chicos sueltos en las calles y los padres no se encuentran por ninguna parte.	It seems to me that some Latino families here do need to learn how to take care of their children because I see their young children loose on the streets and their parents are nowhere to be seen.
Maria: Es cierto que algunos padres no tienen dinero para pagarle a alguien capaz de cuidar a niños. A veces los [los padres] dejan con personas iresponsables.	That's true that some parents don't have money to pay a capable person to take care of their children. Sometimes they [the parents] leave their children with irresponsible people.
Manuel: Lo que comprendo por lo que dicen es que todos tenemos la capasidad de ser responsable pero hay algunos padre que necesitan más ayuda.	What I understand from what you are saying is that we have the ability to be responsible but there are some parents who need more help.
Roberto: Muchas veces las escuelas tienen rasón por lo que dicen de nosotros, los Mejicanos porque uno se debe de presentar con confiansa y ánimo aunque no sepa como navegar al sistema.	Many times schools have a reason to say what they do about us Mexicans because one needs to appear confident and courageous even though we don't know how to navigate the system.
Juan: Pues yo no iba a decir nada pero la verdad es que desde que comensamos a hablar de que tenemos que ir a las escuelas para hablar con los directores, me ha costado mucho sueño. No se como es posible hacer algo así que nunca he hecho solo cuando me llaman con quejas de mi hijo mayor.	Well, I wasn't going to say anything, but the truth is that since we began talking about having to go to the schools to talk to principals, I've lost a lot of sleep. I don't know how it is possible to do something like this which I've never done before except when they call me with complaints about my oldest son.
Rebeca: Usted ya nos ha dicho que tiene miedo ir solo a las escuelas y le hemos asegurado que nadie va tener que ir solo porque vamos en grupo.	You've already told us that you're afraid to go alone to the schools and we've assured you that no one will have to go alone because we're going in a group.

Juan: Yo se, pero aunque me importan mis hijos, es difícil hacer algo así en otra idioma cuando uno no la sabe hablar.

I know, but even though I care about my children, it is difficult to do something like this in another language when one cannot speak it.

Rosa: Me parece que todos nosotros, aunque no hablemos el inglés ni conoscamos muchas de las costumbres de éste país y aquí en Carpinteria, sabemos que nosotros también tenemos una idioma linda, y sabemos respetar y tenemos una cultura que es también valorosa. Así es que debemos presentarnos con ése espíritu.

It seems to me that, even though we don't speak English and don't know the cultural ways of this country and of Carpinteria, we also have a beautiful language and we are respectful and have a culture that is equally valuable. That is why we should present ourselves in that spirit.

Juan: Pues sí, tiene rasón señora. Es cierto que tenemos una idioma que podemos usar para comunicarnos. Aunque sea diferente del inglés.

Well you're right. It's true that we do have a language with which we can communicate even though it's different than English.

Maria: Aprecio lo que dice la Señora Martinez porque a veces nos hacemos menos porque no sabemos hablar inglés muy bien, pero no somos menos y tenemos que tener orgullo por lo que le regalamos a nuestros hijos. Toda la historia de Méjico es parte de nosotros — aunque ya vivamos aquí.

I appreciate what Mrs Martinez says because at times we feel inferior since we don't speak English well, but we're not inferior and we need to be proud of what we can give our children. All of Mexico's history is part of us — even if we live here.

Juan: Sí, Señora Maria, [se usó el primer nombre] ¿pero porqué es que aquí nos hacen menos los maestros y directores que dicen que a nosotros no nos importan nuestros hijos porque no asistimos a juntas o porque llegamos tarde a juntas y varias otras cosas de que nos critican?

Yes, Mrs Maria [first name used in place of last name] but why are we made to feel inferior by teachers and principals who say that our children aren't important to us because we don't attend meetings or because we arrive late to meetings and numerous other criticisms they make?

Roberto: Pues es cierto porque muchos de nosotros nos comportamos como si nos diera miedo al vida. ¿Porqué es que no

Well it's true because many of us act as if we're afraid of life. Why is it that we don't go to the schools if our children matter to us? We need

vamos a las escuelas si nos importan nuestros niños? Tenemos que cambiar esos hábitos que nos impiden acercarnos a la educación de nuestros hijos. Como siempre nos decia la Señora Marquez, las escuelas son de nosotros y debemos de tomar responsabilidad.

to change those habits that impede our presence in our children's schools. Like Mrs Marquez always told us when our children were in preschool, these are our schools so we should act responsibly.

Juan: ¿Cómo se cambian esas costumbres? ¿Cómo podamos aprender hablar el inglés que es tan difícil?

How do we change those habits? How can we learn to speak English which is so difficult?

Maria: No es fácil de cambiar hábitos. Es necesario hablar y discutir entre nosotros y de entender como pensamos.

Por eso estamos aquí para ayudarnos todos — no es que sea fácil pero entre todos hay furerza. Debemos de anotar, por ejemplo, que aunque nosotros debemos de aprender el inglés, también tenemos que hacer a las escuelas que se comuniquen con nosotros en español.

Ya mis niños tienen muchos años en estas escuelas y aunque esten en clases bilingues, nunca veo que nos manden anuncios en español.

It isn't easy to change our habits. It is necessary to talk and discuss how we think.

That is why we are here to help each other — it's not easy but there is strength in unity. We should note, for example, that even though we should learn English, that we should also make the schools communicate with us in Spanish.

My children have been in these schools many years and even though they're in bilingual classes, I never see any notices sent home in Spanish.

And so the issue of communication between schools and families was one of the initial topics which engaged both Spanish-speaking families and educators in what became the COPLA organization. Collective critical reflection helped the parents forge through personal and social doubts, deficit thinking and focus on strengths to shift their perception of themselves and continue learning, thus emerged the principal orientation of the group.

Empowerment of individuals, families and the Latino community at large evolves as the protean self emerges from isolation into connectedness. The notions of proteanism and empowerment intersect and instruct us on the ways that individuals and communities are transformed in a collective process. The protean self conception explains the personal, familial and community shifts observed in Carpinteria. My readings of Robert Jay Lifton's work over several years have influenced my theoretical understanding of how literacy in this Latino community contours their lives and in turn how they create meaning of literacy in their sociocultural context. The people's stories of their cultural identities pointed to struggles of their encounter with middle-class Euro-American sociopolitical ideology. Sociocultural adjustments of Latino families in Carpinteria are compelled by dreams of working hard to provide their children the best education and promise of a more comfortable life than they had as poor immigrants. Personal and collective expansion changed people's beliefs of self, their attitudes toward others and their behavior to act on behalf of the 'greater good' — a process I term empowerment.[5b] The protean self emerges with a new vision through both a personal and collective journey of critical reflection and investment in the individual and the group's pliability and resilience.[6] New concepts of self frame the protean person capable of bringing together incompatible elements of identity for continuous transformation of these elements.[7]

Latinos of Mexican descent have resided in Carpinteria for many generations and share an experience of prejudice and isolation. Recent Mexican immigrant families in Carpinteria have encountered a political climate different from that of past generations. Theirs has been one of educational opportunity resulting from legislation of the war on poverty involving Lau vs Nichols.[8] They have nevertheless, like Chicanos before them, felt prejudice as they attempted to adjust to a new country, to learn a new language and to educate their children. Rather than fold under the pressure and threat of a new system, the self turns out to be quite resilient. Long-time Chicano residents who weathered the undermining and isolation of segregated schools along with the more recent Mexican immigrants in Carpinteria have continued growing and struggling to become active participants in their community and schools. This story shows how Mexican immigrant families have risked, confronted and evolved; it is a story of the self's capacity for functional wisdom within the cultural framework of the family, community and the nation State.

In 1985, I entered Carpinteria to research literacy in Latino family and community settings.[9] Literacy practices in the households provided a point of entry in family-life. My interest as an ethnographer began in the homes with the question of what literacy practices existed in households, schools and the community at-large. Spanish-speaking children were placed in different reading ability groups in school beginning in the first grade. Educators, including some classroom teachers, suspected that the students who were in advanced reading groups had parents who read to them and were more attentive to their school-work than parents of children who were in the novice reading groups. After careful observation of classroom literacy activity in grades 1–3, I followed children into their homes to learn about the family's literacy practices.

A research team of graduate students accompanied me to conduct ethnographic observations and interviews. Although the individuals changed almost year to year depending on their graduate student status, research assistants mastered ethnographic tools to work on the project. The first three years of the Carpinteria study were particularly taxing because the research team, particularly myself, were immersed in the community, culturally and comprehensively. We observed family interactions in literacy events as well as classroom literacy activities.

A better understanding of literacy practices in Latino families and community at large obligated me to present my data of the home literacy activities to a large group of Latino families. Parents participated in ethnographic analysis and in the process became aware of the variance of knowledge which parents possessed about schools. In the process, some of the parents who were part of the group that met to reflect on the data and who were more familiar and experienced with the needs of the Spanish-speaking community organized a parent group for families to support each other.

Data collection in Carpinteria resembled four concentric circles with the community at large as the most outer circle followed by the school as the third circle and the family comprising the second outer circle and the inner most circle representing the individual. Stretching across all of the circles I envision an arrow which for me defined a series of methodological strategies undertaken to examine the form, function and meaning of literacy in Carpinteria. They included observation through audio and video taping, participation observation as a facilitator in COPLA, extensive individual interviews, and group surveys in Spanish. All of these strategies involved children, community members, families, and educators. My participation as a critical ethnographer in the collective community organization in Carpinteria determined my research strategies each step of the study.[10] Reflexive thinking between the researcher and the collaborators in the community highlighed the research questions. The case studies of the original group of twenty families generated volumes of data about literacy in the home which raised a new generation of questions about the nature of parents' participation in their children's education. I examined family interaction in the home, student–teacher literacy activities in the school and observations in community events involving family members of the original case studies. Twenty families were the focus of the daily visits by the research team pertaining to practices involving literacy. I observed adult–child interactions as well as those among siblings and extended family members. Video, audio recordings and field notes captured the family engagements as they carried out daily chores. Usually, only the children were home after school and managed the household tasks until their parents arrived from work. Activities involving written text were examined along with the written text. A new set of questions were posed when the Latino community at-large reflected on the data on literacy collected in the twenty households. Their critical reflection resulted in the formation of the COPLA organization. Families who participated in the initial literacy and critical reflection phases of this ethnography subsequently organized a community parent group, Comite de Padres Latinos (COPLA). Together with other Latino families they met to support each other in their interactions and to provide for their children optimal opportunities for schooling. Educational personnel participated in the study throughout the various phases. Teachers of children in the case studies were interviewed as were principals and district administrators.

To provide a small comparison base between Latino and Anglo parent participation, I interviewed a group of English-speaking parents in the largest school-parents group in the largest elementary school. Through personal interviews of the parents and observations of their meetings, I was able to direct more in-depth study of issues involving Spanish-speaking parents.

Eleven Latino adults, five women and seven men, organized COPLA. COPLA formed a school district-wide group which met weekly for about two months at which point they organized school-site committees. Technically, COPLA includes all Latino parents who have children in the Carpinteria schools although some parents are more active since they attended more meetings and have integrated and applied what they have learned in COPLA.

The data collection process expanded to include COPLA meetings, and school activities involving parents. COPLA became the focus of the research which helped me to understand how parents taught themselves to work with their children and the schools while struggling to negotiate a different culture. Essentially, parents in Carpinteria, organized themselves for the purpose of supporting each other and 'in conversation' they shared historical experience — in their former country, in Carpinteria with their families, and with the schools. Through the conversation process which parents organized which I termed a 'critical reflection process', parents shared their cultural knowledge. This was the wealth they held as heritage to transmit to their children. The intent was to explore how Latinos shaped the organization and its reciprocal, how the organization influenced their lives and the community in general.

The district COPLA group met monthly and together with school-level committee meetings, there was a minimum of one large Latino group meeting per week. Other meetings were spawned as parents met together with school personnel to plan the larger school-level meetings. Parent meetings were audio recorded and, on occasion, also video recorded. COPLA members carried their learning to their homes. Research questions were raised about the impact which COPLA had on the leaders who were quite committed to the community organization.

As COPLA expanded in size, it intensified its work with the schools. Data on Latino families in all five schools necessitated survey strategies to understand their participation in the schools as a result of COPLA. Two years after the inception of the district-wide COPLA, a survey of 215 Latino parents was conducted to ascertain the extent of parent involvement in the organization. The research team designed a questionnaire in Spanish and administered it to parents who attended the COPLA meetings at respective schools. We wanted to learn the extent of COPLA in helping Latino parents to understand the school system and how to support their children. Care was taken not to duplicate parents who may have attended meetings at more than one school as a result of having children in different grade levels. A problem in the survey was a result of the low literacy level of many of the adults. This necessitated conducting the survey in person and instructing the parents how to respond to the survey. Members of the research team read each of the questions to all of the parents present at the meeting. The selection of the meeting was random but the respondents included all Latino parents who attended the meeting on the particular day we designated to survey. As one assistant read each of the questions with the parents, another assisted some parents in marking the appropriate response. The task was complicated by the fact that one of the items was an open ended response. The onerous part of this survey taught us that while we could obtain large set of data through survey, this Spanish-speaking population with low literacy skills and no prior experience in responding to survey-type formats posed complications in obtaining large samples of data with adults who were unaccustomed to school-like curriculum.

COPLA's concern with the underachievement of Spanish-speaking readers prompted the design of the Family Literacy Project (FLP). Parents' frustrations centered on their readings with their children, who seemed unmotivated and who even when interested, found themselves without books. The unavailability of reading materials in Spanish further restricted their reading activity. These concerns emerged as parents and educators negotiated their needs to improve education, not only for Latino but for all students. The Family Literacy Project (FLP) was designed by COPLA and our research team. The goal of the project was to have third and fourth graders read with their parents at home and, as a family, report back to the classroom teacher to evaluate and expectedly improve children's academic literacy performance.

In COPLA meetings parents learned the results of which indicated that by the time Spanish-speaking children reached the third or fourth grade, parents were intimidated by the language barrier posed by an all-English homework curriculum. This intimidation is a distancing factor in the parent–child relationship which is crucial to a supportive system for children.

Three of the active COPLA parents were selected to participate in the FLP. They were trained by the research team to perform three major tasks in organizing eight monthly family literacy sessions. The students selected for the FLP project were in second, third and fourth grade Spanish-speaking students and their families whose teachers identified them as underachievers for their grade level in Weaver and Morton Schools.

Another issue surfaced in the FLP study: because homework consumes most of the children's time at home, parents found little time to do leisure reading with their children. As parents became aware of their literacy practices in the home they expressed an interest in increasing their reading at home with their children; parents who had children who did not excel in reading were especially interested.

Fifty books were screened intentionally for topics that would generate discussion in families in this community. Eight books for the project were non-sexist, non-racist and non-classist stories. They received major consideration. Parent-participants were observed reading to their children in the natural home setting on five different occasions. A recording was made during each of these periods. These occasions provided the researchers with observation and interview data on parent–child interaction regarding literature content. COPLA has made many gains and accomplishments.

Recognition of COPLA's ties to the educational system were noted by the Anglo community. Without directly naming COPLA, *The Carpinteria Herald* ran an article on May, 1990 which acquainted the community with the benefits of the organization. The article entitled, 'A Brighter Outlook' read as follows:

> The Carpinteria School District and the Hispanic parents and students it represents have made tremendous strides in recent years. Other school districts having difficulty motivating their Hispanic communities would do well to study what has happened here.
>
> As recently as three years ago, school officials say, you couldn't get Hispanic parents involved in their children's education. They rarely, if ever, came to board meetings and seemed intimidated by teachers and administrators. Worse yet, there seemed in some Hispanic circles to be an inbred opposition to students distinguishing themselves. A teacher of Hispanic students once said that if one student excelled academically, he would be accused of trying to show the others up.
>
> But all that is changing. It is as if an element of American society that has until now stagnated is starting to jell. In Carpinteria, Hispanic school-parent meetings are so popular that as many as 100 parents attended in one night. Sometimes they draw adults who don't even have children in the classes.
>
> The realization that education is the key to Hispanics moving up in American society seems to be sinking in . . . Carpinteria is a place which is a tribute to those now in charge. The Carpinteria school district, from the superintendent to the school board to teachers and principals, is bending over backward to provide Hispanic students with an enlightened education . . .
>
> As demographic studies show the Hispanic minority in Carpinteria, Santa Barbara and other communities may one day be the majority, we applaud Carpinteria school officials for having made such vital progress in the bilingual field of education.[11]

COPLA's achievement in the above newspaper article evolved through the process of empowerment. My research in Carpinteria has been defined by construct of empowerment which identifies engagement as a negotiable force. I maintain that power is not a tangible commodity to be given or withheld from someone. Empowerment is a process of unfolding ones potential through collective reflection and continuous dialogue where differences give way to mutual purposes and directions — thus transforming lives.

During the years I have spent as a researcher in Carpinteria, I have made many public presentations where people have asked me how much the Latino children in Carpinteria improved their grades as a result of their parents' involvement in their children's education. People have felt unsatisfied when I responded with a lengthy and involved answer which, in essence, meant that learning is a lifelong process and that the COPLA parents have learned a great deal from each other, but it has been through their years together. A change of grade on student report cards and accelerated test scores alone represent a narrow perspective of parent involvement in education. Children's academic accomplishments are born of parents' commitment to support them in their education. Put differently, parents can be quite actively involved in a child's school, at a time of crisis, the test and grade outcome remain unaffected. Even though parents may be actively involved in their children's education, children's grades may plummet at different times during their schooling as a result of complicated circumstances. Yet children have a stronger possibility to socially and academically recover as a result of their family's support. A child may become empowered over time as a result of the parents' consistent intervention and support even though the outcomes are not immediately evident as was the case with Carpinteria families.

Readers searching for panaceas and models to replicate will be disappointed. I propose no recipes for achieving 'effective parent involvement' because the lessons I learned in Carpinteria with COPLA families and the community speak of much more profound connections than simplistic formulas for communication between teachers and parents. COPLA activists created a context in which divergent views came together and gave way to creative means. These borderlands exist as a synthesis of varied worlds unencumbered by space or time. People define and redefine identity, experience, feelings, beliefs and dreams in borderlands. Borderlands transcend rigid ideological and cultural borders which we construct to understand our multiple identities.[12] Within borderlands we create the time, space and context to exchange experiences and learn new identities. As the protean self emerges in the borderlands, people are empowered to experiment with their full potential.

Proteanism in schooling family and community relationships reconceptualize the most basic assumptions concerning family involvement in the schools and seeks to participate in the dialogue with the dominant discourse on culture and education to encourage new pedagogies. Contentious discourses on culturally different families in the schools dichotomize children from their families, family from the school, children of color from the Anglo children, mainstream groups from immigrant and poor communities, and linguistically different communities from English-speaking communities. The COPLA pedagogy encompasses a mutually interactive interchange of knowledge between the parties involved and engaged in transformative understanding of the particular subject.

This story involves many Latinos of Mexican heritage whose first language is Spanish. While English is the dominant language of the school, Spanish-speaking Latino families used Spanish in most of their interactions with bilingual school personnel and community leaders. I have tried to accomplish two main things in using the Spanish language in this book as I did; to maintain the integrity of the people's Spanish language which many Latinos in Carpinteria consider their primary language; and to preserve continuity and a steady flow in the interaction which makes it necessary to represent conversation in English only without the Spanish. Thus, in sections where the Spanish-speaker's dialogue is longer than a couple of sentences, I have chosen to convey it in Spanish and provide an English translation.

I grappled with the decision of writing parts of this text in English, for an academic audience, or Spanish to represent the families' authentic words. I problematize the use of English and Spanish in the text because the majority of the community with whom I worked in Carpinteria is primarily Spanish-speaking. And while English is the primary language in the schools and the community at large, I want to maintain the integrity of the people's primary language wherever possible in this story. In the case of bilingual narrative, I represent the English in parantheses, and in cases where only Spanish was used, I tried to keep the people's words in the primary language and provided a translation on the right column.

I have made a great effort to maintain the integrity of the people in Carpinteria as they would see themselves portrayed in text. The name Carpinteria is used as the true name of the community because I received permission from the school district administrators to identify it by its real name. However, except for the name Carpinteria, I use pseudonyms for all other personal nouns identifying persons, schools, community agencies, geographical locations like streets and stores to honor the wishes of my co-collaborators in the community who choose to maintain their identities private. All of the Latinos who participated closely in my research project during my tenure in Carpinteria are legal residents. Only two adults who were initially active in COPLA were undocumented but were legalized during the time when the amnesty law was enacted in 1988. Furthermore, many Latinos who were born in Mexico have become citizens.

My participation as a researcher and facilitator evolved on a daily basis throughout the course of the ethnographic study. Throughout the study, I accompanied the community's initiatives in reflection on their family life experience in Mexico and Carpinteria as they involved themselves in their children's schooling.

This book unfolds the story of the Carpinteria Latino families and their interaction with Euro-American community on issues related to their children's learning in and out of school. I have spent over fifteen years collecting children's stories from children in the communities where I have conducted research. In this book, I have chosen to have children's stories introduce each chapter. Those which I have selected to include in this book are a few of the countless stories told to me by the children in Carpinteria during the many hours I spent with them and their families. They require no explanation because they speak for themselves. The children's stories reaffirm the humor, values, fears, hopes and lore. They enrich our understanding of how cultures perpetuate and change. Here Latino children show us how their protean culture extends borders.

Chapter 1 describes Carpinteria's sociohistorical landscape including past and current generations of immigrants and their diverse ethnic experience in shaping their family, social, and political networks in Carpinteria. Issues of immigration and segregation offer a background and perspective on schooling projects that have currently made learning Carpinteria a desirable community.

Chapter 2 presents the three phases on how COPLA evolved from its inception. Latino parents' respect for each other and their commitment to learn from each other defined COPLA. Each phase held particular significance in expanding the Latino community's program to work with the schools and support each other and their children's schooling. Their promise to hold their children as the primary focus of their COPLA work frames this chapter.

Chapter 3 depicts true family strengths as parents become more active with each other and with the schools; they relate differently with their children. They recognize that the world view they share with their children in their language is worth the family unity they promote as well as shifts in their interaction with their children and their teachers.

Chapter 4 depicts the Mendez family as they grew through their involvement in COPLA and extended their learning to family members, friends and the community — the quintessential protean and empowerment process. This chapter captures the essence of protean relationships representative of COPLA leaders. What is true is that as parents become more active with each other and with the schools, they relate differently with their children. They recognize that the world view they share with their children in their language is worth the family unity they promote as well as reach out to each other in the way they knew but often failed to convey the meaning of their reality to one another.

Chapter 5 discusses the gains and errors of the Family Literacy Project and the COPLA leadership. This chapter reveals how teachers and parents struggled to work with each other. They attempted to reach out to each other and to break their fear, but their efforts reinforced their historical practices of the school dictating the parents' relationship to the school.

Chapter 6 considers how claiming cultural space and political voice and utopian visions do not by themselves address the rigid structures that propel inequity and sever family–school relationships. Nor can COPLA meetings alone address the challenge or replace the structures of power embedded in capitalism, they are potential counter-hegemonic cultural forms that provide reservoirs of hope and struggle for healthier communities. Insights from the Carpinteria superintendent and other leaders show creative visions for a community that has seized its historical markers for transforming human relationships.

I'm applying the concept of proteanism to the immigrant experience attempting to share with others their knowledge. What allows this to occur is the joining together with others in COPLA with children as their main focus.

Their power emerges from their felt belief to share with each other cultural and ethnic ideals about children, family and education while finding something in common that extends their personal and collective potential. I have grown personally and professionally through my work with the people in Carpinteria and feel compelled to tell their story in a format that best unfolds their proteanism.

I wrote this book in a style that presents the voice of the people in Carpinteria with minimal interruption. Analyses, theoretical discussion and comments are deferred to the endnotes. I maintain that in critical ethnography, the researcher's perception of the collaborators and the collaborators' perception of the researcher are integrally connected.[13] I have written about the integral nature of critical ethnography and the researcher's autobiography, and here I discuss how I changed through my relationship with my collaborators in Carpinteria.[14] I have also interspersed subjective autobiographical perspectives throughout the text where needed to clarify the ethnography.

I maintain that issues involving poor, ethnically and linguistically underrepresented communities deserve to be examined not only with theoretical rigor but also with methodological comprehensiveness that enables us to understand the question in a holistic crossdisciplinary position. The intersection between ethnography and social issues calls for the researcher to assume an interactive position with the people in the research setting.

My participatory relationship with the people in the study taught me that my ethnic identity, gender, class ethos, and personal history converge with the ethnographic process of research and influence the activities in the field as well as the way I, as the researcher, interpret what I observe and tell.

This book describes much of the way in which the Latino families of Carpinteria empowered themselves but my connection to the people and the community underwrites the significance of the research. The porous boundaries between persons and my familiarity with the working class patriarchal family relationships, as well as my knowledge of the psychosocial adjustment to a new language, culture and school profoundly resonated with my own life story.

Born in Chihuahua, Mexico in an adobe house my maternal grandfather built, I was the second oldest of five sisters. I was raised in a strict working class Mexican household where intergenerational linkages extended to grandparents and relatives from Mexico to California. At the age of eight, my family immigrated to the Los Angeles area. Two generations of my mother's family, including herself, her parents and siblings had already lived and worked in California as international agricultural migrants. Although for my mother this was not her first migration, for my father, a construction worker, this was his first migration North.

As children, both of my parents missed out on formal education both in Mexico and again in the US because they worked to help support their families. On their own, they pursued instrumental education to learn English and new skills for employment in the US. Their experience manifested explicit and implicit messages of encouragement, especially from my mother, to study, travel, learn as much as possible and above all to respect myself and others. My identity as a Mexican woman was formed in a household where the Spanish language and Mexican cultural traditions such as love for family were valued along with new rules established by my mother. She expected her daughters to break the confinements of poverty and dependence on patricarchy. In contrast, I was confronted by the tormenting, yet sometimes exciting school community which valued primarily English speaking and mainstream culture. I learned that education and a strong sense of self was the best response to the politics of prejudice. Supported by my parents' sense of discipline, I worked hard in all areas of my life which earned me many awards, scholarships and opportunities to study — exercising my personal power. I hold a passion for knowledge and have practiced encouragement, respect, collectivity, hard work in all of the communities where I have been a teacher, elementary school principal, researcher and professor. My ethnographic work is an extension of my interest in learning about crosscultural perspectives and strengths in children, families and communities as a way to create meaning and connection in pedagogies. Carpinteria, more than any other community I have studied, has led me to examine the fluid boundaries of self-family-school and community resulting in formulations of empowerment in literacy. Power has been a central spirit in my academic and personal concepts of education. I've just begun to theorize about the researcher/collaborator relationship in fieldwork. Here are three concrete examples that illustrate my connection to my current research community in Carpinteria.

1. Through critical reflection with my collaborators, I learned depth of people's insights about their relationship with each other. It changed my theory about what the activities meant to the lives of the people.
2. I learned from family members that they perceived me as having 'faith' in them (see Chapter 4) thus, they felt empowered to share their learning with others.
3. My perception of personal life issues also changed as I applied the process of critical reflection, and empowered myself when I struggled with my health crisis. I forged through the fear by challenging my preconceived notions of outcomes. This deepened my strength, resolve and understanding of the many possibilities open to me and join with others for support.

Although my research builds on existing sociocultural theories explaining the meaning of literacy as well as current discourses on alternative pedagogies, I am conscious of the particular lenses I bring to the study. Suad Joseph, colleague anthropologist and scholar, maintains that given the significance of connectivity, research outcomes may differ depending on the psychosocial dynamic between the ethnographer and the communities we study — class, race, gender, education, ethnicity and specific family histories are always interactive.[15]

Where the researcher ends and the community's story begins remains a constant query grounded in the current debate of anthropology and autobiography and the political responsibility of the researcher conducting fieldwork. My collaborators in Carpinteria participated extensively in the formation of meaning and analyses, and it is my intent to represent their agency to every extent possible. The researcher's part in writing, however, remains problematic. Just as fieldwork data collection demands certain choices of me as an ethnographer, in writing this book, I was obliged to make selections which formed the emphasis found in the chapters that follow. The mutual learning which characterized this critical ethnography verifies that theoretical connections exist between the ethnographer's background, experience, embodied knowledge and a continuing resonance with the collaborators and the final written text.

Notes

1 The term literacy has been the subject of extensive research and of importance here is how the concept is defined. Literacy here is framed as Hymes, 1974, described it, an interactional structure. The event is often centered on relationships between oral and written language strategies and how they are used by participants in order to play, work, and communicate for general use. Literacy as a conceptual tool in sociocultural context has been studied in more references than I can possibly mention here but these are a few significant works which have shaped my thinking about the practice of literacy as I studied it in Carpinteria: Abrams and Sutton-Smith, 1977; Anderson and Stokes, 1984; Botvin, and Sutton-Smith, 1977; Devine, 1994; Freire, 1970; Heath, 1983; Hymes, 1974; Leichter, 1984; Reder, 1994; Schieffelin, 1986; Schieffelin and Cochran-Smith, 1984; Scollon and Scollon, 1980; Scribner and Cole, 1981.

2 For concepts of cultural continuity interweaving culture and education see earlier works by Spindler, 1955 and henceforth through recent publications Spindler and Spindler, 1994. As the key figures, 'parents of Anthropology and Education' they are credited with recognizing that learning is a process of acquiring a culture and schools are entrusted with imparting the culture. Their notion of cultural transmission and continuity and discontinuity has enlightened the field of education to recognize the critical importance of culture in the learning process.

In the 1970s, the analyses of schooling expanded to account for an economic perspective of schools, teaching, curriculum and policy according to class (Marxist) theory. Bowles and Gintis, 1976 were major leaders in this new framework. They argued that the educational system was a product of the Capitalist economic system that also governed the social order of the country. Their work along with that of Carnoy and Levin, 1985, was the springboard for the new ideological direction that followed. Resistance ethnographic research by Willis, 1977, Everhart, 1983, and Foley, 1990, as well as McLaren, 1986, showed that the struggles of working class students in urban schools stemmed from their life in social isolation and exclusion from participation in the mainstream curriculum of schools as a consequence of their poverty. Curriculum is the focus of critical theorists including Apple, 1979, 1993, and Giroux 1992. Feminists including Lather, 1991, Ellsworth, 1989, Grosz, 1988 and Luke, 1992 have extended the critical pedagogical discourse to include women.

3 Postmodernism has been at the vanguard of the debate to rethink the tradition of what constitutes cultural knowledge. Much of the focus on postmodernism and education has been focused on issues of democracy and the role of State institutions as Aronowitz and Giroux, 1991, note. Postmodernism asserts no privileged place, aside from power considerations, for artworks, scientific achievements, and philosophical traditions inquiring whether western cultural interests are legitimate. Hutcheon, 1989, among many other holds that postmodern discourses are defined as the system of relations between parties engaged in communicative activity which, simply stated, means that postmodernism cannot be but political. And, while postmodern has no effective theory of agency that enables a move into political action, it does work to turn its inevitable ideological grounding into a site of de-naturalizing critique (Hutcheon, pp. 3–9).

4 Works by Hooks, 1989, that of Luke and Gore 1992, Lavie 1990, Segura, 1993 as well as Trinh, 1989 deal with theoretical concerns related to feminist pedagogy advancing that differences in race, ethnicity, gender, class, and sexuality must frame the emancipatory classroom, community and nation.

5a/b I discuss the various principles of empowerment in numerous publications, Delgado-Gaitan, 1990; Delgado-Gaitan and Trueba 1991; Delgado-Gaitan, 1992; Delgado-Gaitan, 1993; Delgado-Gaitan, 1994(a); Delgado-Gaitan 1994(b); Delgado-Gaitan, 1994(c); Delgado-Gaitan, 1994(d); Delgado-Gaitan, 1994(e). Each of these publications emphasizes and explores in detail particular aspects of empowerment as it involved families and educators in Carpinteria.

I hold that the critical reflection process is the determining feature of empowerment as a transformative process. Empowerment challenges the asymetrical social relations in order to create a new culture that includes global perspectives rather than a Eurocentric one as Chaudhry (1995) suggests. Empowerment means that people transcend the linear boundaries of a single nation State and identify with multiple nations and cultures. This is particularly important to permanent and temporary international migrants. (In Delgado-Gaitan, 1990, I describe at length how the process of critical reflection in Carpinteria initiated the parent group, COPLA.)

6 Protean-like resilience is clearly the essence of Lifton's work, 1993, but the background of these concepts began with his research discussed in his earlier books. Lifton's brilliant and provocative writings have intrigued me for years. Prior to his 1993 book which was the most recent inspiration for this book, I was inspired by his previous work on the Vietnam War, 1973, Hiroshima survivors, 1967, Nuclear Age 1987 and the Nazi Holocaust. Each of these books (out of his sixteen published books) explores the psychological dimensions of totalitarianism, social change, nuclear weapons, and more generally, death and the continuity of life. As a psychological investigator Lifton develops new theory and method for applying psychological principles to historical events. His long standing interest in the interplay between individual psychology, with historical change, within the psychological process which led him to investigate the psychological effect of the dropping of the Atomic Bomb in Hiroshima. The assertion and establishment of the self which he so intricately and passionately pursues results

of, in his formulation, the self which he envisions as a protean self developing into an elaboration and expansion of self, culminating in the twentieth century tendency toward inventing the individual self by means of the protean pattern of radically imagined extensions, recreating, and mocking caricatures of actual experience.

Proteanism is also a struggle of ideas and beliefs. Individual's or collective ideas and beliefs shift occur constantly. Today, says Lifton, one is likely to hold a variety of ideological, political, and religious positions in a lifetime, not to mention one's aesthetic values and revisions in personal relationships as well as lifestyle modifications. Given these tendencies the protean self evolves, accommodates and transmutes obstacles and pain and remains fluid in a form. Proteus was a minor aged character in Greek mythology. He was a prophetic man healer — a sea God, herder of seals of Poseidon. He foretold the future if anyone could catch him at noon and keep him from changing his form. He was able to change his form from a sea dweller to a land creature, at his will. Whenever he was pursued by anyone to give prophesies, he changed his form to avoid prophesizing the future and when he was caught, he told the truth. In Homer's *Odyssey,* Menelaus held on to Proteus until he informed him how to return to Sparta.

7 Lifton's, 1993, p. 5 focal point is that undergoing continuous change is a central tenet of proteanism. I use the concept of a 'spiraling motion' to describe my construction of empowerment. A diagram of this spiral is presented in Chapter 2.

8 Limited education for limited English-speaking children has long marked the educational system. Lau vs Nichols legislation as discussed in Donato, Menchaca and Valencia, 1991; *Lau vs Nichols,* 1974 (414 US 563,566) and Roos, 1978, was the landmark litigation which dramatically changed the delivery of education to Spanish-speaking children. Although these authors do not discuss the other language groups, the Federal mandate, *Lau vs Nichols* of 1974 has affected the education of all limited English speakers from all language groups. The decision of the law suit was initiated against the San Francisco School Board by the parents of a Chinese student, whose last name was Kenny (English name) Lau. The decision held that public schools had to provide an education that was comprehensible to limited English proficient (LEP) students. The Supreme Court recognized that limited English proficient students had historically been denied 'meaningful' access to learning as a result of only having been taught all of their curriculum in English.

The decision prompted Federal funding for school districts to design bilingual education programs in cases where any one language group per grade level was more than twenty. Other limited-English speakers whose language group did not constitute more than twenty per grade-level, were provided instruction according on an individual plan.

9 As I wrote more extensively in 1990, the initial stages of the Carpinteria study involved community literacy. I examined ways in which Spanish-speaking families interacted with written text and how they interacted with each other around written and oral texts. I did not dichotomize oral and written texts; I did, however, note that some families were less literate in reading written text but were quite literate in oral competency which meant that they involved themselves completely as they could in their children's education in spite of their limited formal schooling.

10 My article, Delgado-Gaitan, 1993, discusses critical ethnographic research in the Carpinteria community and raises issues pertinent to anthropology and autobiography. That is, the ethnographer's autobiography is a harmonious symmetry as Okely and Callaway, 1992, note, I brought into the research site my personal and professional knowledge, which gives my work a particular dimension. My reflexivity as I have written in Delgado-Gaitan, 1993 shaped every step of my research. The more I reflected the more I subverted preconceived notions that the researcher is an impersonal instrument.

11 This article appeared in *The Carpinteria Herald*, May 13, 1990.

12 Anzaldúa's, 1987, concept of 'borderlands' resonates best with my understanding of the experience of what those of us who share multiple cultural and ethnic identities mean by having to straddle and cross many borders moment to moment.

13 Two articles, Delgado-Gaitan, 1993 and Delgado-Gaitan, (forthcoming) describe my subjective interlace with my research topic, the people and my shift in conceptualization about my observations and myself as a researcher.

14 About my own ethnography and autobiography, see Delgado-Gaitan, forthcoming (a) and Delgado-Gaitan, forthcoming (b). For accounts of anthropologists who write on autobiography and anthropology see K. Hastrup. 1992; J. Okely and H. Callaway, 1992 and R. Rosaldo, 1989 for more extensive discussion on writing ethnography and the ethnographer's role in the field and writing of the research.

15 Suad Joseph, 1993, writes extensively about one's relationship to society, in particular issues of connectivity and patriarchy and personhood. Her message is summarized in this quote:

> As scholars begin engaging these complex and contradictory junctions of self and science more critically and reflectively, relational conceptions of knowledges may take shape.
>
> It is increasingly clear, however, that we need alternatives to the Western binary of autonomy/relationality, self/other. We need vocabularies for talking about autonomous selves who are relational, relational selves who sustain autonomy. We also need to investigate the intersections between relationality and structures of domination, as well as conditions of relative equality. Such constructs and experiences of personhood are woven throughout the most basic processes by which we observe and analyze. Therefore, they become a integral part of the fabric of knowledge. If we are to weave science out of stronger cloth, we must understand how the threads are both separate and mesh. (1993:30)

Chapter 1

Community Landscape

'El Perro y el Burro Hablan'

Era un día que muy alegre que un señor fue a agarrar un burro, un lasso y un machete y después se fue al cerro y hizo la leña y venía con el burro que no quería caminar y después el burro dijó, 'No puedo caminar con tanto cargo que me traes.' Se bajó el hombre corriendo y luego el homre le dijo al perro, 'Yo nunca había oido un burro hablar.' Contestó el perro, 'Ni yo, tampoco.' Contestó el hombre, 'Yo nunca había escuchado un perro hablar.' El perro contestó, 'Ni yo tampoco.' Corrió el hombre a su casa. Quedó muy asustado por oír al perro y al burro hablar. Pero su esposa le aseguro que no debia de tener miedo porque no era nada mala. Le dijo que debia de recordar que cuando fue la primera navidad, todos los animales hablaron. El señor se sentió feliz.

'The Dog and Burro Speak'
(Story told by 10-year-old Becky)
It was a happy day when a man got a donkey, a rope, and an ax and then the man went to the mountains to cut wood and on his way back, the donkey did not want to walk and then the donkey said, 'I cannot walk with so much cargo that you have placed on my back.' The man got off the donkey running and then told the dog, 'I have never heard a donkey speak.' The dog answered 'I have not either.' The man heard the dog speak. The man ran to his house. The man was scared to have heard the dog and the donkey speak. But his wife assured him that he should not be scared because there wasn't anything wrong. She told him that he should remember that at the first Christmas, all of the animals spoke. The man was happy.

By the twenty-first century, California's cultural tapestry will have changed dramatically showing Latino children comprising 36 percent of all school children as compared with 42 percent Anglo. Asian Americans will comprise 9 percent, and African American students will be 9 percent while the remaining 4 percent will include many other ethnic groups.[1] California's increasing non-White population includes an ever-growing immigrant group. 17 percent of its new legal immigrant group come from Mexico.

Immigration is not a new phenomenon for California any more than it is for the country as a whole. Let us not forget that this country has its origins with immigrants who committed genocide with Native American Indians. The contradiction is that the labor of these immigrants has built horizons for other immigrants to come. In Lifton's words, '. . . this is a protean nation', in the way that immigrants came, moved forward, and extended. The negative part of the US history, of course, is that its histories suppressed Native American Indian cultures as well as others — African American, Latino, and US citizens tended to foster fundamentalism, racism, and xenophobia to maintain one monolithic culture.[2] How to express the integrity of their culture is the plight of many groups that attempt to make this democracy a culturally diverse one.[3] Immigrant groups as diverse, separate and dissimilar as they are, also share a common experience, their relationship to American institutions. That relationship is a window that helps us learn the importance of culture. The issue of immigration pervades all the social institutions in a community. Educational institutions have been one of the most responsive to immigrants since the beginning of public education in this country. This may be true because public schools in the United States began with a strong intent to 'Americanize' immigrants from Eastern Europe.[4] Latinos who are the focus of this book are unfamiliar with that part of the history of US 'Americanization' since Mexico, which extended to what is all of the south-western United States today, was then Mexico.

Throughout the history of the United States, immigrants have both been credited, and blamed, for the economic condition of the United States. The ebb and flow of Mexican immigration during this century has been explained by the economic needs of the US just as much as the political turmoil in Mexico. The first part of the century saw immigrants leaving Mexico to escape the Mexican revolution. Many were rejoining their families who already resided in the United States for generations some dating back to the times when the Southwest belonged to Mexico. Newcomers worked in agriculture, garment factories and in the meat packing industry. These same people who worked to improve the economy of the country became the victims of discrimination by the same country who once extended a hand to them. Mexicans were deported and accused of draining the economy during the depression. In the early 1950s California's agricultural demands spurred the bracero program which brought single Mexican men and provided a tireless seasonal 'cheap labor force'. Although men were required to return to Mexico, some chose to stay and continued working year-round in smaller ranches and became a part of the low-paid workforce in the agricultural industry.

In the current period of economic down turn, anti-immigrant sentiments have resurfaced as Mexicans remain overly represented in the lower ranks of the labor force and find their children underachieving in excessive numbers in the public schools. A consistent cry from anti-immigrant organizations is that immigrants who are willing to work for lower wages than those demanded by unions and the American labor force in general are taking jobs away from Whites. Increasing crime and unchecked population explosions are also blamed on immigrants because some statistics indicate that the immigrant and US-born

Latino population tends to be younger and have more children than non-Latinos. However, part of this country's proteanism is the acceptance of refugees from war-torn countries.

Current immigrants and refugees must be contextualized in the sociohistorical developments. Testimony before the Select Committee On Statewide Immigration Impact emphasized, 'The U.S. influences political circumstances that create refugee and migrant flows. Repression and human rights violations are important "push" factors . . . past U.S. actions and foreign policy interests in countries such as Vietnam, Laos, Cambodia, Nicaragua, El Salvador, Guatemala, Haiti and Iraq have also contributed to the "push" of refugees and migrants worldwide.'[5] Persistent poverty and unequal distribution of wealth in certain countries will continue to push individuals out of their countries in search of employment to better their economic conditions and opportunities in the US.

The assumption is that Latino families who immigrate to the US are poor. The median age of Latinos in the US is 25.5 years of age. Fewer than 25 percent of these immigrants have a high school diploma and less than 3.5 percent have a bachelor's degree as opposed to 77 percent of the US-born adults who have at least a high school diploma.[6] Crowded schools and poor educational outcomes fall on the immigrant children's shoulders as critics single them out as social culprits. Latino children, including Mexican and Central American children, have posed an educational challenge to California schools to deal with learning in the primary language.[7] Children of immigrants are most likely to become bilingual, speak English fluently and prefer it to their parents' native language. By the second generation children speak mostly English.[8]

To build understanding and communication in an ethnically, racially and linguistically diverse community requires a strong commitment and dependable collaboration between families and schools if we are to succeed as a democratic society. Ethnic research and in particular, ethnography, offer a window of opportunity for researchers to study directions toward democratic. Carpinteria is one example. While every community deals differently with ethnic diversity issues, the schools in Carpinteria have been the research ground that has most consistently brought ethnic and linguistic differences in focus for me.

Born of Immigrants

Mexicans who have immigrated to Carpinteria during the past twenty years know a significantly different community than those who came earlier. Mexican immigrants came to Carpinteria in the early twentieth century when immigration laws were more relaxed and the economic incentive to seek better opportunities was strong. Descendants of this migration wave constitute the present-day Mexican American family population in Carpinteria. The agricultural industry in Carpinteria was a 'fit' for Mexicans who had the desired skills and motivation. It should be noted that the Chumash Indians who resided in Carpinteria since the sixteenth century were hunters and fishermen leaving ample opportunities in agriculture for Mexicans. Land belonging to the Chumash became extinct as their fishing was industrialized in the hands of major fishing companies. The Chumash were then forced into hills where substandard living conditions threatened their survial.

The total population of Carpinteria did not exceed 1,000 residents until the mid-1940s.[9] Predictably, employment differentiated ethnic groups, as did different geographic boundaries. The Mexicans took farm-related jobs and lived in neighborhoods apart from the non-Latino population.

Lemons and avocados were the principal crops worked by Mexicans in the Carpinteria area. By 1950 the bracero program had brought in a new migration of Mexicans to work specifically in agriculture. Dutch, Japanese and a few Mexicans owned ranches which employed Mexicans as laborers. These Mexican men did not immigrate with their families because they were obligated to return to Mexico after their contracts terminated. Many men, however, stayed in Carpinteria and married local women and raised their families in this community.

Mexican workers were valued for their experience in agriculture and provided cheap labor, but that did not grant them equal status in the workplace, in housing, social activities or in the schools. Institutionalized segregation was active in the schools until the early 1970s. According to a newspaper article from a nearby town, Santa Paula, the Carpinteria school board segregated Mexicans because they were classified as Indians and the State of California permitted the isolation of Indians under dejure segregation laws:

> School authorities of Carpinteria have caused considerable interest in all parts of the state with their decision in declining to accept the ruling of Attorney General U.S. Webb that cannot segregate Mexican, Chinese, Japanese and Indian children . . . The Carpinteria school board takes the ground that children of Mexican born parents are Indians . . . In Santa Paula the Mexican situation is handled in a tactful manner, school authorities believe. Many of the Mexicans are going to school in the Canyon and Ventura situated in their own sections of this city . . . the school situated in their own districts take care of the majority of the Mexican children, and special courses of study have been arranged for them. They are said to be happy in their own schools.[10]

Under the guise of this legal interpretation of race, the schools could legally segregate Mexicans into the Weaver School which became known as the 'Mexican School'. Children who attended the school at the time it was segregated recall the harsh treatment for being Mexican on the part of the teachers and principals. Mrs Sanchez recounts her seventh-grade experience when she could not speak Spanish to her friends even during recess without being punished.

> One day we were at recess and the teacher who was supervising at the time did not like it that my friends and I were speaking in Spanish. She took us to the principal's office and we all got spanked by the vice-principal and then we were expelled. Our parents were so angry that they went to the office the next day and complained to the principal but he wasn't there. So, they talked to the vice-principal who told them that they had no right to complain because it was the school's policy not to allow Mexican children to speak Spanish. My mother said that she felt very angry and frustrated because she had gone to talk to the principal to insist that they treat us with more respect but she couldn't say anything because no one listened to them.

Restricted use of primary language compounded with corporal punishment were not isolated activities in Carpinteria schools during that period making the education of Mexican students much like that of other schools where Mexicans were segregated throughout the Southwestern states where schools segregated Mexican students.[11] Mexican immigrants to Carpinteria shared a language, an ethnicity, a history in Mexico, a subordinate social class position and low schooling opportunities in Mexico. In spite of their common culture, families tell a personal story of struggle, adjustment, and endurance in their travels from Mexico to their adaptation in Carpinteria.

An Immigrant Tradition

David Rodriguez and his wife Maria tell their protean immigrant story of life between Mexico and Carpinteria during the past thirty years, a story which includes their three children Hector, Nuvia and Mirea.

Zapote, Michoacan is a small town in the outskirts of Michoacán where David spent his childhood. His family of eight lived in a rancho which required an intense daily routine just to care for the crops which fed their family and which they sold locally to others for a meager income. He completed elementary school in the local school where there was no high school at which time he moved to Potrero, Guanajuato, a nearby town in the adjacent state where there was a high school. During his high school years, he met Maria, who would later become his wife.

Maria's family owned a corn mill where the family ground other people's corn and made 'masa' (cornmeal) for their daily tortillas. As the seventh of fourteen children, Maria worked quite hard around their ranch and in the masa mill. This limited her availability to attend school beyond elementary grades. She was saddened to have to quit school and always admired those who were able to continue. At the age of 16, her aunt took her to Tijuana to work in a factory and she stayed only one year until her mother needed her back in the ranch in Mexico. During her short stay in Tijuana, David made his first trip to Sacramento, California with his mother, a US citizen. He also had brothers in Sacramento. David joined his father who got a job picking carnations in Carpinteria and shortly afterwards both of his parents returned to Mexico. His relationship with Maria evolved through letters and David's periodic visits to Mexico.

Agricultural managers in Carpinteria in the 1970s hired mostly single Mexican men who left their families in Mexico. But by the mid-1970s, many families were reunited in Carpinteria as men sent for the families during the initial amnesty efforts, and nurseries hired them in their expanding industry. David was one of those men who sent for his family. He and Maria were married in Mexico and he returned to Carpinteria without her until he could get enough money for both of them to live. David recalls,

Entonces se podia rentar una casa con poco dinero. Las rentas eran bajas y podia uno vivir con menos dinero. Las familias se visitaban con más frequencia en los domingos. Yo estaba envuelto con el club religioso desde el 1972 que se ocupaba en recurir fondos para la iglesia.

[María dice,]

Cuando me vine yo a vivir aquí a Carpinteria, tenia mucha tristesa porque no tenia mi familia y estaba muy aislada donde viviamos en el rancho. La iglésia tenia tardiadas los dominos y nos juntabamos para estar con nuestras familias. También el equipo de soccer era oportunidad para juntarse con otros.

David jugaba mucho el fútbol y en esos juegos conosí a Rebeca Cortina porque allí jugabamos con nuestros dos niños y luego nos hicimos comadres.

At that time, one could rent a house with very little money. Rents were low and one could live with very little money. Families frequently visited each other on Sundays. I was very involved with the religious club since 1972 that had as its purpose to raise funds for the church.

[Maria adds,]

When I came to live in Carpinteria I was very sad because I did not have my family and I felt isolated where we lived in the ranch. The church had outings on Sunday and we gathered to be united with our families. The soccer games were also an opportunity for us to get together with other people.

David played a lot of soccer and at those games I met Rebeca Cortina because there the two of us played with our young sons and later we became compadres,

[Magadalena became her youngest daughter's godmother.]

David began taking English-as-a-Second Language classes when he first moved to Carpinteria. He continued progressing in his English proficiency until he qualified for US history classes which intrigued him. He worked until 6.00 p.m. in the ranch, went home to have a bite to eat and was in class by 7.00 p.m. When he returned home at 10.15 p.m. read for about an hour then helped around the house for a few minutes and finally went to bed so that he could awaken at 4.00 a.m. to begin work again. 'I learned so much about the history of this country and I enjoyed all of the books so that I began buying many history books myself — history of all the world. Eventually, I took classes that led me toward my citizenship.' I found this rather curious since his mother was a US citizen. David admitted not knowing his rights about already being a citizen since his mother was a US citizen. Had he known that he was already a citizen he would have only had to file numerous forms. 'Maybe it was really better this way because I learned so much in those citizenship classes and I became interested in reading everything that was history related.'

David's family applauded his accomplishment. Maria also began to take English classes at night. Other education classes she took were 'Birthing and Childcare' classes in Spanish when she became pregnant with her first child, Hector. Representatives from Casa de la Raza in Santa Barbara notified her about the classes and offered transportation which enabled Maria to learn about natural childbirth and how to care for her baby's nutrition and health after birth.

The Rodriguez have been quite involved in the schools since their children began preschool. They, however, feel rather dissappointed with the more recent newcomer families from Michoacan. The new arrivals seem to come from remote ranches with virtually no schooling. To compound the problem, they confront unemployment in Carpinteria which was not the case when David and Maria arrived. Adults, particularly the men take to drinking and 'hanging out' in their front yards while children go unattended. Young people find adjustment difficult and turn to loitering the streets and sometimes vandalizing in ways that were never before seen. Solutions to the problem call for aggressive educational support for students from these families, employment, affordable housing and means of assistance for sociocultural change for families to learn how to deal with their US system. David believes that organizations like COPLA are critically important in helping them to stay off the streets. Although David attends more COPLA meetings than does Maria, she helps with the children's homework. She has become so competent in English as a result of helping her children and from taking citizenship classes that she became a US citizen in April 1994. 'I was quite nervous, but my children helped me to study for the exam. Now I can spend a bit more time with the kids when I get home from work. The nursery seems to be quite slow lately anyway so that my hours have been shortened.' Maria's commitment to her children's schooling has been extended through her own example of advancing her education.

Mexican immigrant experience in Carpinteria is diverse. Although immigrants like the Rodriguez have lived an exemplary protean immigrant experience by improving their socioeconomic condition and their children's opportunities for education and employment, other immigrant families have had a different life in Carpinteria. It is for this reason that COPLA is all the more imperative.

By the time that the Rodriguez children began school in Carpinteria the political climate in the schools had changed considerably from the earlier days of segregated schools for Mexicans. Some of the very students who once attended the all-Mexican schools became important change agents in the community as teachers and counselors. Two of those teachers (Mendez and Islas) are part of this study. Islas became a leader in the preschool program, then a bilingual teacher and in 1993 was appointed principal of Martin School.

Another important development in educational reform occurred in the early 1970s when the federal government made funds available to create a bilingual program for limited-English-speaking students. This was a result of the *Lau vs Nichols* Decision which generated Federal funds to create bilingual programs for children with a home language other than English.[12] Thus, Carpinteria employed State and Federal funds to create a bilingual preschool and elementary school program. The children who benefited from these programs had parents who had immigrated in this recent generation. For the most part, these children were born in the US but their parents were predominantly Spanish-speaking.

Cultural Brokers

Just as it is necessary to have professional Spanish-speaking Latinos translate between the two cultures Latino families to Whites, so it is crucial to have Spanish-speaking White educators translate between their ethnic and cultural group to Latinos. Such seems to have been the case with Paul Niles who is the Director of Special Projects in the Carpinteria School District. His work with community groups and Latino families has been a continual stabilizing force especially between Latino families and the schools. He adamantly believes that the current thrust in the school district is to prepare all students to make informed choices about attending a university after high school graduation. Currently, Carpinteria has a 17 percent rate of students who attend a four-year college or university following high school graduation.[13] Long before Director Niles became the school district representative in COPLA, he was a director of the Title VII Bilingual Program with teaching responsibility in ESL classes in the middle and high school. His commitment to working with parents and building strong ties between families and educators stems from his first-hand experience with the bilingual program when it was federally funded.

Carpinteria's bilingual program had a national reputation for its strong achievement record which could be attributed to the enrichment focus on children's first language. While most bilingual programs construed bilingual classes with both Spanish and English curriculum simultaneously, Niles observed the value of having students immersed in Spanish and become proficient learners in their language before being expected to learn in English. Niles also became convinced that bilingual education truly was an enrichment for English-speakers wanting to learn Spanish.

As bilingual director Paul Niles was able to shape the program's philosophy and direction. His background in sales prepared him with skills to present the bilingual program to English-speaking families and interested parents in placing their children in bilingual classes. With 50 percent of the bilingual class English-speaking Anglo and 50 percent Spanish-speaking Latino, Niles established an effective bilingual program where a fluent bilingual teacher taught the entire curriculum in Spanish one day and English on alternate days. The English-speaking parents became strong advocates for the bilingual program because their children learned Spanish and the Spanish-speakers achieved as they learned English. The force that parents exerted to support the program was consistent with Paul's prior experience in Burbank with highly successful bilingual programs. His interest and success in working with parents in advisory committees made his later work with COPLA all the more compelling. He explains why the bilingual program flourished in the late 1970s and began to decline in its effectiveness by the early 1980s.

> One important change in the bilingual program has been a shift in our population. In the years when I first came to Carpinteria, more Mexican immigrant children came from bigger cities and had schooling in Mexico prior to coming here. In more recent years, there are more immigrant children entering our schools who come from poorer rural areas where they have not had any education and they're not as inclined to want to learn English and to become bilingual or to apply themselves in the classes as they did twenty years ago.

Other reasons for the difference in bilingual education include that many bilingual teachers left Carpinteria School District as a result of personal mobility. The district had a difficult time competing with pay which excellent bilingual teachers could receive in neighboring school districts. Exhausted federal funds rendered the school district unable to continue offering full bilingual programs to Spanish-speakers. As a consequence, the direct benefit to students, provision of teacher training and the resources of teacher-assistants were lost. All of these components supported teachers' effectiveness in working with Spanish-speaking students and teachers' assistants. Consistently, the administrative reorganization by a different superintendent between 1986 to 1990 moved the school district from a centralized administration to a decentralized structure where principals, who had little training in bilingual education were expected to assume responsibility for implementing their program. As a result, teachers lost their district-wide coordinator when his responsibilities diversified and divided his attention with other programs.

Precursors to COPLA

One of the programs which Carpinteria implemented in the early 1970s was a bilingual preschool where the teacher, Celia changed the lives of many Spanish-speaking children in the school district. She spoke Spanish and knew well the culture of the families and the community. She, too lived in the Carpinteria. She made the parents co-teachers with her in a way that helped the parents learn to help their children in the home and she also made them accountable to her for helping in the preschool. Most of these parents, all of whom were immigrants from Mexico, have no more than a fourth grade education in Mexico and held jobs as agricultural workers in the nurseries.

Celia taught the parents to read books to their children and encouraged parents to converse with their children by making time to do household chores that involved children. By allowing children to help in cooking, washing dishes, shopping etc. parents could use a great deal of language interplay.

The declining strength of the bilingual program affected grades from first grade to sixth. The long-standing exception to the declining quality of programs which addressed the needs of Spanish-speaking students has been the Bilingual Preschool Program. The teacher in charge of this program provided a rich curriculum (in Spanish) and created a strong relationship with Spanish-speaking families.

When the children left the preschool program, however, few resources existed to help Spanish-speaking parents to bridge the connection with the school. As Spanish-speaking children moved up the academic ladder and learned more English, parents were distanced from their children and the schooling process. Parents reported that by the time their children reached junior high school, they felt as if they were 'living with a stranger'. A parent, Mrs Avila, recounts her experience with Jorge, her son and his teacher on the question of his reading skills.

Jorge was in the third grade and read only in Spanish when he began learning to read in English. He was not doing well in reading but the teacher, Mrs Robins, tried to connect with his parents. She sent notes home with Jorge and told him to tell his mother to call her but weeks passed and the teacher just continued working with him. At home, Jorge's mother knew that he was having problems because he did not understand his homework. She was unable to help him because she did not understand the instructions even though they were in Spanish. The reports sent home by the teacher never reached Mrs Avila because Jorge feared giving them to her. His mother, on the other hand, felt shamed for her limited literacy skills and did not attempt to communicate with Jorge's teacher. She felt at a loss in finding ways to help him which created a distance between her and her son, and between her and Jorge's teacher as well as between Jorge and his teacher. The breakdown in communication isolated everyone in a way that made them have to work harder with minimal gains.[14]

Jorge's case epitomized most of cases involving Mexican parents and the school. Although Jorge's case was not an extremely urgent one characterized by crisis, it was nevertheless a critical one because it became increasingly problematic for parents like Mrs Avila who distanced themselves further and further from the teachers like Mrs Robins. Parents felt more and more constrained as their children moved up the grades and limited to deal with the schools since teachers often assumed that Latino parents did not care about their children's schooling. Given the perpetual sequence, the schism between Latino families and schools was reflected in the children's underachievement and the parents' frustrations as well as the teachers' frustrations because they faced structural limitations when dealing with Latino families. These and more became reasons for Latino parents to organize Comite de Padres Latinos (COPLA).

COPLA bridged the discontinuity between parents like Mrs Avila and teachers like Mrs Robins with students like Jorge. This organization differed in their purpose from other parent groups in the school district. It was not the intent of these Latino parents to have their organization meet legal mandates of the school district which were satisfied by formal-school site committees comprised primarily of Anglo parents who dealt with questions of budget and school policies. Rather, they wanted to support each other so that they could learn how to work with the schools in an informed way and to assist their children in their schooling. They constructed new avenues through which the community could voice their interests and knowledge and become partners with the schools.

Counter-hegemonic Project

In COPLA meetings, parents learned the results which indicated that by the time Spanish-speaking children reached the third or fourth grade, parents were intimidated by the language barrier presented in homework, which was almost totally in English. This intimidation is a distancing factor in the parent–child relationship which is crucial to a supportive system for children.

Reforms achieved through shifting power relations are based on the notion that a group has something that the other needs and wants. Changes that result through the rearrangement of power relations usually have restricted potential for sustaining change. The school is usually intent on maintaining a position of power even though some gains are made toward giving voice to isolated populations. If schools are perceived to have power and the community is perceived as powerless, then the schools and communities will remain oppositional to one another.

Although people's native language, ethnicity, and historical identity are acknowledged in reforms dealing with family and school relationships, schools tend to appropriate the family's home culture to support their goals. Cultural and political consciousness remain to be explored as ethnically isolated families negotiate their silent cultural forces. Community efforts have long been a force in countering hegemonic national policies. 'All politics are local' — has become almost a clichéd line to focus attention on the democratic participation. Major developments in school reform programs such as bilingual/bicultural education are rooted in attempts to provide more equal education only within the framework of the americanization of Mexicans.

Reasons abound as to why Latinos have been excluded from mainstream tracks in public schools.[15] Certainly, Carpinteria educators including Paul Niles who deals with program evaluations admits to the consistent underachievement of English-speaking Latino students. Typically they score within the 10–20 percentile below their White counterparts who score in the 5th percentile in the school district. The 1993 scores for example, show Chicano students clustered in the fifth percentile while White students averaged in the 64th percentile rank. Historically, schools including Carpinteria's, have established relationships with families and communities which position the schools as the authority. The americanization of Mexican students through school has taken place in the educational system and has been tethered to the necessary reconstruction and citizenship building seen as the goal of public schools. The process has been accomplished primarily through isolation in americanization programs of changing the student's language, religion, dress, recreational activities, family traditions and home lifestyle.[16]

Critical Directions in Family–School Relationships

Prevailing interpretations of educational reform have, for the most part, failed to take into account analyses of culture in relation to the State. Examining the role of education in the conflict between dominant and subordinate ideologies and the role of cultural resistance, should serve as a form of counter hegemony — of change in the dominant culture. But this involves the control of schools in relation to the access of knowledge.

Power has a different meaning beyond counter-hegemonic ends. If people discover how they self-construct cultural meanings and identities within and against the ideological frameworks of mass culture, institutional settings and discourses — then students will have the critical tools with which to act in morally responsible, socially just and politically conscientious ways against individual and collective oppression.

Change occurs in a variety of ways. Commonly, times and places of connection between families and schools happen in structured events where the school defines the interactions of the actors. In such settings, educators assume a position of knowledge over the parents or community members. Transactions result in parents having to adhere to the school culture to support their children in school-related tasks. Cultural borders created by structural conditions are rigid boundaries enforced by school policies and practices. In this mode, the pedagogy of change is learned through school-defined structure. Therefore, Latino families as well as other ethnic and poor families who have been underrepresented in schools, continuously crosscultural borders between their knowledge source and that of the school's to a limited end: and an organization like COPLA, creates borderlands where new pedagogy occurs.

Borderlands are terrains of learning through interaction which become inextricably linked to people's identity, place in history and shifting of power relationships by utilizing knowledge and resources differently. Reutilization of knowledge and resources for the benefit of all empowers those involved. While change can occur in any setting through well-designed projects, borderlands change extends beyond the reform efforts and focuses on activities which transform events into empowering situations. Communities accomplish a great deal with, and through, reform projects but empowerment occurs through conscious critique of the conditions in question. Through sharing of collective historical experience, ethnic identity, and their realization of personal strengths, persons involved can transform their situations and accomplish an ultimate protean task. I maintain that COPLA has been a unifying structure for families in Carpinteria because it has created an opportunity for continual learning described in subsequent chapters.

Notes

1 Research on immigration now more appropriately travels under the theoretical concept of 'transnational migration'. Numerous references develop this perspective (see for example, Bodnar, 1985; Goldberg, 1992; Rouse 1989; 1992; Schiller, Basch, Blanc-Szanton, 1992). The concept of transnationalism casts the study of migration in a global perspective. Only by understanding the world as a single social and economic system can we comprehend the implications of the new patterns of migrant experience that have been emerging from different parts of the globe into the US as well as those occurring *in* different parts of the world. Simultaneously, we can understand the individual and collective strategies of adaptation of international migrant people and enables us to observe the migrant experience in process. By expanding the theoretical perspective of immigration to include ethnicity, class, gender and identity in both the homeland and the new culture, we can comprehend the cultural practice and agency of the immigrants. The Carpinteria study, however, is limited by the fact that it does not examine the immigrants in their homeland in Mexico other than through ethnohistorical interviews. For other examples of work on migration from Mexico and adaptation in the US see Achor, 1978 where Achor uses the term Mexican American at the ethnic identity of the group.

I use the term 'Latino' to refer mostly to recent Mexican immigrants and Mexican Americans who have been long term residents in the US and Chicanos who are of Mexican descent and usually born in the US. I chose the term 'Latino' because Mexicans in Carpinteria call themselves Latinos when referring to the group at large. The same people who refer to the group at large as Latinos also call themselves Mexicans when referring to the individual and/or the nuclear family unit. By this I mean that the identity of Latinos in Carpinteria is complex in that they identify by language use, migratory practice, ethnic and class categories. Most of the people I collaborated with in this study used the term Latino to refer to themselves and sometimes used Latino, Mexicano and Chicano to refer to others in their community.

2 In his book, *The Protean Self: Resilience in the Age of Fragmentation,* (1993) Robert Jay Lifton depicts the US as a protean nation in that it has continued to change and

expand yet it has a legacy and history of racism and oppression of many peoples who need to be included in the fabric of democracy.

3 A more culturally democratic society is the heart of research by a team headed by Henry T. Trueba. Their publication, Henry Trueba, Cirenio Rodriguez Yali Zou and Jose Cintron, 1993 researched a Northern California community which chronicles the group of Mexican immigrants who, in spite of their obstacles, learned to participate in the US democratic system to obtain access to the educational system.

4 Historically, we have seen that immigrants whose culture of origin most resembles White Anglo Americans have traditionally had the best reception in this country. By contrast, immigrants from countries whose culture is less known to Americans have always had more or less access to the sociopolitical and socioeconomic system. See Cremin, 1957; Ehman, 1980; and Spring, 1991 for a discussion on the social and political purposes of American education. In Delgado-Gaitan and Trueba, 1991, we present our research on the education of immigrant families in a Northern California community. Our research presents the accounts of the home and community life of the Spanish-speaking families and the school in their lives. We described the potential of human resources as children and their parents undergo cultural and language change and while they maintain fragments of their Spanish language and Mexican and Latino values, still attempt to incorporate new cultural and academic knowledge to obtain socioeconomic and political access. Ultimately, we note the commitment to living and participating in a democracy in spite of the tremendous economic burden and social isolation from the mainstream community.

5 Lina Avidan of the Coalition for Immigrant and Refugee Rights and Services stated in her testimony to the Select Committee in the California Assembly as reported in the Summary Report Prepared for Assembly Select Committee on Statewide Immigration Impact — Assembly Member Grace Napolitano Chairperson — prepared by Assembly Office of Research (#0501-A), Robert L. Bach and Doris Meissner, June, 1990, *America's Labor Market in the 1990's: What Role Should Immigration Play?*, Washington DC, Library of Congress.

According to McCarthy and Valdez 1986 in their study on immigration, with respect to the settlement process of the immigrants, to the educational and occupational integration of their US-born offspring into California Society, McCarthy and Valdez, 1986, concluded in these 3 points:

(a) We found little evidence that immigrants have disrupted California's labor market or displaced native-born workers' instead, the immigrants may actually have provided substantial benefit to the state's economy.

(b) Immigrants' use of public services is not a general problem, although the education of their children (both U.S. and Mexican-born) is subsidized by the state's taxpayers, and communities with substantial concentrations of foreign-born bear a disproportionate share of the costs burden while receiving less than a proportionate share of the tax revenues.

(c) Mexican immigrants are not fostering a separate society; they are integrating into the state's society in much the same way as other immigrants have done.

6 Julian Simon (1989) *The Economic Consequences of Immigration.*

The National Immigration Law Center, Guide to Alien Eligibility for Federal Programs, 1992 reports that undocumented immigrants are eligible for only the following programs: emergency medical services, WIC, school lunch and breakfast, 'Headstart', federal housing and social services block grant. A survey report published by the US Department of Justice, Immigration and Naturalization Service, Report on the Legalized Alien Population, 1992 reported on immigrants who legalized their residence during the 1987–8 Amnesty program. At the time of application, the legalized alien population had used fewer taxpayer and employer-supported social services than the general US population. The study found that fewer than 1 percent of the legalized alien population had received general assistance, social security, supplemental security income, workers' compensation and unemployment insurance payments. Economist Marta Tienda and Leif Jensen, in their report, *Immigration and Public Assistance Participation: Dispelling the Myth of Dependency*, June, 1985 found that family income of immigrants is less than native family income by $1,700 to $3,800, except for black and spouse-absent white families. One would expect significantly higher participation by immigrants in public assistance programs than natives; however, participation in public assistance programs by immigrant families does not exceed their native counterparts' participation rate by more than 5 percent. Immigrants are less likely than natives to become dependent on welfare. Recent immigrants do not use welfare at a higher rate than immigrants who have already been in the US for some time (except for refugees who receive cash assistance from the federal government when they are resettled from abroad).

7 Trueba *et al.* 1993.

8 San Miguel, 1984 and 1987, argues the historical discourse of bilingual education while Zantella debates the fate of Spanish in the US by analyzing language policies and Merino, Trueba, Samaniego, 1993, present the theoretical frameworks for the study of the maintenance of the home language in language minority students.

9 See US Department of the Census, (n.d.) *The Foreign Born Population in the United States, 1990. (CPH-L98)*; Stockton, 1960.

US Department of Commerce, (n.d.) *Population Projections of the United States. by age, sex, race, and Hispanic origin: 1992 to 2050* (Current population reports, P25–1090), Washington, DC.

10 *Santa Paula Chronicle*, 1929:b-6 cited in Menchaca and Valencia, 1990:240.

11 Gonzalez, 1990.

12 Trueba, 1989.

13 School District statistics were supplied by Carpinteria District administrators, usually Paul Niles collected statistics on the students and projects.

14 Parental knowledge about the schooling system is seen as an essential ingredient to effective socialization. The impact in the home provides a powerful link between the family setting and social institutions (Berger, 1991; Blakely, 1983; Clark, 1992; Cochran and Dean, 1991; Coleman, 1987; Comer and Hayes, 1991; Delgado-Gaitan, 1991; Epstein, 1990; Klimer-Dougan, Lopez, Nelson, Adelman, 1992; Lareau, 1989; Phelan, Davidson and Cao 1991; Torres-Guzman, 1991). Immigrant families were the focus of the first part of our study beginning in 1985 which found that Spanish-speaking families experienced isolation from the school because they lacked information about its operations and expectations. This phase of the study occurred prior to the organization of the parent group and helps to explain the changes in family interaction after the family's participation in a community organization. The distance between many of the families and the school created problems for children's schooling told in Jorge's case.

Research has shown academic gains on the part of students when families and schools participate in term projects for a finite period of time to forge strong contact between parents and educators (Davis, 1982; Diaz, 1992; Dornbusch, Ritter, Leiderman, Roberts, and Fraleigh 1987; Gotts and Purnell, 1986; Kohn, 1959; Levy, Meltsner and Wildavsky, 1975; Morrison, 1978; Stevenson and Baker, 1987; Walberg, 1986). School reforms contribute to improved academic results for the period in which they operate but usually stop short of critique of the conditions that created the inequity of resources.

15 Exclusion of Mexican/Chicano students from school has a historical base dating back as early as the late 1800s. Gonzalez, 1990 reports that Mexican children were separated from Anglo-American children, and by 1920 most schools actively practiced 'separate but equal' policies. The concept of Mexican schools as Carpinteria once had were prevalent in communities where Mexicans/Chicanos resided. Segregation of Mexican/Chicano students in schools led to the 1947 landmark legal case 'Mendez vs Westminister' which was the first case ever argued on the 14th Amendment that the premise of 'separate but equal' is unconstitutional.

A first-hand experience was described to me by a participant in my research study in Commerce City Colorado on Latino students who succeed and those who dropped out of high school (see Delgado-Gaitan, 1988 and Delgado-Gaitan and Segura, 1989). Mrs Olivarez, a parent of one of the young girls who dropped out of school, told of her early schooling days in the Colorado school where half of the school population was Mexican. 'I was about six years old and I had just begun school and I loved going to school because my mother braided my hair so pretty and I wore long beautiful ribbons and my grandpa used to walk me to school everyday. All my friends were Mexican because that's the way our school was divided and in my classroom — we were only Mexicans or "Spanish people" as many called us here in Colorado. So, one day I remember getting to school and as soon as the bell rang we went to be filed in line and went into the classroom. Immediately, the teacher asked all of us to line up again because we had to go to the auditorium because the nurse wanted to see us. So all of the students were there and they asked us, the Mexicans to go stand against one wall and they asked the white kids to go the other wall and then they went out of the auditorium and we were left standing against the wall and the nurse came around and untied all of our pretty braids and they proceeded to pour carotene on our hair. All the boys and girls had this done to us because there was a breakout of "piojos" (lye) you know those hair bugs, and they thought that the Mexicans were the only carriers. This happened many times through my schooling there. The humiliation and anger we all experienced still haunts me.'

Desegregation made 'separate but equal' illegal, however, what remained in tack was the practice of tracking which continued exclusion and academic segregation (see Rangel and Alcala, 1972 and Uribe, 1980). Volumes have been written about tracking. Oakes, 1990 writes on the benefits of heterogeneous groups, on the school curriculum, and examines the injustices and travesties in education under organized tracking which is congruent with what Slavin, 1990 reports in his review.

16 Americanization has long been the goal of public education and public programs in the workplace. Gonzalez, 1990 writes that special teachers were hired to direct americanization programs and to go into the homes to help them with their inferior lifestyle as one home teacher stated that Mexicans had a 'tendency to wander and live in a shiftless way which was not checked by the economic conditions in

which this type of family finds itself here.' (Vera Sturges, 'Home Standards among Our Mexican Residents', Los Angeles School Journal 9, no. 4 (28 September 1925:13) Cited in Gonzalez, 1990:54.

In School the americanization programs attempted to eliminate the 'dirty, shiftless, lazy irresponsible, unambitious, thriftless fatalistic, selfish, promiscuous, and prone to drinking, violence, and criminal behavior' (see Garcia, 1978 and Gonzalez, 1990). School principals dictated classroom and school programs based on the culturally deficit hypothesis. An example was this quote by a Phoenix, Arizona school principal, 'Much more classroom time should be spent teaching the [Mexican] children clean habits and positive attitudes towards other, public property, and their community in general . . . [The Mexican child] can be taught to repeat the Constitution forward and backward and still he will steal cars, break windows, wreck public recreational centers, etc., if he doesn't catch the idea of respect for human values and personalities.' (Jessie Hayden, 1934, 'The La Habra Experiment in Mexican Social Education', Masters' thesis, Claremont Colleges, Claremont, CA, p. 27, cited in Gonzalez, 1990:37).

Chapter 2

Participatory Voices

'Conejo y Lobo Se Hacen Amigos'

Había una vez un conejito y un lobo que quería agarrarlo. El conejito corrió y se encontró un huevo. Allí, adentro estaba un pollito y el no sabía. Era huevo chiquito y se encontró una casa solita donde no había nadie y después y allí lo guardó y cuando el lobo vino tocó la puerta y el huevo se quebró. El conejito no sabía y que mira para atrás y mira al pollito. Después se hicieron amigos los pollitos y el lobo. Y el pollito le ayudó al lobo que los cuidara en ves de comerlos como queria el lobo. Después de que estaban fuerte los pollitos el lobo se fue a vivir a otro lugar.

'Rabbit and Wolf Become Friends'
(Story by 5-year-old Anita)
There was once a rabbit and a wolf that wanted to catch the rabbit. The rabbit ran and found an egg. There, inside the egg was a baby chick and the rabbit did not know it. It was a small egg and the rabbit put it in a small and safe house and when the wolf came knocking on the door the egg broke. The egg broke and the rabbit did not know it, and when the rabbit looked back at the egg it saw the baby chick. They became friends and the baby chick helped the wolf to protect them instead of eat them as the wolf wanted to do. Later, when the chics were strong the wolf left and went to live somewhere else.

Family–school connections between Latino families and schools have been the focus of COPLA efforts in Carpinteria. Since its inception, COPLA has undergone numerous phases of development resulting from organizational expansion in size, direction and influence. Three major phases characterize COPLA's development, Phase 1, establishing power base; Phase 2, structural changes in COPLA; Phase 3, redefining and redesigning COPLA. Throughout their work, COPLA members, parents and educators organized around the 'child' as the explicit focus with an implicit ethic of respect for the voice of membership which included people who attended meetings and represented themselves and other families. With the child as the center and respect and egalitarian ethic communication, COPLA moved forward. Although COPLA called itself an organization, it only required one criteria for membership, that people be involved with some level of schooling in Carpinteria. They expected to create a visible presence in the schools with their organization.

COPLA: Developmental Spheres of Influence

Phase 1: Establishing a Power Base

During this period COPLA began a dialogue that has distinguished COPLA as an organization — that of respect between the members and their dedication and commitment to their children.

Part of this dialogue between COPLA and school district personnel has influenced the way in which parents and schools relate to one another. I observed advancements in the frequency and the effectiveness with which Latino parents and school personnel communicated with each other through personal and written contact, and through specific training for Latino parents. Other changes ensued in educational programs which involved Latino students principally in Marina and Weaver Schools.

Latino Spanish-speaking parents began to attend more meetings in the schools and to become active in issues that directly affected their children. Some parents began to assist large meetings while others developed more trust and began to initiate more personal contact with their children's teachers. Their participation was diverse because their learning opportunities varied.

Teachers and principals reported more communication between teachers and parents. Parents reported more communication between themselves and teachers such that they better understood what the teachers expected of their children. This has been the heart of COPLA's success. Many parents attended COPLA meetings. In this book, various examples will include COPLA members present at those meetings. Although many parents attended the district COPLA meetings as well as the local school meetings, the leaders were most frequently present. Here is the list of the parents and school personnel who comprised the district-wide COPLA committee for the first two years of its activity.

At the meetings, people usually addressed each other by the first name. Initially, however, parents addressed school personnel by Sr (Mr) or Sra (Mrs)

Table 2.1: Members of district Comite de Padres Latinos: COPLA

Parents	School personnel
Maria Rosario	Paul Mills: special projects director
Rosa Martinez	Ramiro Marquez: Weaver School
Antonia Suarez	Kay Paton: principal, Morton School
Ofelia Torres	Sally West: principal, Marina School
Rebeca Cortina	Kevin Lane: principal, South High School
Ramon Mendez	John Sosa: migrant coordinator
Roberto Rodriguez	
Manuel Pena	
Juan Ramirez	
Beto Ruiz	
Lalo Robles	
Mario Solis	

and the reverse was the practice until a few months later. Both parents and the school personnel addressed each other by their first name. Parents, however still addressed the other parents by their formal title Sr (Mr) and Sra (Mrs). Thus, they will appear as such in the data examples. Although the meetings all took place in Spanish, I have chosen to translate this following interactions and other to English except where Spanish is necessary.

COPLA Meeting

Weaver School was the usual meeting place for the district-wide COPLA meetings. The group met for about ninety minutes. At the district COPLA meeting, 12–1–1989, eight people were present including two administrators. During the meeting parents dealt with the issue of not being informed enough about their children's reading program to understand how to assist their children at home. Sr Mendez read the agenda for the meeting and noted that they were to discuss the question of teaching parents how to deal with reading when they did not understand classroom curriculum was the first part of the agenda. Sr Marquez, the principal, commented that Marina School should be doing more of that kind of training for the families because there are no problems with the reading program at Weaver. He added, 'The problem we have here [at Weaver] is one of English. Our students in the 4th–6th grades need more help with math and English.'

Manuel suggested, 'If we could read the books the children are reading at school, we could help them.'

Maria noted, 'but all parents don't have the skills and abilities to read the difficult books, or to comprehend them. What can they do if they don't know how to manipulate the meaning of the story and the words. Actually, maybe that's what we as COPLA leaders can do, help the parents to understand how to help their children with those tasks.'

'Here at Weaver, we're trying to get the teachers to work with the parents of their own English and Spanish-speaking students', explained Mr Marquez. People listened attentively and after Mr Marquez spoke, two others raised their hands and Ramon acknowledged both by saying,

'We'll hear from Mrs Cortina then from Manuel Peña.'

Rebeca Cortina proposed, 'Maybe we should meet with the Marina School principal and the teacher can meet with COPLA parents to present to them the classroom reading curriculum. Rebeca Cortina as did other parents knew lexicon like 'curriculum' and steps to take like 'meeting with the principal' because they had been active in the schools.

Final comments were made in a 'once around' process which was suggested to them by Paul Niles. At the end of every meeting, each member made a brief comment about the meeting related to something they learned or something that impressed them or even a critique.

During Phase 1 of the research study involving COPLA, the Carpinteria School District accepted more bilingual students into the Gifted and Talented Education Program (GATE) after lengthy discussions between program leaders, principals and parents who believed that their children should be in (GATE) classes because they met the cognitive criteria even if they were bilingual.

COPLA began to organize a group in each school. The satellite groups in every school were clearly in place, but had more visibility in two elementary schools, Marina and Weaver. Progress was slower in Morton School as well as in the South Middle and West High School. Some Latino parents who were not active in COPLA criticized those who were because they believed them to be 'busy bodies' with little else to do. This confirmed the need for organizations like COPLA to assist Latino parents to become more knowledgeable about their role as advocates for their children. The irony of course is the fact that even children of critics benefited from the initial efforts of COPLA.

Two high-school Latino parents convened a meeting and invited teachers from English-as-a-Second Language (ESL) classes. Their end was to establish a COPLA committee. Mr Lane, the principal, grilled 'carne asada' for over fifty parents who attended. He also made a green salad and asked a couple of parents to bring Mexican rice and tortillas. This was the largest gathering of Latino parents ever seen at the school. Dinner was served at 6 o'clock and by 7 Mr Mendez, president of the District COPLA committee began the meeting by introducing himself and admitted that he was nervous about addressing a large group of people but that it was encouraging to see such a large number of Latino parents attend a meeting about issues related to their children's learning.

Nosotros, que trabajamos con el Comité de Padres Latinos hemos tenido que aprender como hacer muchas cosas. Aunque muchos de nosotros no tenemos mucha escuela, nos hemos apoyado a hacer presentaciones para animar a los padres Latinos que se envolucrecen en las escuelas. Nuestros niños nos necesitan a nosotros y necesitamos toda la información posible sobre el modo en que operan las escuelas aquí para poderles ayudarles.	We, who work with the District COPLA Committee, have had to learn how to do many things. Even if many of us have not been schooled, we have supported each other in learning to address Latino parents and to encourage them in getting involved in the schools. Our children need us and we need to be as informed as possible about the way schools operate here and how to help our children.

He introduced three other members of the district committee and the two teachers, Mrs Hill and Mrs Johns who would make the presentation about the high school's curriculum for Spanish-speaking students including the school's expectations regarding absences, class grades, tests and high-school completion requirements.

In their presentation, the teachers outlined the various courses offered in the ESL track designed for students who were limited in English. The teachers made numerous strong points about the need of parents to remain aware of their children's school attendance, but the parents also shared their concern about the schools failure to notify them that their children were skipping classes. Ultimately, this issue unified both parents and teachers that night as they both learned that thèy had to find a way to communicate directly with each other not because the students were incapable of being honest, but rather they needed to know that both of their parents and teachers held the same goals and standards for them. Adults in that meeting spoke to this issue and began to break the barriers between them. They realized that both teachers and parents had to address the students' needs and problems together and to adhere to school policy and procedure. Parent responsibility for getting students to attend class everyday was futile unless both showed caring and personal interest in the students' daily activities. Mrs Martinez epitomized their sentiment.

Si nosotros [como padres] no sabemos donde estan nuestros hijos a las 10:00 p.m. de la noche durante la semana, entonces es nuestra responsabilidad de asegurar que esten en la casa descansando y preparandose para el siguiente día de escuela.

If we don't know where our children are at 10.00 p.m. at night then it's our responsibility to make sure that they are home getting ready for bed and for school the next day.

Si tu eres una maestra que no sabes donde esta el estudiante a la hora cuando debe de estar en tu clase entonces tu tienes la responsabilidad de hacer todo lo posible para que ese estudiante se interese en tu clase.

If you're a teacher and don't know where the student is when she or he should be in your class then it's up to you to do everything possible to find out why that student does not attend your class.

Pero porque el estudiante es la responsabilidad nuestra ambos [padres y maestro] entonces debemos trabajar juntos y comunicarnos con el estudiante para informarle que los dos [padres y maestros] estan interesados en su éxito

But because they're both of our responsibility, we must all work together to communicate with the students and let them know that we're both on her or his side.

Teaching Each Other Leadership

At a meeting at Marina School library, February 3, 1989, the District COPLA committee, Paul Niles, the School District Director, Marina's principal and a first grade teacher attended as did thirty parents. The meeting was held to assist Marina's COPLA committee to elect officers. Prior to the meeting, Ramón Méndez, a Marina School parent and active in the District COPLA met to set the agenda.

Mr Méndez, the District COPLA president addressed the Spanish-speaking parents at Marina. He began the meeting by thanking people who attended and apologized about how nervous he was which occurred whenever he spoke to a large group of people in the early stages of organizing Latino families. He presented the goals of the organization by talking about their role as the children's first and most important teachers.

Nosotros conocemos a nuestros niños y tenemos mucho que ofrecerles en trabajar con ellos. En COPLA estamos aprendiendo uno con otro. Estamos alcansando a resolver diferencias entre padres y maestros y cooperar con uno al otro.

Una de las metas es de nombrar un comité para dirijir a COPLA en cada escuela. Asi es que estamos aquí en la escuela Marina esta noche para asistirlos a elegir un comite para que trabaje con la directora para organizar actividades en español para padres Latinos.

Estamos tratando de enseñarles a padres de los programas escolar que se ofrecen para nuestros niños y para conseguir la cooperación de otras agencias de la comunidad.

Una de las metas es de nombrar un comité para dirijir a COPLA en cada escuela. Asi es que estamos aquí en la escuela Marina esta noche para asistirlos a elijir un comité para que trabaje con la directora para organizar actividades en español para padres Latinos.

Estamos tratando de enseñarles a padres de los programas escolar que se ofrecen para nuestros niños y para conseguir la cooperación de otras agencias de la comunidad.

We know our children best and have a great deal to offer them as we work with them. In COPLA we are trying to learn from each other. We're trying to resolve differences between parents and teachers and to cooperate with each other.

One of the goals is to name a committee to lead COPLA at each school. That is why we are here at Marina School tonight to assist you in electing a committee to work with the principal to organize activities in Spanish for Latino parents.

We're wanting to teach parents about educational programs offered to our children and to obtain cooperation from other community agencies.

One of the goals is to name a committee to lead COPLA at each school. That is why we are here at Marina School tonight to assist you in electing a committee to work with the principal to organize activities in Spanish for Latino parents.

We're wanting to teach parents about educational programs offered to our children and to obtain cooperation from other community agencies.

Mr Manuel Peña from the District COPLA group suggested to Ramón Méndez that they ask the parents if they understood. When Ramon asked them if they had any questions, a father raised his hand and asked if Marina School had a representative in the District COPLA. Ramon answered that they had some parents who had children in Marina like himself, but as of yet they did not have a person who had been elected by the parents in Marina. And parents' vote was necessary and important in COPLA. One parent asked about the kind of activities that Ramon meant. Mr Mendez gave invited guests as an example. 'You can invite people to speak about a theme which is of interest to the parents.' Mrs Paton (who had followed the proceedings of the meeting through translation) said that it could be someone to talk to the parents about 'reading'.

Mrs Rosario called Mr Mendez's attention to the time. It was now almost forty-five minutes into the meeting and they still had to hold an election. Mr Mendez's asked the parents to nominate people for three positions, president, vice-president and secretary. He explained that the person who served as vice-president would work closely with the president during one year so that they would assume the president's position the second year. Parents said that they did not feel comfortable in nominating people because they didn't know other parents well enough. Others commented that they didn't feel experienced enough to assume such leadership responsibilities. Rosario assured the parents that COPLA did not require previous leadership experience and that what was important was commitment to work with the aim of helping the children to receive maximum support in their schooling.

Mrs Rebeca Cortina reiterated that what people need to know to work in the COPLA committee is revealed to them each step of the way. Rebeca again reminded them not to allow the word 'president' to scare them because what are needed is willingness and interest in learning as much as helping the children. Manuel suggested that parents put down their nominations on a piece of paper and if the people accepted, the names would be put on the board and people would vote. Vicente told the parents, 'All of you who say that we don't know each other, well here's the chance to get to know each other by working together.'

By now the meeting was an hour-and-a-half long and the group continued to discuss strategies for electing their COPLA officers. Another idea for nominating and voting on people was proposed to the group by Rosa who said that maybe the names could be put in a hat and someone could choose the names. Ruben objected to the suggestion because it would not constitute an election. He felt that people needed to vote for the candidates. Antonio, a parent from Marina school, felt that already too much time had been spent on the election process. Three people stood up and prepared to leave the room claiming to have other meetings. Another woman raised her hand and told the group that she would have to leave soon because her childcare provider had to go home. Other people shifted their position, stretched their backs away from the small wooden library chairs. Sighs were heard and people looked around the room. Ramon agreed that too much time had been spent electing the COPLA committee and that maybe they could just go ahead and vote for the candidates and learn from the process. He proposed that they list the eight names on the board and that people write down the name of one person and that the top three votes would become the officers respectively.

Nine names were submitted and only one person declined to have his name on the board: Antonia, Manuel, Vicente, Jose, Martina, Fidel, Rosa and Juan. Mr Manuel Peña became president, Fidel Ramos, vice-president and Martina Romero was secretary. Two representatives to COPLA were also elected. Ramon reminded them that all of them would attend the monthly District COPLA meetings.

And the meeting continued. Ramon told the group that two areas remained on the agenda, to discuss communication in Spanish and to respond to parents' questions about their children. On the topic of communication in Spanish, Ramon emphasized the need for the new COPLA committee at Marina to deal with the issue of school communication to Latino parents in Spanish.

Ramon presented the last item on the agenda as a critical mission of COPLA in learning and supporting each other. People were invited to submit a concern regarding their children. A woman raised her hand and explained that her daughter in the first grade didn't pay attention and she felt that the child was more advanced than she demonstrated and that possibly her inattention was due to the teacher's low expectations. Another woman spoke about her daughter in the third grade also being in a classroom with low expectations. She suggested that what Latino parents should do is to visit the classroom and check to see what materials are used with the students and to make sure that a challenging curriculum is taught. 'Furthermore,' added another parent, 'we as parents also need to work closely with our children at home so that they know that we care how well they read.'

Mrs Kay Paton, principal, said that it was necessary for parents to communicate directly with teachers about those questions and that possibly as a COPLA activity, the bilingual teachers can meet with the parents and explain the literature program as well as other curriculum. She had prepared a written text in Spanish with the help of Paul Niles to read to the parents, 'Yo estoy muy feliz que ustedes estan interesados en la educación de sus niños. Yo quiero hablar más con ustedes. Sus preguntas son muy importantes y aquí estamos para ayudarles.' [I'm very happy to see that you're interested in your children's education. I want to talk with you more. Your questions are very important and we're here to help you address them.]

Parents acknowledged her statement by clapping and then a parent asked if COPLA could sponsor a drawing contest for kids. The question was not answered and Maria suggested that the issue be raised at the next meeting. 'That's it. We should end the meeting.' Suggested Maria.

Ramon apologized for the long election process and reminded everyone that they were all still learning and, 'It's all for the kids, so we can stand to be patient.' He thanked everyone for attending and the meeting ended. People lingered and talked with each other about how tired they were and how late it was while they hoped that future meetings would be shorter. Others were heard continuing the meeting by making comments about their children and the need to talk with the teachers about the books they read.

Up to this point in the history of the Latino parent participation in the

Carpinteria schools, they had been active in a variety of ways that enhanced their children's education.

The first phase of the COPLA development added a crucial dimension to the possibilities of communication between Latino families and schools indicated on Figure 2.1, below.

Phase 2: Structural Changes in COPLA

During this period of the development of the COPLA organization, the nature of the dialogue between COPLA and the schools characterized the success of an advocate organization. The way in which parents interacted with each other and with the school personnel identified COPLA as a viable community leadership group. One of the things that COPLA was able to accomplish during this period was to extend its sphere of influence.

COPLA school committees were established and they successfully resolved major issues, including correspondence in Spanish to Latino parents, criteria for admitting bilingual students in the Gifted and Talented Program (GATE) and English as a Second Language (ESL) curriculum. Numerous community organizations had visited the District COPLA meetings to inform them of the services available to the Latino families. Various community groups from neighboring Santa Barbara towns learned about COPLA and its successes with building communication between the Latino community and the schools and called upon members of the organization to meet with them to help them to organize parents in their respective communities. COPLA school committees as well as the District COPLA group began inviting community programs to meet and work with them in the local schools.

Outreach and expansion of COPLA's efforts to develop an informed Latino parent community is evident in the COPLA agenda of November 2, 1990. The COPLA satellite school committees reached out to connect with community organizations. The meeting began with Mr Mario Fernandez, the high school's COPLA president reported that two weeks prior the high school COPLA had a successful meeting where sixty parents attended including fifteen Latino students from ESL classes. The topic was teenage alcoholism where the Klein Bottle organization held a discussion with the parents on the theme of alcoholism which had been requested by the parents.

The parents representative from Weaver School reported that twenty-five people attended the last meeting where they worked with staff from a popular community newspaper from the Santa Barbara area that wanted COPLA schools to contribute interviews and articles about their efforts to organize Spanish-speaking Latinos. In addition, they also decided to spend three meetings on the topic of children's self-esteem led by a bilingual psychologist and a bilingual teacher. Family Math Project was also adopted as a project for Weaver families. Members from a University of California Math Department research

Figure 2.1: Critical interaction between parents their families and schools

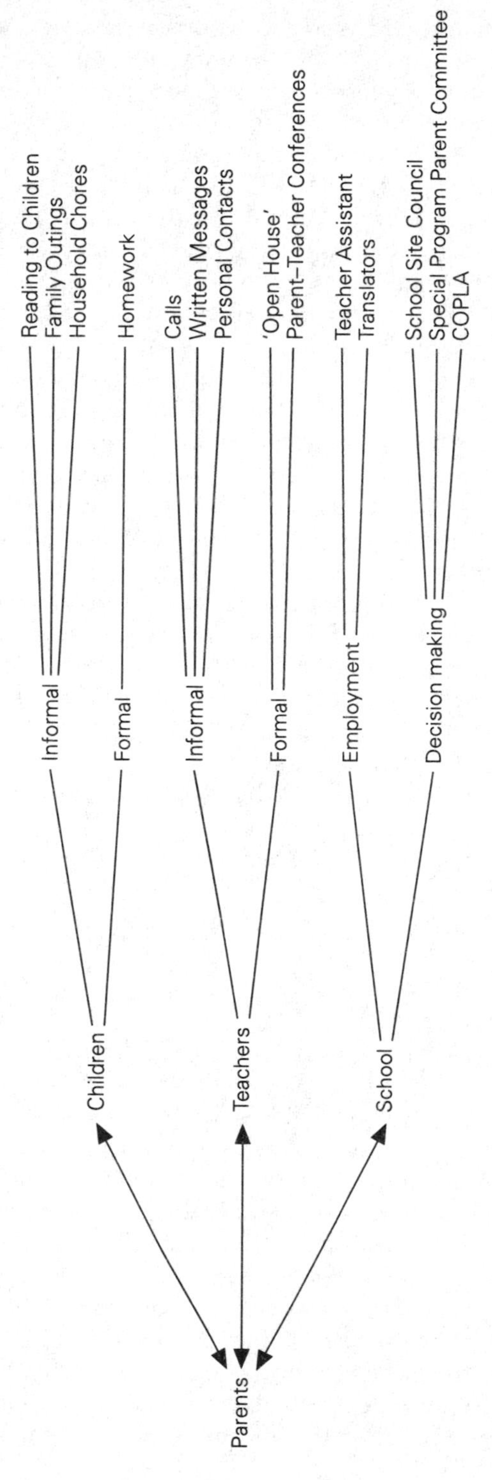

Note: Another version of this graphic appears in Spanish-Speaking Families' Involvement in Schools in C.L. Fagnano and B.Z. Werber (Eds) *School, Family and Community Interaction*, p. 91.

project on Family Math would assist the parents in the workshop on math with their children. Weaver School COPLA parents had connected with the university and local community agencies to expand their knowledge about ways to assist their children succeed in school.

Marina School representative, Manuel Peña reported that over 100 Latino parents attended the school COPLA meeting the previous month. The meeting included questions and answers directed to the principal about school programs and objectives for learning including concerns about the discipline policy.

Manuel also commented on the questions raised by parents at the end of the meeting pertaining to their individual children. A father wanted to know where he could find children's literature books in Spanish. He had been unable to get interesting books for his children and the school kept saying that he should read with them but they neither allowed books to be taken out of the school and he could not find books in the library or stores. Other parents shared his concern. They told him that the problem was indeed real. However, there was a small bookstore in Oxnard which sold children's books in Spanish and they discussed the possibility of getting a list of the books at the store and pulling together in carpools to make trips to buy books.

A mother then asked for assistance in ways to deal with her Kindergarten daughter who was afraid to go to school. At the meeting she was guided by COPLA leadership first to go to speak with her teacher, and then to find out what the teacher may know about the child's fear. If the problem were not resolved, then she was to speak with the principal. Ramon Mendez also a representative from Marina School added that he had tried to follow up to see if the woman had attempted to reach the teacher. Apparently, the woman went to the school but did not get to see the teacher because she had left the school. Ramon added that they responded to the parents' questions about personal problems as a way to guide parents to think about the necessary steps to resolve the problem. In other words, although parents share personal experience in helping others resolve their obstacle, the purpose is to get them to think about how the schools operate so that they become knowledgeable in resolving their own problems.

The Martin School representative Roberto Rodriguez extended the discussion of specific individual problems raised by Martin School parents. Latino parents seemed to have concerns with some teachers who were not bilingual and were consistently insensitive to working with Latino children and their parents. Parents of a fourth-grade boy complained about the child failing to return homework. Parents were aware that the child did his homework because they helped him with it, but the teacher never received it. Parents wanted to have a meeting with the teacher but were intimidated because in past meetings, the teacher has become quite angry about their son's presumed 'laziness'. Both Roberto and Antonia of the school's COPLA committee, made suggestions on how to approach the teacher. They reminded the parents that in a case where they did not feel satisfied with the results of their meeting with the teachers, they should contact the principal. Usually, someone on the COPLA committee informally followed-up with the parents who raised concerns at school meetings.

Four of the five schools reported on their respective school COPLA meetings. The middle school was conspicuously absent because the parents in charge of organizing the middle school had difficulty convening regular meetings due to the administrators' disinterest.

Following the school reports, the main topic on the District COPLA meeting's agenda was the presentation by a University of California, Santa Barbara representative who wanted to talk with the District COPLA about a possible meeting with Latino parents in the high school. The guest from UCSB spoke with the members of the committee.

Guest: Vine esta noche para hablarles del programa que tenemos el la Universidad para estudiantes Latinos que califican para la Universidad.	Tonight I came to speak to you about the program which we have to qualify Latino students for the university.
Ramon: Gracias por su visita. Si, nos interesa mucho su presentación porque las familias Latinas nos estamos reuniendo para enterarnos de los programas que benefician a nuestros niños.	Thank you for your visit. Yes, we're very interested in your presentation because our Latino families are meeting to become knowledgeable about programs that benefit our children.
Maria: Yo creo que nuestros hijos tienen que tener toda la oportunidad para tomar los cursos que los van a preparar para la Universidad.	I think that our children need every opportunity to take classes that will prepare them for the university.
Y ahora yo sé que muchos de nuestros hijos no saben como entrar a esos cursos y nosotros no sabemos como ayudarles para que entren a esas clases. Algunos de ellos califican pero por el hecho de que hablan principalmente español, no pueden tomar clases como química y física. Yo voy a alegarles a los directores de la High School que deben de tener clases para niños bilingues pero obviamente no lo consideran importante.	And I know that many of our children don't know how to get into those classes, and our program accepts only Latino students who have taken the required courses to enter the university. Some of them qualify but because they speak only Spanish, they can't take classes like chemistry and physics. I go to argue with the high school principals who should have classes for bilingual children but obviously they don't think it's important.

Guest: Nuestro programa acepta solamente a estudiantes Latinos que ya han tomado los requisitos para la Universidad.

Our program accepts only Latino students who have taken the required courses to enter the University.

Rebeca: Yo diria que es importante que hable con los estudiantes Latinos de la High School porque algunos de ellos son bilingues y han podido aprender inglés a punto que han entrado en las clases avansadas.

I would say that it's important to talk with Latino students in the high school because some of them are bilingual and they've learned English to a point that they can enter more advanced classes.

Juan: Yo también digo que cualquier información que se les ofresca a los estudiantes Latinos seria importante.

I too would agree that any information that our Latino students can receive would be important.

Manuel: Parece que el Señor Ramirez (guest) necesita que nosotros le demos permiso para presentarse a los padres Latinos en la High School. Es cierto que nuestros estudiantes pueden beneficiarse con este programa pero también estoy de acuerdo con los que han dicho que este asunto nos urge a nosotros que consideremos como es que puedamos preparar a nuestros estudiantes mejor para que puedan entrar a esas clases que requieren las universidades no solo La Universidad de California en Santa Barbara.

It seems as though Mr Ramirez (guest) needs our permission to present to the Latino parents in the high school. It's true that our students can benefit from this program but I also agree with those who have noted that this is an urgent issue for us to consider as to how we can best prepare our students to enter those classes that the universities require not only the University of California, Santa Barbara.

Guest: Yo se que otras comunidades Latinas también piensan igual y se preocupan por los estudiantes en la High School.

I know that other Latino communities also think the same and they worry about the high school students.

Ofelia: Yo estoy al tanto de las clases que toma mi hijo y son todas en inglés y a veces no se siente preparado para cierta clases de matematicas y historia. Cuando le

I'm on top of the classes that my son takes which are all in English and sometimes he doesn't feel prepared for certain mathematics and history. When that has

ha pasado eso, a tomado clases en el verano para adelantarse y sentirse más en control de su materia. Que no seria posible tener ese como plan para los estudiantes de habla-español?

occurred, he has taken classes in the summer to advance himself and to feel more in control of his subject. Wouldn't it be possible to have that as a plan for the students who are Spanish-speaking?

Rosa: Me gusta mucho esa idea como algo para proponerle al distrito escolar. Nuestros niños también se tienen que apoyar uno al otro como nosotros nos apoyamos. Y los estudiantes pueden ayudarse en programas de verano como modo para adelantarse en sus cursos del otoño, y tiene buen sentido para mi.

I very much like the idea to propose to the school district. Our children also have to support one another just like we support each other. The students can help each other in summer programs as ways to progress in their fall courses, and that makes sense to me.

Manuel: Sí, es cierto, y a la mejor podemos discutir este asunto como más tiempo en otra junta pero por hoy como lo tengo entendido, el Señor Ramirez de la universidad no nos puede ayudar a resolver este problema. Sólo nos puede ayudar a adelantar a los estudiantes Latinos que ya, como se dice, estan en camino.

That's true and maybe we can discuss this issue with more time in another meeting but today, I understand that Mr Ramirez, from the university can't resolve this problem. He can only help to advance Latino students who, as we say, have already made it.

Paul: Yo puedo hablar de parte del distrito [escolar]. Y todo lo que han dicho esta noche tocante a clases apropriadas para estudiantes bilingües es importante. Unos de los problemas que hemos encontrado es que no tenemos los numeros de estudiantes en clases para abrir clases en español en história, física y otras materias.

I could speak on behalf of the [school] district. And everything that's been said tonight regarding the appropriate bilingual classes is important. One of the problems that we have found is that we don't have the numbers of students that we need to offer history, physics, and other subjects taught in Spanish.

Maria: Comprendemos que ese es problema del distrito pero mientras nuestros niños que pueden beneficiar de clases bilingües no tienen oportunidad.

We understand the problem which the district has but meanwhile our children who can benefit from such bilingual classes don't have the opportunity.

Ramon: Pues yo no tengo niños en la High School así es que no se mucho de lo que han discutido aquí.

Pero sé que lo importante es que tenemos que considerar aquí es lo que es mejor para los niños.

Asi es que no cabe duda que el distrito nos tiene que considerar modos para avanzar a nuestros niños en la High School.

También lo que veo es que es necesario para el Señor y Señora Fernandez que son representates de COPLA en la High School que propongan este tema como algo urgente y debian envitar a los estudiantes y al Señor Sosa del programa migrante para que puedan discutir las necesidades de los estudiantes más abiertamente.

Ahora, me parece que como presidente tengo que pedirles su permiso a todos y a ver si podemos llegar a un acuerdo para dirijir al Señor Ramirez en modo para trabajar con el comité COPLA del la High School.

Well, I don't have children in high school so I don't know much about what you've discussed here.

But I do know that the important thing for us to consider here is what's important for our children.

Therefore, it stands to reason that the district has to provide us ways to advance our children in the high school.

Also what I see is that it is necessary for Mr and Mrs Fernandez, who are the COPLA representatives in the high school to deal with this question as something urgent and they should invite the Migrant Education students and director, Mr Sosa to more openly discuss our students needs.

Right now, it seems that as president I have to beg your permission and see if we can come to some agreement about the purpose of Mr Ramirez's visit which is to work with the high school COPLA committee.

Celia: Pues, si me parece importante que la siguiente junta de COPLA envitemos al Señor Ramirez y también toquemos el asunto de clases bilingües para adelantar a nuestros niños.

Nosotros [Mr Fernandez y yo] también tenemos niños en grados elementales no solo en la High School. Y yo creo que esta información de becas para la Universidad deben de aprovechar todos los padres para que sepan como aconsejar a sus niños desde los grados elementales.

Well, I think what's important is to invite Mr Ramirez to the next COPLA meeting [at the high school] and to also deal with the issue of bilingual classes to advance out students.

We [Mr Fernandez and myself] also have children in the elementary grades not just the high school. I think that all parents should benefit from this information on scholarship for the university so that they can learn how to advise their children from the beginning in elementary grades.

Ramon: Sí, seria bueno que abrierarmos esa discusion con el Señor Ramirez a todos los padres interesados.	Yes, it would be good that we open the discussion with Mr Ramirez to all interested parents.

Ramon closed the meeting which began at 6.30 and ended at 9.00 p.m. The meeting concluded with a process they called 'once around'. Parents took turns commenting about their impressions of the meeting. Most parents noted that they had felt frustrated by realizing that while some opportunities for scholarships were available for Latino students, the issue of language and bilingual classes had yet to be resolved in the Carpinteria high school. Although COPLA was cooperating with a community that also supported Latino students, parents were finding that often resolving some problems revealed other problems. In so doing, the parents continued to stretch and grow beyond their organizational parameters in order to assist their children.

As COPLA increased its visibility through linkages with other community organizations and strengthened its connections with the respective schools, talent and skills of its members were spotlighted. A critical form of outreach to Latino families on the part of COPLA through the workshops was led by members of the District COPLA committee.

One of the first community conferences which involved COPLA members as presenters was held jointly by the District Migrant Program and COPLA. Information about the conference and pre-registration forms went out to the parents from the Migrant Program. The conference was held in the Weaver School. The gray, cloudy, cold day in November did not discourage the conference participants from attending. Over 100 parents from the five schools registered for the conference at 8.00 a.m. Ofelia and Rebeca led a workshop on 'Communication Among Parents', Maria and Ramon led the workshop, 'Helping Children with Homework'. Other workshops by Celia, the preschool teacher and representatives from community agencies included, 'Alcoholism', 'Discipline in the Family', and 'Sexuality'. Parents selected from two of the five workshops and attended one in the morning and the second one after lunch. With the assistance of two students, I video taped the two workshops led by COPLA parents.

Parent-to-Parent Communication

Ofelia and Rebeca met a couple of times before the conference for preparation. Their topic demanded an interactive format where the presenters could engage the parents in discussing their needs and ways to form social networks that could be resourceful in their children's education. They had about twenty people in both of their workshops. Rebeca and Ofelia confessed feeling nervous, as parents began to enter the room for the workshop. Nevertheless, they walked to the door and greeted the people, invited them to take a seat, and then took their positions at the front of the room. After introducing themselves, they explained that their work in the COPLA organization led them to take an interest in teaching other parents about working with each other as Latino parents interested in their children's education. They presented the topic and format for their workshop.

Collectively, the parents formulated a list of obstacles which they felt prevented them from advocating for their children.

1 No hablamos inglés. [We don't speak English.]
2 No tenemos transportación. [We don't have transportation.]
3 Tenemos miedo ir solas a las escuelas. [We're afraid to go to schools by ourselves.]
4 No sabemos como ayudarle a los niños con la tarea. [We don't know how to help our children with homework.]
5 No tenemos cuidado de niños. [We don't have child care services.]

Secondly, Ofelia elicited comments from the parents and Rebeca wrote listing the rights that they knew parents to have in the schools.

1 Derecho de preguntar. [The right to question.]
2 Derecho de comentar. [The right to comment.]
3 Derecho de participar en hacer dicisiones. [Right to participate in making decisions in the school regarding my child's education.]
4 Derecho de saber. [The right to know.]
5 Derecho de comunicarnos con nuestros hijos en nuestra idioma. [The right to communicate with our children in our own language (Spanish).]

These parents seemed knowledgeable about the rights that parents had in the schools. Although quite general, they seemed to understand the parent presence in the school in spite of having detailed their obstacles. After discussing each of the rights, on a clean sheet of large clipboard paper, they began listing responsibilities which they felt parents had in their children's education.

1 Responsabilidad de abogar por nuestros hijos. [Responsibility to advocate for our children.]
2 Responsibility de ayudar a nuestros hijos con su tarea. [Responsibility to help our children with homework.]
3 Responsabilidad de hablar con sus maestros. [Responsibility to speak with the teachers.]
4 Responsabilidad de buscar ayuda para nuestros niños cuando nosotros no puedamos. [Responsibility to seek assistance for our children when we're unable to assist them.]
5 Responsabilidad de aprender inglés para hablar con nuestros niños siendo que ellos van aprendiendo más y más inglés y olvidando el español. [Responsibility to learn English to enable us to communicate

with our children since they're learning more and more English and forgetting Spanish.]

That each section of the discussion had about the same number of points, meant nothing in and of itself. The workshop leaders and participants listed only those specific points which they discussed extensively. Ultimately, Ofelia and Rebeca got the parents to consider how it was possible to overcome their perceived limitations by working with other parents to support each other. Parents recognized that COPLA provided them with the opportunity to join with others who had similar historical and cultural experience to examine their current community environment and possibilities for change and development.

Homework

Maria and Ramon presented on the topic of homework. Twenty-one parents attended the session on homework. Eight of the people were couples and in addition, four men and nine women comprised the group. Their objective was to raise concerns about their children's homework which parents shared. The presenters introduced themselves as interested parents involved in COPLA. Maria identified the areas to be covered in the workshop: Problemas con la tarea (Problems doing homework); Strategias para resolver los problemas de tarea (Strategies to resolve homework problems). Parents raised a variety of problems which haunted them in helping their children to do homework; parents' lack of formal preparation, excessive amount of homework at nights without sufficient instructions, children who don't want to do homework, teachers who don't want to help parents do homework, plus the fact that students were penalized too harshly for errors made on homework tasks. Ramon wrote the list on the flipchart as Maria elicited comments from the parents and they embellished each other's statements as people corroborated each other's comments with stories that conveyed frustration.

A mother who brought her 10-year-old daughter with her told of her daughter receiving so much homework that she was unable to play with her friends and then her daughter felt discouraged when the teacher would just collect them without giving her any feedback so she didn't know whether or not she was doing the pages correctly. Another parent agreed that teachers often assigned too much work and she believed that it had little meaning if the children didn't know how to do it. 'Yo sé que los maestros quieren que los estudiantes practiquen la materia pero no es posible cuando los niños no tienen suficiente explicación sobre lo que tienen que hacer. La tarea resulta siendo sólo algo para frustrar a los niños y a nosotros. [I know that teachers want students to practice their subjects, but it's not possible when they don't have sufficient explanation about what they have to do. Homework turns out being work only to frustrate children and us (parents).]' While concerns and problems were quickly forthcoming, Ramon and Maria also encouraged the parents to talk with each other in pairs to explore possibilities for action.

Workshop participants advanced ideas for dealing with homework that had interaction between parents and teachers at the center. Parents wanted teachers to provide more instruction on how to do homework tasks. In addition to how parents could communicate with teachers, Maria and Ramon also helped the parents to think about ways to advocate for their children by uniting with each other. They accomplished getting their important message to the parents which made them responsible for seeking resources other than their formal educational background to assist their children with homework. Parents recognized that although they felt frustrated about their children's homework situation, they could seek more support for the children's schooling. This point was synthesized in one parent's comment, 'Yo creo que no nos debemos de culparnos por no saber inglés. Yo diría que debiamos de conseguir a alguien quien pueda ayudar a ellos y muchas veces puede ser la maestra pero requiere que yo me comunique con ella. [I don't think that we should blame ourselves for not knowing English. I would say that we should find someone who could help them and oftentimes it could be the teacher, but it requires me to communicate with her.]' Ramon and Maria underscored her comment and emphasized the importance of meeting with other Latino parents in COPLA who had similar experiences with their families and their children's teachers. Latino parents need not feel isolated and can discover ways to effectively deal with their children's educational needs by becoming active in COPLA and learning ways to deal with their schools.

The workshop sessions had a very pragmatic mission, to raise Latino parent consciousness on communication and homework. COPLA leaders intended for the participants to feel that they could deal more effectively with their individual problems and be able to take steps to work collectively with other families in COPLA. Their message was strong about dealing with problems in two different ways, as an isolated family or as a united group which could be more resourceful in a continued effort to support families.

As satellite COPLA groups became stronger in each of the schools, they took on particular forms of operating depending on the principal's ability to work with the Latino community and the specific educational needs of the children in the respective grade levels. The organization expanded by joining forces with other community groups that also advocated for Latino families and education of Latino students. Among these organizations was the Latino for Better Government (LFBG) group which is comprised of professional Chicanos in Carpinteria who also have as their focus, increased success of minority students and the hiring of Latino personnel (especially teachers and administrators) in the school district. Through their joint efforts with other organizations COPLA, during this phase of its development, became a recognized voice in the schools such that when there is hiring of personnel, COPLA members are involved as representatives of the Latino community. This is a new development in recognizing the importance of the Latino community voice in hiring school personnel. Both LFBG and COPLA were involved in the selection of the new superintendent, Dr Pablo Seda who was hired during the summer of 1991.

The united Latino community voice also became important in the community council level as well. An issue arose in the City Council which ignited the Latino community in the spring of 1992. The Council voted to enforce a city ordinance which had been in the books but had not been strictly enforced. Essentially, the ordinance called for imposing a fine on households which had unused cars (or even parked cars) in front of the house. According to Carpinteria Latinos, part of the ordinance included penalties for households with a large number of residents. They felt that the Latinos were the target because they were the largest poor population requiring them to house extended families in small-sized apartments and houses. More accurately the issue was affordable housing.[1] A leader in the District COPLA group described the situation best,

Desgraciadamente es cierto que muchos Latinos que sobre todo cuando éstan jovenes pasan tomando afuera en los patios o lo que sea. Y el Latino que es más vago hace más fiestas y fuman más el sabado y el domingo cuando tienen barbacoas. Entonces a los Americanos no les gusta ver, no les agrada tanto ruido y entonces tratan de quitar que haiga más gente y suben las rentas.

Luego viene gente con más dinero y que pueden comprar las casas de más alta categoría. Unos de los problemas que presentaron los que quieren enforsar ésas leyes es de decir que Latinos tenian mucho abuso de niños porque vivian muchos juntos en una casa.

Claro que no es cierto de todos pero si es abuso. Pero eso se debe de negociar con la ley separadamente porque hay muchas personas que no más son pobres y solo necesistan un lugar donde vivir con sus familias.

Unfortunately, it's true that many Latinos above all young people stay out late outside in their front yards or whatever. And some Latinos are fun-loving and smoke at their outdoor parties on Saturdays and Sundays when they have BBQs. So Anglos don't like to see this and they don't like so much noise and they want to raise the rents.

Then, other people with more money want to buy the places that are higher priced. One of the issues that council persons who are in favor of enforcing the ordinance argued that a great deal of child abuse was found in households with a large number of people living in one house.

It's true there is child abuse in some families, but that issue should be handled legally and separately because there are many more people who are just poor and need a place for their family to live.

Representatives from Latinos for Better Government and COPLA met to decide on ways to respond to the Community Council regarding the issue. At the council meeting, a member from LFBG presented arguments against the ordinance and hundreds of Latinos attended as a result of COPLA's organizing efforts. While the City Council failed to resolve the issue with any concrete decision, it appears that the Latino community formed stronger linkages on behalf of justice. COPLA also seized the opportunity to request from the school district more training in the area of child development. Dr Seda, the superintendent, proposed and funded a series of workshops for the Spanish-speaking Latino families. The plan was for Dr Santana to train COPLA leaders who would in turn train other parents on topics of child development.

Phase two in COPLA's evolution, advanced the organization forward as it expanded its networking strategies to better educate and support Latino children. Accomplishments with COPLA meant a stronger voice for Latinos in the schools as school-site committees formed stronger connections among Latino families. As they learned to share their experience with each other for their children's gain, they developed leadership to head school-site committees and encouraged more involvement on the part of Latino parents to resolve some of their children's schooling problems through collective work with each other.

Phase Three: Redefining and Redesigning COPLA

During this period of development, COPLA continues to negotiate with the school and bring about improvements in the educational programs including the hiring of Spanish-speaking personnel. The middle school finally hired a Spanish-speaking secretary for the front office. After five years of COPLA expressing concern in this area, the middle school has recognized its importance.

With the hiring of a new superintendent, Pablo Seda, the school district's central administrator has made new commitments to work with the Latino community as well as with other parent groups. As part of this new commitment to parent involvement, the district administration hired Dr Santana to train the COPLA leader on child development and finding strengths of the family. The leaders who have trained with Dr Santana have begun to organize other parents to extend their training. The second tier of trainees will then select a third cohort to train.

In spite of the many developments in the schools and increased participation of parents in their children's schooling, new dilemmas surfaced in COPLA. The District COPLA leadership faced the problem of decreased parent attendance at the local COPLA school meetings. At a fall, 1993 COPLA meeting parents posed various analyses on the question of declining attendance.

Parents critiqued the organizational directions, activities and their leadership as well as the school's expectations. After examining their organizational commitment, they offered two pointed explanations for the apparent decline in attendance at meetings. One was that the focus of the organization had changed from the awareness to actual practice and that many parents had become more active in their children's schooling. They had become directly involved at the level of parent–teacher communication which explains the decline in parental attendance. Another interpretation is that the COPLA leadership had neglected to educate new families in the community as their children began school largely due to the fact that COPLA spent much of its attention in expanding and linking with other community organizations. It overlooked their organizational commitment to incorporate new families in the schools.

Leaders spoke to this issue as an urgent phase in restating their objectives for working together in an organization for parents focused on improving their children's educational opportunities by enriching their own. In the fall meeting, parents raised critical questions which would direct their future work as an organization: How can COPLA continue existing as an organization? What are the most important objectives? What are the obstacles that preclude COPLA from achieving its goals? How do we propose to deal with them? What's the most important things we've accomplished during the past five years? Although they raised these major questions for themselves, they managed to answer a significant one, that they genuinely wanted to continue growing and learning how to help their children in their schooling.

COPLA has continued to operate as an organization and they have continued to reach out to parents in the local schools. While the local committees exist, they draw fewer people to the meetings. There is more connection between teachers and parents around children's daily concerns in the classroom. Principals have also become more engaged in dealing with their respective school site COPLAs as a result of Superintendent Seda's objective to evaluate principals on their success in instituting strong family and school relationships. Together school personnel and parents have a greater task before them, to reach out to Latino families who still feel isolated and to convince them that they too can be leaders, rebuild the strength of COPLA as they did initially when the group of seven Latino parents first began the District COPLA to teach each other and to connect with other families in the five schools. Although COPLA has neglected to reach out to the isolated Spanish-speaking families as was originally their intent, they never abandoned their primary focus which was the child.

In the third phase, COPLA leadership has become more involved in activities that provide children social activities in the community in the absence of affordable community resources. Rebeca organized a folkloric dance group with the assistance from a dance instructor from Santa Barbara who offered classes to the children in the dance group. Rebeca organized fund-raisers including community dances on Saturday nights to pay for the children's costumes, lessons and transportation for children to perform. She also solicited Carpinteria businesses to sponsor the children's performances. Parents whose children danced in the folkloric group also often attended COPLA meetings. The parents who help organize the folkloric group tell the children, 'Nosotros no queremos nada para nosotros, es para ustedes. [We don't want anything for ourselves, it's all for you.]'

El grupo de baile ha trabajado muy bien. Las mismas niñas que estan bailando, son las niñtas que aveces andaban en la calle. Ahora no tienen que andar. Ay unas niñas que antes me las encontraba en las calles y yo les preguntaba que hacian en la calle tan tarde y me decian que andaban caminando. Pero no era hora para que ellas anduvieran caminando.

Ahora van al baile folklórico y de allií se van a su casa. Cuando menos, ya no veo esas seis parejitas allí en la calle de vagas. Y los papas también saben que estan bailando. Una de las mamas que nunca se preocupaba por su niña que ahora esta en nuestra grupo, el jueves pasado vinó a ver a su hija bailar.

The dance group has worked out very well. The same girls who are now the dancers are the same ones who used to wander the streets. Now they don't have to hang out in the streets. There are some girls whom I used to encounter on the street and I would ask them what they were doing out so late and they would tell me that they were out walking. But it wasn't a time when girls should be out walking.

Now they go to the dance and from there they go home. They don't need to be on the street. Their parents also know where they are dancing. One of the mothers who never cared where her daughter was came to visit the dance class last Thursday to watch her dance.

Rebeca's dance group paid five dollars a month to dance. Local Mexican stores sponsored from four to five months of dance classes for children who could not afford the classes. While young boys danced in the folkloric group, other boys found soccer more to their liking. Ramon organized a soccer league for young children of three age groups, 8–11, 12–14 and 15–18 but he got his brother-in-law and other people to coach because he was still quite involved in COPLA leadership and had assumed parent directorship of the Migrant Education Program.

Challenging the School Culture

The most significant finding during these three phases of parent involvement development in Carpinteria is that Latino parents explicitly state that the success of COPLA is based on their learned culture and ability to be supportive advocates of their children through school. It is that knowledge which they want to share with other parents. Throughout COPLA'S development, parents stayed focused on their children as the fundamental impelling force of their work. Even as the organization proliferated, the parents remained sincere about their efforts to work together in projects for their children as the end.

By constructing new discourse norms in a common space in this specific historical point in time between the schools and families, Latino parents created a voice for themselves as they became aware of their children's conditions in schools, and their rights. Beginning in 1988, Latino parents organized to join with others to share their life experience, the need to cooperate with the schools, and to create change through improved programs and policies situated in the culture, language and politics of the community. This awareness led to continued dialogue between the schools and the families. The district-wide group proliferated into the schools, and within a year the parents in the district committee joined with other Latino parents in every school in the district and formed local school-site COPLA committees.

Five major features of COPLA frame its identity:

- Continuous critical reflection on the part of COPLA members allows for systematic growth for the organization as the group pursues new goals and directions to learn from each other ways to work for children;
- Parents and school personnel hold 'the child' as the key mutual stake;
- An egalitarian mode of interaction allows for shared power between parents and the school personnel;
- Parents address multifaceted social needs which impact on the family, classroom and community at large and;
- Continuous dialogue extends beyond the crisis issues.

Integral to the discourse of change is the critical reflection process which brings people's experience and concerns to a conscious level as Freire describes in his work. Through continual dialogue, parents and school personnel transformed practices and policies related to Spanish-speaking Latino children. Inherent in the critical reflection structure is the conviction that individuals have strengths and that learning new roles provides people with access to resources. The learning of those roles occurs through negotiation and participation in new social arrangements.

The critical reflection process which engaged Latino families in Carpinteria as a supportive network has given the Latino community a recognized voice — thus power. Ultimately, three things occurred: parents changed their view of self, they changed the way they saw each other, and they acted to change conditions. This empowerment process evolved through focused interaction which changed the individual's perceptions of themselves; changed the perceptions on the part of the individuals toward others, and acted to alter their circumstances. The change that has ensued as a result of the collective and personal awareness, evolves and accounts for changes in local policies and programs while continuously reflecting on the change process.[2]

Underrepresented people, including women and ethnic and linguistically subordinate groups of which women constitute a significant size group, must participate fully in all facets of society. Opportunities to participate exist in the process of educating Latino children as demonstrated in Carpinteria. The role of the community is recognized as prominent in the empowerment process. An understanding of the history of a given community or group, including the language, values and traditions associated with role allocations, is indispensable to determine appropriate strategies for creating equality.

Figure 2.2: Spiral continuum on the empowerment process

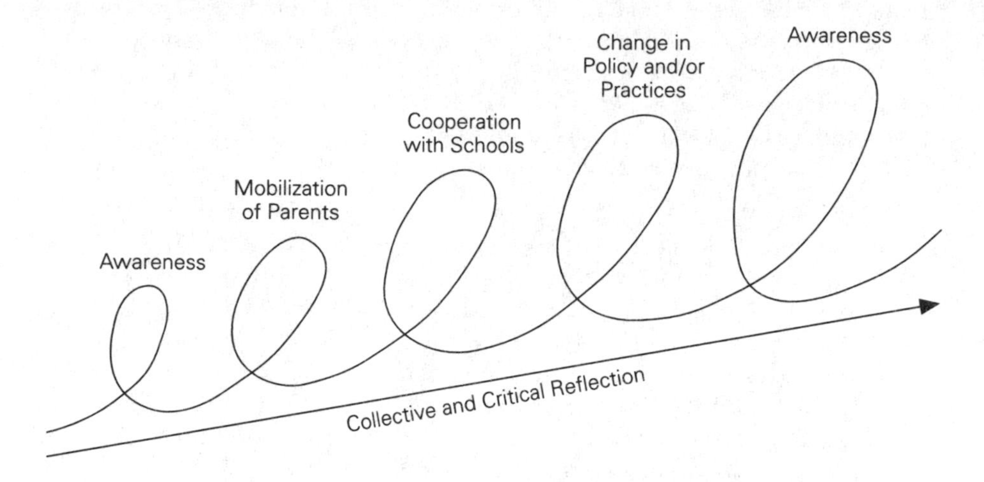

Note: Another version of this graphic appears in Spanish-Speaking Families' Involvement in Schools, in C.L. Fagnano and B.Z. Werber (Eds) *School, Family and Community Interaction*, p. 93.

COPLA is one context in which Latino Spanish-speaking families participate and build consciousness about oppression. They see their liberation as a process of ongoing dialogue, where political awareness of the system is learned along with skills to participate in it.

Latino parents initiated the process of critical reflection on issues of their children in the schools. Reflection for Latino parents developed through a collective effort because the events leading to their organization involved collective processes. However, the context for critical reflection cannot be identified solely with a collective context given that individuals can reflect on their issues pertaining to them personally which result in changes of the social ecology in which they live. Such was the case with changes observed in Latino families in Carpinteria where parents were involved in reflection on the improvement of education such that family units transformed.

Notes

1 High rents for families with low incomes have been a contentious issue in Carpinteria on more than one occasion. The local nurseries have been the target of disapproving council members. A local newspaper wrote:

'In Carpinteria, nursery housing projects become an exercise in politics when the Carpinteria City Council and County Board of Supervisors (1st District) have thus far failed to provide leadership on the issue of affordable housing. The issue is one involving Edward Van Wingerden, owner of Ever-bloom Nursery in Carpinteria which employs about 25 Latino workers on a year-round basis, all of whom live in

Carpinteria. Due to Carpinteria's lack of affordable housing, these workers are forced to live with extended family members who can contribute to the rent. The idea of a nursery owner footing the bill to provide his workers with quality living conditions at an affordable rate is both honorable and worthy. This appears to be the ideal situation for both the city and the workers.

The plans for the housing project called for the northern end of Santa Ynez Road to be granted by the city. The neighbors along the road rejected the project because it would increase the traffic as a result of twenty new housing units. Apparent was the fact that the Mexican/Latino community remained virtually silent. In essence, they have no active voting bloc exercising their rights against nursery workers who have no voting status which the politicians didn't overlook.' (*Vos Popular*, July 1990)

2 The social change in the Carpinteria families, schools and community is grounded in research and theory addressing social, cultural and political assumptions leading to critical reflection and dialogue at a community level. These authors who have influenced my conception of empowerment include Allen, Barr, Cochran, Dean, Greene, 1989; Barr, 1989; Delgado-Gaitan, 1990; Freire, 1970 and 1973; Lather, 1991; Lifton, 1993 and Williams, 1989.

The respective concepts represented by these authors confluence such that they ensue a process as central to the empowerment premise which, I maintain, spotlights inequality in society and holds the individual central to the process of change which involves critical reflection both individually and collectively and also builds on the people's strengths and undergirds the full expression and participation of the individual or collective. Each of these theorists contributes an important principle to the process which I term empowerment:

1. The critical reflection process enables people to envision their place in society and in their community and appraises their strengths and, through their continual reflection, can create a vision to expand their potential to learn (Allen *et al.* 1989).
2. Conflict reinvents power to a win–win position as opposed to a winner–loser (Barr, 1989).
3. A critical ethnographic approach is essential in understanding literacy and how empowerment operates in ethnic and linguistic communities which have been underrepresented and isolated (Delgado-Gaitan, 1990).
4. Literacy is a process of reading not only written text but of one's social position in the world in which we live. Through literacy we learn critical consciousness (Freire and Macedo, 1987).
5. The concept of proteanism helps to understand the individual's resilence and ability of continual change (Lifton, 1993).
6. Education means 'giving to the ordinary members of society its full common meanings, and the skills that will enable them to amend these meanings, in the light of their personal and common experience.' (Willams, 1989, p. 14).
7. In response to the question, 'What is to be done?' theory nurtured by action is the premise of *praxis* which leads us to take action in the world and become creative through our activity (Lather, 1991).

Chapter 3

Building on Family Strengths

'El Perico de la Señora'

Una mujer tenía un perico y luego fue y dijó al perico, 'Voy a ir de compras, si viene alguien, dices todo que sí.' Que llegaron las tortillas, 'sí' dijó el perico y luego llegó la leche ye dijó 'si' el perico. Llegó el pan, 'sí' lba pasando un borrachito. Luego dijó 'Quieres unos fregadazos?' Dijó 'sí' el perico 'sí'. Luego llego la dueña del perico y le dijó elia. ¿Proqúe estás morado?' y le dijó 'Porqúe andaba diciendo que sí y mira lo que me pasó. Luego dijó la señora que dijera otra vez que no. Llegó la leche, 'no'. Llegó el pan, 'no'. Llegaron las tortilla, 'no'. Pasó de vuelta el borracho. 'Oye, ¿te dolieron los fregadazos que to di? y él dijó, 'no' y le pego du vuelta.

'The Woman's Parrot'
(Story by 7-year-old Susana)
A woman had a parrot, and then she told the parrot 'I am going shopping, if someone comes say "yes" to everything.' When the tortillas were delivered the parrot said 'yes' and when the milk was delivered the parrot said 'yes'. The bread was delivered, 'yes', there was a drunk person passing by. Then he said 'Do you want to get hit?' The parrot said 'yes'. Then the parrot's owner arrived and she said 'Why are you bruised?' and the parrot said 'because I was saying yes and look what happened to me.' Then the woman told the parrot to say, 'no'. The milk was delivered, 'no'. The bread was delivered, 'no'. The tortillas were delivered, 'no'. The drunk person passed by again and said 'Hey you, did it hurt when I hit you?' And the parrot said, 'no' and the parrot got hit again.

Familiar Networks

Just as I have known many families like those in the leadership of COPLA, I have met and worked with numerous others who feel stuck in pain as a result of their isolation and feeling of hopelessness. They have lost their jobs. Maintaining a healthy family becomes increasingly difficult. They too live in crowded apartments. With larger families, the household often was filled with fear as a result of an alcoholic father or mother who abused the family.

Members of these families live with a gag over their mouths because of the shame and isolation they feel.

For many children who live in these families, going to school is their only outlet away from a fear filled environment. Yet, their ability to be comfortable enough to learn in school is often impeded by their emotional stress compounded by unresponsive schools until this cycle is interrupted. And *how* can families like these who face oppressive difficulties find their source of strength and power? Better yet, how does proteanism emerge under these conditions? How to tap those strengths has been to confront stressful situations related to their children's connectedness with others in a supportive situation redirects their pain outward rather than inward.[1] No simple formulas exist for becoming a protean individual, family or community. I'm convinced that everyone regardless of color, religion, socioeconomic standing, place of residence, ethnicity or educational attainment have strengths and power.[2]

How to tap those strengths has been illustrated to us by the Rodriguez family (Chapter 1) and others involved as COPLA leaders (Chapter 2). They have harnessed their ability to confront stressful situations related to their children's connectedness with others in a supportive situation and have managed to redirect their pain outward rather than inward. Parents find support in dealing with problems of schooling their children by being active in the COPLA group.

What we know of the sociohistorical dynamics of these groups for these families active in COPLA, is that people can't always find their power when their lives feel out of control. However, it is important to recognize that one's experience of isolation and oppression is not unique, and that by sharing with others there is potential for us to change our lives — be it in relation to the larger community or on a much more personal level, such as smaller social units like family or other social groups.[3]

Social networks provide opportunities for people in Carpinteria to become connected with others around common issues to learn that they were not alone in dealing with their problems — as overwhelming as they may seem. With others we gain a different perspective on problems which then enables us to act differently. We get to open doors and see the possibility of solutions by reaching out and finding access to those resources which lead us to new directions that translate to more love within our families and community.

Among COPLA families, building community included intimate family gatherings, church social organizations, Alcoholics Anonymous (AA) active participants, soccer games, (or team matches) and workplace related socials. This is a way of noting that various avenues existed for families to communicate with each other and to maintain and to confront their issues about their common and different values within communities. They shared family, and employment resources, including children's educational options. To the extent that families are able to socialize around their personal interests, there existed a means of building a cohort to support their cultural values. Proteanism, in Latino families in Carpinteria was built just as much of their own strength as on their collective endeavors.

Religious Activities

In Carpinteria these involve two Catholic churches which draw from the east and west side of the freeway respectively although many Latino families lived on the east side. Carpinteria has two churches which has members from the east and west sides. Mrs Angeles commented on her learning from west-side families in their contacts with extended families and their community as much as their own. She taught a Saturday morning class for children preparing to make First Communion in the Catholic Church. One of the reasons she enjoyed working with COPLA was that she had such a difficult time working with parents in the church. According to Mrs Angeles, some parents did not study with their children yet expected them to make their First Communion even when they did not know their lessons. She recounted a situation which occurred with one of the parents in her class. Mrs Angeles had a class of twenty-six children with children of ages 6–7 years old. Parents left their children at 9.00 a.m. and picked them up at 11.00 a.m. She decided that it was time to confront the parents on the question of helping the children to take more responsibility for helping their children learn the Catechism for their First Communion. She contacted the parents and asked them to attend a meeting one Saturday at 11.00 when they picked up their children. Of the twenty-six children only three parents came into the room forcing her to cancel the intended meeting. Mrs Angeles decided that the following week she would ask the parents or whoever picked up the children to come inside the room and pick up their children and stay for a few minutes to talk about how they had to assist their children to read their lessons and prepare for their test the following week otherwise if the children did not pass their test, they would not be able to make their First Communion.

Twenty parents (some fathers and others' mothers) and four older siblings came to pick up their younger brothers and sisters from the class. The children watched as Mrs Angeles talked with the adults. She reminded them that the time for First Communion was approaching and all of the children had to pass the test which would be given the following week. This called for a commitment on the parents' part to help the children prepare for the test. Mrs Angeles had the cooperation of all of the children's parents although she could not count on getting all of the children to pass their test. After all the other parents left, one parent remained to talk with Mrs Angeles about his daughter who had been having problems reading. Mrs Angeles began by informing him about ways to help his daughter to remember her lessons for the First Communion test. The parent said that he felt confident that she could probably pass the test since it was oral, but his concern had to do with her reading problem at school. His daughter used to like reading but her mother died during the year and his daughter fell behind in her learning. Now, he said, she's quiet most of the time and doesn't even want to try. Her sisters and brothers are also having a hard time. He had thought of sending them to back to Mexico to their aunt because it was difficult for him to do it alone even though they had some friends from their home town who helped them daily. Mrs Angeles directed him to the Migrant Education teacher in Marina to help his daughter with her reading, but she also suggested that he attend COPLA meetings so that he could become more informed about resources in the school. Mrs Angeles said that it might be a good idea for him to take his daughter to a counselor who could help the family to deal with the mother's death. She suggested raising this need with the priest who could help them find someone to assist the family in that specific area.

At the next COPLA meeting, Mrs Angeles called this parent and she encouraged him to attend. He said his car had broken down and needed a ride. So she went by his house and picked him up. He thanked her for taking such an interest in his daughter's schooling and informed her that his daughter was beginning to like school again since she passed the test and was able to make her First Communion. Mrs Angeles asked about the other children and whether he had sent them back to Mexico. He said he would wait until the end of the school year to evaluate the situation again and that maybe he would send for his sister to come up to help him instead of sending the children back to Mexico. He did not want them to leave their classes while school was still in session because, as he remembered, his wife always felt that education was the top priority for their children.

Through her teaching of the Saturday, First Communion classes, Mrs Angeles formed linkages with families and between families and appropriate agencies. Latino parents related to one another through their day-to-day encounters at the laundromat, the grocery store, soccer games on weekends, at their employment places in the nurseries in spite of the scrutiny of other employers who were usually white.

Spanish-speaking Latino families relate in limited ways to Whites in Carpinteria because of the different languages. While most contacts are cordial and non-consequential, some incidents are born of misunderstandings like the one involving two Latino children who were found by the local police, playing tennis at the middle-school playground. In the spring of 1993, the police were called by a neighbor who saw a number of children in the playground and called the police to investigate. The neighbor arrived at the playground with the police and the police interrogated the children and asked them who they were and the adult was who accompanied them. The Latino counselor identified himself and said that he was a counselor in the school and that he had brought the children to the playground to help the children practice their tennis. The neighbor woman said that maybe there wasn't a problem right now with the children playing tennis but they (Latinos) should all be sent back to Mexico because they occupied too many jobs and cost the country too much money. Contacts such as these between Latinos and Anglos in Carpinteria make relationships hostile at best since Latinos, especially children, feel confused about the blame hurled unjustly at them.

Adult Latinos complain of becoming more isolated as a result of tense confrontations with Anglo residents. Both groups, poor Spanish-speaking Latinos and Anglos coexist in much of their daily activities including shopping in the same grocery stores, doing their laundry in the same laundromats. Occasionally, an attempt is made by Anglos to contact Latino parents to meet about school issues. This usually occurs around planning time or school carnivals. Earlier interest in working together occurred when COPLA was organized, Anglo parents attended COPLA meetings to learn how the group was organized and how they define their task. Nevertheless, distant relationships prevail as language differences prevent extensive and involved interactions among English and Spanish-speakers.

The Workplace

The workplace has been the site of much conversation about family activities. Women who are active in COPLA work in nurseries, factories, schools and other locations alongside those who are not as aware about schooling in the US. For example, a co-worker approached Mrs Rodriguez about the problems her children encountered in school. The parent hesitated to go to the school when the teachers called her to complain about her daughter, and Maria Rodriguez told her and other women to go to talk with the teachers. They used to tease her about caring too much and insisted that teachers should know how to do their job. Maria would explain how necessary direct communication was between parents and teachers. Now after a few years they don't tease her anymore but they don't attend COPLA meetings either. Neither does Maria attend meetings — it's David who attends.

Leisure Activities

Leisure activities provide another meeting ground for Latino families to ask questions of their children. One day after a children's soccer game, a mother of one of the players stopped Maria to ask if she knew about a school where they could put their young teenage son because no school wanted him. He had been suspended from school so many times that the school district authorities refused to accept him again and the principal suggested that the child attend the county alternative school in Santa Barbara. Maria advised them to go and speak with the administrators and to find out as much as possible about the alternative school and about the son's rights to return to the district school. The boy's parents accepted her advice and went to the school to speak with the principal where they learned that the district did not have an obligation to accept back the boy unless they could show that he had made exceptional progress for at least one academic year at the alternative school and even then, the son would be accepted on a probationary basis. This example shows how Maria as well as other COPLA leaders made every event an opportunity to share with their social network their knowledge about educating their children.

What to Expect

Adults who were leaders in COPLA reported shifts in their family relationships as a result of their participation in COPLA. They became aware that their low school attainment in Mexico need not interfere with their high expectations for their children's education but they also realized that high expectations were insufficient. Hard work was required. Accepting new responsibilities in their children's education meant revisions within their families.

'Lo más que queremos para ésta vida es que nuestros hijos vayan por un buen camino, que puedan hacer más que nosotros. [The most that we can expect of our lives is that our children take a good road and accomplish more than we have.]' Maria Rodriguez epitomizes the feelings of parents that highlight the value of the system underlying the socialization of children in their families.

As parents become more active with each other and with the schools, they relate differently with their children. The world view they share with their children in their own language is recognized as worthy of the family unity they promote. Between families and relatives, and their communities.

Initially, they worked only minimally with their children on school-related tasks. Homework and parent–teacher conferences were always given top priority in these households. Other educational activities were only occasional occurrences but not part of regular family activities. After a couple of years of working in the leadership of COPLA, parents extended their list of activities in each household which promoted their children's schooling. Homework occupied a great deal of parents' time with their children. Some helped their children by sitting down with them to complete their nightly tasks while others just asked the children to report to them upon completion.[4]

As the chart indicates, homework was only one arena for parent–teacher connections. Other contacts were made through teacher–parent conferences, parent-initiated calls, parent-and-teacher initiated written reports. Parents observed that their children made a great deal of progress as a result of their participation in COPLA.

Table 3.1: Text-related family activities

1. Parent–child homework activity
2. Parents' oral literacy related talk
3. Parents reading with children
4. Parents motivating children to read
5. Parents discuss completed homework
6. Parents discuss school reports with children
7. Personal literacy materials (letters, etc.)
8. Parents study English as a second language

Note: Another version of this graphic appears in 'Spanish-Speaking Families' Involvement in Schools.', in C.L. Fagnano and B.Z Werber (Eds) *School, Family and Community Interaction*, p. 92

Mr Lopez told me about his son in tenth grade.

A mi me parece que mi hijo pone un poco más de empeño por lo que yo le digo. Y eso me hace sentirme muy feliz.	It seems to me that my son tries harder and pays more attention to what I tell him. And that make me feel good.

Mrs Alonzo told me of how her son in the fourth grade and daughter in the seventh grade have benefited from her activism.

Yo estoy viendo que mis niños si estan aprovechando que yo este al tanto de lo que pasa en su escuela y a ellos les gusta que yo vaya a la escuela a ver como trabajan.	I've noticed that my children have benefited from my attention to what happens in their school and they like it that I go to their school to watch them work.

Mrs Hernandez recognized that her son's work in the tenth grade had improved some due to her participation in COPLA.

Les hablo para que se levanten en la mañana y les doy su desayuno. Y tocante a sus tareas, ahora tratan a superarse más en sus tareas.	I call them to wake up in the morning and prepare their breakfast. With respect to their homework, they now try to get ahead in their work.

Some parents like Mr Morales have seen their children bring home higher grades.

Lo principal es que nos traen buenas notas y ya nos dicen problemas que antes no nos comunicaban. Asi es que tenemos más comunicación entre nosotros en la familia.	The most important is that they bring home good grades and they tell us about problems while before they did not communicate. As a result we have more communication in our family.

Other parents commented about the progress they witnessed in their family communication which meant significant changes in their children's education through family support. Mr Mendez is particularly elated about the developments within his family.

Ahora que participo con COPLA, le hago saber a mis hijos lo importante que es una buena educación, me comunico con los maestros de mi hijo para ponerme a trabajar con	Now that I've been participating in COPLA, I've made it known to my children how important a good education is. I communicate with my son's teachers so I can work

ellos y hacerles saber que ellos son parte de nuestra vida.

Les hago saber que me interesa todo lo que ellos hacen, les motivo para que den lo máximo en la escuela. Les hago sentir que son muy importantes, que son inteligentes, y que ellos pueden ayudar a otros niños. Por ejemplo a mi hijo le gusta compartir sus conocimientos, y yo lo animo para que de alguna manera transmita a otros los que el sabe hacer. Lo animó que lea cuentos a su hermanita y que le enseñé a contar, a colorear etc. De esa manera el se siente que es muy importante.

with them [the children] and to let them know that they're a part of our lives. I try to make them know that I'm interested in everything they do.

I motivate them to give the most they can in school and to help other children too. For example, my son likes to share his knowledge and I encourage him to somehow transmit to others what he knows. I encourage him to read stories to his little sister and to teach her to count, to color, etc. By doing so, he can feel important.

Some students enjoyed having their parents involved in their schooling both in and out of school as indicated by their direct and explicit communication to their parents and their improved grades.

Even in more challenging situations, communication and participation, improve results. Mrs Suarez's son had been sexually molested and she had been trying to find ways to help him deal with his emotional distress around the incident which affected his entire life and specifically his schooling.

Mi hijo se ha hecho más responsable y toma más interés en participar en los eventos escolares. Se siente más feliz ahora que yo este más involucrada en la escuela. En mi primer año en COPLA el se mejoró bastante. Con tan poco tiempo he visto buenos resultados. Yo creo que ha sido tan difícil para el y para todos que yo siguire buscando el modo para ayudarle sea lo que sea. Y confio que el va a seguir para adelante.

My son has become more responsible and takes more interest in participating in school events. He is happier now that I'm more involved in the school. In my first year in COPLA he improved tremendously. Within such little time I have seen good results. I believe that it has been so difficult for him and all of us that I'll continue finding the way to help him in whatever way I can. I'm confident that he'll continue moving forward.

Parents who assist their children in their homework report that much of the work cannot be completed without parent intervention or special tutors.

Children's work can be quite demanding, especially if the children are in GATE classes as Manuel Peña tells.

Yo he aprendido que tengo que sentarme con mi hijo que ahora esta en el cuarto grado en GATE. Me gusta mirar que es lo que esta haciendo. No es que no tengo confianza en el, es porque quiero saber que tipo de materia tiene como asignatura. Yo no estudie en este país y apenas complete la primaria asi es que a la ves que le estoy ayudando, también estoy aprendiendo.	I have learned that I need to sit with my son who is now in fourth grade in the GATE program. I want to know what he is doing. It's not that I don't trust him, it's because I want to know what curriculum he's assigned. I didn't attend school in this country, and I barely completed primary school so while I'm helping him, I'm also learning.
Yo Quiero estar pendiente de todo lo que hace mi hijo. Aunque he aprendido mucho de COPLA también se que no puedo pasar todo mi tiempo en juntas porque quiero pasar tiempo con mi hijo. Mi esposa no asiste a las juntas de COPLA pero esta pendiente con las maestras de mi hijo y ella se comunica con ellas y me avisa a mi de lo que necesita estudiar Roberto.	I want to be on top of what my son does. Even though I've learned a great deal from COPLA, I also know that I cannot spend all of my time at meetings because I want to spend time with my son. My wife does not attend COPLA meetings but she talks with my son's teachers and she communicates with them and then tells me what Roberto needs to study.

Although the Peña and other parents could not help their children with the complex tasks their children brought home, other parents were able to help their children who were in the early primary grades. Mr Garcia who had only a fifth grade education in Mexico prided himself in helping his sons in high school by finding words in the dictionary.

Yo, si puedo, me siento con ellos [mis hijos] y les ayudo en sus preguntas o les ayudo a buscar en los libros los ejemplos que necesitan.	If I can, I sit with them [my sons] and I help them with their questions or I help them look in the books for the examples they need.

Mrs Martinez raises an important point which I observed to be present in the households where I spent a great deal of time documenting the small details which united a family.[5]

El punto que quiero tocar es que en el hogar debe haber 'reglas' — tiempo para levantarse [en la mañana] — tiempo para desayunar,	The point I want to make is that in one's home there should be 'rules' — time to get up [in the morning] — time to eat breakfast, time to

tiempo para prepararse, y salir a la escuela. Tiempo para regresar de la escuela, tiempo para hacer la tarea, tiempo para mirar un poco de televisión, tiempo para juntos poder comentar y leer un rato.

prepare and to leave for school. Time to return from school, time to do homework, time to watch a bit of television, and time to talk and to read a while.

Parents have motivated each other and their children to make sense of a system from which they previously felt alienated. Most significantly, Latino families turned their attentions inward to learn more about their children, their schooling activities and the means of connecting the family and the school. COPLA was credited differently by parents who participated more actively. For some, COPLA provided a forum to discover more about the schools. Others like Mr and Mrs Ruiz are a prime example of people who cared a great deal about their children, COPLA provided ways to more effectively assist their children at home about school issues. They were quite active in the organization of COPLA and, while Mr Ruiz always participated in the meetings, it seemed that he was quite knowledgeable about the avenues to take advantage of programs the school offered. Both credited their activism in COPLA sharing with other parents about their children, for their increased consciousness. However, Mr Ruiz revealed an interesting vignette about his expanded awareness.

Quiero ser sincero con usted porque yo podia engañarla. Pero yo seria el autoengañado. Yo no les he ayudado nada a mis hijos en la casa. Ha sido mi esposa quien toma la responsabilidad. Yo tengo un gran defecto, mi carácter porque siempre ando de mal humor. Pero ya poco a poco empiezo a platicar con ellos ya les prometí que voy a cambiar. Ahora ya les digo que la educación es la única herencia que vale la pena.

I want to be sincere with you because I could deceive you. But I would only be fooling myself. I haven't helped my children at home at all. It has been my wife who takes all the responsibility. I have a great character defect, my bad temper. But little by little I am beginning to talk with them and I have promised them that I will change. Now I tell them that education is the only legacy that's worth anything.

As they noted, the Ruizes reached out to their children in ways more meaningful than they knew before they joined with other parents to share their mutual history while they strive to make sense of their children's schooling.

Family Decisions

Communication between parents and children was unquestionably the more developed sphere in the Latino households of the active COPLA members.

Their children's future became a more concrete possibility as they tailored family conversations around the exploration of plans for college, employment, and even marriage. The Torres family of six, including four children and the parents, Ofelia and Marcos, faced the tensions and joys of their children's decisions for careers.[6a] The Torres family had always shared their dreams and hopes with each other. Ofelia made every effort to maintain a strict schedule which would bring the family together every night for dinner followed by a homework session where they all sat together at the kitchen table and the living room couch to help each other with the homework. Although both parents assisted their children in their work, only Ofelia provided direct assistance since Marcos was illiterate and could not read the written curriculum. However, both Mr and Mrs Torres held the children accountable for completing their work and getting themselves ready for school. Most of the work fell on Ofelia as she coordinated everything the children needed including clothes, books and medical appointments. Marcos assured that the children got to bed at a reasonable hour and helped them to put together a meal when Ofelia was not home. From the time the children were in elementary school, both parents listened to their children's dreams of what they were 'going to be' when they graduated from high school. The Torres parents did not impose their desires on their children for a choice of profession. Their only wish was for their children to get an adequate education that would prepare them for a job beyond what they had with limited schooling. Ofelia was pleased about her children's expectations and plans for a career. Javier, the oldest son for example, wanted to go to college to study law. Cecilia talked about plans to become a teacher. Mario, the next youngest was interested in art and thought about including it in a career somehow. And Celia the youngest, was in middle school at the time this was written, and had begun inquiring about beautician work.

Shortly before Javier's graduation day, he came home and before dinner time he asked his mother and father to sit down and that he wanted to talk to them. They sat at the kitchen table and announced to them that he was seriously considering going to the Marines after graduation. Apparently, Javier's friend had enlisted in the Marines and was sent to fight in the front lines in the Persian Gulf War. Javier believed that he too should enlist and do his part in the service while getting a free education. Mr and Mrs Torres expressed their ambivalence to Javier about his decision. First his father shared his thoughts and then his mother spoke about her fears for him.

Mi hijo yo no creo que me gusta la idea de que vayas a los marines. Yo pensaba que tenias planes de ir aquí al colegio. Tu mama y yo nos preocupamos por ti y esta es una decisión grande. Si estas aquí cerca en el colegio sabemos como estas.

Son, I don't like the idea about your going into the Marines. I thought you had planned to go to college here. Your mother and I worry about you because this is a big decision. At least you are here in college nearby where we know

Pero allá tan lejos y en tanto peligro, cómo vamos a saber de ti?

how you are. But if you're so far away and in so much danger, how will we know how you are?

Papá, yo se que ay peligro en lo que voy hacer pero yo siento que es mi deber. Y si voy a los Marines puedo tomar classes para mi carera. Me gustaria hacer algo que tiene que ver con servicio del govierno.

No se que significa eso en lo que necesito para entrenearme ahorita pero me interesa mucho ese campo. Mis calificaciónes no estan suficientemente fuertes para entrar a la universidad así es que puedo estudiar a la misma ves.

Father, I know that what I want to do is dangerous but I feel that it's my duty. And in the Marines, I can take classes toward my career. I would like to do something that has to do with government service.

I'm not sure what that means or how much training I need, but that field interests me a great deal. My grades aren't strong enough for me to enter a college or university and this way I can study at the same time.

Mi hijo yo tengo mucho miedo por tu decisión. No quiero que vayas aunque siempre te hemos permitido libertad para que hagas tus decisiones. [Los ojos se le llenan de lagrimas.] Pero ay va hacer tan difícil para todos nosotros, mi hijo.

Son, I'm very scared by your decision. I don't want you to go even though we've always given you the freedom to make your own decisions. [Tears well in her eyes.] But — oh — it'll be so difficult for everyone, dear.

Yo sé, mama, [movió su silla cerca de ella y la abrazo.] pero es también una oportunidad para estudiar. Yo les dije a los representantes de los Marines que ustedes podian firmar para que yo entrara a los marines.

I know mom [He moved his chair next to her and put his arm around her shoulder.] but it's also an opportunity to study. I told the Marine recruiters that you would sign for me to enlist in the Marines.

Neither Mr and Mrs Torres wanted to sign the document that night. Marcos admitted not wanting to see his son leave for a far away land if he was sent to fight in the war or even if he would be stationed in a far-away state. However, a few days later, they conceded and signed Javier's permission to enlist in the Marines for two years but not before Ofelia dealt with the torment she felt about Javier's decisions. For the days that followed she talked with her work mates about young men they might know who have enlisted in the armed forces. She was not consoled much with their stories about how much their sons or nephews matured when they went into the service. More than sorrow over her son's decision, she was emotionally torn because she had always told her children to respect their inner direction and to follow their heart. Now she did not approve of his leaving home to join the service because it would be dangerous. What if he was to get sent into the front lines of the war? Mrs Torres admitted making a visit to the priest to ask for advice about allowing Javier to pursue his intentions.

Ultimately, she felt some resolve that Javier learned decent values having grown up as part of their family. And if he was so intent in joining the service to pursue his education, then he must be making the right decision even if it was hard for them to accept it. Ofelia also considered that the family could not afford to pay for his college education and that Javier was convinced that he could pursue the profession of his choice while in the Marines.

Once Javier left home to begin his two-year term, the family missed him terribly and the parents had a change of heart about his decision. They were proud of Javier and his achievements in the service. His letters and phone calls to Ofelia and Marcos convinced them that he was happy and benefiting from the educational programs offered by the government although he did complain about the rigorous routine that woke him up at 5.00 a.m. every morning.

The Torres family faced a different conflict when, in the following year, Cecilia began dating a young man, a few years older. He wanted to marry her. Ofelia and Marcos did not wait for any announcements from Ofelia, rather, Ofelia anticipated surprises and sat Cecilia down to let her daughter know that she supported her in her plans to attend college and prepare to become a teacher. Cecilia was in the eleventh grade at the time and her mother had already warned her to spend more time on her studies and less with her boyfriend since her grades, although quite average, were not representative of her ability. In defense of herself, Cecilia said that most of her time was spent in working at McDonald's and she felt that it was unfair to restrict her from her boyfriend when he actually supported her. A mother–daughter talk had been prearranged by her mother; the designated Friday night finally arrived. Cecilia returned from her part-time job at McDonald's still reeking of onions and French fries. Her mother was dressed for bed. Both sat down at the kitchen table and sipped soft drinks as they talked. When Ofelia talked with Cecilia, she had only reassuring words for them.

Yo no me quiero casar ahora. Yo quiero trabajar y ahorar mi dinero y graduarme de la high school.	I don't want to get married right now. I want to work and earn money and to graduate from high school.
Tu papa y yo pensabamos que querias estudiar para ser maestra. Eso requiere que vayas al colegio. ¿Qué no?	Your father and I thought that you wanted to study to be a teacher. That requires you to go to college. Doesn't it?
Si se que tengo que ir a la universidad. Pero tengo que tener alguna libertad para entretenerme.	Yes, I know that I need to go to the university. But, I have to have some freedom for entertainment.

Queremos hacer lo que podemos para ti, mi hija. No es que queremos detenerte. Tienes que saber que tu nos importas mucho y no queremos que te cases hasta que tengas tu una carrera para ti.	We want to do what we can for you, dear. It's not that we want to limit you. You need to know that you're very important to us and we don't want you to get married until you have a career for yourself.

Cecilia and Ofelia accomplished what they wanted in their brief conversation on this critical topic. And Cecilia held to her word about going to college after high school, except that she began at the local community college because she did not have the funds or grades to leave home and attend a university.

While little research exists on family socialization of Latino girls where educational values and support exists, Carpinteria families provide a window into parents' feelings about educating their children according to gender differences. Latinos have long been underrepresented in the educational ranks from early years of schooling to the university graduate level. The Torres, as did many Latino immigrant families in Carpinteria expected both their sons and daughters to have a good education and the opportunity to pursue their dreams to the extent they desired.[6b] Some parents however felt that their daughters did not need as much education as their sons.

The Torres represented one side of Latino family beliefs about gender distinction in their children's education. They wanted all their sons and daughters to continue their education beyond high school. When they first became active in COPLA, some parents, believed that boys should have more education until they changed their mind through their participation in COPLA. Educating 'all of our children' was a topic raised from the very initial meeting of the organization. The message was explicit — that both daughters as well as sons deserve their parents' dedicated attention and encouragement to advance their education. Raising this issue to the forefront of the education of Latino children remains to be fully explored in COPLA and the Carpinteria School District.

Work in and out of Home

Traditional gender roles in the household are not radically altered when Mexican families, who work in the agricultural industry, immigrate to the US. While working full time and having children, women continue managing the household thus doubling their workload.[7] Traditional responsibilities can shift as a result of social interventions which raise a new consciousness about gender roles. COPLA provided a context for that shift in Latino families of Carpinteria. Although not all adults involved in COPLA felt convinced of the need to reorganize their gender-defined roles in their households, Latino women active in the COPLA leadership more readily found the need to openly discuss with their husbands questions regarding evening meetings, children's homework and adjustments to their share of division of labor. Some husbands increased their chauffeuring duties as wives worked longer hours to help support their children. Other husbands accepted more responsibility in tasks like doing the family laundry more often as women attended afternoon meetings with their children's teachers. Other women like Rebeca Cortina complained about their husband's unwillingness to help them around the house. Rebeca's husband hurt his back at his job and was on disability for two years before he was strong enough to resume work, although he was forced to change his employment because he was unable to lift heavy loads. When he was home, however, Rebeca said that she expected him, at least, to wash dishes and do light work like dusting and occasionally boil potatoes, but he refused, using his disability as a pretext. During that period Rebeca was vice-president of COPLA and she was working two jobs to pay for a computer and flute which her daughter, Sonia, needed for her Gifted and Talented Program (GATE).

Rebeca managed the ordeal with her husband's disability and reluctance to help her around the house, and shortly after he returned to work, she was able to convince him that his assistance with housework was just as important to the maintenance of the family as her employment outside of the house was to the economic support of the family. Admitting that he felt stronger and could help with light housework, he now washes dishes and occasionally performs other minor household tasks. Rebeca was quick to give her husband credit on issues of supporting the children in their schooling tasks. He always encouraged both Sonia and their son Miguel to do their best in the academic arena and he actually assisted them in their homework when he could intervene. He even coached Sonia on her baseball technique so that she could make the team. Miguel received special attention when he went out for the soccer team. Rebeca, nevertheless, held most of the responsibility for meeting with teachers and teaching other parents to work with schools.

The Cortina story resonates with other activist women in COPLA, while the activist men told a different story in their teamwork to educate their children. Ramon Mendez and his wife Chela learned to work with each other's demanding schedules by dividing their tasks related to their children's schooling and the household chores. Chela felt more comfortable with helping their children Pablo and Mona. Chela had only a second-grade education in Mexico and felt rather insecure about her communication with schools but could understand some of their children's homework when they were in kindergarten, first and second grade. Once Pablo began to get more English curriculum in the third grade she deferred to Ramon, who completed the equivalent of high school in Mexico. Pablo sometimes waited till late at night when his father was at COPLA or other school-related meetings. There came a point when Ramon's meetings kept him out of the house so much that Chela taught him to heat his meals and even make some quick snacks for himself because he came home too late to expect her to get him something to eat. Another reason was that he sometimes came home before her and then left for meetings before she arrived from work so that he had to prepare something quick to eat. Ramon brags about his terrific salsa.

Chela me enseñó hacer una salsa muy buena para comer con mis tortillas o se la pongo sobre algo que caliento en el microwave. Sólo rebano poco tomate, chile jalapeno, cebolla, poquita sal y unas hojitas de cilantro. Luego hecho todo en la liquadora y sale muy sabrosa. Ella cocina muy bien y algunas veces yo hando de carreras, pues así no me paso hambre.

Chela taught me to make a good salsa to eat with my tortillas or to put on whatever I heat in the microwave. I just chop a bit of tomato, jalapeno chile, onion, a bit of salt and a few cilantro leaves. Then, I put everything in the blender and it turns out very tasty. She's a very good cook and sometimes I'm running around so this way I don't go hungry.

Ramon laughed at his story of how he had come this far to have become so active in educational groups that he can make salsa. He recognizes that while he and Chela and him have agreed that he should take the leadership and involvement in their children's schooling and in organizational leadership, he also admists that his wife still handles the most difficult of all household jobs, the family economics. In spite of their division of labor with respect to schooling and household matters, both Ramon and Cecilia agree on their values to raise and educate their children as intelligent bilingual children with a vision to learn how to explore the world and assist others in doing the same.

A Collective Effort

That people change when they immigrate to a new society is not even a question. Cultural change is inevitable and immigrant families adapt to a new society to the extent that their local communities recognize their social and economic potential. Latino families have had more support in their dealings with social institutions including the school than did Chicanos who lived in Carpinteria when the schools and the community were more segregated. Although everyone is inclined to change given their specific family, community and personal direction, cultural proteanism occurs only through collective work and through vision for common goals that empower individuals, families and communities — a trust assumed by COPLA in supporting those with common history and experience. Through their work with COPLA parents display their strengths. Their assessment of their collective accomplishments reveals their respect for each other's work and their gratefulness in extending support and knowledge which enabled them to learn the power of their cultural values. As active members of COPLA, the safety to adjust to different practices empowered them politically as a community.

The COPLA format has been an important context for learning criticism, communication and confidence which many parents believe they are able to transfer to the empowerment of their families.

Participar en COPLA me ha ayudado bastante no sólo en tener más conocimiento de cómo funciona la escuela y cómo ayudar mejor a mis hijos si no también a tener más seguridad en mi misma.	Participating in COPLA has helped me not only to better understand how the school functions and to help my children but [COPLA has helped me] to have more confidence in myself.

Antonia Suarez believes she has grown along with COPLA. When she first became involved with the organization, she felt shy about speaking up at meetings. Although her attendance was consistent she remained quiet at meetings. However, she was not inactive in her associations with others including her neighbors and her family. Antonia talked with parents of students in her children's classes. Her reaching out to them kept her busy teaching them everything she learned at meetings. Not only were other parents her objective — her family too benefited from her knowledge of the educational process. She began communicating with her children more directly and honestly which compelled her daughter and son to trust her in obtaining guidance. At the end of every COPLA meeting parents, one-by-one, commented about the meeting. Antonia always acknowledged how strong she felt her own family communication was becoming due to what she learned at COPLA. She was particularly convinced that her strength in working through her family also helped other families in the community who came to her for guidance and advice about their children and their education. Antonia usually shared her delight at being a part of a group like COPLA. Her communication skills were developed in COPLA and evolved to the point that in 1994 she became the president.

Family communication also enriched Ramon Mendez in his pursuit of knowledge about schooling and other opportunities for his family including his brothers and their families. He extended his new found consciousness to others by respecting them and himself as well.

Con mi participación en COPLA he aprendido a saber valorar las opiniones de otras personas. Las críticas las acepto y las tomo de una manera positiva, algunas veces me ayudan para seguir adelante. Ahora, aprecio y escucho a cada persona y creo que tiene algo bueno que aportarme.	My participation in COPLA has taught me to value the opinions of others. I accept criticisms as something positive, and sometimes they help me move forward. Now, I appreciate and listen to everyone and believe that they have something good to teach me.

En COPLA he aprendido bastante de otros padres de maestros de los medios que hay para motivar a mis hijos a estar en la escuela. Además he aprendido a comunicarme con mis hijos de una manera efectiva. También tengo mucha comunicación con los maestros de mis hijos y con mi pareja.

In COPLA I have learned a great deal from other parents on ways to motivate my children to stay in school. Additionally, I have learned to communicate with my children in a more effective way. I also have much better communication with my children's teacher and with my wife.

Ramon's assessment of what COPLA has accomplished confirms his protean development in his personal life and that of his family's which permits him to impart his knowledge and affection with his co-workers and other families.

Con mi participación en COPLA he aprendido a forjarme metas. He aprendido que no debo de darme por vencido tan facilmente. Sé que aunque hay metas difíciles de lograrlas me han dado más confianza alcanzarlas con mis esfuerzo.

Me siento muy contento de participar en esta organización y si puedo y tengo algo que aportar para otros padres. Me he dado cuenta de la importancia que es el compartir mis inquietudes con otros padres y maestros.

También me he dado cuenta que la mayoría de nosotros tenemos las mismas inquietitudes y luchamos con un mismo fin — el brindarles una buena educación a nuestros hijos.

In COPLA, I have learned to develop goals. I have learned that I need not feel like a victim. I know that even if we have difficult goals to achieve they have given me more confidence to be able to reach them with my effort.

I feel happy to participate in this organization and [hope] that I have something to share with other parents. I have become aware of the importance of sharing my conflicts with other parents and teachers.

I have also noticed that the majority of us have similar conflicts and that we struggle with the same objective — to provide our children with a good education.

His world view changed to encompass a more promising vision and positive approach to working with other families to reach mutual ends.

Otra cosa que me ha gustado es la manera tan optimista con la cual hemos emprendido diferenetes tareas. Realmente para mi ha sido muy importante estar en esta

One of the other things I have liked [about COPLA] is the optimistic way we have launched our various tasks. Actually, for me it has been very important to be in this organization.

organización. He cambiado bastante en mi hogar, en mi comunidad, en la escuela de mis hijos. Otro de los cambios que yo he tenido es que miro las cosas con mas objetividad. Ahora busco lo bueno que puedo obtener de cada persona en lugar de mirar los defectos.	I have changed a great deal in [the relationships with] my family, with my community and with my children's school. Another of my changes has had to do with the way that I see things more objectively. Now I look for the best in each person instead of looking for defects.

Thinking differently about oneself and others as did the families of Ramon, Rebeca and Antonia along with other COPLA activists, represents an empowering accomplishment. The foundation of transformative action is the belief system undergirding it. Families transmute adversity in their households and workplaces. As they applied themselves to overcome hardships in their daily lives, they adapted wholly to the strident changes. They exemplify a case of proteanism.

Notes

1 Redirecting one's pain outward rather than inward is a concept that has been explored in Lifton, 1993.

A different form of outward expression in dealing with one's pain has been documented in the resistance movement. Resistance is a way of confronting and dealing with the hopelessness of oppression and can serve as a way out of their oppressive conditions. See Willis, 1977; McLoed, 1987; and Foley, 1990.

Resistance often creates negative thinking on the part of Chicano students. This behavior is often the only resort available to the community when their culture is denigrated. See Delgado-Gaitan, 1988. Foley, 1990, has also noted that resistance is the only option available to Chicano students when Capitalist forms of education undermine their language and culture in the midst of poverty.

2 Publications, Delgado-Gaitan, 1990, 1991, 1992, 1993 discuss the position of power in Latino families including the researcher's role in the process. My research on immigrant families including Latino, Russian and Indochinese has departed from the premise that poor families are 'culturally deficient' and uncaring about their children because they lack formal education and are therefore unable to raise their children. My position on empowerment begins with the rejection of the 'deficit theory'.

3 Although I do not have the space here to name the extensive list of publications on this topic of social networks related to Latinos, I need to include a note on seminal work on the question of Mexican social networks: Vélez-Ibañez, 1983 and 1988. The social networks reported by Vélez-Ibañez differ from the nature of the COPLA organization but the informal networks offered social and economic support for the Mexican communities in Arizona. The 'Funds of Knowledge' concept is a response to social and cultural adjustment which has been documented in Tienda, 1980, 1983, Tienda and Guhleman, 1985.

Unjust blame of immigrants for the economic decline of the US economy is explained by Simon, 1989, as a seminal study that helps us understand the political dimension of immigration serving capitalists' interests.

4 Accountability for homework is examined in schools where Latino children attend and in households where Spanish-speakers interact around questions of education. Delgado-Gaitan, 1992 describes the strengths of the family examined in their daily interactions in household and community contexts. Allexsaht-Snider, 1991; Reese, Goldenberg, Couck, Gallimore, 1989; and Vasquez, 1989 take a qualitative approach to the questions of family–school communication and offer an integrated view of parents' and teachers' efforts to promote bilingual children's leaning.

5 Documenting details of the family in the privacy of their home required trust for the researcher, extensive and triangulated strategies as well as constant critical perspective on the researcher's role involving the participants' self-critique, see Delgado-Gaitan, 1993.

6a/b Latino parents are criticized for not 'pushing' their children into careers thus creating underachievement in a generation when students require all of the direction they can have to achieve the most in this society. However, parents in this study, have shown that they encourage their children as much as they can into a career to the extent they are knowledgeable about resources that permit their children to enter a specific career. Underrepresented Latinos in education are noted by Baca-Zinn, 1980, 1983 and Delgado-Gaitan and Segura, 1989.

7 Carpinteria parents active in COPLA expected both their daughters and sons to be educated. Poor immigrant parents are criticized for holding lower expectations of their children. The case is that such critiques do not take into account the socioeconomic and historical context as well as the particular community in which the children live.

Chapter 4

Shapeshifting: A Self of Many Possibilities

'Cesar y Agustina'

Había una vez dos personas, Cesar y Agustina. Cesar le dijó a Agustina que el techo estaba roto pero que el no tenía dinero para areglarlo. Agustina le dijó, 'Tu tienes un violín.' Cesar le respondió, 'Sí, pero no recuerdo donde lo deje.' Luego, Agustina le dijó, 'No te preocupes, yo me voy a dormir.'

Agustina se acostó y dijó, 'Podemos ganar dinero si tu tocas el violín y yo canto.' En ves de dormir, Agustina bajó para abajo y comenzó a buscar el violín y lo encontró. Entonces, subió para arriba a llevarle el violín a Cesar y le dijó, 'comineza a practicar tu violín.'

Cesar comenzó a tocar el violín. Luego en la mañana, Agustina dijó, 'yo voy a ponerme un vestido nuevo.' Cesar le dijó, 'voy a vestirme y salimos a cantar.' Se pararon en la esquina el la calle y comensaron a cantar y luego Agustina cantaba y la gente en la calle comenzó a escucharla y darle dinero. Entonces, ellos coleccionaron mucho dinero y compraron nueva ropa, zapatos, y helados.

Se olvidaron del techo y

'Cesar and Agustina'
(Story by 7-year-old Miguel)
Once there were two people Cesar and Agustina. Cesar told Agustina that the roof was rotting but that he had no money to fix it. Agustina told him, 'You have a violin.' Cesar responded, 'Yes, but I don't remember where I put it.' Then, Agustina told him 'Don't worry, I am going to sleep and you should go to sleep.'

Agustina laid in bed and then said, 'We can earn money if Cesar plays the violin and I sing.' Instead of going to sleep Agustina went downstairs and began to look for Cesar's violin and she found it. Then, she went upstairs to take the violin to Cesar and she told him, 'Start practicing your violin.'

Cesar began to practice his violin. Then in the morning Agustina said 'I am going to put on a new dress.' Cesar said, 'I am going to get dressed, and we will go out and sing.' They stood on a street corner and began to sing and then Agustina sang and the people in the street began to listen and give them money. Then they collected a lot of money and bought new clothes, shoes, and ice cream.

They had forgotten about the roof

regresaron a la casa con comida cuando Cesar se acordó del techo y dijó, 'Oh no, va a llover.' Entonces Cesar y Agustina se pararon en sillas para cubrir el agujero en el techo con un trapo. Entonces, Cesar martilló la tabla sobre el agujero y luego el pusó un sarten en el suelo para que no le caiga el agua en el píso.

and returned home with food when Cesar remembered about the roof and said, 'Oh, it is going to rain.' And then, Cesar and Agustina stood on chairs and covered the hole in the roof with cloth. Then, Cesar nailed the wood over the hole in the roof, and then he put a pan on the floor so that the water would not drip all over the floor.

The portrayal of the Mendez and Rosario families here was influenced by scholars who have argued for the complex humility of the people like those with whom I worked in Carpinteria. The context is one of an unwelcoming American society where fear of immigrants abound. In this text, I show ways that Ramon and Chela Mendez and Maria Rosario assert their accounts of identity reinforcing the position that belonging and connectedness is never beyond power. In this light, the stories of these individuals reject any idealization of family or community because they shift between discourses restating a major position in this book that no action has a single effect. Our cultural history provides a broad canvas on which we construct the self — meaning that — the self is never separable from context.[1] Here I posit that identities on the individual level resist closure and reveal complicated, shifting, multiple facets.

Two COPLA leaders, Ramon Mendez and Maria Rosario and their respective families take center stage in this chapter. Community activism extends from the individual's personal values and history which motivate their concern for opportunity for their children as well as equity for extended family and community members. The meaningful events which Ramon and Maria share about their lives convey their strength and openness to learn a new language, a different culture, and to face themselves as they ferret through incessant adversity in their lives and then to shift their perception and actions to include wider possibilities for growing and expanding their potentiality.

Ramon and His Family

On the dining room wall of their two bedroom Mendez condominium, hang four plaques of commendation for Ramon's work in the Carpinteria community and schools. In 1991, COPLA awarded him a plaque with an inscription 'En Reconocimiento a su Magnifico Labor Como Presidente de COPLA 1989–1991. (In Recognition of Magnificent Labor as President of COPLA.)'

The three other plaques were given to him by Director of Special Projects, Mr Paul Niles and Superintendent Pablo Seda, in 1992, by the Director of Migrant Education, in 1993 and by Dr Mario O. Solis in 1992 for his participation in leadership classes on 'Families in Society'. All of Ramon's accolades praise his contributions to families and schools of Carpinteria.

Ramon's achievements have grown along with him in the forty years of his life that began in Zacualco de Torres, Jalisco which is just south of Guadalajara en route to Manzanillo. His family worked in agriculture growing beans and corn in their small ranch to feed their family. Ramon's family ran a small tortilleria. Since the age of 8, he helped in the ranch during the week before and after school. On weekdays, before going to school, he had to sweep around the house or go to the corn mill. School began at 9.00 a.m.

On weekends, he helped in the family tortilleria for a couple of years until he began to sell popcicles. He awakened mornings at dawn in order to get a push-cart to sell his popcicles. He pushed the cart from 6.00 a.m. to 5.00 p.m. and earned about twelve pesos for the day which at the time was the equivalent of one dollar in the US.

Ramon liked school a great deal especially math since he had quite a bit of practice in the streets as a young entrepreneur, and math was his ticket to survival even if it were for a mere few cents. At the age of 10, Ramon made small gelatins to sell. He bought the gelatins for $.20 and prepared them himself. He put them in small plastic cups to sell for two pesos per gelatin. He had an attractive profit margin. He had to sell them the same day because he did not have refrigeration. Then, he began to sell cookies and candy from the same stand for about one year.

All of this happened in Zacualco. It was a town of approximately 15,000, a bit bigger than Carpinteria. It had a primary school, one high school, one business institute that taught typing, and eight Catholic churches. It seemed that Ramon always liked math, and selling treats was one way that he could stay close to computation. His uncle offered him the opportunity to work in his store. Ramon worked there five hours after school for two years while he was in high school. He also liked writing which, like math, was a necessary skill in his early business career. He became so engrossed in his uncle's business that he abandoned his studies at school at which point his uncle posed an ultimatum, either attend school or quit work. Reluctantly, Ramon returned to high school and graduated. In retrospect he feels appreciative of having completed high school because most children in Zacualco stopped attending school in the third grade due to the families' need for children's labor such that children often lost initiative and lacked supportive motivation. Most however, completed primary school because it was compulsory. Throughout primary school Ramon received high grades as a model for his younger brothers and sisters. When his interests shifted to work in the stores, Ramon recalls how his grades in school dropped.

Cuando me puse a trabajar con mi tío no sobresalía más que en lo que estaba muy fuerte, en matemáticas y en español, y ortografía. Pero de

When I began working with my uncle I didn't succeed like I used to in Math and Spanish and writing. But from that point forward, I only

hay en más, iba otras clases nada más y iba sobre llevando las clases de biología, física, química. Se me ponía más difícil. En México, yo creo que me faltaba más el empuje que se le diera al estudiante y hacerlo importante. Nos quedábamos nada más en lo que era del pueblo. No podíamos mirar más lejos que lo que había en Zacualco. Era todo nuestro mundo.

Lo que pasaba es que los maestros no nos hacían ver las oportunidades que habían para otros lados. Era siempre, ¿cómo le diré? Se dedican los maestros nada más a su materia y no, te van preparando como para que vayas, como algo vocacional que busques algo que te ayude. Simplemente nada más te dan tus clases y son buenos maestros, pero siempre como que faltaba de que le dieran a uno la visión.

attended classes and survived biology, physics, chemistry and it was more difficult. In Mexico, I think that I needed more of a push than what I received as a student to make the student feel more important. We only dealt with what concerned the town. We couldn't see beyond what we had in Zacualco. That was our entire world.

What happened was that the teachers did not help us see opportunities that we had around us. It was always, How should I say? They dedicated themselves just to their material and they don't prepare you like to go into a vocation, or to find something to help you. They only taught classes, and though they were good teachers, it was always like a vision was missing.

After completing high school, Ramon had the distressing task of notifying his parents, who had counted so much on him for economic support of the family, that he planned to leave town to study at the 'preparatoria' which is the equivalent of a community college. His uncle, who owned the store where Ramon worked, offered him a loan to begin his own store. Ramon then decided to remain in Zacualco and open his own small store where he worked for two years. Subsequently, Ramon became interested in attending the university in Guadalajara and was accepted along with ten of his friends. But he failed to convince his parents who, according to Ramon, said they could not support him in his decision to go to the university.

Me dijieron mis padres que apenas tenía para lo de la casa y que no me íban a poder ayudar. Me dijó mi papá, '¿Para que te voy ayudar? Te voy a decir que vayas pero no te puedo respaldar con dinero.'

Yo creo que aveces porque no hay el medio económico o el dinero suficiente para respaldar, los padres

My parents said that they barely had enough for household expenses and they would not be able to help me. My father said, 'Why should I help you? I'll allow you to go but I won't be able to support you with money.'

I believe that sometimes because there are no economic means or sufficient money to help, parents

le niegan a uno su apoyo. Pero aveces es que antes los papas no sabían y no creían que era tan importante el estudio.

deny children their support. But the truth is that sometimes it's that before, parents didn't know and they didn't believe that it was important to study.

Creían que nomás con enseñarlos a trabajar, a ganar para ayudar a la familia ya era suficiene. Esa es la mentalidad que había. Aun todavía.

They thought that by teaching us to work and to earn enough to help the family, that it was sufficient. That was the mentality at the time. And, it still is.

Ramon believes that his parents did not know how to support him in what he wanted to do because they were too busy worrying about their daily survival.

Chela's parents, much like Ramon's, have had to make monumental shifts in their understanding of their children's independence and education with Chela's youngest sister who wants to be a teacher and needs not only their emotional but also their economic support. This was particularly difficult for Chela's parents because they had always worked hard just to keep food on the table. Ramon recalls when he first met Chela's family they planted cucumbers and beans and they lived in desperate poverty.

Chela era la tercera de diez hijos. Y son muy pobres. Es una pobreza que tienen que estar trabajando cada día. No hay ni siquiera trabajo estable. Ya tienes para una semana o para 15 días. Ahí, como comes hoy, mañana, quien sabe.

Chela was the third of ten children in her family. And, they're very poor. It's a poverty that keeps you working every day. And, there isn't even steady employment. You might have something for a week or two. You may eat today but you don't know about tomorrow.

Ramon admires her tenacity and strength for her creative strategies to work her way out of destitute poverty. He credits her with breaking the poverty cycle of their family which consisted of working, marrying another poor person, having many children and then caring for ill parents and the cycle continues. But Chela persevered through the hunger which the family faced almost on a daily basis. She followed her interests to work in a restaurant away from home.

Ramon describes two points of view of how some people remain caught in the vicious poverty cycle while others chose to leave in order to be able to help themselves and others.

Hay dos visiones muy diferentes. Una manera de ver nuestra situación cuando somos pobres es de tratar de detener a los hijos como mis

There are two different visions. One way to see our situation when we're poor is to try and hold back our children like my parents who didn't

padres que no querian apoyarme cuando quería ir a la Universidad porque sabian que no podian seguir apoyandome con fondos. Asi es que me desanimaron. Y en la familia de Chela, los padres no querian que estudiara la sobrina de ella porque los padres necesitan que les ayude a la familia en el campo.

Y Chela y yo pues nos tuvimos que ir de nuestras casas para poder concocer más y hacer por nosotros. Yo me vine para acá, los Estados unidos y ella salió a trabajar afuera de la casa en la loncheria porque le gustava el negocio de comida y restaurate.

Yo creo que nosotros ahora estamos en mejor posición para ayudarles a nuestras familias y a otros que si nos huvieramos quedado en el rancho con todos allí.

want to support me to go to the university because they knew that they could not support me financially. So they discouraged me. And in Chela's family, the parents didn't want her niece to study because the girl's parents needed her to help the family in the fields.

And, Chela and I, well we had to leave our homes to learn more and to help ourselves. I came here to the United States and she went to work outside of her own home in the taqueria because she liked the food and restaurant business.

I think that we now are in better position to help our families and others than if we had stayed on the ranch with everyone.

Just as Chela found the strength to leave home, so did Ramon when he followed his father to the United States. As the oldest of nine children, seven boys and two girls, he lived at home in the ranch or in his small store and helped to raise the younger children until the age of 19 when he left to come with his father to work in agriculture in California. Ramon's father came to work in the Sacramento area with the bracero program. He stayed and became a citizen. His father came to California after working in Arizona and brought Ramon with him for the first time.

Ramon's route to Carpinteria was paved by his father's brother-in-law who came to work in Los Angeles. About that time Ramon was feeling a bit restless in his home town of Zacualco where his small business was successful to some degree but not without a price. Ramon came to join them to work in LA and when they came up to work in Carpinteria, he followed his cousin.

Cuando estaba allí en la tienda iba bien el negocio. Ya había pagado lo que le debía a mi tío. Este, ya estaba yo solvente en gastos. Pero había bien mucha pobreza. En el pueblo hay bien mucha pobreza y este tiene uno . . . Pues su gente de

When I was in the store the business was good. I had paid the debts I owed to my uncle. I was quite solvent in my expenses. But there was a great deal of poverty. In the town, there is lots of poverty and one has to . . . Well, the

uno ahí van a la tienda, al mercado, y van con poco dinero y a veces necesitan lo más basico. Que azúcar. que arroz. que frijol. Y no tienen dinero. Unos porque trabajan en el campo y a veces el trabajo es temporal y no paga bueno.

townspeople go to the store, to the market, and they have little money and sometimes they need just the basics. Sugar. Rice. Beans. And, they don't have money. Some because they work in the fields and its seasonal work and the pay is not good.

Otros porque se lo gastan en el alcohol. Entonces las personas vienen mucho a que les fíes. Me pedian, '¿Me puedes fiar dinero?' '¿Me puedes fiar comida?' 'Y te pago y te pago.' Pero no.

And, others because they spend it on alcohol. So many want credit. They asked, 'Can you loan me some money?' 'Can you give me some food on credit?' 'I'll pay you. I'll pay you.' But they wouldn't.

Así me la pasaba. El corazón de uno no es muy duro y les fiaba cosas y luego muchas veces no me pagaban. Me estaba yendo bien pero era mi ilusión de tener más grande la tienda y de tener un poco de dinero.

And, that's the way it went. My heart isn't very tough and I gave them things on credit and manytimes they didn't pay me. I was doing well, but it was my illusion to have a larger story and to have a bit more money.

Y así fue como decidí para venirme. Este, mi ilusión era nada más trabajar un año, agarrar mi dinero y regresarme y trabajar alla en mi tienda. Además que el local no era propio. Tenía que pagar renta, y para entonces ya me estaban pidiendo el local a cada rato la dueña porque miraba que había negocio.

And, that's the way I decided to come [to the US]. My illusion was to work only one year, earn some money and return to work in my store. But the place wasn't my own. I had to pay rent and by then, they were asking for the place because they saw that there was business.

El dueño me dijó. 'Y me pagas más o dejas el negocio.' Y no tenía contrato, era solamente de mes a mes. Pero esa era mi intención de venir un tiempo nada más y regresarme a estar en la tienda. Y ya van como 20 años aquí.

The owner said, 'You pay me or leave the business.' I didn't have a contract, it was just month to month. But, that was my intention to stay a while and return to stay in the store. Now we've been here twenty years.

The first visit home to Zacualco after being in the US was a fifteen-day vacation during which time he met Chela. At that time she worked in a restaurant and they spent nine days together then he returned to Carpinteria.

Zacualco, Jalisco was a long way from Carpinteria, California and even farther since he had romantic interests that occupied his mind. Chela recalls that he sent an average of one letter per month.

By the time Chela met Ramon, she had already experienced many difficult times in her early childhood. She left school in the second grade because her parents did not have money to send her to the doctor for recurring headaches. Chela finally tired of not being able to read and write in school and at home. Her absences became frequent. She left school after the second grade and helped her parents to do work in the ranch to help support the family. Without money her parents could not take her to a doctor. Chela's mother convinced her that the headaches were mere excuses to avoid attending school.

No me salí de la escuela. Deje de ir por dolor de cabeza. Lo único que me dijó mi mamá, 'Bueno, si tu no quieres ir a la escuela no vayas. Yo no te obligó. Si no quieres, tu sabrás.' Pero ella si me dijó, 'Es muy importante las escuela.' Y ahora lo miro que si es.

I didn't leave school. I stopped attending because of my headaches. The only thing my mother said was, 'Well, if you don't want to go to school you don't have to go. I won't insist on it. If you don't want to, it's up to you.' But she did say, 'School is very important.' and now I see it's true.

Sí, es muy importante porque a veces el niño me pregunta cosas que no puedo ayudarle. Pero, pues no había dinero también para curarse uno. Después, cuando yo entre a la loncheria, fuí a Guadalajara y me adaptaron lentes.

It's very important because sometimes my son asks me things and I can't help him. But there wasn't money to cure oneself. Afterwards, when I went to work in the taqueria, I was able to go to Guadalajara and I get fitted for glasses.

A couple of years after leaving school Chela began working for a woman who owned a store. She swept and mopped the store.

En la loncheria donde trabajé la señora vendía sena ahí es donde comencé a trabajar de niña. Yo creo que tendría unos once años cuando empecé a trabajar ahí limpiando. Era poquito lo que me daba pero servía para algo en la casa. Y ya después entre a una tostaderia como por un año a hacer tostadas.

The woman's Café opened for dinner. That's where I began working as a child I think I was 11 years old when I began working there, cleaning the place. She paid me a meager amount, but it helped my family a bit. Later I began working in a tostaderia (taqueria-like place where they made tostadas). I was there for a year making tostadas.

Casi nunca me gusto [hacer trabajo] de criada. Decía yo no me meto a trabajar en casa no me

I never liked working as a housekeeper doing housework in people's houses. I used to say that I

gusta. A mi me gustó mucho lo de negocio. El negocio si me gusta.

would not go into any house to work. I used to like working in businesses.

Y pues estuve como un año ahí en la tostaderia. Me salí de ahí. Y a los 15 años entonces yo entré al restaurante ahí y me salí para casarme a los 23. Casi duré 8 años trabajando ahí.

And, so I stayed about one year. I left there and went to a factory where I stayed for a brief time. At the age of 15, I went to work at the restaurant. Then, I left at 23 to get married. I worked there 8 years.

Chela feels pleased to have had the opportunity to work even though it was difficult for her at times since the hours were long and the pay was low. Nevertheless, she was able to keep a little bit of money for herself. Most of the money she earned went to her parents but she felt that it was important to keep at least a small amount for herself because she felt a bit of independence. She also felt grateful that she did not have to contribute all of her money to her family as did all of her older brothers and sisters to support the household as the family was quite large.

All of her siblings had to work in the family farm that grew corn and beans and still had to work outside the home. By the time Chela began working, there were fewer children living at home and although they often went hungry, it was less severe than her older siblings faced. With tear-filled eyes Chela recounts some of the most austere times in her home as a child.

Aveces no había nada que comer. Y luego a un punto mi papá se enfermó cuando le picó una vibora.

Sometimes there was nothing to eat. Then at one point my father became ill when a snake bit him and he could not work.

El pasó dos años. Siempre había más pobreza para los mayores que para nosotros porque tenian más personas que mantener.

He spent two years sick in bed. There was always more poverty for the oldest ones than for us because they had more of us to support.

Cuando yo comensé a trabajar, habían solamente cuatro, dos mujers y dos hombres. Para entonces mi papa podía trabajar y los días de hambre fueron menos.

When I began working, there were only four of us kids remaining at home, two girls, and two boys. By then, my father was able to work again and our hungry days were fewer.

Nuestra casa era de nosotros porque la heredamos de mi abuela quien fincó esta casa de un solo cuarto y se la dejó a mi mamá. Siquiera no teniamos que preocuparnos por casa. Pero era la pobreza que veía diario.

Our home was ours because we inherited it from my grandmother who built this one room adobe house and left it to my mother. At least we did not have to worry about a home. But it was the poverty that I saw daily.

Me decia yo, 'Si algún día me llego a casar si dios quire y si no, me quedo trabajado, decía yo porque no me quiero quedar como mis hermanos. Un niño por aca, otro por la mano, otro cargado en el otro brazo.' Eso es muy duro. Es muy duro. Es una vida muy dura.

I said to myself, 'If some day I marry or if God wants me to [marry] and if not, well, I'll just remain working because I don't want to end up like my brothers and sisters with one kid here and another by the hand, and holding another in the other arm.' That's hard. That's a hard life.

Todos ellos [mis hermanos] dicen lo que dicía mi mama, 'cada niño viene con su torta.' Pero ahora ven que no es cierto.

All my brothers and sisters used to say what my mother said, 'All children come with their own food.' But now they see that it's not true.

A desire to improve their economic educational opportunities drove Ramon and Chela to Carpinteria where they both work in the agricultural industry and became legalized during when the amnesty law was enacted. Twenty years after their arrival to Carpinteria, work, marriage and three children, Miguelito (11 years old), Mona (8 years old) and Marcos (3 months old) occupy their time. Ramon continues to work in a nursery in charge of outdoor plants. Chela works in a factory making dried flower arrangements. And, while Miguelito and Mona have experienced a great deal of academic success, their parents have learned along with them as to the best way to help their children in school.

Chela feels limited by her lack of formal education and admits to feeling shame when Miguelito asks her why she is always encouraging and urging them to value school when she herself didn't even go to school. 'Yo le explico que me salí de la escuela porque no podía estudiar en el dolor de cabeza y la pobreza me pohibió poder ver a un doctor. (I explain to him that I left school because I couldn't study due to my headaches.)'

Chela feels the need to return to school but now her limitations are time since she is quite committed in caring for Ramon, the three children, and working full-time to pay a mortgage which they encumbered two years ago. Although this sounds as if she feels powerful about her situation, that is not the case. She reads self-help books in Spanish and tries to study English. In fact, it was Chela's ingenious skill with finances, planning, discipline, and her tenacity that enabled the family to save enough money to buy a small two-bedroom condo where they now live.

Ramon credits the stability of the family to Chela who spends a great deal of time with the children while he's at night meetings. She also helps her niece in Mexico with money and support to study psychology in the university in Guadalajara and to prepare to become a teacher. Ramon also credits Chela for maintaining the emotional warmth of the family which was a part of her own family's way of relating to one another. Ramon feels that the family has a lot of faith in God, and especially appreciates conversations in Chela's family which occurred but to a lesser degree in his family. Although, he did remember his mother telling him she loved him. But when Chela's family gets together Ramon says, 'Uno sabe que hablan con el corazón. (One knows they speak with their heart.)'

Chela revels on the love she and her children share but she also feels strongly that sometimes poor parents expect too much of children because they worked hard as children and later want their children to support them. Chela believes that such expectations create too much pressure for children and may disillusion them from studying in school.

Yo quiero hacerlo diferente a como fue mi familia y como se ve en muchas otras familias. Algunos padres esperan que los hijos los mantengan cuando los niños trabajen.

Es que yo no espero a mis hijos que me mantengan cuando crescan. Yo solo quiero que ellos estudien y llegen a ser personas bien educados y que se dediquen a una carrera.

I want to do it differently from that of my family and many other families. Some parents expect their children to support them when the children start working.

I do not want my children to support me when they grow up. I only want them to study and to become well-educated individuals and to devote themselves to a career.

Ramon's participation in COPLA inspired in him a new way of thinking, about himself, his family and community such that he has committed himself to mobilization of Latinos. He believes that people must engage in their local settings to improve conditions for education of children and to build a major community. He attributes part of his new found political and social consciousness to a personal search, part of which has been revealed to him in the workplace. He has grown through the conflicts in the workplace and in turn the workplace has improved as a result of Ramon's tenacity.

Yo creo que una de las cosas que he ayudo ajustarme [a la cultura Americana] es como que andaba buscando algo.

Como que aquí [en Carpinteria] habia la posibilidad de progresar. No tenía que depender de otras personas como, se te da el valor que, como personas.

Y a veces como que antes me sentía que mi valor dependía de lo que tenía no de lo que era. Ahora me siento que tengo valor por lo

I think that one of the things that has helped me to adjust [to American culture] rapidly has been my questing about something.

And, here [in Carpinteria] I feel like here I found many possibilities to progress. I feel like I don't have to depend on anyone for my worth.

Before, I felt like my worth depended on what I had, not on how much and what I had, rather than who I am as a person. I feel

que soy y lo que puedo hacer. Aprecio la libertad que tiene uno para hacerlo sin miedo. Yo creo que eso es lo que me más ha influido.

He aprendido muchisimo de usted y de la Sra. Rosa Martinez, usted la conoce, y de otra gente en las escuelas y de las amistades de mi esposa.

Todo lo que he aprendido de todos ustedes me ha ayudado parar de tomar y poder estudiar y encontrar más recursos para mis niños. En mi trabajo es donde paso la mayoría de mi tiempo. Y es cierto que he tenido tiempos muy duros.

Por ejemplo, cuando el supervisor nos apresionaba mucho y no quería que nos comunicaramos con el patrón. El mayordomo nos hacía miserable la vida con la pressión que nos ponía y nos prohibía hablar con el patron.

Pero, ví el cambio en el mayordomo cuando fuí a la escuela a aprender el inglés y así podía comunicarme con el patrón. Han cambiado las cosas en el trabajo. Hasta el supervisor parece como persona diferente. A la mejor sabe que hizó mal. En el fútbol también siento que ha sido muy importante para mi. Yo creo que ahí es donde más, más he influido. Antes, la mayoría tomaba y ahora la mayoría a dejado d tomar. Yo ya no tomo. Ya tengo teimpo.

Antes tomaba un poco y, de un tiempo para acá ya no he tomado. Y así siempre es lo que les ha llamado la atención de que porque no lo podian hacerlo ellos. Y algunos lo han hecho. Han dejado de tomar.

validated by who I am and what I want to do. I appreciate the freedom to do what I want without fear. I believe that's what has influenced me the most.

I have learned a great deal from you, Mrs Rosa Martinez, you know her, and from people in the schools and from my wife's friends.

All I've learned from all of you, has helped me to stop drinking and to study and to find more resources for my children. At my job I've spent most of my time. And, it's true that I've had some difficult times.

For example, when the supervisor put a lot of pressure on us and didn't want us to communicate with the manager. He made our lives miserable with the pressure he put on us and forbid us to talk with the managers.

But, I saw change in the supervisor when I went to school and learned English and then I could communicate with the top boss. Things have changed around the workplace. Even the supervisor seems like a different person. Maybe he understood that he was doing wrong. Also in soccer I think it's been very important for me. I think that is where I have had the most, most influence. Before, the majority [of the adult players] drank; now they have stopped drinking. I no longer drink. It's been a while now.

Before, I used to drink and for sometime. That's what has always got their attention, why it was that I could do it and they couldn't. And some have done it. They've stopped drinking.

Although soccer has been a learning as well as a healing experience, Chela continues to struggle with Ramon because of the time he spends away from home while she's left at home with all of the household responsibility and the family. She's aware that Ramon has improved opportunities of their family and others in the community. However, some of his commitment to the community has shaken some of their personal stability. As I complete this chapter she has talked about her feelings of emptiness and aloneness which was heightened when she found herself alone at the hospital having her third child. It seemed that she went into labor on Saturday and could not find Ramon because he was at a weekend part-time gardener job and Chela did not have that phone number. Fortunately, her sister-in-law drove her to the hospital. Chela had the baby within forty-five minutes and Ramon did not arrive in time for the birth.[2]

Soccer game, Migrant Education meeting, COPLA meeting or not, the Mendez family has made time for a couple of weeks during the summer to visit their families in Mexico. Their families look forward to Ramon and Chela visiting with their children, because they receive so much from them. By this, I do not mean the material goods that the Mendez generously bestow on their family but they look to them for advice and guidance. One of the ongoing issues in the family has been the question of Chela's niece attending the university while the parents need her to work and contribute to the family support. During their 1994 vacation in Zacualco, Ramon talked with his brother-in-law that the family had to support Chayo, Chela's niece.

Le dije que lo más importante que puedes hacer es darle la confíanza a tu hija. Le dije que ella tiene muchas ganas de superarse y aunque no le puedas ayudar economicamente si le puedes ayudar mucho moralmente. Díje, 'Ayudala, apoyala, apoyala. No te vas a arrepentir. Buscale la manera.'

I told him that the most important thing that he could do was to give to his daughter his confidence. I told him that she wants very badly to develop herself and even if you can't help her economically, you can help her with moral support. I said to him, 'Help her, support her, support her. You won't regret it. Find a way.'

Chela and Ramon both take money down to their families. Usually it's money which Chela has managed to save during the year. She had some humorous anecdotes about taking clothing down to their families.

Miguelito y Mona tienen muchas cosas que pueden compartir con sus primos en Mexico. Llevan jugetes, ropa y materiales de escuela. Pero una de las cosas poco chistosas es que Miguelito dice algo como así,

Miguelito and Mona have lots of things they share with their cousins in Mexico. They take toys, clothes and some school materials. But one of the funny things is that Miguelito will say something like 'Thanks to

'Gracias a dios tenemos mucho y podemos regalarles cosas a nuestros primos.' Mientras que Mona se pone más resistente para regalar. Ella me dice, 'Ya te dí muchas cosas y me dejas sin ropa.'

Yo le digo que le compro más y ella me dice, 'No, no te lleves estos, son bonitos y me gustan y son mios. Me gustan y me gustan así es que dejalos aquí.' Así es, y así es. Pero de cualquier manera, les llevamos bastante a nuestros familiares.

God we have so much and we can give some things to my cousins.' Mona, on the other hand, is more resistant to giving. She'll say to me, 'I've already given you lots of things and you're leaving me without any clothes.'

I tell her that I'll buy her some more and she says, 'No don't take these, they're pretty and they're mine. I like them so leave them here.' That's the way she is but anyway, we take plenty to our relatives.

Both Ramon and Chela feel very grateful for all that they have received in life and feel even more privileged to be able to share it with other family members, friends and people brought into their life in a variety of ways. Just as they are quick to acknowledge their opportunities to give to others, they are just as appreciative to others for what they have received. Ramon expresses his gratitude to those whom he believes have influenced the changes in his life.

Nosotros hemos aprendido mucho de usted [Concha]. Yo siempre le he dicho, ¿sabe qué? Usted me tuvó confianza y eso vale bien mucho.

Me abrió a saber que yo podia y de saber que debo de estar abierto y ser positivo porque todos tenemos nuestra fortaleza. Y así he seguido aprendiendo del Señor Niles. Y así es seguido siempre abierto para todas las personas y me he hecho más sensible. Y me a hecho mejor. Me siento mucho fuerte.

We have learned a great deal from you [Concha]. I have always said that. Do you know what? You have had confidence in me and that's worth a great deal.

It has opened my consciousness to know that I could do whatever and to know that I needed to remain positive because we all have our own strengths. And that's the way I have continued learning from Mr Niles. And that's the way I have remained open to all people, and I have become more sensible. I've become a better person. I feel much stronger.

As president of the Carpinteria School District Migrant Education Parent Committee, Ramon has maintained his integrity in terms of his goal for getting people to collaborate with each other on behalf of all children in the school district. His specific advocacy is for Spanish-speaking Latino students who have continued to be overrepresented in the lower academic ranks.

Although Ramon spends a great deal of time away at school and community meetings, his top priority has always been and remains his children. Manuelito, who is now in the sixth grade, waits for him to return home on nights when Ramon has meetings so that he can help Manuelito with homework. He has been known to wait quite late, but he prefers to do that. Ramon's favorite task is to return home at night and help his children with his homework or, if they've completed their homework, he enjoys reading them a story. Chela says her stories to the children are shorter because even with glasses, she still gets bad headaches when she reads a lengthy piece. Ramon has a special story which he learned at a parent conference. All five, Ramon, Chela, Manuelito, and Mona sit and listen to the bedtime story told by Ramon.

English summary of bedtime story

This story tells of a mother's relationship with her son to whom she sang and rocked him to sleep since he was an infant. As the son grew, regardless of how old he was, she would sing to him and rock him to sleep. When he became an adolescent, she tolerated his loud music, crazy friends and odd-looking clothes. But when he came home late, she walked into his room and sang to him and rocked him to sleep. The mother continued her devotion to care for her son even when he left home and married and had his own children. When she became old, her son visited his mother and when his mother could no longer finish the familiar song which she sang to him, he finished it for her. And on the day she died, her son took his mother in his arms and sang to her and rocked her and then he went home and walked into his little daughter's room just as his mother always did with him. And, he took her in his arms and sang the same song he heard from his mother throughout his life and then rocked her back and forth, back and forth just as his mother always rocked him all of his life.

Story in Spanish

Una madre cargaba su nuevo bebé y muy despacio lo arrullaba de aquí para alla y de alla para aca. Y mientras lo arruyaba le cantaba, 'Para siempre te amaré, para siempre to querre. Mientras en mí halla vida siempre serás mi bebé.' El bebé crecía, crecía y crecía. A los dos años el niño corría por la casa. Jalaba los libros de los estantes. Sacaba toda la comida del refrigerador y cogía el reloj de su mamá y lo tiraba en el suelo. Algunas veces su mamá decía, 'Este niño me esta enloqueciendo.' Pero cuando llegaba la noche a aquel niño de dos años finalmente tranquilo, ella abría la puerta de su cuarto. Caminaba cuidadosamente hasta su cama y miraba a su hijo desde ahí abajo. Y si realmente el estaba dormido, ella lo levantava y lo arrullaba de aquí para alla y de alla para aca.

Y mientras lo arrullaba le cantaba, 'Para siempre te amaré, para siempre te querré. Mientras en mí halla vida siempre serás mi bebé.' El niño crecía y crecía. A los nueve años nunca quería llegar a cenar. Nunca quería tomar un baño y cuando llegaba la abuela de visita, siempre decía palabras muy malas. Algunas veces su mamá deseaba venderlo al zoölogico. Pero cuando llegaba la noche y el muchacho estaba dormido. La madre silenciosamente abría la puerta de su cuarto. Caminaba cuidadosamente hasta su cama y miraba a su hijo desde ahí abajo y si realmente el estaba durmiendo, ella levantaba a aquel muchacho de nueve años y lo arrullaba. De aquí para alla y de alla para aca. Y mientras lo arrullaba le cantaba, 'Para siempre de amaré, para siempre te querré. Mientras en mí halla vida siempre serás mi bebé.'

El niño crecía, crecía, y crecía. Crecía hasta que llegó a ser un joven. Tenía amigos raros. Se vestía con ropa rara. Escuchaba música rara. Algnas veces la mamá sentía estar en un zoölogico. Pero cuando llegaba la noche y el joven estaba dormido, la madre silenciosamente abría la puerta de su cuarto, caminaba hasta su cama y miraba su hijo desde ahí abajo. Y si realmente él estaba durmiendo, ella levantaba a aquél muchachote y lo arrullaba de aquí para alla y de alla para aca. Y mientras lo arrullaba le cantaba, 'Para siempre te amaré, para siempre te querré. Mientras en mí halla vida siempre seras mi bebé.' Aquél joven crecía, crecía y crecía. Crecía hasta que llegó a ser un hombre. Entonces se fue de la casa y se cambió para una propiedad para el otro lado del pueblo. Pero algunas veces cuando las noches estaban muy obscuras, la madre sacaba su automóvil y se dirijía especialmente a la casa de su hijo. Y si estaban apagadas las luces en la casa de su hijo, ella abría la ventana de su cuarto. Entraba caminaba cuidadosamente por el piso y miraba a su hijo desde ahí abajo. Y si realmente ese hombre bien grande estaba dormido ella lo levantaba y lo arrullaba. De aquí para alla y de alla para acá. Y mientras lo arrullaba le cantaba, 'Para siempre te amaré, para siempre te querré. Mientras en mí halla vida siempre seras me bebé.' Bueno, atraves del tiempo aquella madre envejecia, envejecia. Un día llamó a su hijo y le dijó, 'Sería mejor que vinieras a verme porque ya estoy muy vieja y enferma.' Entonces su hijo fue a verla. Cuando él entro a su cuarto, ella trató de cantarle la canción. Para siempre te amare, para siempre te qurre. Pero ella no pudo terminar la canción porque ya era demasiado vieja y enferma. El niño se acercó a su madre. La levantó y la arruyó de aquí para alla y de alla para aca. Y mientras la arrullaba le cantó, 'Para siempre te amaré, para siempre te querré. Mientras en mí halla vida siempre seras mi mamá.' Cuando el hijo regresó a su casa esa misma noche se quedó pensativo por largo tiempo a lo alto de las gradas. Luego entró a la casa y entró al cuarto de su hija y se le acercó. La levantó y la arruyó de aquí para alla y de alla para acá . . .

Ramon admits that of everything he has learned in his years of community activism, his connection with his children has been the most critical. Even if in his own school years he did not appreciate reading very much, as a parent and family advocate with the school, he recognizes the value of family literacy and the closeness of sharing time together. The repetition of language in this story conveys rhythm, not only in language but also in the love and care shared between the parents and children.

Maria and Her Family

Maria and her family were one of the first families in Carpinteria with whom I made contact. I met her in 1985 through her son who was in preschool. In my observation of the bilingual preschool parent meetings I could not miss Maria's eloquent and caring statements on whatever the topic was discussed. Quickly she became a valued collaborator whose insights about her life, her family's life, and the life of the community propelled the study in Carpinteria. I trained her along with other community members to assist me in data collection involving specific interviews throughout the years of research.

When I first met Maria, her husband, Alfredo and three children, Armando, Gloria and Raul lived in a one-room recreational trailer which was parked in a lot for recreational vehicles in the outskirts of Carpinteria. When the children were younger and smaller the Rosarios managed much better than when the children grew taller and bigger and their need for privacy was crucial. They creatively added more space for their oldest son by erecting a small tool shed adjacent to the trailer. This angered the lot owner to whom they paid rent to park their trailer and he tried to evict them. Unable to afford an apartment or home, the Rosarios were forced to remove the fixture until the owner forgot the incident, and they attempted it again and again and again. This and other strategies were common on a regular basis to manage their survival on a slim budget where a two-income is sufficient for food and small rent.

Alfredo, Maria's husband has a steadier job than Maria. He has been employed by a printing company where he has continued to advance. Maria's employment, on the other hand, has been irregular. Upon arriving in Carpinteria in 1982, she worked in McDonald's but left the organization when she tired of conflicts with the manager who insisted on dumping extra food while Maria insisted on taking the excess bread to poor families she knew were hungry. Thereafter, she worked part-time in a community preschool where she began to apply some of the preparation in developmental psychology which she learned in the University in Mexico. Although she only spent one year at the university, she always desired to resume her studies.

Maria's involvement in COPLA later helped her to meet school personnel who recognized her skills and knowledge about children which helped her get a job as a part-time teacher assistant in a bilingual classroom.

Maria loves and understands children so well in the classroom that, after extensively working with her family, I learned that her work in the classroom was an extension of her love and care for her own children. Maria's childhood was filled with books and expectation to learn and nurture others. She was the eldest of ten children, four boys and six girls, all born in Mexico City. Her family were people of modest means but her parents managed to provide Maria with a loving homelife that held high expectations for her to be educated and to follow a career.

Mis padres siempre querian que estudiaramos y nos apoyaron con libros. Teníamos muchos libros de literatura en nuestra casa.

Todos mis hermanos y hermanas también les gustaba leer y estudiar. Un hermano es abogado y una hermana es física y yo quiero seguir preparandome para ser maestra.

My parents always wanted us to study and they supported us with books. We had many literature books in our home.

All of my brothers and sisters also loved to read and study. One brother is a lawyer and a sister is a physicist and I want to continue my preparation to become a teacher.

When Maria and her family immigrated to Carpinteria she believed in a dream and hopes of great economic and academic success for all of her family. Soon she began to realize how difficult the road would be to fulfill her dreams.

Yo tenía mucho miedo, pues desconocía el sistema y el idioma. Mis hijos tuvieron la fortuna de entrar imediatamente a la escuela, yo estaba contenta por eso. Pero, muy pronto descubrí que mi hijo el mayor, que había entrado en el cuarto grado, estaba teniendo problemas. Así que acudí a la escuela donde el asistía para ver que pasaba.

I was very scared because I was unfamiliar with the system and the language. My children had the good fortune to begin school immediately, and I was happy about that. But, soon I discovered that my oldest son who had started in the fourth grade had problems. So I went to the school he attended to see what was happening.

Al llegar ahí en la escuela me sentí presa de miedo pues nadie hablaba mi idioma más que la directora y una maestra que entonces no conocía.

When I arrived at the school, I felt imprisoned by my fear because no one spoke my language except for the principal and one other teacher whom I did not know at the time.

Cuando hablé con la directora, pues no podía comprobar que era cierto lo que se sopone que habían hecho los niños.

Lo que aprendí fue que ella, la directora, no hacía caso de los

When I spoke with the principal, well she couldn't prove that the boys had done what they supposedly did.

What I learned was that she, the principal, did not pay any attention

niños que no hablaban el inglés. Ahí empece a pensar ideas de la manera para que nosotros los Latinos fueramos escuchados — cuando menos en las escuelas.

to students who did not speak English. There I began to think about ways for us Latinos to be heard — at least in the schools.

The struggle continued with her oldest son in the school as he went up the grades. Armando is very talented in art and was quite interested in history. However, in other subjects, he needed a great deal of motivation and teachers, particularly in junior high, failed to help him make the connections to his subjects. Armando became so disinterested in school that he found himself in remedial classes when his ability exceeded grade level in both English and Spanish.

By the time Armando entered high schools Maria had learned of his resentment against her and Alfredo for uprooting him from Mexico where he loved his friends and grandparents. In a conversation with him about the matter, he told me that he was interested in learning but he didn't think anyone at school cared about what he liked.

A mi me gusta mucho leer y aprender pero no me gusta del modo en cual estos maestros creen que uno porque es Mejicano no sabe nada. Me interesa la historia del arte y yo la leo acá aparte de la escuela porque no encuentro ninguna clase que me acepté lo que me interesa a mi.

Sí es cierto que no me gusta aquí los Estados Unidos porque, no sé, allá era diferente y siquiera me entendían mis amigos.

I like reading and learning but I don't like the way that these teachers believe that because one is Mexican that we don't know anything. I like history of art and I read it here away from school because I don't find any class at school that accepts what interests me.

It's true that I don't like it here in the US because, I don't know, it was different over there and at least my friends understood me.

When Armando was in high school Maria found that she was spending a great deal of time in school helping Armando negotiate his classes so that he could get the teachers whom she knew cared about students more than others. What Maria learned through trial and error and through the assistance of Paul Niles about ways to help her son later became gifts she brought to COPLA as Latino parents organized. Armando graduated from high school and went to work in the same printing company as his father. Many parents with children in the high school had similar problems as did Maria with Armando.

Maria's middle child, Gloria, presented the school and her parents with problems which made Armando's seem pleasurable. When in the sixth grade she began having problems with some classmates who kept challenging her to defend herself physically and so Gloria struggled with herself about giving in to their taunting. Finally, her mother, Maria, helped her to rise above these issues that kept distracting her from her schoolwork. Maria reinforced her unwavering love and trust in her as a person.

Yo le aseguró que nosotros estamos aquí para ayudarla y que ella tiene que confiar en nosotros porque la queremos. Le digo que tiene que seguir su corazón y deje esas amistades que le aconsejan cosas malas.

Yo le recuerdo que una amistad es una persona que desea lo mejor para uno y que si alguien le dice que no estudies o que tome drogas o que haga mal que esa persona no es amistad.

I assured her that we are here to help her and that she has to trust in us because we love her. I tell her that she has to follow her heart and stop listening to those friends who misguide her.

I remind her that friends are those people who want the best for us and that if someone tells her not to study or wants her to take drugs or do wrong that person is not a friend.

Gloria's academic and social problems persisted in school, but they seemed manageable to Maria until one night when she found herself driving her daughter to the hospital to pump her stomach because she had taken an overdose of pills. After extensive counseling, Gloria appeared to feel better about herself and her studies, or so it seemed to her mother, until she found Gloria intoxicated and had to call the doctor.

Maria, meanwhile continued not only her daytime job but additionally, assumed another part-time job selling natural products. She had hoped to save enough money to buy a larger trailer or maybe even procure a small house of their own to end the daily squabbles at the trailer court and their congested situation. Years passed, however, and Maria and her family were still in the trailer court because many life crises interfered with the family's ability to accumulate enough money for a down-payment. She occasionally made comments to me such as the following which led me to believe that her tenacity had roots deeper than her dreams: 'Cuando estábamos en la Ciudad de México, había oído decir que aquí [en los Estados Unidos] se disfrutaba de mejor vida y educación para los niños. Lo que no me dijieron era que todo eso me costaría muchas lágrimas y sufrimientos. (When we lived in Mexico City, I had heard that here [in the United States] one could enjoy a better life and education for the children. What no one told me was that it would cost me many tears and suffering.)'

Maria's collaboration with other parents and her work in the schools provided her with a voice to express her knowledge and experience of family, learning and hope which she believed to be possible even through the daily strife of poor immigrant life in Carpinteria. Meanwhile, she and Alfredo struggled with their family problems such that she was forced to minimize her participation in COPLA events. Although she attended few COPLA meetings, she continued her commitments to the organization by serving on the committee for the selection of a new superintendent which eventually hired Dr Pablo Seda. While this level of participation in the superintendent selection committee, was difficult for Maria, as one of the representatives from COPLA, she believed it was necessary to involve herself in the selection of the key administrator in the school district. Her painful experiences of discrimination in schools was due to the absence of non-Spanish-speaking personnel to communicate with Latino families. Maria's commitment to children and communication between families and schools made COPLA a viable unit in which to collaborate with others.

En mi experiencia con mis hijos en sus escuelas, he tenido muchos problemas con personal que no habla español. Y creo que todos los demas Latinos también han tenido ese problema.

Lo que yo no me explíco tan facilmente es porque todos los padres no toman acción como deben por sus deberes. Me he dado cuenta de la aucencia de participación de padres Latinos.

No solo en COPLA pero en todo mi trabajo me he dedicado a preguntar a otros padres la razón de su apatía asi las reuniónes escolares.

Antes de COPLA, muchos padres me han contestado de esta manera, '¿A qué vamos? si no entendemos nada de lo que dicen. Preferimos llegar a comer y descansar a la casa después del trabajo.'

In my experience with my children in their schools, I have had many problems with personnel who don't speak Spanish. I think that all other Latinos have also had that problem.

What I don't understand so easily is why it is that parents don't take action like they should for their children's rights. I've become aware of the absence of participation of Latino parents in schools.

Not only in COPLA but in all of my other work I have dedicated myself to asking other parents as to the reason for their apathy regarding their school-related meetings.

Before COPLA, many parents answered in this way, 'Why should we go? We don't understand anything they say. We prefer to go home and eat and rest after work.'

Maria's involvement in COPLA was characterized by a sense of honesty and critical questioning about parents assuming responsibility and presence in the schools. She was always known to provide a wide perspective and understanding of the issues at hand. That is, just as she was inclined to ask parents who complained about the teachers when was the last time that they visited the classroom in question, she was just as quick to ask the school personnel about their plans to rectify whatever problem was at hand. Maria holds all parties responsible for correcting whatever problem may impede children's opportunity for learning.

Her youngest son, Raul, currently in junior high, receives most of her attention because Armando, the oldest graduated from high school and is working. Gloria, left high school to marry and have a child.

Mi hijo más pequeño ha tenido mejor suerte en sus estudios porque ha tenido buenos maestros desde el principio en el Preschool.

Ha tenido la suerte de estar más adelantado en sus clases. Recibe buenas notas en casi todas sus materias. Tengo mucha esperanza en que salga con una carera buena.

My youngest son has had better luck in his studies because he has had good teachers since the beginning in preschool.

He has been fortunate to be more advanced in his classes. He gets good grades in almost all of his classes. I have a lot of hope that he can get a good career.

Maria attributes Raul's academic achievement in school to his successful start with Mrs Celia Marquez who taught the bilingual preschool. Maria believes that if Armando and Gloria had been able to have Celia as their teacher that maybe they would have received a stronger foundation in their education. Celia has been credited by Maria and many other parents with compassion and belief not only in students but in their families. Celia's strength has always been to make the parents co-teachers with her. However, Maria's wishes did not manifest except in the case of her youngest son, and she's equally committed to all children's learning both in the primary grades where she is and has been for years a bilingual teacher assistant and out of school with the families of students whom she befriends. One case stands out in Maria's work with children and their families outside of school.

Maria tutors a young third-grader who was disabled and because she had missed a great deal of school, the student was quite behind in her academic achievement. Most of the time, the little girl, Sonia, used a wheel chair, but at home she could not use it because they lived in an upstairs apartment. Her sister had to carry her on her back to move her around the house and up and downstairs. During Sonia's time with Maria as her tutor, she befriended Maria who became her confidante. Sonia kept Maria informed about her home life and the problems her mother faced trying to keep food on the table and a roof over their head. Sonia's father abandoned the family and her mother had finally found a job. And, to help the family financially, Sonia's mother had accepted that her brother, Sonia's uncle stay with them. Sonia did not like her uncle because he was mean and yelled at her and her older sister when he was intoxicated. Sonia's older sister cared for Sonia at home. She helped to bathe her and cooked her meals and helped with other care while the mother worked. Maria had tried to help Sonia to deal with her anger about the uncle who was mean and out of the kindness of her heart she visited Sonia's mother to relay Sonia's fears about the uncle. The mother was quite aware of the difficult situation under which they were forced to live, but she did not see a way out of the predicament.

Maria informed Sonia's mother about community agencies which were affordable and had Spanish-speaking staff who could help her to deal with her problems at home. Maria noticed improvement with Sonia's emotional and psychological frame of mind which seemed more stable and enabled Sonia to concentrate on her work. However, one day Sonia's appearance was quite disheveled and she seemed quite unkempt. Sonia reported to Maria that she thought that her uncle had molested her older sister because she heard all of it from her room where she spent most of the time in the house. Maria inquired in great detail about this matter and paid a visit to the mother who became enraged to hear of this. The mother called the police and had her brother arrested. Sonia's ability to concentrate was unstable for days following and then stabilized such that Maria believed they were finally able to make real progress in her reading.

Maria knew that the ordeal wasn't over when Sonia showed up to the tutoring session and announced that her sister feared she was pregnant. Maria could not stay quiet about this either and so she visited the mother who was overwhelmed about the problem and felt powerless because she had no money to take her daughter to a doctor. Maria intervened and gave the mother the name of a clinic in Santa Barbara where she could receive free service if she could not pay. It turned out that Sonia's sister was not pregnant although she did have anemia and other health problems. Maria continued tutoring Sonia and noticed her progress more steadily as some of the severe home problems abated. Maria was assigned to assist in the preschool and discontinued her tutoring assignment with Sonia. However during the time she tutored her, Maria's faith in Sonia's ability to learn kept Maria in touch with Sonia's family to help in whatever way to assure Sonia a bit more peace of mind and therefore a stronger frame of mind with which to learn.

¡No es fácil! Pero dios puso en mi camino a una profesora de la universidad que trabajó con COPLA y aparte de todo, me ofreció su amistad y la aprecio como oro en polvo. Y aunque se cambió cerca de San Francisco, nunca se olvida de los padres de Carpinteria y sigue colaborando con su asesoramiento y guía con nosotros.

A partir que COPLA entró en acción, el distrito escolar en esta ciudad ha mejorado y sigue mejorando.

Pues ahora ya tenemos

It isn't easy! But God put in my way a professor from the university who worked with COPLA and aside from everything else, she offered me her friendship and I cherish her like gold dust. And even though she moved near San Francisco, she never forgets the parents in Carpinteria and continues to collaborate with us through her professional guidance.

Since COPLA mobilized, the school district in this city has improved and it continues to improve.

Now we have bilingual educators,

profesorado bilingüe, podemos contar con empleados en las escuelas que hablan nuestro idioma, los estudiantes disfrutan de los previlegios que antes no contaban y con asesoramiento y tutorias en sus diferentes materias.

we can count on staff using our language in the schools, students enjoy privileges that before didn't have and with advisors and tutors in various subjects.

Se han dado más becas a nuestros estudiantes y también se han visto más hispanos graduados de High School y entrar a una universidad.

More scholarships have been given to our students and we have also seen more Hispanic students graduate from high school and enter a university.

En cuanto a nosotros como familia, hemos tenido más comunicación entre nosotros, y mi esposo se ha portado más comprensivo con mis hijos y participa más en su educación.

Where my family is concerned, we have more communication among ourselves, and my husband is more compassionate with my children. He participates more in their education.

Algo que me dá mucha satisfación es que mi esposo mismo ha progresado en su trabajo y le han dado deseos de estudios alguna carera.

Something that gives me great satisfaction is that my husband has progressed in his work and is thinking of studying for a career.

As for Maria, she is currently feeling quite happy as a teacher assistant in preschool. Her most exciting recent accomplishment is being able to clear some of her evenings to attend classes at the community college that will lead towards a teacher credential. She feels particularly hopeful that with her teaching credential, she will be able to remain close to children and families to help them advance their personal and political consciousness and thus continue contributing to the community.

Notes

1 Anthropologist, Kondo, 1990 specifically argues that selves are crafted in processes of work and within practices of power which reflects the position that experience and practice are inseparable.

2 Two months following my last formal interview with Chela and Ramon Méndez they contacted me and wanted to talk openly about their marital problems. Initially, they merely wanted me to listen to them because they did not have anyone else to talk with them about this question and the priest they had already consulted didn't feel he had anymore to offer on the subject. I was hurt by the case because they were like family to me and marital counseling was not one of my skills. I, nevertheless, felt honored that they would trust me enough as a friend to discuss their very sensitive personal life with me in hopes that I could assist them. Once I moved

passed my emotional attachment to thinking that I had to 'fix' their marriage, I had an intellectual curiosity about their approach to resolving their marital problem since I had been privileged to see their strategies in solving other issues in their life that involved their identity to their community and their cultural adaptation to a new language, a new community and a new society. I had three conversations with them personally and on the phone and on the third one, I recognized that their problem was intensifying beyond what I as a friend who lived 700 miles away could effectively do. I recommended a Spanish-speaking counselor in Santa Barbara. They were most grateful because they felt they were ready to talk to someone professionally. They called me after a couple of visits and they wanted to inform me that they were doing all right and that their problems were by no means solved but they were willing to start talking like friends and maybe through the friendship that they felt they always had, they could learn ways to solve their marital problems. They are currently working on becoming friends again and beginning to talk to each other more openly on this level of communication to redefine their relationship with each other and their family and the pressures of community activism.

I do believe that their process in solving their marital problems conforms with the protean directions they employed through their lives to overcome strife and adversity and exemplified the love and care which defined their community activism with COPLA and other community activities.

Chapter 5

Protean Pedagogy

'Nuevos Amigos'

Había una vaz un gatito que no podía caminar pero un perrito fue a salvarlo y se fueron a descansar. Después, el gatito no quería quedarse en la casa solo. Después, el perrito se lo llevó a la casa de él. Él le pusó una curita y después cuando se la quitó, ya podía caminar el gatito y podía jugar. Después, encontró al Pato Donald en el parque donde estaban jugando y el gatito fue a jugar con ellos dos — el Pato Donald y el perrito. Se hicieron amigos los tres. Cuando acabaron de jugar 'Simon Says', se fueron a sus casas los tres y se hablaron por teléfono.

'New Friends'
(Story told by 8-year-old Roberto)
Once there was a little cat that could not walk, but, a dog saved the cat and they went to rest. Later, the little cat did not want to stay at the dog's house. So then the dog took the little cat to its home. The little cat put on a band-aid and when the cat took it off he could walk and play. Later the cat met Donald Duck in the park where they were playing. Later the little cat went to play with Donald Duck and the dog. The three became friends. When they finished playing 'Simon Says', they each went to their own home and called each other on the telephone.

With reference to family–school relationships, concerns of the bilingual teacher often coincide with those of non-bilingual teachers. In Carpinteria, parent involvement appears to be more widespread among the primary grade teachers (Kindergarten, 1st, 2nd and 3rd) although upper grade teachers mentioned various ways they involved parents in their classroom.[1] Overall, an underlying agreement existed in the way that these teachers related to families — that home–school relations are very important and that each situation had the potential to change parent's involvement in their child's schooling that ensued.

Communicating With Traditional Means

Both bilingual and non-bilingual teachers revealed that home–school communication was important in some way. Without initially providing parents with a connection to the school, it would be very difficult to maintain communication. Many teachers described holding Parent–Teacher conferences and doing 'Back to School Night' as their most successful efforts to communicate with parents.

Since these are mandatory events for teachers, they were quick to point out the importance of these events as a way to establish some kind of relationship if the parents attended. Next to meeting personally with parents, teachers noted specific activities which they used to communicate with parents. Most often teachers sent home weekly letters or individual notes on each student while phone calls usually meant negative reports of student behavior. If parents are illiterate and do not have phones, this activity would serve little purpose. More creative methods of contacting parents would then become necessary to communicate with some parents. Both bilingual and non-bilingual teachers assigned homework to involve parents or members of the family. Parents' volunteering in class was most popular with non-bilingual teachers.

Teachers expressed their concern for what kind of time parents spent with their children at home. Many teachers, especially those who had taught for more years, believed that parents did not work at home with their children to the extent that their children needed their support.[2] The lack of parenting skills or the lack of time to spend with their children was described as a problem. Teachers believed that parents should be clothing, feeding, bathing, talking to and providing necessities for their children. Many children come to school hungry, dirty and ill. 'They come from places that could not be defined as homes and arrive at school very unprepared to learn or behave properly.'

In recent years, teachers in Carpinteria have become more vocal about their beliefs that parents, in general, have relinquished much of their parenting to the school. In fact, some teachers felt indignant about the public's expectation to have them replace the parents' role. Teachers expected parents to provide children with their basic needs like food, health, emotional, psychological and academic preparation.[3] Along with having parents supply children's physical needs, teachers also wanted parents to support the school by helping children do homework and to acquire primary literacy skills prior to entering school. By defining parent expectations, they limited their role as teachers to imparting information.[4]

Demarcating school and family roles suggested a curriculum which separated the home from school interests. In interviews conducted with forty bilingual and non-bilingual teachers in the primary grades Kindergarten to sixth, 98 percent indicated that parent involvement was, in their terms, 'very important, vital, critical, most important, crucial, and a strong need in the curriculum.'

Teachers commented that communication between parent and teachers is most active in the earlier years. Kindergarten teacher Mrs Vaca, a bilingual teacher who works with Latino parents believes:

> Good home–school communication makes the job easier for the teacher. If parents work closely they will know the teacher's expectations, and

the students will know that the parents and teachers are working together, using rewards and punishment with consistency between parents and teachers. Weekly letters, phone calls, positive notes home, eighteen parent volunteers in the classroom, and help from parents at home are some of the ways I establish and keep home–school relationships. Parents also have my telephone number and they know they can call me until 8.30 in the evening. There is almost 100 percent participation at 'back to school night' and at that time I make a big deal about helping, and much positive reinforcement is given for the parents.

Getting Past Obstacles to Family–School Communication

Thinking of obstacles to good home–school relations was not a problem for most of the teachers. The most common obstacle which teachers identified was the parents' lack of time for their children. Non-bilingual and bilingual teachers cited similar obstacles to communication with parents. However, bilingual teachers, specifically noted that Latino families lack confidence and understanding of the school system including their inability to speak English. Obstacles occur for various reasons even in early grades as Kindergarten teacher, Mrs Stone, a bilingual teacher, confronted.

> I have encountered many obstacles such as parents who cannot read and do not know anyone who they feel comfortable asking for help, parents who do not have phones and do not work or who change jobs so often it is almost impossible to contact them when an issue arises, parents whose overcrowded living situations provide difficult 'home' situations for this relationship to work, and some parents are abusive, alcoholic, and basically absent from their child's life in general.

Mrs Stone credited COPLA for their support in helping Latino parents communicate with their children's teachers. However, teachers need just as much support to stay in close communication with their children.

> Teachers would need more release time to work with parents. Teachers could hold parent-education meetings and workshops. There should also be a community liaison to educate parents in any areas which are foreign or difficult for them. Talented teachers should be given release time to give parent–teacher workshops.

Both bilingual and non-bilingual teachers in all of the primary grades admitted that many obstacles between teachers and parents could not be readily eliminated such as parents' economic positions, unhappy marriages, large families, unsafe living conditions, parents' illiteracy, and the pre-existing attitude that the school is supposed to do it all. A fifth-grade non-bilingual teacher, Ms Smith, who taught both Latino and non-Latino students, felt that parents' attitudes about their role was the issue in conflict with the school's actual role.

> Some obstacles have been that parents lack realistic attitudes. They shouldn't be doing homework for their kids, and shouldn't have the attitude of 'My child can't change because he is just like his father.' If that's the case then what do they expect us to do? They need to expect their children to be able to improve. With single-parent families, kids are not the highest priority, and parents tend to give up on their kids.

Teachers' perceptions and judgments about parents' ability to work with their children such as those represented by Ms Smith raised the question of family–school relationships a high priority. The issue demanded the attention of both families and schools since it was a mutual concern to both. COPLA served that role between Latino parents and the school. Working on a literacy project brought together teachers and Latino parents to deal with questions of underachieving readers.

Family Literacy: Bringing the School Home

The parent organization COPLA in collaboration with me designed a project to assist the parents whose children were underachieving in reading with their children at home. As the researcher, I worked with COPLA and the school district to coordinate a two-year project where the first year was dedicated to teaching the families a literacy program. The second year, parents practiced their reading in the home with their children and my research team visited them periodically to examine how they progressed with their reading. A specific feature of the project involved COPLA parents in the leadership of the family project. Maria Rosario and Antonia Suarez were two of the parents who assisted with the planning of the family literacy classes.

Three major premises guided the family literacy project. These were discussed at COPLA meetings as we talked about the issue and planned the development of the project: (1) That all literacy is based on specific social practices. (2) That children become empowered through interaction with parents about the story text that utilize their personal experience. (3) That intervention involving families must consider the home cultural niche.[5]

COPLA parents became convinced that the more that parents read with children the better readers they become.[6] Many of the parents had participated in the preschool workshops when their children went through the Carpinteria Bilingual Preschool. They believed that during the reading activity with children, parents could teach sociocultural knowledge based on their own experience. Parents convey values, a world view about their position in society and a sense of confidence to their children that they are important enough to receive their parents' attention. Until parents openly discussed these issues with each other in COPLA, they were unaware of the sociocultural knowledge which they shared with their children through reading together.

To understand how to apply this knowledge (knowing one's status and experience in society), the adults wanted to have primary experience in examining texts for their own purpose. COPLA parents concluded that they were more able to teach their children how to reflect on their own experience in relation to storybooks if they, as adults, have been able to practice this with written text of interest to them.

The books selected were: *Rosa Caramelo, A Donde Vas Osito Polar, Historia de los Bonobos con Gafas, El Primer Pajaro de Piko-Niko, Tio Elefante, El Perro Del Cerro, Mira Como Salen Las Estrellas, La Rana De La Sabana* and *Monty.* The books varied in length and the project began with shorter stories and progressed to longer ones.

A variety of questioning strategies were taught to parent-participants for eight sessions. They learned how to discuss book content with their children. At monthly sessions, held at Morton School, parents were given a children's literature book and taught the four types of questioning strategies which would improve their child's involvement in reading.

At each monthly meeting parents discussed the new books, and working in small groups, asked each other questions to model possible ways of interacting with their children. Maria Rosario had a great deal of experience in reading with children and in working with the COPLA parent group. She assisted in the literacy classes while Antonia Suarez organized childcare and children's story hour during the parent literacy meetings. By involving active parents in a variety of capacities, the FLP was strengthened as a result of parents involved in a project designed for their community. Parent leaders served a critical part to those learning new practices regarding their children's schooling. Their participation strengthened the families who participated in the family literacy project.

Parents and teachers met to discuss children's literacy progress. Meetings were usually initiated by parents as recommended by the FLP instructors. Children of the parents in the FLP project were in novice reading groups in their respective classes and parents were encouraged to talk frequently with the teachers and report to them what the children had read at home and their reading sessions at home. In addition to frequent meetings with their child's teacher, families were required to keep a calendar of the materials they read and to report on it at the monthly classes. Therefore, although the FLP class met only once a month, families had a great deal of homework to do including nightly reading sessions, meeting with the child's teacher, recording all of the reading materials and meeting at least once during the month with the research team for an interview and video tape of the parent–child reading together.

Video sessions were scheduled beforehand with the families. Usually, the preferred hour was after dinner or right after school when the parent could sit down with their child to share a book. When we first began video taping the families in their home, they showed reluctance to being observed reading with their children. It was evident in the way that parents and children sat with more distance between them than we noticed in later months of the project. Nonetheless, the interaction around the story revealed that parents felt increasingly comfortable reading with their children. As the months passed the complexity of their discussions enhanced. Parents became more comfortable talking with their children about their own beliefs, perspectives, attitudes, criticisms, likes and dislikes. In turn, children engaged in discussing their views about the stories they read. In a reading session with his father at home, Sergio Olivarez, a third grader, shared his ideas about the story.

A mi me gusto mucho el libro del osito que se perdió en el polo del norte. Me puse muy triste cuando el osito no encontraba a su mama osa y flotaba solo en un pedaso de hielo en el oceano buscandola. Me hizo pensar que triste fuera si yo perdia a mi mamá o papá.

I liked the book about the little polar bear who got lost in the North Pole. I got very sad when the little bear lost his mother and by himself floated on a small piece of ice in the ocean searching for her. It made me think how sad it would be if I lost my mother or father.

Children expressed how the stories touched them emotionally. Such was the case involving the book, *Historia de los Bonobos con Gafas*, in which the male monkeys made the female monkeys do all of the work like pick their food and feed them while they lived comfortably in the trees. Then the male monkeys went on a trip to learn a new language and returned with sunglasses and they positioned themselves as the élite group including using new words which the other monkeys did not understand and refused to share what they learned with the female monkeys. One day the females decided to take their babies and move to another forest, and the male monkeys had to gather their own food and do their own work. After exhausting their resources they left in search of the female monkeys and no one knows what really happened, but some people tell stories about the males reuniting with the female monkeys and that they learned to help them with the daily work so that they lived happily ever after. But we may never know.

Parents read the story with their children and discussed the issues related to gender-role distribution of household tasks. Children responded to questions about the fair distribution of housework between men and women, about the élite behavior on the part of the 'bonobos' who didn't share the new language they learned, and about the male aloofness to their children. Children's opinions were solicited. Yolanda Romero, a fourth-grade student, commented about her dislike of the bonobos' chauvinistic behavior. Her teacher was one who commented about the enormous development she noticed in Yolanda's literacy since her family participated in the FLP. Her shyness became overshadowed by her critical thinking about the books she read.

Yolanda: Yo no se porque los bonobos tienen que portarse así.

I don't know why the male monkeys have to act like this.

Father: Ellos no querian compartir nada con ellas, y ellas tenian que hacer todo el trabajo.

They didn't want to share anything with them [the female monkeys], and they had to do all of the work.

Yolanda: Ellas hicieron bien en buscar otro bosque. Yo no dejaría que me hicieran hacer todo el trabajo como la bonobas tuvieron que hacer. Hójala que ellos [los changos] nunca las encuentren [a las changas] porque ellas pueden vivir muy feliz sin ellos que eran tan flojos. Papá, ¿no crees que es injusto que hagan eso?

They did right by going to another forest. I wouldn't want them make me do all of the work like the female monkeys had to do. Hopefully, they [the male monkeys] will never find them [the female monkeys] because they can live very happy without those monkeys who were so lazy. Dad, don't you think that it's unjust for them to do that?

Father: Sí mi hija, es injusto. ¿Qué harias tu en ese caso de las bonobas? Yo les aventaria con las frutas que me hacian recoger. [Father chuckles.] Lo importante es que no te vas a dejar que te traten injustament, mi hija.

Yes dear, it's unjust. What would you do in a case like that of the female monkeys? I would throw at them with the fruit they made me pick. [Father chuckles.] The important thing is that you would not allow them to treat you unjustly.

Theoretically, we expected that Spanish-speaking children and their parents would become empowered when they learn to interpret literature in relation to their own experience and reality.[7] Yolanda's exchange with her father exemplified protean learning. To achieve this, the research team and the parents of Spanish-speaking children planned to have parents read children's literature books to their children and pose a hierarchy of questions designed to generate discussion between children and parents.[8] We extended the premise of becoming analytical readers and reading for meaning by having parents and children decide their own questions and interaction during their story-reading session.

Four types of questions framed the interaction between adults and children: descriptive, personal interpretative, critical phase, and the creative phase: Descriptive questions solicited factual recall for example, 'What did the female elephants wear?' Personal interpretative questions asked the reader to think about their personal experience in relation to what they read, for example, 'Have you ever felt that you were prevented from doing things that others had permission to do? How did you feel?' Critical type questions revealed the child's ability to analyze the text in terms of a sociopolitical perspective, for example, 'Could the male and female monkeys have divided the work and responsibilities better?' Creative questions made the reader think about ways that they would resolve similar questions to those in the story, for example, 'If you had been one of the female monkeys, what could you have done to improve the situations?' During the evening classes, parents practiced asking these questions of each other in small groups led by COPLA parents and members of the research team. Discussions ensued about the topic of the books such as this brief excerpt represents on gender differences in the book *Rosa Caramelo.*

Yo digo que Rosa Caramelo hizó lo que debia de hacer para liberarse. El modo de que su papá la encarcelaba en el jardín pequeño con las otras elefantitas y no la dejaba jugar en los jardines más amplios donde podian jugar los elefantes gris o sea los hombres. Lo importante en este libro era que Rosa no sólo se libero ella sola pero también animó a las otras que se rebelaran.	I would say that Rosa Caramelo did what she had to do to liberate herself. The way that her father constrained her in the small garden with the other female elephants and did not allow her to play in the larger meadows where the male elephants played. The important part of this book is that Rosa not only liberated herself but she also encouraged the other female elephants to liberate themselves.
Pues, yo no estoy de acurerdo que debiamos de darles ideas así a nuestros niños porque Rosa desobedeció a sus padres. Y me parece que esos no son los valores que debemos dar a nuestros hijos.	Well, I don't agree that we should give our children ideas about disobeying their parents. And, it seems to me that those are not values which we want to give our children.
Pero Rosa no se rebelaba solo por desobedecer a sus padres. Era que había desigualidad entre los que podian hacer los hombres o sea los elefantes gris y las mujeres que eran los elefantes color rosa. ¿Qué debo de hacer si mi hija decide tomar el punto de vista de Rosa y yo no estoy de acuerdo con ella?	But Rosa didn't rebel simply to disobey her parents. It was that there was inequality in what the males [grey elephants] were able to do as compared with the females who were the pink elephants. What do I do if my daughter decides to accept Rosa's position and I don't agree with her?
Yo diría que lo que debemos de hacer es insistir que nuestros hijos expresen su ideas aunque sean diferentes a las de nosotros como padres. También nosotros tenemos derecho a nuestras ideas y debemos explicar porque tenemos esas ideas.	I would say that what we need to do is to help our children express their ideas even if they are different from ours. We also have a right to our ideas and we should explain to them why we have our ideas.
No siempre es necesario tratar de convenser a nuestros niños de nuestros puntos de vista pero si es necesario explicarles las rasones y a	We don't always have to try and convince our children of our point of view, but it is necessary to explain our reasons and at the same

la ves debemos de ayudarles a expresar sus ideas y que examinen su conciencia.

time help them express their own ideas and examine their conscience.

Results from the FLP intervention showed parents' and children's growth in literacy practices as they achieved closer communication between the families and the classroom. In spite of these successes, the questioning strategies which were taught to the parents in the FLP classes bore limitations on the FLP goals. The parents were apparently overly conscientious of the academic aspect of the project, that of the labels of the category of the questions. Some parents were confused by the hierarchy of the questions — not that they could not ask the various questions, it was more a confusion of the appropriate match between the label of the category and the type of question.[9] For example, in the creative category the type of question might be, 'How would you handle the situation if you were Rosa Caramelo?' Parents were not accustomed to working with academic strategies most likely to be employed by teachers in their instruction of literacy. In our final analysis, they might have benefited more by becoming aware of their own process and using their own frameworks of interaction to initiate discussion about the literature books. Overlooking the families' native literacy left the cultural part of the project wanting. Put differently, families nurtured their children with stories as chapter 4 exemplified and a more cultural integrity in the FLP. Criticism of the school curriculum in COPLA meetings cited the absence of home culture in the school curriculum and then the FLP neglected this critical aspect of the home culture. Comments from parents, however, confirmed the success of the project.

A mi me ayudó mucho este programa porque me hizó ver la importancia de leer con mis niños con más frequencia. También veo lo necesario de hablar con los maestros tocante a la lecutra y asignaturas diarias que les dan a los niños.

Antes [que tomaramos la clase FLP] me esperaba hasta las conferencias con los maestros para hablar con ellos. Pero ahora, aunque no haiga problema, voy a hablar con ellos [los maestros].

This program was very important for me and it made me see the importance of reading more frequently with my children. It also reminded me of the necessity to talk with the teachers specifically about the daily reading assignments they give the children.

Before [I took the FLP class] I used to wait until parent–teacher conferences to talk with teachers. But now, even if there isn't a problem, I go to talk with them [the teachers].

Although such comments were forthcoming from the parents from the beginning of the FLP, a frequent comment disturbed me. It signaled the parents' confusion about the questioning categories we taught them in the FLP classes. Stories which children learn from parents or other relatives indicate a strength in family literacy which existed prior to the Family Literacy Project. Had the FLP incorporated family stories as part of the curriculum the academic questioning categories could have been taught differently and minimized the conflict which lasted for the adults long after the literacy classes ended. This is not to say that the parents could not learn the importance of the questioning categories, rather it means that the questions may possibly have been learned much more easily had family literacy been used along with the commercial children's literature books.

In Carpinteria I learned how children's power of story undergirds the dynamics of culture. Children just as much as parents learn through the favorite stories told to them and which have an impact on their thinking, enough to retell the stories to each other in the classroom and in their play areas, including their playground. Children without a doubt look to their teachers and parents as the predominant figures of authority. Parents and teachers are the important custodians of children's minds and our only error was to overlook this. Although COPLA was involved in shaping the FLP the omission of family story indicates their need to authority to the researcher. It's difficult to tell whether the FLP would have been organized differently but it does point to the need to include more family culture and literacy in school-oriented projects.

Cultural Parent and School Relationships

Teachers and parents sometimes feared each other. They reached out to each other in the way they knew best. Essentially, culture undergirds the classroom curriculum and it is the most critical aspect of family–school relationships. Just as Mrs Stone incorporated parents' diverse talents in her classroom, she also organized her teaching to reflect cultural diversity.

> It is very important to incorporate the home culture in the curriculum so that parents and students feel good about who they are, where they come from, where their fellow students come from, and to feel good about the language they speak. We use star of the day and star of the week students spotlighting, books, songs poems and artwork from other cultures. We do the back to back program with two non-bilingual kindergarten teachers so the children are integrated and exposed to different types of children. We also openly talk about issues that are happening at home, both the positive and negative ones. Respect for all cultures is a general theme in all areas of learning. If children learn to see the good in all people, they will most likely see it in themselves.

COPLA meetings particularly at Marina School (preschool through second) brought together teachers and parents who would learn about each other. Many meetings took place over the past seven years of COPLA activism.

Teachers and parents at Marina School have gathered to talk with each other about children's education. Early years of schooling have long had the attention of researchers because parents tend to participate more actively in their children's schooling during the early primary-grade school years.[10] Marina School's bilingual program, from Kindergarten to second grade, has enjoyed years of Latino parent participation through the efforts of COPLA. Teacher–parent meetings were initiated by bilingual teachers who desired to work closely with parents. They were held in the respective classrooms where teachers presented the class-literacy curriculum to the parents. Parents interacted actively with each other and the teachers as they together attempted to learn to resolve homework problems which may result from miscommunication between teacher and students or from lack of knowledge about the classroom curriculum.

In one teacher–parent meeting, Ms Jeffrey met with the parents of her bilingual class. About thirty parents attended on Thursday evening. The teacher read the book, *Salvador y Señor Sam* to the parents. She posed questions to them as she read the story to demonstrate question-asking strategies. After reading the story, she opened the discussion about the story and invited the parents to raise any concerns about their personal cases. Parents expressed their critiques about the book and requested information about where to find more books in Spanish to read with their children.

Ramon Mendez spoke about his appreciation for the meeting and presentation and asked Ms Jeffrey to explain why homework was difficult for some students like his son, Pablo, who was a very good student. Pablo's grades had been high in math but he required more help in his literacy skills.

Yo tengo un problema que con mi hijo, Pablo, que no le gusta hacer su tarea de lectura.

I have a problem with my son, Pablo, who doesn't want to do his homework on reading.

La maestra preguntó, ¿qué problems tiene con Pablo, Señor Mendez?

The teacher asked, what problems do you have with Pablo?

Pues, cada noche cuando él debe de ponerse hacer su tarea, no quiere y luego yo me pongó estricto con él y él comiensa a temblar. Luego, yo me siento tan mal porque él, como que tiene miedo.

Well, every night when he should be doing his homework, he doesn't want to do it and then I get very strict and he begins to tremble. Then, I feel terrible because he, like he's afraid.

Es posible que Pablo no tiene mucha confiansa en su lectura. Aúnque es buen estudiante, no tiene mucha confiansa en si mismo en esta materia. Y si usted es muy estricto con él, se siente ansioso.

It's possible that Pablo may not feel confident about his reading. Although he is a good student, he doesn't have a great deal of confidence in himself where that subject is concerned. And if you're very strict with him, he may feel anxious.

Sí, es posible que soy demasiado estricto con el porque yo también tengo poca ansia con esa materia. Las matemáticas no son tan dificil para mi porque siempre me gustó y supé como hacer cuentas, pero en lectura pues no sobresalí como con las matemáticas.

Yes, it is possible that I'm overly strict with him because I too am too anxious about reading. Math is not as difficult for me because I always liked the subject and I could compute, but where reading was concerned, I didn't excel.

También Pablo es buen estudiante en matemáticas y ahora sé porque tiene tanta diciplina en esa materia. Es porque a usted le gusta y le ayuda a el sobresalir con esa materia.

Pablo is also a good student in mathematics and now I know why he's so disciplined in that subject. It's because you enjoy it and you can help him advance in that subject.

Tiene rasón, maestra. Mejor espero que él me pida ayuda si necesita en ves de yo insistir que me lea su lectura.

You're right, [Ms Jeffrey]. Maybe I'll just wait for him to ask for assistance rather than to insist that he reads to me.

The exchange between Ms Jeffrey and Ramon about Pablo impelled further conversation among the parents. A discussion ensued until many parents made comments in sequence of each other without interruption so that Ms Jeffrey was able to respond to them individually. Remarks seemed to affirm their interest in working with the teachers and their need to meet and talk about ways to support their children.

Para mi, lo importante es que este grupo de padres [de COPLA] siempre ha querido por mejor diciplina y que los niños no tengan malas ideas ni vicios.

For me, the important thing is that this group of [COPLA] parents has always wanted good discipline for our children and so they don't learn bad habits or vices.

He aprendidó a comunicarme más con mis hijos. Todo el tiempo les pregunto por su tarea. Les ayudo en lo que puedo y me siento muy contento cuando los puedo ayudar.

I've learned to communicate with my sons. I always ask to see their homework. I help them in whatever I can and I'm glad whenever I can help.

En estas juntas con ustedes maestras y con los demás padres de família puedo ejercer mis ideas en la exposición de temas que se presentan. Me siento muy apoyado.

In these meetings with you teachers and with the other parents I can express my ideas and in the variety of themes presented here. I feel very supported.

Lo más importante es conoser las estrategias para ayudarles a nuestros niños con sus estudios. Así los padres y maestros podemos estar de acuerdo con lo que se les enseña a

The most important thing is to learn the strategies to help our children in their studies. That way parents and teachers can agree with what is taught to our children. I

nuestros hijos. Yo digo que cuando los dos trabajamos juntos, los niños tienen mas apoyo.

would say that when we work together, the children have more support.

Nuestras hijas nos han mostrado un trabajo en sus estudios desde que su mamá y yo nos hemos hecho más activos en su escuela.

Our daughters have demonstrated some wonderful work in their studies ever since their mother and I have become more active in their schoolwork.

Ahora quieren leer, escribir, y hacer sus cuentas en matemáticas que antes ni quería que nosotros le ayudaramos. Ahora parece que tienen más diciplina porque saben que nosotros las asistimos porque aprendemos en estas juntas con su maestra. Mi esposa y yo hemos aprendido como diciplinar la mente de nuestros hijo. Así puede enfocarse en sus estudios.

Now they want to read, write, and do their math which before they didn't even want us to help them. Now they seem to have more discipline because they know that we assist them by coming to these meetings to learn a great deal with their teachers. My wife and I have learned how to keep our son's mind occupied. That way he stays focused in his schooling.

En nuestras juntas con usted maestra Jeffrey, yo he aprendido como dar cariño y castigar a mi hija cuando es necessario. Y aparentemente este equilibrio ha sido importante porque [ella] sigue sobresaliendo en sus materias.

In our meetings with you, Ms Jeffrey, I've learned how to love and discipline my daughter when it's necessary. Apparently this balance seems important because she continues excelling in her studies.

Yo aprecio que estas juntas con usted como maestra me han ayudado a reclamar mis derechos como madre de niña en esta clase.

I appreciate that these meetings with you [teacher] have helped me reclaim my rights as a mother of a child in this class.

Sharing knowledge with each other and respect for cultural practices help parents and teachers reach an understanding for communicating. While parents and teachers agree that they need to communicate with each other, both sides claim their share of limitations in their work together and apart. Latino parents have learned to communicate with their children's teachers, many more parents, however remain to be drawn into the school–family connection. The reverse also appears to be the case where parents want teachers to learn about the home culture so that they respect their children. They also want the school curriculum to reflect their home culture.

Notes

1 Parent involvement has been a focus of extensive research which requires much more space than I will take here to list all of the publications which merit

acknowledging. I must however recognize a selective few references which are important studies because they are theoretically grounded such that offer us the opportunity to engage in the discourse of 'parent involvement' issues beyond a mere portrayal of strategies for involving parents in the school, which I regarded limited in its understanding of the complexity of the subject. On that note, see, for example, Allexsaht-Snider, 1991, Bronfenbrenner, 1978, Cochran and Dean 1991; Coleman, 1994; Comer, 1984, Delgado-Gaitan, 1994; Delgado-Gaitan and Allexsaht-Snider, 1992; David, 1989; Epstein, 1994; Levin, 1987; Lareau, 1989; Phelan, Davidson, and Cao, 1991.

2 Many teachers know that if a child is underachieving, parents cannot bear the entire responsibility. I would not presume to imply that teachers, categorically, blame parents when children underachieve. In fact, in my research, I have taken care to carefully describe those cases where teachers are knowledgeable and professional in their relationship with families and in integrating home culture in the curriculum. As I have written in this book and in numerous other publications, the relationship between parents and schools is too complex to simplistically point the finger at either the school or the family when children face learning problems. When I first began my study in Carpinteria in 1985, I observed in many classrooms and I was told by most of the teachers that bilingual children had learning problems in reading because their parents did not care. Some of the teachers were careful to note that most Latino parents worked hard and long hours and could not read English which made it difficult for them to read with their children. As my study progressed over the years, I documented how teachers actually dealt with parents differently and that as the COPLA organization became more active, many of those same teachers who once criticized parents now began to reach out to the Latino parents differently and recognized that they did and do care about their children and schooling and found ways to better communicate with parents.

3 Realistically, parents should provide their children with all of the basic needs. No one can argue with that, but blame cannot be hurled at families as if they are isolated from society's power on the family including economic, politics and cultural influence. A common wish expressed by many educators and the public in general is that families should return to the 'traditional family'. In Coontz's 1992, book by a title in response to the popular wish, 'the way we were' — *The Way We Never Were: American Families and the Nostalgia Trap*, the author presents an excellent historical study examining two centuries of American family life and shatters the myths that so often burden modern and postmodern families. Pressures from dwindling resources to families compound intrafamily interactions and organization. Studies by Baca Zinn, 1983; Saragoza, 1983; Segura, 1988 and Williams, 1990; Ybarra, 1983 on Mexican/Chicano families adequately examine these questions.

4 Most parent-involvement efforts are intended to endorse the schools' policies with little regard for the parents' understanding of the school's operations and for their voice.

5 In the reading, acts between parents and teachers, parents teach more than the mechanics and strategies on reading. See Ferdman, Weber, Ramirez, 1994.

6 The need for frequent reading by parents to children is studied in emergent literacy research involving family in linguistically diverse communities by Delgado-Gaitan, 1994; Goldenberg, 1987; Heath, 1982; Pease-Alvarez, 1991; Schieffelin and Cochran-Smith, 1984; Scollon and Scollon, 1981; Taylor, 1983; Trueba, 1984; Trueba,

Jacobs, Kirton, 1990; Vasquez, 1989. Here again the list of exceptional research in emergent literacy in culturally and linguistically different communities is enormous so I've selected only these few, but I do not mean to ignore the multitude of other excellent, critical and cross-discipline research on literacy.

7 Following Freire and Macedo (1987) concept of liberation with his work on literacy with Brazilian peasants, Alma Flor Ada attempted to have parents learn how to motivate their children to practice the four questioning strategies in order to teach their children how to read a story by reflecting on their own experience and liberation.

However, my research team departed somewhat from the recommendation of Flor Ada in her curriculum simply because the review of some of the books used in the Pajaro Valley project could not be used with this parent group because the print was cursive and therefore not clear to children, or it was believed that some illustrations (e.g., a partially naked mermaid) might be found offensive by the parents. Furthermore, we thought that some of the themes were not interesting enough to generate discussion. We did overlap with Flor Ada's recommended list when our criteria fit.

8 Ada, 1988, designed a series of questions for each of her selected books. The questions were actually intended for teachers to use with Spanish-speaking children, and the same set of literature books and questioning strategies were suggested for the parents to use in the home with their children.

9 Part of what my research team and I learned in our work with the FLP was that the hierarchy of questions designed by Flor Ada were effective where the project involved classroom teachers as the key teachers in the reading program. However, as we designed the project to focus on parents as the key educator relative to reading with children, we needed to have allowed the 'question' classifications to emerge from an ethic perspective. In the FLP classes we observed that parents had keen insights about their relationship with their children not only where reading written text was concerned but also in the case of parents sharing oral stories with their children. Parents also had strong opinions about topics and themes surrounding the stories we read in each class. Therefore, I had to intervene during the second year — 'follow-up' — year to explain to the parents that the most important part of their learning was not the category of questions but what they practice as close interaction in reading with their children which was the most important.

10 Notions about liberation, learning, literacy, communication, schools, and families are a composite of my years as an elementary school teacher, elementary school principal and as a researcher in various immigrant communities.

Chapter 6

Dimensions of Change

'Buscando Una Casa Nueva'

Había una vez un gatito que se llamaba Nuve. Su dueña que se llamaba Anita se enfermó y se murió. Nuve se quedó solo y quería encontrar a un dueño para que le cuidaran y para que le dieran de comer y lo bañaran y le peinaran. Nuve salió de su casa y se perdió. Luego lo encontró un hombre viejito que le dijó que el queria ayudarle a cruzar la calle. Luego se hicieron amigos y el gatito Nuve estaba feliz.

'Looking For a New Home'
(Story told by 8-year-old Ramon)
Once there was a little kitten whose name was Cloud. His owner whose name was Anita got sick and died. Cloud was left alone and wanted to find someone to take care of him, to feed him, bathe and comb him. Cloud left the house and got lost. Then he was found by an older man who told him that he wanted to help him cross the street. Then they became friends and the kitten, Cloud was happy.

While teachers expect the administration to support the importance of this part of their classroom curriculum through release time, community liaisons and support of skills to work more closely in the area of home–school connectedness, parents also expext the Carpinteria School District administration to meaningfully build communication with the community on all levels. The administration in general has evolved in their way of dealing with the Latino community.

Superintendent Dr Pablo Seda, who served in the position from 1990–4 recognized the importance of working closely with parents and the community. Upon his arrival to the school district, he formed a council of parents representing various interests in the community. He meets with the groups monthly. In those meetings he solicits their views on current issues while he shares his own vision of education for its students.

Dr Seda's background prepared him for this leadership position in Carpinteria. He taught Spanish in a high school and coached basketball before becoming an assistant principal. During the time he was principal of Garey High School, he remained active as a community coordinator for the City's Hispanic Youth Task Force. After receiving a doctoral degree in education from the University of Southern California, Pablo became Assistant

Superintendent for Secondary Instruction in the Santa Barbara High School District during which time he continued speaking in community agencies and conducting workshops to train parents to work more effectively with schools and to learn ways to help their children to reach greater academic success. As a superintendent in Carpinteria, Dr Seda remains connected with the community at large through his column in the local newspapers in which he communicates his perspectives on education.

In his article, 'What Do Children Learn In School?' Dr Seda comments.

> In reality, children learn much in school about how they are and they are frequently reinforced by teachers and peers of the self concept they acquire somewhere between kindergarten and twelfth grade.

Children learn and/or acquire leadership skills, self confidence, empathy for others, appreciation for life, responsibility for their actions, self discipline, and such values as honesty, integrity and perseverance. They learn these traits, skills and habits from their teachers, peers, parents and other adults. However, sometimes children fail to learn these lessons, and instead, they learn that they are not able to learn.

> ... A teacher is so important! A teacher relates to the child why learning and school are important. A teacher helps a child to make the connection between school and his future. A teacher is also an advocate for the child and believes in the child and convinces him/her that he/she can learn. The teacher is also available at the hard and difficult times when things just don't go right and love and protection and sheltering are necessary.
>
> I look around and see where our society is going and it is somewhat frightening at times. And so my wish is that teachers always wish the best for their students and do all that's necessary to make sure they succeed ...

His wish for teachers to live and teach the essence of empathy for others reveals his beliefs that teaching should promote truth, courage, knowledge, work, stability, balance and joy. These assertions about the teacher's place in children's learning leads into Dr Seda's understanding of teachers' responsibilities in what he terms the 'Greatest of All Professions' in his November, 1991 article.

> ... I am convinced, that if our society and our country are to maintain its excellence, it will be done by teachers who are committed to making a difference everyday. Willie Stargell, former major league baseball player, was once asked for his autograph by a child. Mr Stargell turned to the child and said 'You should instead seek the autograph of your teacher. He (she) will do more for you than I ever will.' Willie Stargell knew about teachers and the difference they make.

. . . As a teacher, I can think of nothing more exciting and satisfying than knowing that I have made a positive difference in a child's life. Recently, I saw a former student of mine whom I had in my class in 1971 in San Diego. It has been years since I had seen him. I spent a great deal of time with Kirk, but his parents divorced and later drugs contributed to his downfall. When I saw him recently he told me during all the bad times in his life he could always remember he could win and succeed. I taught and coached him for three years and it was that experience he kept going back to until he finally made it. Now he is drug free, happily married, the father of two beautiful girls and successful in business. That's what teaching is all about. It's about making a difference.

Teachers touch hundreds, maybe thousands of lives in their careers. Sometimes even unknown to the teacher, a child may make a great discovery that will change, his/her life because of something positive the teacher said or did. In the movie 'The Boy Who Could Fly' a girl talks about her teacher, 'He made us believe in ourselves again, now when I feel like giving up and not trying, all I have to do is think of what he taught me.' Teachers know all children are special and that all can fly.

I recently heard of a judge who has saved over twenty men on death row from their execution and so far he has not gotten one thank you card. I am sure he doesn't feel appreciated, but he goes on anyway and does what he thinks is right. Teachers have the same problem. They touch hundreds, maybe thousands of lives in their careers and they receive little recognition for their efforts. Their salaries are low and receive few incentives to continue to strive and make a difference, but they do it anyway. Because what is important is that each teacher knows he/she is doing all that is possible to have the students experience success.

I remember a few years back I was unhappy with who I was. I had sold myself short and given up on my dreams. I was just kind of going along. I was living, but nobody was home. So I decided to take a look at myself and see who I was and where I was going. I decided that as hard and painful as it was I was going for the finish line and I was going the distance. Anytime we look at ourselves and work at expanding our experiences we experience fear. I choose to say that I experience fear, but I will not give in to say that I am afraid. I now live in the present and I enjoy every moment of my life and live everyday as if it were my last. Every night before I go to bed I can look at myself in the mirror and say. 'Today I made a difference in this world. Today I made a difference in someone's life.' I have this experience because I had some great teachers in my life. Alice, Mitch, Jack, Mr S., and Priscilla were all there for me. They made me their project. They believe in me and convinced me I was unique and special. They were my teachers and they made a difference in my life. I am a better person because I was their student.

Teachers do make a difference. Teaching is the greatest profession of all because it allows for teacher and student to go for their potential and be the best they can be. A teacher can make a difference every day in the lives of children.

Dr Seda's candid account of his teaching supports his belief in the importance of teachers in children's lives. Such expectation of teaching and learning was further expanded in his article, 'We Are Able to Overcome Expectations of Others.'

During World War II, Victor Frankl, Jewish psychiatrist and author of the book, *Man's Search for Meaning*, was sent to a concentration camp. His parents, brother, and wife died there. Naked and alone in a room, one day he became aware of what he later called the 'last of the human freedoms'. Noticing a far away home he saw a light inside. He chose to see his light as a sign of God and that he was heard.

From that day on, Frankl decided the Nazis could never take away his chosen freedom. Through that freedom he learned that he could decide within himself how his present situation affected him.

Between what happened to him (his stimulus) and his response, he found a vast world he could control. He used visualization and his mind (imagery) to project himself lecturing after the camp experience was over. He, little by little, disciplined himself (mind and emotions). His tools were primarily his imagination and memory. Slowly he exercised his new freedom until it grew larger and larger, even larger than that of his Nazi captors. He told himself that no matter what they did to him he would always have his dignity, his integrity, and he would survive to tell about it. He did!

Frankl discovered that between stimulus and response, man has the freedom to choose.

In our places of work and in our homes, we often face negative stimuli. Lack of money, demands from insensitive people (be it a parent, administrator colleague, spouse, or child), and complaints from people who lack empathy, contribute to the negative environment in which we often live.

We can choose to react to this stimuli by being negative, angry, upset, sad, by giving up, blaming, by saying, 'If only I had more money' or 'if we had a commitment from the district.' 'If I had a different boss . . . A different husband . . . a different superintendent.' Or we can choose to be proactive, to stand and realize that we can create our own response. We have the freedom to choose. We can say, 'I choose, I prefer. I will, I can, let's look at the alternatives.'

> We, too, must accept the fact that we can change our environment and our perceived realities and accomplish anything we want if we believe in our power to overcome negative stimuli.
>
> All children can become whatever they set out to be and accomplish whatever they want if they learn to utilize the power that exists within them.

People's unique inner power was the focus of Dr Seda's expectation for students, educators, and parents. Such were the expectations of Latino parents with each other in their COPLA organization. Cooperation is one of the values inherent in the empowerment process which enabled people to work together. The issues are further explored in his article, 'Winning Isn't Always Defeating Somebody.'

> . . . We are as a society preconditioned to compete. We think that for us to win someone else must lose.
>
> We don't clearly understand the concept of win–win. We think of a tie as half a loss. Some even say that if it doesn't matter who wins, then we shouldn't play at all. . . .
>
> Winning is very important to us. Otherwise, why would professional teams be willing to pay an athlete $30 million? . . .
>
> Winning is fun. It brings us happiness. We jump, we cheer, we laugh, and our disposition improves. However, when we lose, the opposite occurs. . . .
>
> When we lose, we become philosophers. We say, 'It is just a game anyway.' A loss forces us to meditate, reassess and change so we can turn our defeat into a future victory.
>
> . . . We want to rank ourselves so we can tell others we are at the top. Of course, when one is at the top, someone must be at the bottom.
>
> It is OK to rank students when one is among the top, but how would we like to be 499th out of 500? Where does it say that we must have so many A's, so many B's, C's, D's and F's? School is not a football game where for one to win, another one must lose!
>
> School can and should be a place where all can succeed, where all can win. There should be nothing wrong with all students earning A's.
>
> Universities then would probably want to rank students some other way so they can decide who to admit and who to refuse.
>
> Likewise, if we truly believe that education is the answer to our society's problems, then we would want all classes, all schools, and all districts to win. We all win in education when all students learn and reach their potential. . . .
>
> . . . Schools need to teach children that life is not a game about

winning or losing arguments, scoring points, winning games, or collecting toys.

Winning in life is about living full out, going for our potential, reaching for the stars, being a good person, giving all we have to give, and lobbing everyone with all our heart and soul. That's really winning! . . .

Leadership, for this superintendent meant a commitment to motivate others to make the same promise to education which he brought to Carpinteria. His protean approach to education began with an appraisal of his own strengths and a value to work towards negotiation in a collective way. Collectively, cooperation, excellence and forthright communication and inclusion were congruent values with those of COPLA's organization and leadership. Dr Seda's educational philosophy has been available to the community but his critics believe that is just that — a philosophy. They have been less than patient with his efforts to decentralize management responsibilities.

For example, on the issue of parent involvement, teachers have requested assistance from the district administration in order to establish closer communication with parents. Teachers felt they needed a parent liaison to help them reach difficult children whose families required frequent home visits. Additionally teachers wanted release time to meet with parents and to bridge closer partnerships with families including composing weekly classroom newsletters. To these petitions, the central administration felt that such a request was the responsibility of each school principal since they should be the ones to assess their school curriculum and staff needs. Dr Seda has been able to appoint school principals who are now beginning to initiate projects tailored to the specific needs of their school population.

Consistent with his educational philosophy, Dr Seda's response to teachers' needs allow people the freedom to make decisions and choices for themselves even if it entails more time and the process takes more time and requires more patience and work on everyone's part than one would want if the decisions were made in a centralized fashion. As Dr Seda has commented, 'One way to empower teachers is to welcome them in the decision-making process. They too are leaders and as such should be involved in the decisions affecting their future. The superintendent has, however put in place an accountability feature in his evaluation of principals. Beginning this school year 1994–5 principals will be evaluated for their progress in establishing strong family–school connectedness.

Just as Dr Seda's belief in including teachers in the educational decision-making process so is his interest in involving parents and staff, 'Parents and staff members are also very important. They too must become part of the solution by being involved in the decision-making process and in planning the goals to form the strategy which will create a new structure to meet the vision and purpose of our schools.'

In his article 'Carpinteria Toward the 21st Century' Dr Seda writes,

> Carpinteria — The 21st century is about students and their performance. Excellence is achieved when all students reach the peak of their abilities. By identifying the levels of skills, abilities and knowledge desired for each student, we can ascertain our schools' level of success. Carpinteria — The 21st century is about all our students knowing they are capable to reach their potential and every student being engaged daily in the learning process to make that potential a reality. It will take an effort by the entire Carpinterian community to make Carpinteria — The 21st century a reality. It is not just the job of the educators . . . All of this could happen, but only if we choose to take a stand and hold hands together to make Carpinteria — The 21st century a reality.

Dr Seda's vision for Carpinteria may still come to fruition, but it will happen without him as superintendent. As I complete this book Dr Seda has just left Carpinteria to take a superintendent position in Southern California. And so the spiraling motion of empowerment takes still another twist as a new chapter awaits COPLA as they participate in the selection of a new superintendent. Mr Paul Niles threw his hat in the ring and came up number two of five candidates. The newly selected superintendent is an outsider to Carpinteria and new opportunities await everyone in the community. One area of parent education begun by Paul Niles and then by Pablo Seda will continue, however, by the bilingual counselor whose goal was to work with small cadres of parents and train them to train others in areas of parent–child relationships. His next assignment with the district will focus on the high school Latino students and their parents and teachers. The intent is for them to receive separate trainings then come together and learn from each other.

Protean Literacy and Directions in Family–School Connectedness

My research in Carpinteria did not begin with set theories about learning, literacy or family–school relationships. I did, however, take into the research setting specific notions about culture, literacy, families, learning, schools and liberation. Throughout the years I spent in Carpinteria, these notions evolved such that now as I culminate this phase of my research I can suggest certain general principles which describe what I understand protean literacy to mean.

1. Literacy is a basic tool and vehicle that enables people to participate in society and obtain agency.
2. We need literacy to gather information and to discover the alternatives available.
3. Through literacy, people gather information to make conscious choices for ways to conduct their lives.

4 Literacy is a sociocultural process designed by our context and is therefore malleable, ever shifting and never ending.
5 Literacy extends beyond written text; it is one's knowledge to competently utilize innate power in socially constructed contexts.
6 One's ability to participate actively in social contexts permits the expansion and development of one's cultural knowledge.
7 Protean literacy is achieved through an empowerment process.

During my decade of research in Carpinteria, I conclude that Carpinteria educators and families embodied the nature of empowerment through their efforts to work collectively and make 'the child' their fundamental purpose for literacy and for relating cooperatively with one another.

I maintain that the most critical act which we must implement is a reflexive assessment of our local conditions. This compels a new vision that is all encompassing and creates a process of inclusion in contrast with what we experience in these modern/postmodern times. A set of empowerment principles undergirds the protean work accomplished in Carpinteria.

1 Underrepresented groups included women, ethnic, linguistically different and poor people who are assigned unequal status in society. A truly democratic society is organized to provide all people of diverse backgrounds choices and opportunities to exercise power.
2 All individuals have strengths and cultural change should emanate from that position to advance personal and collective agency.
3 An understanding of the history of a given community or group, including the knowledge of language, cultural values and conventions associated with cultural meaning, are indispensable to determine appropriate strategies for reducing inequality.
4 Learning new roles provides people with access to resources and the learning of those roles occurs through participation in those new settings.
5 Collective critical reflection is an integral process to participation and empowerment by bringing social and cultural concerns to a conscious level.

The empowerment process manifests three dimensions of power including a collective process, critical reflection, and mutual respect expanding the dimensions of personal and collective identity.

> Empowerment is an ongoing intentional process centered at the local community. Mutual respect, critical reflection, caring and group participation, allow people equal access of valued resources gain greater access to and control over those resources through awareness of their social conditions and their cultural and personal strengths. They determine their choices and goals. Action is taken to unveil one's potential

as a step to act on one's own behalf. Implicit here is consciousness of, and responsibility for, one's behavior and willingness to take action to shape it through a social, familial and personal process.

In the Carpinteria research project we learned to think of ourselves differently. Yes, I include myself as a researcher. I learned along with the families that what makes us look at our same circumstances differently is deeper than political knowledge, it's about our deep and fundamental values. During the time I studied Carpinteria, the community, schools and families as well as individuals have accomplished a great deal that had encouraged them to collectively create a context for learning and empowerment.[1]

Family interactions were enhanced, specifically between parents and children. Dialogue about educational issues opened up as parents learned more about schools while children shared their school events, conflicts and successes. Through family literacy activities children and parents shared awareness knowledge and vision. Together children and parents built a stronger confidence in the possibilities for a fuller education. Although parents have always been the children's most important teachers, through increased parent–child communication parents have become even more efficacious advocates.

Schools are organizations designed to support the learner. They are effective to the extent that they benefit the members. To make this possible schools in Carpinteria have become more responsive to the Latino community who have experienced a history of isolation and underachievement. COPLA has influenced Carpinteria schools by urging them to hire bilingual personnel to communicate with Spanish-speaking families. Additionally, schools have continued to implement a strong bilingual program as a result of COPLA parents' informed presence in their children's classrooms. All schools have organized a COPLA Latino parent group to work with administrators and teachers on issues pertaining to Spanish-speaking children. Teacher–parent communication has increased over 60 per cent since the inception of COPLA as both parents and teachers have reached out to each other in order to further strengthen children's learning. Educators have begun to implement effective school–family communication, for example, the school district's response to the Latino community by establishing GATE program for Spanish-speaking students.

Community agency was increased through numerous COPLA efforts to involve the Latino community in sociopolitical activities, to build consciousness and presence in Carpinteria and to unify Latinos in supportive collectives that enabled them to buy cheaper food in bulk communities near Oxnard, California. COPLA parents united to devise activities to involve children in creative activities after school and on weekends as measures against boredom leading social problems since no organized activities existed in Carpinteria that catered to poor Latino children who were unable to pay for membership. Soccer teams and folkloric dance groups have become increasingly popular and successful, building on children's self esteem, skills and collectivity while maintaining their cultural traditions.

Individuals active in Latino organizations like COPLA participated in a collective empowerment process of critically examining their common social and cultural history in Mexico and in the United States. Their analysis of their experience as poor and underschooled individuals convinced them that although they lacked formal schooling in the US, they recognized their cultural power and the strengths they had to raise their children as well as their caring to help them succeed in their schooling. They dismissed cultural stereotypes of personal self imposed on them by the community at large including school personnel and which they had internalized including assumptions of being 'uncaring parents' and 'always late for meetings'. Active COPLA leaders have reached out to assist and encourage family members, friends and acquaintances to get an education. They have enhanced communication with others by learning to listen to others and to speak up in public meetings.

Families and educators active in COPLA didn't get lost in the battle. They maintained a vision which continues because it's not a single one-time or short-term project, their vision is an ongoing dialogue based on moment-to-moment assessment of the issues to be addressed. Negotiation becomes their major focus.

By way of a conclusion, to appreciate the personal, cultural and political struggles which Latinos in Carpinteria have faced, we need to consider how the historical context helps to shape the educational outcomes and the socio-cultural opportunities that play a role in the personal and collective transformations that transpire.

In claiming their rights, including both political and cultural space as part of the community, Latinos challenge old conceptions of American educational practices while attempting to participate fully in the process, and are thus reshaping old concepts of education, of Latinos and of family–school relationships. Thus the making of new citizens demands consistent participation in a new, more equitable society.

Claiming cultural space and political voice and utopian visions do not by themselves address the rigid structures that propel inequity and sever family–school relationships. Nor can COPLA meetings alone address, challenge or replace the structures of power embedded in capitalism. They are potential counter-hegemonic cultural forms that provide reservoirs of hope and struggle for healthier communities and in general, a better society.

There are no fixed formulas that lead to protean literacy and empowerment, only possibilities located in our perception and understanding of the conditions in which we find ourselves. And through collective engagement, we find meaning and potentiality to resolve whatever situations confront us. When we participate meaningfully in our families and community — if we find an emotional connection we can change. Love transforms relationships — we are transformed through love. Some question that a more cooperative, progressive society, whose goals are the preservation of the species in human and ecological form, may not be achieved through community and family-level empowerment efforts. But, transformation cannot occur without them. Although COPLA is not a panacea in the community-development impetus, it has been a pebble in the water that has produced ripples outward to create opportunities for people to expand on the face of dissonance. Proteanism charts that transformation.

Notes

1 COPLA is certainly not a panacea in the course of the educational restructuring of a school or social change at a community level. It does, however, offer a language of possibility defined through focused, interactive activity. Numerous comparable empowerment efforts, nationally and internationally, corroborate the success of this type of empowerment process. One case study demonstrating success was carried out in Annie Strack Village, a private non-governmental residential facility for children. It serves sixty children and has a staff of thirty. The educational level of the childcare workers varies between standards six and ten (grades 8–12). In-service training and National Diploma — the basic qualifications in childcare are mandatory standards for all childcare workers.

Prior to the empowerment model, the village functioned on the 'family-system-model'. The role of the childcare workers was that of substitute parent, or what often resembles 'glorified nannies'. Problems were described as high staff turnover or tired, frustrated and low-paid workers with no autonomy. During a general staff meeting, it was decided to conduct an evaluation.

During the evaluation process, the staff identified the problems, brainstormed alternatives. And finally made decisions about actions and implementation. The evaluation report was then presented and discussed with the management board. If mutually accepted, the plans were implemented and revised as specified. This process developed into a refined and very effective participatory decision-making process and service-review model. The most significant outcome of this process was the empowered people that is 'generated'. This case has meant that, together with many concrete changes (such as staff structure, improved salaries, and goal-directed intervention programs), the 'glorified nannies' were transformed into primary intervention agents. That is, they became full partners in all the decisions that affected their own lives and the lives of the children. Once more, their voices were heard and this enhanced the efficacy of the service professionals (Allen, 1990).

A different empowerment effort can be cited as an exemplary effort against crime and drugs affecting the Mattapan neighborhood of Boston. Residents have lobbied and succeeded in retaining an abandoned building for a recreation center. The success thus far can be attributed to a core group of involved tenants getting involved during five years of effort during which they have mobilized broad-based support within the community.

International community empowerment efforts have been documented in Barbados with the Women and Development Unit (WAND) in the School and Continuing Studies of the University of the West Indies. Women have been able to build the capacity of other women to take control of their lives by launching an ongoing adult education program based on curricula defined by the community, and income-generating projects as well as a preschool and day-care center (Cochran, 1991).

Barbados' endeavors have been joined by other communities in other countries, including the Black Health Center in Cape Town South Africa, the Department of Social Studies and Organization in Aslborg, Denmark, the Community Health Center in Hamilton, New Zealand, the School of Child and Youth Care, Victoria, British Columbia, Canada: Centro de Educación y Comunicación, Managua, Nicaragua, and the Home and Day Care Education Project, Joensuu, Finland. The principles common to the empowerment work in all of these communities is the inclusion of those who have been isolated. Indigenous and subordinate cultures are valued. Further, it is believed that educational communities should support the goals of the communities they serve through continued collective thinking and cooperative dialogue that is committed to enabling personal and structural change (Barr, 1992; Cochran, 1991).

References

ABRAMS, D.M. and SUTTON-SMITH, B. (1977) 'The development of the trickster in children's narratives', *Journal of Amerian Folklore*, **90**, pp. 29–47.

ACHOR, S. (1978) *Mexican Americans in a Dallas Barrio*, Tucson, University of Arizona Press.

ADA, F.A. (1988) 'The Pajaro Valley experience: Working with Spanish-speaking parents to develop children's reading and writing skills through the use of children's literature', in SKUTNABB-KANGAS, T. and CUMMINS, J. (Eds) *Minority Education*, Philadelphia, Multilingual Matters LTD, pp. 223–38.

ALLEN, J. (1990) 'Experiencing the empowerment process: Women and development', *Networking Bulletin*, **1**, 3, pp. 1–17.

ALLEN J., BARR, D., COCHRAN, M., DEAN, C. and GREENE, J. (1989) 'The empowerment process: The underlying model', *Networking Bulletin-Empowerment and Family Support*, **1**, pp. 1–12.

ALLEXSAHT-SNIDER, M. (1991) 'Family literacy in a Spanish-speaking context: Joint construction of meaning', *The Quarterly Newsletter of the Laboratory of Comparative Human Cognition*, **13**, 1, pp. 15–17.

ALLEXSAHT-SNIDER, M. (1991) 'When School Goes home and Families Come to School: Parent–Teacher Interaction in a Bilingual Context,' Dissertation-University of California, Santa Barbara, Ann Arbor, Michigan, University Microfilms International.

ANDERSON, A.B. and STOKES, S.J. (1984) 'Social and institutional influences on the development and practice of literacy', in GOELMAN, H., OBERG, A. and SMITH, F. (Eds) *Awakening to Literacy*, Exeter, New Hampshire, Heinemann Educational Books, pp. 24–38.

ANZALDÚA, G. (1987) *Borderland-La Frontera: The New Mestiza*, San Francisco, California, Spinsters/Aunt Lute Book Co.

APPLE, M.W. (1979) *Ideology and Curriculum*, Boston, Routledge.

APPLE, M.W. (1993) *Official Knowledge: Democratic Education in a Conservative Age*, New York, Routledge.

ARONOWITZ, S. and GIROUX, H. (1991) *Postmodern Education: Politics, Culture, and Social Criticism*, Minneapolis, Minnesota, University of Minnesota Press.

BACA ZINN, M. (1980) 'Employment and education of Mexican-American women: The interplay of modernity and ethnicity in eight families', *Harvard Educational Review*, **50**, 1, pp. 47–62.

BACA ZINN, M. (1983) 'Ongoing questions in the study of Chicano families', in VALDEZ, A.V., CAMARILLO, A. and ALMAGUER, T. (Eds) *The State of Chicano Research in Family, Labor and Migration Studies*, Stanford, California, Stanford Center for Chicano Research, pp. 139–47.

BACK, R. and MEISSNER, D. (1980) *America's Labor Market in the 1990's: What Role should Immigration Play?*, Washington, DC, Library of Congress.

BACH, A.R.L. and MEISSNER, D. (1990) Report Prepared for Assembly Select Committee on Statewide Immigration Impact, Assembly Member Grace Napolitano Chairperson, Prepared by Assembly Office of Research, #0501, June.

BARR, D.J. (1989) *Critical Reflections on Power*, Cornell University Project, Department of Human Services Studies, College of Human Exology, Ithaca, NY.

BARR, D. (1992) 'Understanding and supporting empowerment: Redefining the professional role', *Networking Bulletin*, **2**, 3, pp. 3–8.

BARRERA, M. (1979) *Race and Class in the Southwest: A Theory of Racial Inequality*, Notre Dame, University of Notre Dame.

BERGER, E.H. (1991) 'Parent involvement: Yesterday and today', *The Elementary School Journal*, **91**, 3, pp. 209–19.

BLAKELY, M. (1983) 'Southeast Asian refugee parents: An inquiry into home–school communication and understanding', *Anthropology and Education Quarterly*, **14**, 1, pp. 43–68.

BODNAR, J. (1985) *The Transplanted: A History of Immigrants in America*, Bloomington, Indiana University Press.

BOTVIN, G.J. and SUTTON-SMITH, B. (1977) 'The development of structural complexity in children's fantasy narratives', *Developmental Psychology*, **13**, pp. 377–88.

BOWLES, S. and GINTIS, H. (1976) *Schooling in Capitalist America: Educational Reform and the Contradictions of Economic Life*, New York, Basic Books.

BRONFENBRENNER, U. (1978) 'Who needs parent education?', *Teachers College Record*, **79**, 4, pp. 767–87.

CAMARILLO, A. (1992) 'California and ethnic/racial diversity', *La Nueva Vision*, 1, 2, Stanford, Stanford Center for Chicano Research, pp. 1–11.

CARNOY, M. and LEVIN, H. (1985) *Schooling and Work in the Democratic State*, Stanford University Press.

CARPINTERIA HERALD (12 May 1990) 'A Brighter Outlook', Editor's Section.

CHAUDHRY, L. (1995) 'Marginality, Hyberdity, Empowerment: Education as a Site of Resistance for Pakistani Women in the U.S.', Unpublished Paper.

CLARK, R.M. (1992) 'Critical factors in why disadvantaged students succeed or fail in school', in JOHNSTRON, J.H. and BORMAN, K.M. (Eds) *Effective Schooling for Economically Disadvantaged Students: School-based Strategies for Diverse Student Populations*, Norwood, New Jersey, Ablex Publishing Corporation, pp. 65–77.

COCHRAN, M. (1991) 'Child care and the empowerment process', *Networking Bulletin*, **2**, 1, pp. 4–15.

Cochran, M. and Dean, C. (1991) 'Home–school relations and the empowerment process', *The Elementary School Journal*, **91**, 3, pp. 261–9.

Coleman, J. (1987) 'Families and schools', *Educational Researcher*, **16**, 6, pp. 32–8.

Coleman, J.S. (1994) 'Family involvement in education', in Fagnango, C.L. and Werber, B.Z. (Eds) *School, Family and Community Interaction: A View From the Firing Lines*, San Francisco, Westview Press, pp. 23–38.

Comer, J.P. and Haynes, N. (1991) 'Parent involvement in schools: An ecological approach', *Elementary School Journal*, **91**, 3, pp. 271–77.

Comer, J.P. (1984) 'Home–school relationship as they affect the academic success of children', *Education and Urban Society*, **16**, 3, pp. 323–37.

Coontz, S. (1992) *The Way We Never Were: American Families and the Nostalgia Trap*, New York, Basic Books.

Crawford, J. (1989) *Bilingual Education: History, Politics, Theory, and Practice*, Trenton, New Jersey Crane.

Cremin, L. (1957) *The Republic and the School*, New York, Teachers College Press.

David, M.D. (1989) 'Schooling and the family', in Giroux, H.A. and McLaren, P.L. *Critical Pedagogy, the State and Cultural Struggle*, New York, Suny Press, pp. 50–65.

Davis, K. (1982) 'Achievement variables and class cultures: Family schooling, job, and forty-nine dependent variables in cumulative GSS', *American Sociological Review*, **47**, October, pp. 569–86.

Delgado-Gaitan, C. (1988) 'The value of conformity: Learning to stay in school: An ethnographic study', *Anthropology and Education Quarterly*, **19**, 4, pp. 354–82.

Delgado-Gaitan, C. (1990) *Literacy for Empowerment: The Role of Parents in Children's Education*, London, Falmer Press.

Delgado-Gaitan, C. (1991) 'Linkages between home and school: A process of change for involving parents', *American Journal of Educational*, **100**, 1, pp. 20–46.

Delgado-Gaitan, C. (1991) 'Involving parents in the schools: A process of empowerment', *American Journal of Education*, **100**, 1, pp. 20–46.

Delgado-Gaitan, C. (1992) 'School matters in the Mexican-American home: Socializing children to education', *American Educational Research Journal*, **29**, 3, pp. 495–513.

Delgado-Gaitan, C. (1993) 'Researching change and changing the researcher', *Harvard Educational Review*, **63**, 4, pp. 389–411.

Delgado-Gaitan, C. (1993) 'Research and policy in reconceptualizing family–school relationships', in Phelan, P. and Davidson, A. (Eds) *Cultural Diversity and Educational Policy and Change*, New York, Teachers College Press.

Delgado-Gaitan, C. (1994) 'Spanish-speaking families' involvement in schools', in Fagnango, C.L. and Werber, B.Z. (Eds) *School, Family and Community Interaction: A View From the Firing Lines*, San Francisco, Westview Press, pp. 85–98.

Delgado-Gaitan, C. (1994) 'Consejos: The power of cultural narrative', *Anthropology & Education Quarterly*, **25**, 3, pp. 298–316.

Delgado-Gaitan, C. (1994) 'Parenting in two generations of Mexican-American families', *International Journal of Behavioral Development*, **16**, 3, pp. 409–27.

Delgado-Gaitan, C. (1994) 'Russian refugee families: Accommodating aspirations through education', *Anthropology and Education Quarterly*, **25**, 2, pp. 137–55.

Delgado-Gaitan, C. (1994) 'Socializing young children in immigrant and first generation Mexican families', in Greenfield, P. and Cocking, R. (Eds) *The Development of Minority Children; Culture In and Out of Context*, Hillsdale, New Jersey, Lawrence Erlbaum Associates.

Delgado-Gaitan, C. (1994) 'Sociocultural change through literacy: Toward the empowerment of families', in Ferdman, B., Weber, R.M. and Ramirez, A. (Eds) *Literacy Across Languages and Cultures*, New York, Suny Press, pp. 143–70.

Delgado-Gaitan, C. (forthcoming) 'Dismantling borders', in Peterson, P.L. and Neumann, A. (Eds) *Reflexivity and Research in Education: Self and Work in Academic Women's Lives*.

Delgado-Gaitan, C. (forthcoming) 'Beyond the bedtime story: Reflecting on oral and written narrative', in Zamora B. (Ed) *Divided Language, Divided Self*.

Delgado-Gaitan, C. and Allexsaht-Snider, M. (1992) 'Mediating school cultural knowledge for children: The parent's role', in Johnston, J.H. and Borman, K.M. (Eds) *Effective Schooling for Economically Disadvantaged Students: School-Based Strategies for Diverse Student Populations*, Norwood, New Jersey, Ablex Publishing Corporation, pp. 81–100.

Delgado-Gaitan, C. and Segura, D. (1989) 'The social context of Chicana women's role in children's schooling', *Educational Foundations*, **3**, 1, pp. 71–92.

Devine, J. (1994) 'Literacy and social power', in Ferdman, B.H., Weber, R-M. and Ramirez, A.G. (Eds) *Literacy Across Languages and Cultures*, New York, SUNY Press, pp. 221–39.

Diaz, R.M. (1992) 'Research takes a close look at home–school conflicts', *La Nueva Vision*, **1**, 2, Stanford, Stanford Center for Chicano Research, pp. 5–12.

Donato, R., Menchaca, M. and Valencia, R.R. (1991) 'Segregation, desegregation, and integration of Chicano students: Problems and prospects', in Valencia, R.R. (Ed) *Chicano School Failure and Success: Research and Policy Agendas for the 1990's*, London, Falmer Press.

Dornbusch, S.M., Ritter, P.L., Leiderman, P.H., Roberts, D.F. and Fraleigh, M.J. (1987) 'The relation of parenting style of adolescent school performance', *Child Development*, **58**, pp. 1244–57.

Ehman, L.H. (1980) 'The American school in the political socialization process', *Review of Educational Research*, **50**, 3, pp. 99–119.

Ellsworth, E. (1989) 'Why doesn't this feel empowering? Working through the representative myths of critical pedagogy', *Harvard Educational Review*, **59**, 3, pp. 297–324.

Epstein, J.L. (1990) 'School and family connections: Theory, research, and implication for integrating sociologies of education and family', in Unger, D.G. and Susan, M.B. (Eds) *Families in Community Settings: Interdisciplinary Perspectives*, New Jersey, The Haworth Press.

Epstein, J.L. (1994) 'Theory to practice: School and family partnerships lead to school improvement and student success', in Fagnango, C.L. and Werber, B.Z. (Eds) *School, Family and Community Interaction: A View From the Firing Lines*, San Francisco, Westview Press, pp. 39–54.

Everhart, R. (1983) *Reading, Writing and Resistance: Adolescence and Labor in a Junior High School*, London, Routledge and Kegan-Paul.

Ferdman, B.M., Weber, R-M., Ramirez, A.G. (Eds) (1994) *Literacy Across Languages and Cultures*, New York, Suny Press.

Foley, D.E. (1990) *Learning Capitalist Culture: Deep in the Heart of Tejas*, Philadelphia, University of Pennsylvania Press.

Freire, P. (1970) *Pedagogy of the Oppressed*, New York, Continuum.

Freire, P. (1973) *Education for Critical Consciousness*, New York, Seabury Press.

Freire, P. and Macedo, D. (1987) *Literacy: Reading the Word and Reading the World*, New York, Bengin and Garvey.

Garcia, M. (1978) 'The Americanization of the Mexican immigrant', *Journal of Ethnic Studies*, **6**, 2, pp. 53–70.

Garcia, P. (1991) 'Teaching: The greatest of all professions', *The Carpinteria Herald*, 27 November.

Garcia, P. (1991) 'What do children learn in school?', *The Carpinteria Herald*, 30 October.

Garcia, P. (1992) 'Carpinteria reaches toward the 21st century', *The Carpinteria Herald*, 17 September.

Garcia, P. (1993) 'We are able to overcome expectations of others', *The Carpinteria Herald*, 18 February.

Garcia, P. (1993) 'Winning isn't always defeating somebody', *Montecito Life* (local newspaper), 21 January.

Giroux, H. (1989) *Border Pedagogy*, New York, Routledge, p. 125.

Giroux, H. (1992) *Border Crossings: Cultural Workers and the Politics of Education*, New York, Routledge.

Goldberg, B. (1992) 'Historical reflections on transnationalism, race, and the American immigrant saga', in Schiller, N.G., Basch, L. and Blanc-Szanton, C. (Eds) *Towards a Transnational Perspective on Migration*, New York, The New York Academy of Sciences, pp. 201–17.

Goldenberg, C. (1987) 'Low-income Hispanic parents' contributions to their first-grade children's word-recognition skills', *Anthropology & Education Quarterly*, **18**, pp. 149–79.

Gonzalez, G.G. (1990) *Chicano Education in the Era of Segregation*, Philadelphia, The Balch Institute Press.

GORE, J. (1992) 'What we can do for you! What can we do for "You"? Struggling over empowerment in critical and feminist pedagogy', in LUKE, C. and GORE, J. (Eds) *Feminist Critical Pedagogy*, New York, Routledge, pp. 54–73.

GOTTS, E.E. and PURNELL, R.F. (1986) 'Communication: Key to school–home relations', in GRIFFORE, R.J. and BOGER, R.P. (Eds) *Child Rearing in the Home and School*, New York, Plenum, pp. 157–200.

CROSZ, E.A. (1988) 'The intervention of feminist knowledges', in CAINE, B., GROSZ, E.A. and DE LEPERVANCHE, M. (Eds) *Crossing Boundaries: Feminisms and the Critique of Knowledges*, Sydney, Allen and Unwin, pp. 92–104.

HALL, S. and HELD, D. (1990) 'Citizens and citizenship', in HALL, S. and JACQUES, M. (Eds) *New Times: The Changing Face of Politics in the 1990s*, London, pp. 173–88.

HASTRUP, K. (1992) 'Writing ethnography state of the art', in OKELY, J. and CALLAWAY, H. (Eds) *Anthropology and Autobiography*, London, Routledge, pp. 116–33.

HEATH, S.B. (1982) 'What no bedtime story means: Narrative skills at home and school', *Language and Society*, **11**, 2, pp. 49–76.

HEATH, S.B. (1983) *Ways with Words*, New York, Cambridge University Press.

HERMAN, J.L. and YEH, J.P. (1983) 'Some effects of parent involvement in schools', *The Urban Review*, **15**, 1, pp. 11–17.

HOOKS, B. (1989) *Talking Back: Thinking: Thinking Feminist, Thinking Black*, Boston, South End Press.

HUTCHEON, L. (1989) *The Politics of Postmodernism*, New York, Routledge.

HYMES, D.H. (1974) *Foundations in Sociolinguistics*, Philadelphia, University of Pennsylvania Press.

JOSEPH, S. (1993) 'Fieldwork and psychosocial dynamics of personhood', *Frontiers*, **XIII**, 3, pp. 9–32.

KLIMER-DOUGAN, B., LOPEZ, J.A., NELSON, P., and ADELMAN, H.S. (1992) 'Two studies of low-income parents' involvement in schooling', *The Urban Review*, **24**, 3, pp. 185–202.

KOHN, M.L. (1959) 'Social class and parental values', *American Journal of Sociology*, **68**, pp. 471–80.

KONDO, D.K. (1990) *Crafting Selves: Power, Gender, and Discourses of Identity in a Japanese Workplace*, Chicago, University of Chicago.

LAREAU, A. (1989) *Home Advantage*, London, The Falmer Press.

LATHER, P. (1991) *Getting Smart: Feminist Research and Pedagogy With/in the Postmodern*, New York, Routledge.

Lau v. Nichols (1974) 414 US 563, 566.

LAVIE, S. (1990) *The Poetics of Military Occupation*, Berkeley, University of California Press.

LEICHTER, H.J. (1984) 'Families as environments for literacy', in GOELMAN, H., OBERG, A. and SMITH, F. (Eds) *Awakening to Literacy*, Exeter, New Hampshire Heinemann Educational Books, pp. 38–51.

LEVIN, M.A. (1987) 'Parent–teacher collaboration', in LIVINGSTONE, D.W. *et al. Critical Pedagogy and Cultural Power* , Massachusetts, Berin and Garvey Publishers.

LEVY, F., MELTSNER, A.J. and WILDAVSKY, A. (1975) *Urban Outcomes: Schools, Streets, and Libraries*, Berkeley, California, University of California Press.

LIFTON, R.J. (1967) *Death in Life: Survivors of Hiroshima*, New York, Random House.

LIFTON, R.J. (1973) *Home from the War: Vietnam Veterans Neither Victims nor Executioners*, New York, Simon and Schuster.

LIFTON, R.J. (1987) *The Future of Immortality and Other Essays for a Nuclear Age*, Basic Books, New York.

LIFTON, R.J. (1993) *The Protean Self: Human Resilience in an Age of Fragmentation*, New York, Basic Books.

LIFTON, R.J. and MARKUSEN, E. (1990) *The Genocidal Mentality: Nazi Holocaust and Nuclear Threat*, New York, Basic Books.

LUKE, C. (1992) 'Feminist politics in radical pedagogy', in LUKE, C. and GORE, J. (Eds) *Feminist Critical Pedagogy*, New York, Routledge, pp. 25–53.

LUKE, C. and GORE, J. (1992) *Feminisms and Critical Pedagogy*, New York, Routledge.

MCCARTHY, K.F. and VALDEZ, R.B. (1986) *Current and Future Effects of Mexican Immigration in California*, Santa Monica, California, RAND.

MCLAREN, P. (1986) *Schooling as a Virtual Performance: Towards a Political Economy of Educational Symbols and Gestures*, London, Routledge.

MCLOED, J. (1987) *Ain't No Makin' It*, Boulder, Colorado, Westview Press.

MORRISON, G.S. (1978) *Parent Involvement in the Home, School, and Community*, Columbus, Ohio, Charles Ell Merrill.

OAKES, J. (1990) *Multiplying Inequalities: The Effects of Race, Social Class, and Tracking on Opportunities to Learn Mathematics and Science*, Santa Monica, California, Rand Corp.

OGBU, J.U. (1987) *Minority Education and Caste: The American System in Cross-Cultural Perspective*, New York, Academic Press.

OKELY, J. and CALLAWAY, H. (1992) *Anthropology and Autobiography*, New York, Routldege.

PEASE-ALVAREZ, L. (1991) 'Oral contexts for literacy development in a Mexican immigrant community', *The Quarterly Newsletter of the Laboratory of Comparative Human Cognition*, **12**, 1, pp. 9–13.

PHELAN, P., DAVIDSON, A.L. and CAO, H.T. (1991) 'Students' multiple worlds: Negotiating the boundaries of family, peer, and school cultures', *Anthropology and Education Quarterly*, **22**, 3, pp. 224–50.

RANGEL, J.C. and ALCALA, C.M. (1972) 'Project report De Jure segregation of Chicanos in Texas schools', *Harvard Civil Rights-Civil Liberties Review*, **7**, pp. 310–9.

REDER, S. (1994) 'Practice-engagement theory: A sociocultural approach to literacy across languages and cultures', in FERDMAN, B.M., WEBER, R-M. and RAMIREZ, A.G. (Eds) *Literacy Across Languages and Cultures*, New York, Suny Press, pp. 33–75.

REESE, L., GOLDENBER, C., LOUCK, J. and GALLIMORE, R. (1989) 'Ecocultural Context, Cultural Activity, and Emergent Literacy: Source of Variation in Home

Literacy Experiences of Spanish-Speaking Students', Paper Presented at the Annual Meeting of the American Anthropological Association, Washington, DC.

Roos, P.D. (1978) 'Bilingual education: The Hispanic response to unequal educational opportunity', *Law and Contemporary Problems*, **42**, pp. 111–40.

Rosaldo, R. (1989) *Culture and Truth: The Remaking of Social Analysis*, Boston, Beacon Press.

Rosaldo, R., Flores, W.V. and Silverstrini, B. (1993) *Identity, Conflict and Evolving Latino Communities: Cultural Citizenship in San Jose, California*, Report to the Fund for Research on Dispute Resolution, November.

Rouse, R. (1989) 'Mexican Migration to the United States; Family Relations in the Development of a Transnational Migrant', Ph.D Dissertation, Stanford University, Stanford, California.

Rouse, R. (1992) 'Making sense of settlement: Class transformation, cultural struggle, and transnationalism among Mexican migrants in the United States', in Schiller, N.G., Basch, L. and Blanc-Szanton, C. (Eds) *Towards a Transnational Perspective on Migration*, New York, The New York Academy of Sciences, pp. 25–53.

San Miguel, G. (1984) 'Conflict and controversy in the evolution of bilingual education policy in the United States — an interpretation', *Social Science Quarterly*, **65**, pp. 5–518.

San Miguel, G. (1987) *Let All of Them Take Heed: Mexican Americans and the Campaign for Educational Equity in Texas, 1910–1981*, Austin, Texas, University of Texas.

Saragoza, A. (1983) 'The conceptualization of the history of the Chicano family', in Valdez, A.V., Camarillo, A. and Almaguer, T. (Eds) *The State of Chicano Research in Family, Labor and Migration Studies*, Stanford, California, Stanford Center for Chicano Research, pp. 111–38.

Schieffelin, B.B. (1986) *How Kaluli Children Learn What to Say, What to do, and How to Feel*, New York, Cambridge University Press.

Schieffelin, B.B. and Cochran-Smith, M. (1984) 'Learning to read culturally: Literacy before schooling', in Goelman, H., Oberg, A. and Smith, F. (Eds) *Awakening to Literacy*, Porstmouth, New Hampshire, Heinemann, pp. 3–23.

Schiller, N., Basch L. and Blanc-Szanton, C. (1992) 'Transnationalism: A new analytic framework for understanding migration', in Schiller, N.G. Basch, L. and Blanc-Szanton, C. (Eds) *Towards a Transnational Perspective on Migration*, New York, The New York Academy of Sciences, pp. 1–25.

Scollon, R. and Scollon, S. (1980) 'Literacy as focused interaction', *The Quarterly Newsletter of the Laboratory of Comparative Human Cognition*, **2**, 2, pp. 26–9.

Scollon, R. and Scollon, S. (1981) *Narrative, Literacy, and Face in Inter-ethnic Communication*, Norwood, New Jersey, Ablex.

Scribner, S. and Cole, M. (1981) *The Psychology of Literacy: A Case Study Among the Vai*, Cambridge, Harvard University Press.

SEGURA, D. (1988) 'Familism and employment among Chicanas and Mexican immigrant women', in MELVILLE, M.B. (Ed) *Mexicanas in Work in the United States*, Houston, University of Houston, pp. 24–32.

SEGURA, D. (1993) 'Slipping through the cracks: Dilemmas in Chicana education', in DE LA TORRE, A. and PESQUERA, B.M. (Eds) *Building with Our Hands: New Directions in Chicana Studies*, Berkeley, California, University of California Press.

SIMON, J. (1989) *The Economic Consequences of Immigrants*, Cambridge, Massachusetts, Blackwell Publisher.

SLAVIN, R.E. (1990) 'Achievement effects of ability grouping in secondary schools: A best evidence synthesis', *Review of Educational Research*, **60**, pp. 471–99.

SPINDLER, G.D. (1955) *Education and Anthropology*, Palo Alto, California, Stanford University Press.

SPINDLER, G. and SPINDLER, L. (Eds) (1994) *Pathways to Cultural Awareness*, Thousand Oaks, California, Corwin Press.

SPRING, J. (1991) *American Education: An Introduction to Social and Political Aspects*, New York, Longman.

STEVENSON, D.L. and BAKER, D.P. (1987) 'The family–school relation and the child's school performance', *Child Development*, **58**, pp. 1348–57.

TAYLOR, D. (1983) *Family Literacy: Young Children Learning to Read and Write*, Exeter, New Hampshire, Heinemann.

TIENDA, M. (1980) 'Familism and structural assimilation of Mexican immigrants in the United States', *International Migration Review*, **14**, pp. 383–408.

TIENDA, M. (1983) 'Market characteristics and Hispanic earning: A comparison of natives and immigrants', *Social Problems*, **31**, 1, pp. 59–72.

TORRES-GUZMAN, M. (1991) 'Recasting frames: Latino parent involvement', in MCGROATY, M. and FALTIS, C. (Eds) *In the Interest of Language: Context for Learning and Using Language*, Berlin, Germany, Mouton de Gruyter.

TRINH, M-H. (1989) *Woman, Native, Other*, Bloomington, Iowa, University of Indiana Press.

TRUEBA, H.T. (1984) 'The forms, functions and values of literacy: Reading for survival in a barrio as a student', *NABE Journal*, **9**, pp. 21–40.

TRUEBA, H.T. (1989) *Raising Silent Voices: Educating Linguistic Minorities for the 21st century*, New York, Harper and Row.

TRUEBA, H.T., JACOBS, L., KIRTON, E. (1990) *Cultural Conflict and Adaptation: The Case of the Among Children in American Society*, London, Falmer Press.

TRUEBA, H.T., RODRIGUEZ, C., ZOU, Y. and CINTRON J. (1993) *Healing Multicultural America: Mexican Immigrants Rise to Power in Rural California*, London, Falmer Press.

URIBE, O. (1980) 'The impact of 25 years of school desegregation on Hispanic students', *Agenda: A Journal on Hispanic Issues*, **10**, 5, pp. 3–35.

VASQUEZ, O. (1989) 'Connecting Oral Language Strategies to Literacy: Ethnographic Study among Four Mexican Immigrant Families', Unpublished Doctoral Dissertation, Stanford University, Stanford, California.

VÉLEZ-IBAÑEZ, C. (1983) *Bonds of Mutual Trust*, New Brunswick, New Jersey, Rutgers University Press.

VÉLEZ-IBAÑEZ, C. (1988) 'Networks of exchange among Mexicans in the U.S. and Mexico: Local level mediating responses to national international transformations', *Urban Anthropology*, **17**, 1, pp. 27–51.

Vos Popular, July 1990.

WALBERG, H.J. (1986) 'Home environment and school learning: some quantitative models and research synthesis', in GRIFFORE, R.J. and BOGER, R.P. (Eds) *Child Rearing in the Home and School*, New York, Plenum, pp. 195–20.

WILLIAMS, N. (1990) *The Mexican American Family: Tradition and Change*, Dix Hills, New York, General Hall.

WILLIAMS, R. (1989) *Resources of Hope: Culture, Democracy, Socialism*, London, Verso.

WILLIS, P.E. (1977) *Learning to Labor: How Working Class Kids Get Working Class Jobs*, New York, Columbia University Press.

YBARRA, L. (1983) 'Empirical and theoretical developments in studies of the Chicano family', VALDEZ, A.V., CAMARILLO, A. and ALMAGUER, T. (Eds) *The State of Chicano Research in Family, Labor and Migration Studies*, Stanford, California, Stanford Center for Chicano Research, pp. 91–110.

ZENTELLA, A.C. (1985) 'Language variety among Puerto Ricans', in FERGUSON, C. and BRICE HEATH, S. (Eds) *Language in the USA*, New York, Cambridge University Press.

Index